A Moment of Tenderness . . .

"Can you walk?"

He felt a slender arm go about his splintered ribs and he groaned loudly.

"Don't expect me to feel sorry for you," Joelle warned crisply as she propelled him forward in a stumbling shuffle. His legs had gone to jelly. Raising his head took a major effort, like lifting a boulder atop a straw.

"Where . . . ?" he mumbled in confusion. He had the impression of warm firelight, and then there was an endless fall into a chair.

"Sit still and let me clean you up a little," she said. "I should have let you stand out there until you froze to the spot."

He reached out an awkward hand and caught her wrist. "Why . . . why didn't you?"

Joelle looked from the curve of his fingers to the mess Guy had made of his face. The clogging fullness returned to her throat. She forced a whispering voice to cut through it.

"Because you needed help and you were there for me when I needed someone . . ."

TEMPEST WATERS

NANCY GIDEON

BERKLEY BOOKS, NEW YORK

TEMPEST WATERS

A Berkley Book / published by arrangement with
the author

PRINTING HISTORY
Berkley edition / March 1993

ISBN: 0-425-13758-9

A BERKLEY BOOK ® ™ 757,375
Berkley Books are published by The Berkley Publishing Group,
200 Madison Avenue, New York, New York 10016.
The name "BERKLEY" and the "B" logo
are trademarks belonging to Berkley Publishing Corporation.

PRINTED IN THE UNITED STATES OF AMERICA

10 9 8 7 6 5 4 3 2 1

For my home state,
where I was born and raised
and where I am still content;
and
for all my
Michigan readers.

1

1865 COPPER HARBOR, MICHIGAN

LAKE SUPERIOR NEVER gave up its dead. The chill blue waters stayed at forty degrees year round, and if a person died in their depths, there was no decay, and therefore a body didn't rise to the surface.

Such knowledge provided no comfort for Joelle Parry as she watched the box being lowered before her father's marker. The lovingly crafted pine casket would rest empty through eternity beside the mortal dust of her mother. Lyle Parry would be preserved somewhere in the remote lake, denied the dignity of a decent burial. And Joelle would never have the chance to weep over his remains.

She stood at the grave side, listening to the shrill words of the parish priest as he shouted to be heard above the moaning wind. His assurances gave no more warmth to her spirit than her heavy mackinaw did to her slender form, huddled inside against the whip of November weather. Both her spirit and her body were numb, and stiff with denial, determined to hold the shivers at bay. When the first shovel of freshly spaded earth thudded atop the casket in a very final epitaph, the handful of mourners who had braved the slicing of the elements were quick to offer condolences and rush toward the shelter of their homes, until only Joelle and the priest stood watching the gravediggers push the yet warm ground in over the empty box. Each muffled thump echoed through the hollow misery in her soul.

He was gone. That knowledge savaged Joelle as harshly as the sudden turn of the November skies from benevolence to fury. He would not be returning to her any more than his body would be resting beside her mother. Fate had denied them both his presence. She stared at the newly disturbed earth and felt an inappropriate anger churn inside her. *How could you? How could you leave me? You promised you'd be back. How could you break your word to me and Mama? Now I don't even have your body to bury next to her.*

"Miss Parry?"

The small voice jerked her from her fierce study of the grave. The little priest recoiled when her glare lifted. He'd expected to see grief, not fury, etched upon the young woman's face. For a moment he was stunned into silence. Then the compassion of his calling made him overlook yet another odd facet of this unconventional female.

"Is there someone waiting in town for you?" he queried gently. Her head shook as she pulled a worn knit cap over her bobbed hair. "No family?"

"Just an uncle. He's at the Hewlett and Barnes mine. My mother's brother-in-law," she added defensively, as if to explain why he was not there at the grave beside her.

"You came alone?"

Because there was no censure in his words, Joelle answered with less sharpness. "Papa wouldn't have wanted the work to stop because of him. I thought I should be here, even if he . . . is not." Her features tightened for a moment but betrayed no softening of delicate line. Then she realized that the little priest was quaking with cold within his somber robes. She managed a small smile. "Thank you for performing the service on such a day. I won't keep you any longer."

Still the man hesitated, drawn by duty. "Please come back with me, Miss Parry. My housekeeper would be most happy to put you up and provide a hot meal. Darkness will fall in a few hours." He let that statement linger meaningfully.

"Thank you, but I have business to attend at the docks, and then I'll be on my way back down to Eagle River."

Her tone clearly indicated she would entertain no argument. She sounded as if she were used to having her decisions obeyed. As he had no authority over this stony-faced seventeen-year-old, what could the priest do? He nodded unhappily. He would say a prayer that those who staggered along the streets of Copper Harbor in the day's waning hours and hunched in the shadows along the wharf would not see beyond the gruff exterior she presented in her mannish garb. Clutching his dark raiment, he hurried from the ill-kept cemetery, black vestments fluttering around him like the wings of a nocturnal demon instead of a messenger of God. He glanced back once toward the straight figure forlornly set amid the curls of icy fog. He shook his head, and his lips began to move by rote in a quick prayer for her protection. She wasn't his problem, but surely someone should watch over a young lady like her.

Alone with the slight mound of loose soil, Joelle sighed. She knew she should cry. It was expected when one buried family. But no tears would come. Just as well, for in the frigid air they would have quickly frozen to her cheeks. How like her to behave so sensibly even at such a desperate time.

Carting the ornate box all the way up the nearly impassable road just to see it laid empty in the ground had not been sensible. Her father would have laughed at such sentimental ceremony. He would have said, "Let me lie under the waves at no cost to anyone. Save the space for some poor soul who needs it." But Joelle knew her mama would have wanted it this way. Even if she could barely remember more than the warmth of her mother's smile, she recalled her last wish—to have her husband share the barren plot of ground beside her. Joelle hoped the frail Bridgett Parry would never know he'd not kept that promise any better than the one he'd made to leave the woods and return with her to her native Detroit. But then, perhaps her mother would understand and be forgiving. She'd never complained when one season stretched into the next, and all plans to follow the lower lakes back to civilization faded—just as her health had faded in the chill clime. But Joelle wasn't sure she could be as forgiving. That wasn't in her nature.

How like Lyle Parry to disregard the objections of others in pursuit of his own ambitions. He knew the risk of sailing

Lake Superior so late in the year. He'd scoffed at Joelle's warning that the rise in water along the shore of the Keweenaw Peninsula foretold of the gale to come. Just a week or so, he'd said. Then he'd be back. The weather would hold that long. He was sure of it. The steam barge he was looking to buy in Duluth, to transport Superior timber, wouldn't last more than a few days on the market with competition being what it was. He had to go now or lose the chance to better profits. He'd waved aside her oft-made suggestion that they look to the Hewlett & Barnes instead of shipping so far abroad. Her Uncle Tavis worked there, and Lyle had no liking for the man or the mine. End of argument. Only a stubborn man would build in the wilderness as he had. A stubborn man was needed to forge a logging company of sturdy reputation. Lyle Parry was proud of Superior Lumbering, and he was proud to claim his own obstinacy, for it had got him where he was today.

It had got him into an early grave.

"I'm sorry, Papa," she said somberly to that vacant grave. "You had your way, and now I'll have mine."

With those final words she hunched her shoulders and turned into the biting wind. Unlike the tenderhearted priest, she never looked back, but rather ahead, to the weaving streets of Copper Harbor. Ahead to the future of Superior Lumbering.

Lyle Parry had come to Copper Harbor in the 1840s. A rough mining camp on the rocky top of the Keweenaw Peninsula, it was on its way to becoming the booming capital of copper country. Then, as now, the oval, landlocked harbor was white with sails. Its crisp days rang with the clatter of hammer and ax, with the shouts of the stevedores and teamsters, with the shriek of the whistles at the mines and the rumble of constant blasting in the hills, just as its nights roared with the carousing and fighting of rough-handed, rough-talking miners. And behind that bustling town, for one hundred-odd miles, a serrated range of mountains ran down that tip of northernmost Michigan. They stood as silent and stern and untouched as they'd stood when the Jesuits first beheld them. Wilderness was at Copper Harbor's back and winter at its throat.

Though residents might joke that the region suffered through ten months of winter and two months of poor sledding, their situation was a serious one. The waterways were all that linked them with civilization; that and two hundred miles of overland through snow-covered forest on snowshoe or dogsled. The Peninsula's mining towns were isolated from the Michigan cities down below. It didn't seem that way when the harbors were crowded with boats sailing westward across the cold blue waters of Lake Superior during the summer months. For five months, however, from December to April, the Northern winter with its cold and snow and ice closed that water highway. For five months, no black smoke from steamers, no flutter of white sails, could be seen, and the rest of the world seemed far away indeed.

The sailing vessels Joelle saw in the harbor were the last of the season. The food and supplies they carried were all that stood between the isolated point and the threat of starvation. There would be no other ships until spring. Even those being unloaded at the docks ran the risk of being stranded by the weather. This late in November, the waves could rise as high as those on the distant seas. Amid rain and snow and borne hither and yon by blustery whirlwinds, sailors aboard that final fleet found their hands and feet frozen. Without warning, they could be overtaken by a thick fall of powdery snow driven against them by violent winds, as had likely happened to Lyle Parry and the *Sally Dale*—and countless others before them. It was a race against the unpredictable temper of nature, and there were always those who thought they could win it. Those like her father.

The haste to be under way was evident as sailors and dock wollopers shifted cargo by hand from deck to dock. None of the workers near the *Saint Soo* paid any mind to the slight figure twining between them. They answered her soft-spoken question without a glance toward her.

"Marshall Cameron? Aye, he were aboard," one of the longshoremen growled. "Kin find him over at McGinty's. Said he wanted to stand the captain one for getting him here in one piece."

Joelle frowned. McGinty's. A saloon. Bracing her shoulders against the chill, she thanked the laborer and ambled toward the noisy establishment. The street had yet to freeze and was scored with muddy ruts. She picked her way around the worst of them to reach.the board-sidewalk running in front of several gambling hells. She paused when she reached McGinty's.

There was little Joelle Parry wouldn't face down once she'd put her mind to it. Even dressed as she was, like a shabby choreboy, however, she couldn't make herself step beyond the heavy doors into the drinking hall. Her father's one unbreakable rule had been that she never, ever go inside such a place. Though curious and tempted at times to see what went on amid the noisy miners and satin-clad fancy women, she'd never quite dared cross the line her father had drawn at the doorway. And she wouldn't now. Marshall Cameron would have to come out eventually, and here she would wait.

Frigid air whipped across the lake and on down the main street of Copper Harbor. A swirl of snow danced upon the water. By morning it would be a measurable depth. By morning, Joelle hoped to be back at camp, where such a sight would be welcomed. Loggers knew the more snow, the better. Then the roads could be kept in shape with no hindrance in the woods from deer flies, mosquitoes, or pesty nosiums. But now, huddled beneath the scant shelter of an overhang and with a twenty-mile trip back to camp awaiting her before she could find sleep in her own bed, Joelle was scowling fiercely. How long could one drink take?

Hours, it seemed.

Joelle cast a nervous eye toward the deepening gray tones of the sky above. Snow fell steadily now, the accumulation forming miniature drifts in the wagon ruts. She estimated an hour, maybe two, of remaining daylight. Two hours in which to convince Marshall Cameron and return to Eagle River. Still time, if she could do most of the convincing en route. The streets of Copper Harbor were almost deserted. Its citizens were sitting down to dinner, and those within McGinty's appeared content to remain. Rubbing her mittened hands together, she glanced at the double doors again. What was to stop her from just boldly going within? In truth, the thought of a good stiff bracer of whatever they served over the counter was enough of an incentive. She could find Cameron before anyone was the wiser.

But her father would know.

Somehow he would know, and the thought of his disapproval held her helpless and slowly freezing upon the porch.

Lord almighty, what could the man possibly be doing in there?

One answer became immediately clear as the doors banged open. A staggering miner reeled out almost totally supported by the ugliest woman Joelle had ever seen. She was tall and impossibly blond with eyes so heavy with kohl, that she looked like a backwoods raccoon. Her womanly flesh had been stuffed into a dress that any decent female would not have worn in public. Joelle stood rooted to the walk, openly staring at the mammoth display of bosom.

"Like whatcha see, boy?" the garish female slurred out through rouged lips. A slight movement of her torso sent the bulging breasts jiggling with obscene vigor.

"Doan go wasting it on a runt like that," her gentleman friend complained good-naturedly. "They's already done paid for. 'Sides, wouldn't know what to do, from the look of him."

"Another time, sweet treat," the whore promised before allowing the impatient miner to prod her down the street. Over his shoulder, she called back with loud encouragement, "The name's Tina. Doan go forgetting it now, you hear?"

No. Joelle didn't think she would ever forget the woman named Tina and her abundance of charms. Unconsciously her hand rose to the front of her mackinaw. She couldn't imagine being so—so exposed. She kept the evidence of her own ripening figure a guarded secret beneath the bulky fit of her clothing, hating the budding, the swelling that signaled her approach to womanhood. Surrounded by a camp of men, she did everything she could think of to keep her sex from becoming too apparent. Of course, they all knew she was Lyle Parry's daughter, but she didn't want them to notice that she'd evolved beyond the tomboy who tagged along beside them with a swaggering stride. She'd rather be respected for the swing of her ax than admired for the curve of her figure. Deep down, she'd been terrified that Lyle would some day look over at her and discover he had a young woman on his hands instead of a child. Then things would change. And that she wouldn't allow.

The northwoods were all she knew. The thought of taking up permanent residence in town was terrifying. The threat of being sent to Detroit had hung over her head as it must have her father's for many long years, and she vowed she would not be shipped there for refinement among her mother's unknown relatives. The logging life was a part of her, a passion in her blood. It was his French-Canadian heritage, her father used to brag, handed down through generations. Lyle never complained, and she had done her best to fill the spot of a treasured son. She'd gone timbering with him every year she could remember, doing any odd job that needed doing. She could handle a team on an iced road and limb a fallen tree with the ease of a man at his morning shave. She'd flip buckwheat cakes if one of the cookees fell ill and cut holes in the ice to bring up the wash water at four o'clock while the shantymen still huddled in their beds. But mostly she did what none of the men, including her father, could do as well. She worked the numbers for Superior Lumbering.

Her mother had seen to her education during the summer months when work was slow, and by the time she was eleven and the fever took Bridgett Parry, Joelle was keeping books for the company. She kept the tally of the branded log butts, counting the *S*s seared into the lengths of timber as they came in from the river drive. She figured the pay for each logger according to his position and sent them off on their sprees when all the cutting work was done. She stood alongside her father when they bartered for a price once the timber had been laid out in smooth, sweet-smelling board lengths. Mostly he listened to her advice when it came to company money matters, but not when it pertained to the issue of the Hewlett & Barnes. Lyle set his jaw and wouldn't budge, and see how his stubbornness had served him. If he had listened to her, he might still be alive.

But he wasn't coming back.

Joelle felt a sting upon her cheeks and was surprised to find tears icing up on them. She drew a quick breath of panic, but it was too late. The dam suppressing her emotions gave way with a shuddering force. The pain of loss banded so tight about her chest that she feared her ribs would crack. She gulped back the well of sobs, trying to pull them tighter inside herself, but she'd lost all control. *Oh, Papa, what am I going to do without you?* Never again would she feel his large, rough hand ruffling through her bobbed hair as she bent over the books; hair as black as his own. The wad of misery in her throat thickened. Never again would she hear his roar of "Timber!" echo through the woods, dance to the wheeze of his accordion, or experience the comfort of his solid presence. The enormity of her plans staggered her into a moment of doubt. How could she do all the work without him? Never had she been so aware of how powerless it felt to be female, of how frightening it felt to be alone.

She stood on the empty sidewalk, shaking with cold and grief. Her tears continued to fall, one atop the other into twin, glistening tracks from lashes to chin. When she thought of Lyle Parry somewhere beneath the indifferent breakers of Lake Superior, she wanted to crumple with disbelief. He was really gone.

Just then the doors to McGinty's opened, and the large figure of a man strode out into the blinding brightness of snowy twilight. With one abrupt turn he crashed into her. Joelle gasped as she felt herself falling. Then two hands caught hold of her by the elbows, steadying her balance while her world continued to whirl. The impact had stunned her. She could taste the warmth of her own blood where her lip had mashed up against her teeth. And to her everlasting humiliation, a small sound escaped her. It was a low wail of despair.

"Say, are you all right, son?"

The compassionate tone, the firm grip, the manly presence enveloped Joelle. She collapsed against his chest, burying her face in the warm, scratchy wool of his coat, allowing the sobs to overtake her. She felt him stiffen in brief shock, then his arms came up in a bracing circle, holding her close.

For the moment all her defenses fell before that indescribable sensation of comfort. She clung as if she were the one who was drowning. And he, this stranger who'd nearly bowled her over, let her weep, let her clutch, all the while offering his silent support. In that brief moment warmth was restored, not just to her body but to her spirit as well. The heat of his fine frock coat thawed her cheeks. The strength of his arms eased her pain. In that instant when Joelle was humbled by the need to be held, her thoughts spun with a dizzying clarity. How good he smelled, not of wood chips and tobacco, but of clean, manly leather and good worsted material. Her hands ceased their convulsive kneading and lay flat on his vested abdomen. Though he wasn't overly tall or overly broad, this man, this stranger, seemed perfectly fitted to her form, and she experienced for the first time in her young life the desire to linger in purely feminine contentment against the harder contours of the male physique.

She sighed.

It was that submissive sound that woke her fully to what she was doing. Merciful heavens, she was all but prostrate upon the fellow! She felt the hot binding power of the hands curled over her shoulders and thought with a wild embarrassment of the painted harlot, Tina, sidling up to her paying customer. Whatever must this man think of her? What on earth was she about?

Alarmed and angry at her own weakness, Joelle jerked away from the comforting plane of wool and warmth. The sudden snap of cold air against her face was just the slap she needed to wake her from her teary daze. The stranger—a real dandy he was, too—slackened his arms to allow her brusque retreat, but his fingers, she noted with mounting indignation, still anchored her before him. He was smiling.

"Better now, ma'am?"

The tolerant amusement edging that sympathetic query brought blood flaming to her cheeks. Mortified, she glared at him because he was one all-fired handsome man, and at first he'd thought she was a boy.

She reached for one of her ready retorts and found to her utter dismay that none came to mind. Wordlessly she stared up at him, her humiliation growing. There was no way to deny her loss of composure, to pretend she hadn't been wailing on his shirtfront like a silly, mewling girl. Why did he have to be so danged fine-looking, and why did her female curiosities pick such an awkward time to start buzzing with annoying fervor? To offset both observations, her temper grew positively prickly.

"You should've been watching where you were going," she snapped testily. "You nearly ran me down."

His grin widened. Oh, dear! Were those dimples? She felt her heart flounder recklessly within her chest. That, added to the devastation of melting dark eyes and a most attractive set of straight white teeth, scrambled her senses. He snatched off his hat with polite deference, revealing a sweep of dark blond hair. His bow smacked of insult after he'd openly mistaken her for a lad. For once that error fired her with unreasonable irritation.

To regain her equilibrium, Joelle looked beyond the pleasing face to the figure of the man. Never mind that she'd not found it lacking in the least while pulled up against him. His manner of dress immediately told her he was an Easterner. The open front of his black wool frock coat revealed a cutaway suit, also in black wool. His nicely fitted trousers were of the same color and fabric. His fancy gray-and-mauve brocaded vest sported a double row of brass buttons and a heavy gold watch chain. In his hands—hands that were soft and uncalloused for all their apparent strength—he held the brim of a funny little hat. From his starched white collar and wide, gray silk cravat to his glossy square-toed shoes, he was every inch a dapper gentleman.

There was a cultured drawl to his soft voice. It rasped upon her senses with a disturbing familiarity, the way his coat had felt beneath her chilled, damp cheek.

"I do beg your pardon, Miss . . . ?"

She squinted fiercely and growled, "I don't go bandying my name about to strangers. Especially strangers who knock me down when coming out of a saloon."

He chuckled, and the feeling of warmth intensified in her bones. "Again, forgive me. Allow me to introduce myself. I'm Marshall Cameron. And you are . . . ?"

She left his question dangling. Marshall Cameron? This . . . this greenhorn was Marshall Cameron? This man with the genteel manner that would serve him better in a Boston parlor than on the rugged Peninsula? She almost laughed aloud in disbelief. Her father would have never let her hear the end of it. This was the man upon whom the future of Superior Lumbering rested. God help them.

Remembering herself and her purpose, she too, doffed her knitted cap. Squaring her shoulders and projecting a steely confidence in her direct gaze, she said with stunning candor, "Mr. Cameron, I'm here to see to all your needs."

2

"INDEED?" A HEAVY brow arched high.

Marshall Cameron wasn't quite sure what to make of the offer. Considering the unconventional source, the obvious interpretation seemed implausible. Even here on this northern tip of the godforsaken end of the earth, the professional women inside McGinty's still dressed like women. He couldn't imagine a female plying her trade in less likely garb. A quick glance took in the red-and-black-checked coat, shapeless cap, baggy trousers, and heavy boots. The coat hung off narrow shoulders the way it would sag upon a too-small clothes hanger. Its cuffs engulfed her mittened hands. It was easy to see how he'd taken her for a slender boy. Until she'd leaned upon him. Her softness, her rounded contours, had made the truth shockingly clear that this was no stripling lad he'd comforted.

Examining her upturned features, he knew he wouldn't have made the mistake had he seen her in full daylight. In spite of the rough clothes and a ragged and truly awful haircut, there could have been no doubt of her gender. While she didn't have the fragile loveliness of the women he'd known in Boston, there was a definite appeal in her gamine face. Her thin black brows and the thick fringe of her lashes emphasized her slate-gray eyes, the color of an angry, threatening sky filled with a wintery chill. Her wide cheekbones and sharp jawline contrasted with a delicate nose and full, pouty lips, now pursed in haughty challenge. Her expression was a mix of youthful innocence and bold arrogance. The mix intrigued him along with the masculine garb on her womanly figure and, the rude stare that had replaced the desperate tears of a moment before. She was certainly more interesting than anyone he'd expected to find in this place civilization had forgotten.

Since she was forthcoming with no information, he boldly asked for some.

"Are you with the mine?"

She sniffed at that with obvious disdain. "Now, why would I be wanting to burrow in a hole like some varmint? But I'll take you there if you'll be quick about grabbing your gear."

Her brusqueness surprised him. Not a man to jump to a snap decision, he studied the situation. "I'd planned to get a room and a hot bath for tonight and head down in the morning."

"Roads might be closed by then. It's snowing, if you hadn't noticed. This ain't Boston. Up here, you get whilst the getting's good. You coming or not? I can't stand here jawing with you. Got to make time whilst the light holds out."

Logic told him to stick with his original schedule. Warm room, hot meal, steamy bath, a bed that didn't roll with the waves. But something in her stormy gray eyes provoked him beyond logic. And he did want to get to the mine as soon as possible. If she was right and he was in danger of being cut off by the snows, her offer could be as provident as it was intriguing.

"My bags are at the dock. Do you have a carriage?"

Her grin flashed. "The best transportation known to these parts."

It didn't take him long to understand the meaning of that grin. Only a few miles. By then, he was sure every vertebra in his back had been displaced. He clung to the hard plank seat of the wagon and tried his best to brace for the bangs and bounces as the vehicle traveled the track southward. To call this a road would have been a misnomer. If this was what his driver considered passable, he shuddered to think what her idea of impassable was. His teeth clacked together as the front wheels struck another gouge in the dirt.

He glanced at his silent companion, determined to make conversation before the urge to commit murder overtook him. To think he'd allowed her to kidnap him from the joys of a soft bed. And he still didn't know her name.

"This is the best mode of transport you have to offer?" he muttered.

She grinned a second time but spared him a direct look. "Were you expecting a trolley?"

"I was expecting to arrive with my spine in one piece," he grumbled in reply.

"You will." She laughed. "Just lean back and leave the driving to me."

Since leaning back was out of the question, he settled for studying her hands. Her grip on the reins was firm and capable. Despite his first assumption that she was steering for ruts out of sheer determination, he could see that she avoided the worst of them with a skilled touch. The team responded to the slightest twitch of the reins, and he didn't doubt she was in complete control upon the treacherous path. She made quite a teamster—he wondered what else she could do well.

"Where did you learn to drive a team?"

"My papa taught me. Since he wouldn't let me man a cross saw, driving gave me a way to be useful. I trust the horses, and they trust me. Gets us where we're going. In one piece."

He smiled ruefully. She had a sharp tongue, this little ragamuffin. "And who might your papa be?"

"Was Lyle Parry. I buried him this afternoon."

The gruffness of her tone couldn't disguise the fresh slash of pain. This news explained her tears, her willingness to seek comfort from a stranger. "I'm sorry," he said softly. She shrugged off his sympathy. "You said you weren't with the mine. Was he a lumberjack, then?"

Pride welled up in her voice, lending it a thick, warm quality. The sound jolted him. "He could fell a tree so accurately it would drive a nail set in the ground." He'd begun to smile at that cocky boast when she added, "Perhaps you've heard of Superior Lumbering." Now she had his complete attention.

"Yes, I have. Could you introduce me to the owner there?"

She cast him a sidelong glance and answered noncommittally, "Maybe. What would a mine agent be wanting with the Superior?"

"Timber, of course. Hewlett and Barnes used 2,600,000 feet of pine and 6,000 railroad ties in its tunnels last year alone and is projected to . . . Sorry," he said with a condescending smile. He mistook the reason for her tension. "I don't mean to bore you with details."

"I'm not bored," she replied easily. "And it was 13,000 ties." She was pleased by his startled silence. Before he could question her knowledge, she continued casually, "So you're meaning to take up a contract for Superior lumber?" Did she sound too eager? Joelle hoped not. It wasn't business-like to show too much enthusiasm, even if such an offer would save her and her company. Her excitement traveled down the reins, and the team picked up their pace on the snow-covered road. But not being as attuned to her mood as the twin sorrels, Marshall Cameron thought she was simply being polite in her interest. He was a bit eager to show off his new authority.

"More a buy-out than a contract, actually. The H and B can easily absorb such a small operation and use of its timber production. That's one of the reasons I was sent up here."

"To crowd out anyone in your way?"

Marshall was too smug in his own thoughts to note her brittle tone. "To make things work efficiently. With properly skilled logging teams, the H and B could manage an enormous profit off the Superior's timberland."

"Is that right?" The horses tossed their heads restlessly as the reins bunched up in their driver's hands. "Properly skilled teams. And where you meaning to find 'em? On the street corners in Boston?"

He laughed good-naturedly at her sarcasm. "I don't imagine they get any better than your father. I'll keep on the most qualified and hire the best the northwoods have to offer. Under good management, it should turn out to be a real paying merger."

Joelle didn't like what he was getting to and cut right to it with a blunt chill. "Good management meaning you?"

"That's what they sent me here to do."

How confident he sounded. To Joelle his words were a threatening rumble of bad things to come. She glanced again at the greenhorn beside her and fought to keep the angry fear from her voice. "And you know logging, do you, Mr. College Man from Boston?"

The insinuation made him stiffen. "I know business, Miss Parry."

The bumpy ride progressed in silence for some miles. For much of that time, Joelle seriously considered pushing this arrogant obstacle from her wagon. A man like him wouldn't survive an overnight in his fine frock coat and leather shoes. Perhaps a taste of northland hospitality was what he needed to wake him to the reality of this world far from Boston. But hurting him wouldn't further her plan. She needed Marshall Cameron and the Hewlett and Barnes mine. But she was very afraid that they didn't need her. This man, Cameron, was not the city softy she had at first supposed. She'd heard the hard edge to his words just as she had felt the hard strength in his body. The memory of the broad wall of his chest and the steely circle of arms pressing her against it awoke a sudden traitorous shiver along her limbs. A chill, nothing more. Marshall Cameron hadn't stirred that curious tremble, yet rebellious eyes canted in his direction, sketching his classic profile, appreciating the ruddy color burned into his cheeks by the cut of the wind. *Shove him out,* a panicked voice sounded from deep inside her. *He's dangerous.* He was the kind her father had held out against for years, the kind he'd warned her to stay away from, a ruthless representative of the profit-hungry East. People there didn't know pine from pansies. They only recognized the dollars at the bottom of a tally sheet.

As she forced her eyes not to stray from the white ribbon of road ahead, Joelle refused to admit the truth to herself. Marshall Cameron was dangerous not because of what or whom he represented. He was a threat because of what he was—the first man she'd ever responded to as a woman. That quite simply scared the stuffing out of her.

During the awkward lapse in conversation, Marshall allowed his attention to be pulled from his paradoxical driver to the harshness of the surroundings. The team was straining upward along a trail that disappeared within fifty feet into a powdery swirl of snow. Were they going straight up into the mountains then? He experienced a slight tremor of uncertainty. After the pitching ride over Lake Superior, he didn't think any power on earth could discompose him with that same terror. He wasn't much of a sailor so he'd excused those cramping spasms as mild *mal de mer*. How, then, could he explain away his queasiness now? Just the thought of his first impression of the Peninsula from out on that roiling inland sea was enough to instill the belief that he was truly crazy. The land rose along a wooded shore into rocky, broken precipices, barren of all but a severe grandeur. What a stern, forbidding welcome from the place his father called home.

He had a difficult time juxtaposing the romantic wilderness Colin Cameron spoke of with this jagged ridge of rock. Yet his father's voice never failed to soften with a trace of longing when he talked of his years on the Peninsula. Perhaps it had something to do with the fact that he had met and married Marsh's mother here. True love must have helped to gloss over the most depressing conditions, he supposed. Or maybe these stony cliffs reminded Colin, a half-starved homesick emigrant, of his native Cornwall. Whichever, Marshall had a hard time believing the urban boardroom executive Colin Cameron had become would look back upon these severe surroundings with anything but distaste. It was as hard to understand as his father's insistence that he come here to serve in an odd apprenticeship before taking his place on the H&B board. Colin had pushed him toward an engineering degree. Marshall knew his education would benefit him in Boston committee meetings, but it had not prepared him for toiling in the wilds of the Keweenaw Peninsula. But he loved his father and had always respected his judgments. Now he wondered if Colin Cameron had fallen prey to the nonsensical fantasies of his youth, for what else would explain this desolate trip to the edge of nowhere?

Wintering in the Michigan northwoods hadn't sounded so terrible when he and his father discussed it in a snug Massachusetts parlor. It had taken on a whole other meaning when he stepped off the last link to civilization at the Copper Harbor dock. For five months he would be stranded here, a world away from his comfortable life in Boston, a world away from his plans to wed Lynette Barnes, the daughter of his father's partner, and to assume his inherited spot on the H&B board. Of what possible benefit could this cold and isolated internship be? As his father never did anything without reason, Marshall forced himself to look beyond the obvious explanation—utter madness—to find some saner motive. He could arrive at none. For five months this was to be his home, and he would make the best of it, although the best the Keweenaw had to offer was grim fare indeed: five months in cramped quarters with hundreds of grimy, illiterate miners.

Then he glanced once more at the enigmatic creature at his side. Where did she fit in? With her father newly buried, he wondered what her future would be like. It couldn't be a kind or encouraging one considering her father's trade. He wondered if she had anyone to look after her—a mother, a beau, a husband. That last made him frown unaccountably. Surely she was too young to be wed, no more than sixteen or seventeen. But in these parts, where women were scarce and life so very hard, perhaps that was old enough. Too bad that such a spirited little hoyden would soon be broken beneath the hardships of her fate. He couldn't help remembering how soft and vulnerable she'd felt cozied up against him. It was the only positive impression this land had made upon him thus far. Slowly freezing upon the unyielding plank, unsure of what lay ahead for him at the H&B, Marshall was tempted beyond reason to sample that warming welcome a second time.

Joelle gave a start when her passenger's arm circled about her shoulders. A casual flex of those well-remembered muscles brought her closer to him. She gasped at the sudden wave of sensations inside her; a crazy collection of fright and excitement, outrage and submission. Her confusion flamed the short wick of her temper.

"Here now! What is it you think you're doing?"

"I thought you might be cold."

"Well, I'm not." That gruff disclaimer was followed by a discouraging jab of her elbow. To her surprise, his grip tightened.

"Well, I am. Damn cold and willing to sidle up to the Devil himself if it would break the chill."

Joelle quit her squirming. He probably was fair to frozen in his useless Eastern finery. Though part of her felt he deserved the misery, another offered up sympathy. Whether it was the logic of his argument or the knowledge that there was nothing intimate in the gesture, she felt duly chastened. "See that your hands don't stray anyplace they don't belong," she growled in surly resignation.

"Yes, ma'am."

Was he grinning? She guessed he was, but she wouldn't allow him the satisfaction of a sidelong glance. Instead she stiffened her posture and urged the team to a faster pace. Never had the trip between Copper Harbor and Eagle River seemed so long or so aggravating.

Or so stimulating.

She felt warmer nestled close to him on the hard seat. Huddled together, they made a fairly efficient windbreak, but that didn't account for the heat Joelle found simmering within herself. That, she feared most dreadfully, had to do with this man. She couldn't understand what there was about Marshall Cameron that made her innards quiver and her senses about as stable as the first thin crust of ice on the surface of the lake. She'd grown up around every face, frame, and form of the male species, and none of them had caused this giddy breathlessness she felt now. She had nothing but contempt for the few Easterners she'd met, And there was no man—northern woodsman or Boston gentleman—she'd ever allowed to treat her person so familiarly. To this point, she'd considered a man's touch with a neutral degree of tolerance. She'd wrestled them, she'd danced with them, she'd treated them for frostbite, and even shared the humid heat of the sauna with them, with emotions held in controlled indifference. But there was something about this one that left her winded and gasping, like the sudden full-force smack to the face of a howling winter gale. The harder she struggled into that raging wind, the more difficult it became to pretend she could keep her balance. She disliked Marshall Cameron intensely for flinging her senses into the teeth of that tearing turmoil.

"Do you have a home in Eagle River, Miss Parry?"

His simplest questions set her back into a defensive crouch. Her words came out tersely. "I don't have a home, Mr. Cameron. I've spent my life following the logging camps."

"But now that your father is . . . gone, surely a young lady like yourself shouldn't be allowed—"

"Allowed?" She shot him a frigid glare. "It is none of your business, but I can take care of myself."

"I didn't mean to imply—"

"Didn't you?"

Of course he did, and they both knew it. Marshall had no right to pry into her affairs. They were strangers. But then again, they weren't. For a moment, outside McGinty's, he'd known her more fully and completely than any other had. He sensed from her plucky stance and hard-bitten arrogance that she never let anyone see the side he'd been privy to in that moment, the side of her that was female and young and vulnerable. Knowing that her gruff manner hid softness, he felt oddly protective of the independent miss who claimed she needed no one. He knew better, and he knew she didn't like him knowing.

"It isn't any of my business, but did your father leave you well provided for?"

Joelle looked at him, readying a sharp reply. But words again failed her. She saw sincerity in his dark eyes that overwhelmed her for a moment. Finally she was able to respond. "I'll manage."

Marsh smiled at her tight reply. Yes, she probably would manage. If Parry had left her penniless and adrift, she'd find a way to continue on. In spite of that, he found himself saying, "If you should need anything, come to me, Miss Parry. All you have to do is ask."

She gave him a small smile. For the briefest instant her eyes thawed from cold steel to soft pewter. Then the edge was back, though not as keen as before. "I'll remember that, Cameron." Just as she turned her attention back to the team, he thought he heard her chuckle over some private amusement.

His offer to help her had been impulsive, but he felt better having made it. He didn't like to think of any female, no matter how capable, fending for herself in the inhospitable north country. Not that he thought for a moment she would take him up on the suggestion of aid. She seemed too altogether proud. And while he couldn't agree with her desire to control her own destiny, he did respect her for her courage. As soon as she met the right man, she'd give up her haughty notions quick enough. No woman would chose a solitary way of life when she could be the contented wife of some caring gentleman, if there was any man who qualified as such up here. Anyway, that was not his concern.

From out of the trees and the mist of blowing snow the outline of the Hewlett & Barnes mine rose like a squatting predator. Joelle steered the wagon down the ragged row of company houses. Each pine-board cottage was painted red with a stovepipe sticking through its steep roofline. In near darkness the settlement looked like a forgotten ghost town until a tremor shook the ground, followed by an explosive sound. Joelle shrugged off Marshall's encompassing arm and drew the team up before one of the grimy shaft houses.

"Here you be, " she stated unnecessarily. How hollow her voice sounded to her ears. Did he notice? He seemed to notice too much. Their meeting and the ride down the range had distracted her from the grief resting heavy in her heart. Now she had to face the aloneness, the anguish of missing her father awaited her. She would return to the rooms they had shared and find them empty of laughter and love and life. These last few miles would be the hardest she'd ever driven, knowing that nothing and no one awaited her. She wondered as she cast a glance at Marshall Cameron's handsome face, now set in intriguing shadow, if the memory of his embrace would see her through the long hours of the night.

"I thank you for the ride," he said gratefully. It had been most interesting. He paused on the seat, suddenly unwilling to let her go. "Do you have far to travel yet? You could stay—"

"I've just a piece to go, and people are waiting for me," she told him. It wasn't as curt a refusal as he'd expected. She seemed almost as reluctant to part as he was. With a rough clearing of her throat, she became her former prickly self. A mittened hand gestured toward the shaft house. "Just go on in there and ask for Tavis Lachlan. He's the mine captain. He'll see you settled."

"Tavis Lachlan," he repeated, instilling the name in his memory just as he was instilling the image of her piquant features. Having no reason to linger or to hold her up while darkness fell, he jumped from the wagon onto wobbly legs. He felt as weak as he had when disembarking from the Superior sailing ship. When his bags were on the ground at his feet, he craned up to see her studying him most intently.

"Good night, Miss Parry. Will you accept some remuneration for the trip? You did get me here in one piece, after all."

He'd expected—he'd hoped for—one of her rare smiles. Instead he found her expression unaltered from its somber lines.

"I'm recalling you to your offer, Cameron," came her forthright statement. "There is something you can do for me."

There was a challenge in her eyes, as if she were waiting for him to withdraw his pledge. To assure her of his serious intent and to offset his own surprise that she would call upon him for a favor, Marshall made his reply firm and unwavering.

"Name it."

"I will. Come see me when you want to discuss lumber."

With that perplexing claim, she snapped down the reins, and the wagon was quickly lost to the dusky, shifting snows. Just then he realized that he had never asked her first name.

Smiling to himself, Marsh picked up his bags and headed toward the welcoming shelter of the mine.

3

TAVIS LACHLAN WAS as hard as the rock he worked. Everything about him was rough and gritty, from his miner's clothes to his craggy features. When Marshall had met him coming off his seven-to-six shift down under in the mine, he'd been covered with hematite and already in a temper. He wasn't a tall man, but he was built as square and solid as one of the one-ton kibbles used to haul rock out of the mines. The lines and angles were chiseled into his face as if scored there by powder blasting. He'd sized up the H & B's new agent through eyes impenetrable as granite while he extended a ham-sized hand. Though he felt sure that every bone in his own was ground to powder in that brief, crushing shake, Marsh refused to wince. Tavis hadn't been impressed by his display of stoicism. He merely growled the directions to his quarters and told him to be up with the sun if he expected a tour of the mine. This morning found the underground-foreman cleaner but no less unpleasant.

"Yer late," he claimed tersely even as the whistle sounded to disprove it.

Without comment Marshall took the protective hat thrust at him and with a glob of clay affixed a candle to its short bill. Then, he followed the stocky captain through the throngs of miners donning their work clothes in the shaft house and began the climb down the ladder into the belly of the H & B.

The climb took an hour.

Between his schooling and his father's stories, Marsh had become familiar with every detail involved in mining. He knew the H & B was situated over a bed of amygdaloidal deposits. Unlike the Peninsula's first big producer, the Cliff, which brought up tons from fissure veins rich in mass copper, the H&B blasted through solid rock to extract the ore from where it had settled in gas bubble holes left behind as an underlying flow of lava cooled. Burrowing down through the unyielding layers of earth was hard, costly work, a process virtually unchanged in over twenty years of production. The drilling was done by hand. One man held and turned the drill while two others pounded it downward with their weighty sledges, until it was deep enough to fill with a charge of black blasting powder. Explosions shattered rock, and the shafts sunk downward, with drifts and crosscuts running outward from the main shaft like suckers from a taproot. At first the tons of rock were lifted out by a horse whim. The animals walked endlessly, winding cable about a large drum to pull the heavy sleds of ore up from the caverns below. The blasting went on until the tunnels stretched farther than the streets of the mining town above, honeycombing in a network of drifts, shafts, rises, and crosscuts. When the shafts reached depths of over one thousand feet, horsepower could no longer do the hoisting and was replaced by steam-powered windings engines. But those cars weren't safe for the transportation of men. They had to climb one thousand feet of ladder, increasing their workday from eight to ten hours to allow time to get to and from the underground levels.

Marsh knew these facts, but that knowledge didn't prepare him for the experience of actually descending into the bowels of rock. After the first few hundred feet, his calves began to complain, and a claustrophobic panic overtook him. He was no coward, by God, but there was something about descending that ladder that bothered him. Knowing there was an adequate air supply didn't keep him from taking labored breaths. Knowing the timber bracings could withstand the blasting tremors didn't stop him from clinging to the ladder as it shivered with vibration. He needed considerable willpower to keep from bolting upward. Besides, he would have had to shinny over the backs of all the miners above him heading to the bottom. Cold surface air penetrated through the shaft, stiffening his fingers and knees and making short vapor plumes of each shallow breath. Light from the candle on his helmet flickered to make an irregular pattern on the wall of rock as he continued down.

Down.

Down.

When he thought they'd surely reached the very doorway to Hell, Marsh touched bottom. It took a full minute for his legs to stop quivering. He used the time it took to gather his strength and composure to assay the mammoth cavern blown into sedimentary stone.

"How far down are we?"

Tavis Lachlan smirked at the betraying tension in the other man's voice. He could have made this trip easier on him. The feeling of being swallowed whole was a common reaction to going underground for the first time. All the new workers felt it for the first few days, but Tavis had no sympathy for this invading Easterner. This was his domain, and he wasn't about to let go of his advantage.

"Almost twelve hundred feet of solid rock atop us. One fine grave, wouldn't you say?"

Marsh didn't say anything. He was too busy trying to force a natural breath from his constricted lungs. This could be his grave. Deep, dark, desolate. A hole in the ground separated from air and light and living. His panic twisted inside, cramping his belly, tightening the vise about his chest.

A grave. That image brought back the face of a young woman who had recently laid her father to rest. He thought of her incredible courage—such commanding strength when faced with tragedy and despair. How quickly she'd appeared to face the hard life ahead of her. She had laughed at him in his fine coat, with his proper manners, and his ambitions, and he could picture her reaction to his weakness now. He could almost see her supple mouth taking a wry turn of amusement at his expense. But he could hear his arrogant response to her expression of doubt. *I know business.* A lot of good that knowledge did when it couldn't keep him from quaking in his expensive shoes like a greenhorn Easterner. Damned if he'd suffer a loss of face before those cynical gray eyes.

"Let's get on with it, Lachlan. I want to see what the H and B can do in a day."

Tavis frowned at that command, but he nodded. He had to take orders from this know-nothing, at least for now. But that would change. He'd see to it.

After eight hours underground, Marsh felt reborn as he emerged from the mine. He drew great lungfuls of the sweet air, forcing out what had been fouled by blasting, candles, and the breath of hundreds of other men. He couldn't easily shake off the clammy feel of suffocation, of closeness, of being crushed by the tonnage of rock overhead. But he'd survived, thanks to the image of taunting gray eyes and a challenging smile. He'd carried the memory of the fiery Miss Parry the way some of the superstitious miners held tokens of luck close to their hearts. He grinned. Wouldn't she hate knowing he had made her his charm, making it possible for him to remain where she had made it clear he wasn't welcome. Should he tell her? Perhaps, just to see the indignation fire in her fine gray eyes. He wasn't a quitter. If she and men like Tavis Lachlan thought he would quickly scramble back to Boston, they did not know him. He was nothing if not determined. Even the most unsavory task would not go unconquered once it was put in his path. If that meant climbing a ladder down into the cold belly of the earth each day, he would. He wouldn't like it, but he would do it. The sooner they understood that, the better for them all.

The rest of Marshall's belongings arrived a week after he had. The little spitfire had been right; the wagon had a devil of a time getting through on the snowy roads. At least he had his possessions about him now—his books, his brandy, the more cherished of his luxuries. If he was to winter here, he would do it like a gentleman, with as many comforts as possible. Not that he couldn't do without them, but there was no need for him to make too many sacrifices. Severing all ties to civilized company was sacrifice enough.

With a few scattered touches of humanity, he could make do in the company dwelling. It was a far cut above the boardinghouses rented out to the workers at a total of a quarter

to half their income. His was a small yet cozy house built of
pine board for utility, not entertaining. As if he'd be doing any
of that here. He'd had only his own voice to break the silence
this last, long week. Who would he ask to sit before his fire
to share cigars and sherry and companionable conversation?
Certainly not the surly mine captain. No pleasantries there.
Even matters of business were forced at best. The man had
taken an unreasonable dislike to him. Unbidden, the image
of the quixotic Miss Parry came to him. Would she come
if invited? She would probably appreciate a good cigar more
than his presence. That made him smile as he turned back
to his sullen guest, a glass of whiskey in either hand as he
prepared to hear his mine captain's first weekly report.

Tavis Lachlan was regarding him through hooded eyes. He
took the glass with a wordless nod and drank from it like a
man who knew his liquor. A sigh escaped him.

"A shame it will be to water down the likes of this," he
murmured.

"Why on earth would I do that?" Marsh asked as he settled
into an opposing straight-backed chair.

"Can see you got a lot to learn about life up here. You
have to make things stretch to last till April—your food,
your coffee, your liquor—everything. Once the lanes close,
what you got is all you have."

Contrarily Marsh drank deeply from his glass with the full
intention of pouring himself another. One did not dilute one's
pleasures. Better to go without.

Tavis noted his defiant gesture and shrugged. This one'd
probably be snowshoeing it out in a panic by the time January's short days and long nights were upon them. He wouldn't
be the first to be driven by that mad desperation. Only the hard
survived a northern winter, and this city-bred softy wasn't
made to last. He would be glad to see this one go.

"So," the H&B's underground foreman drawled out, "what
do you think of the finest copper mine in the world?"

The man's pride was unmistakable, as if he were referring
to the accomplishments of a beloved child. Marsh had seen the
way he swaggered below, accepting the title of Captain from
his men as simple due. His father had warned him to tread
lightly here. A mine boss came up from the ranks, earning

the respect of his crew with his ability to lick any man and to know mineral from rock. The presence of a textbook engineer often suggested that the Board was worried about his success in scenting out ore. No great wonder that the burly Cornishman regarded the new agent with a fear-laced contempt.

Since he was more of a businessman than a politician, Marsh was blunt with his summations. With each added comment, Tavis Lachlan's features notched a degree tighter.

"It *could be* the finest copper mine in the world," Marsh allowed in response to his foreman's boast. "But not as it stands. Everything I've seen so far is painfully outdated. It's a wonder we're producing at the rate we are."

"Care to spell that out, sir?" The "sir" was a tag of scorn nearly spat from the man's lips. "I dinna think there was anything wrong with this year's profits."

"I'm not concerned with this year's. It's next year's that has me worried. I look to see the price of copper drop like a hot rock."

"And why would it do that?"

"With the war at an end, the government will be disposing of some five thousand tons of old war materials, enough copper to meet one third of the demand. If that's not crippling enough in itself, the new import trade will soon force our prices in line with theirs. If we're to survive, we have to do whatever possible to cut costs and man-hours. We have to be prepared to face up to a fifty percent drop."

"That's your opinion," the Cornishman said with a sneer. "Times is good, and they'll be staying that way. Work on Number Sixteen will more than make up for any losses."

"I'm suspending work on Sixteen."

That calm claim brought a quick clenching of the mine captain's fists. "The *hell* you say!"

"Geological surveys show little likelihood that any sizable amount of ore is there."

Fury seemed to transform Tavis Lachlan into a hulking beast. He roared, "Paper! You're talking pieces of paper. The ore is there. I gots me a nose for it."

Marsh never faltered. He remarked sensibly, "Then what you're sniffing is low-grade copper not worth the time and money to mine. Sixteen is down, at least until I've implemented my plans."

This may not have been the best time to expect cooperation, but Marsh was eager to get things under way. Ignoring the miner's florid features and the threatening movements of his big fists, Marsh began listing what he saw as necessary improvements.

"I mean to replace the one-ton kibbles with skids that will hold two and a half tons of rock. Man-engine elevators will eliminate the use of ladders and will cut forty-five minutes off the time it takes the crew to get in and out of the main shaft each way. With a locomotive instead of horses to pull the ore to the stamping mill, we'd save on the expense of two men and four horses. I'd like to bring in steam stamps made by Ball machinery and replace the old ties at the washing end of the mill with an automatic jiggling machine. They're called Collums washers and will save the maximum amount of copper in fine ground sands. Smelting locally would spare the expense of paying the teaming, shipping, and canal charges of sending masses and minerals to the lower lakes. I've heard the smelting works in Hancock has a new reverberatory furnace that will reduce the mineral from sixty-five to ninety-nine percent purity."

Marshall had thoroughly researched each of these areas. He had little else to do in the evenings other than pour over charts and graphs and projections. He could predict the coming plunge in ore prices as if it were inscribed upon Tavis's cherished rock and was impatient with the man's sheer stubborn refusal to hear reason when it was laid out bluntly before him. He could tell by the way the man breathed in and out like one of the laboring shaft ventilators that his research had not made the least impression.

Tavis let out a jeering laugh. "And you think by spending a fortune to replace a perfectly good system you'll be saving the H and B. You book types are all the same. Can't stand to let well enough alone. Gots to have your hands in it. Well, you can damned well keep your hands out of my tunnels."

Marsh's tone was deceivingly soft. "Mr. Lachlan, might I remind you that I have complete authority from the Board to do whatever I wish? I will be sending my recommendations with this week's report, and I'm confident the directors will be in agreement and so confident of my judgement that I may begin implementation as soon as the necessary equipment orders and financing can be arranged."

"A lot you'll get done without my workers underground. All your fine talk'll not get you one miner, one miner's assistant, one trammer nor timberman."

"Are you threatening a strike, Mr. Lachlan?" That cold conclusion sat poorly with the Cornishman. He and his countrymen were clannish and fiercely loyal to their mine and its company. Outside influences such as the labor organizations that the Finnish were so fond of were staunchly resisted. A strike was unlikely, but the loss of cooperation was indeed a danger Marsh would see promptly quashed. He made his words succinct so there could be no misunderstanding his seriousness and authority to carry them out. "Should there be any shirking of duty below ground, I will hold you responsible, sir. I understand dismissal this late in the season could mean a very long, cold walk. Do I make myself clear?"

Tavis was silent but Marsh was not fool enough to believe he had convinced him. Lachlan was simply not in any position to argue. Even without overt rebellion, the man could make things difficult for him, and that Marsh wanted to avoid. He was better with figures than management problems. But Tavis Lachlan was a bit like H&B bedrock. Immovable.

Thinking hospitality and a healthy splash of spirits might lighten the tense mood, Marsh refilled their glasses. He frantically sought a topic less explosive to explore.

"With all the timber we use annually, I think you'll agree that buying up our own source would be an advantage."

Tavis gave a curt nod.

With as much nonchalance as he could manage, Marsh commented, "I have heard of a local company, the Superior."

"I know it."

"Is it your opinion that it would suit our purpose?" Besides trying to get in the man's good graces, if there were indeed a good side to Tavis Lachlan, Marsh did want to hear his suggestions. Timbering was not something he knew a great deal about, as Parry's daughter had recently pointed out to him. He would defer to experts in the matter.

"Oh, I think the Superior would suit nicely. It's local, and I be of the mind that it could be available for purchase. For the right price. With the right means of persuasion."

Marsh didn't catch the subtle inflections in that statement. He was thinking of other things; of a pair of startlingly direct gray eyes. *Come see me.* "And whom would I see about making these arrangements?"

Tavis took a long drink and assessed the Easterner with a slight smile. "There might be a bit of a problem there. You see, the owner recently met with a mishap upon the big lake. He's dead. I suppose the one holding the strings would be his only surviving kin."

Marsh had a sudden surge of intuition. It couldn't be. "And who might that be?" he prompted with a suspenseful quiet.

"His daughter. Joelle Parry."

Joelle. Her first name was Joelle. An unusual name. A fitting name. He struggled hard to concentrate, to hold his enthusiasm in check.

"And do you know this woman?"

Tavis grinned. "I should. She be my niece."

Arrogant pup.

Tavis stomped the distance to his own quarters in a high temper.

Imagine the greenling thinking to usurp his power, to condemn his methods, to question his nose for ore. By God, it was too much!

When he'd heard that the H&B board was sending an agent, he'd not been worried. He'd expected a timid, bookish sort who could be bullied by presence and experience into causing no trouble. His men would rally behind him, sharing his contempt for the intellectual's approach to mining. What did an outsider know, after all? Had he been raised upon high, rocky ground? Had he been weaned on hematite? Could he boast of calluses before he was out of short pants? Was tunneling in his blood, in his ancestry as far back as time?

And then the board sent him Colin Cameron's son.

He had the look of him, the boy did. And of her. That made it all the harder to stomach.

Tavis stalked into his company house. His pallid little wife came running as soon as she heard the door slam. He took in her rail-thin body and her faded features, and his temper flared.

"Fetch me supper, woman," he snapped, and Sarah scuttled spiritlessly into the kitchen to see to his command. Her very obedience nettled. His wife. A curse to the memory of the one he'd loved. A daily reminder of what he'd lost and Colin Cameron claimed. And now their son was here to score that bitterness deeper with a new, fresh pain.

Damn Colin. His friend. Tavis had brought him over from Cornwall. When the H&B was looking for workers, he was quick to recommend his own "Cousin Jack." They had worked side by side in the mines of Cornwall and in the mines of the Keweenaw. Both became shift bosses, then Colin had been promoted to mine captain. He was a hard, industrious worker and his friend, so Tavis tried not to be envious. What was a promotion compared to near kinship?

The difference in work status hadn't come between them. Marion Hewlett had. Tavis could still close his eyes and see her as she looked when she stepped off one of the first side-wheelers hauled over the portage at Sault Ste. Marie. Her father was one of the speculators who crowded its decks. He'd come with pockets full of Boston money, eager to sink it deep in search of Peninsular copper at his new mine. Tavis had loved her from the start. She wasn't a great beauty—oh, aye, she was fair, but it was her inner fire that set him to boiling. Colin, too, and he'd won her. He'd sailed back with her that very summer, giving her his name and taking the right to claim her wealth and the power to run the H&B.

Now Colin was out to set him back again, this time in the person of his pompous son who seemed to forget that Tavis and his father had been made from the same mold. Colin had cost him his one love and his chance to rise above the chambers of the mine. He'd be damned if he'd now lose his position of authority to that man's snotty brat of a boy. Colin Cameron was far beyond the reach of his revenge, but Marshall was not. Marshall would be the means for venting his long-festering spite. He would see that proper puppy fail and fail miserably.

But how?

He pondered that question all during dinner, scowling so ferociously that his poor wife didn't dare utter a word. How could he give the blighter the knockdown he deserved, and by dealing him low, strike at the father as well? He couldn't very well sit still and have his respect and seniority stripped from him. He'd suffered that once at the hands of a Cameron. No one would ever lord over him again.

A knock came at the door, and there was his answer.

"Joelle, dear," Sarah called out gratefully. She rightly feared her husband's dark mood and looked to his niece to cheer him from it. As much as Tavis disliked Lyle Parry, he truly adored his daughter. At times Sarah wondered if he made such a fuss just to remind her that she'd given them no children of their own. At least her sister Bridgett had seen fit to present her husband with a babe, girl-child though she was. It wasn't Tavis's fault, after all, that he could not be made to love his wife.

"I'm not intruding, am I?"

"No, of course not. Please come in. I was about to pour coffee." Sarah cast a nervous glance at her husband for approval. He was smiling slightly, so she fled into the kitchen for an extra cup.

"Joey, how be you, girl?" Tavis growled in a friendly manner. "Sorry I was not to be there when you laid your father to rest. A fine man, Lyle Parry. Always thought so."

If he had, he'd never shown it while her father lived, Joelle mused tolerantly. The two men had never gotten on. She'd never understood that, for she loved them both, fiercely. She dropped into one of the dining chairs and blinked back the tears that were ever waiting to spring forth at the mention of her papa. "I hope he's at rest, Tavis," she said with a sigh. She never called him Uncle, at his command. And he never called her by her proper name, always preferring the masculine nickname. "I can't be sure until I do something about the Superior."

"As bad as that, girl?" He sounded sympathetic as he leaned forward on his elbows. His slitted eyes gleamed with betraying speculation, but his niece was too distraught to notice. She might not have believed what she saw there anyway.

"It's time to be sending crews to their new location in the woods. If I don't have the promise of orders and some way to purchase supplies and pay them, we all might well be starving come spring."

She sighed again, but this time her uncle suspected it was for effect. The chit had a talent for building up to something by way of the heartstrings. And his, jaded though they were, weren't totally immune. He waited for her to play out her hand, watching the skillful rise and fall of her shoulders as if they were about to buckle beneath the strain they bore. Nonsense, of course. Her shoulders could support a whim collar without a twitch. But he was patient, hoping her direction might be the same as his.

She glanced up at him carefully through a dark fringe of lashes. Joelle sought and found his affectionate expression of concern, then continued with feigned indifference.

"What do you think of Marshall Cameron?"

"That whelp?" He snorted his opinion. "He'd best be sticking to his parlor patter and leave the tunnels to men who know 'em."

"You know how often I tried to get Papa to accept a bid from the H and B for timber frames and how stubbornly set he was against it."

"Hardheaded customer, your daddy," Tavis muttered not unkindly.

"I have to make those decisions now, and I'm thinking of listening to what Cameron has to say."

"You'd sell to the likes of him? Joey, your papa'd be turning in his grave, were he in it."

Joelle's features pinched in displeasure and dismay. She knew he was right. "Papa's not here, and I'm in charge of the Superior. I have to consider what's best for my crews. And myself. Do you think this man Cameron would listen to reason?"

What was that funny glimmer in the girl's eyes? Why it looked to be an odd mix of female flusters. From his Joey? Unheard of. Unless . . .

Then he recalled the similarly strange way Cameron had referred to his niece, as if something had already sparked between them. At first he was outraged by the mere thought of that and was about to say so. Before he spoke out, however, a more cunning logic caught back his words. He needed Cameron out from underfoot if he was to undercut his authority. And what better distraction than a pretty, blushing package.

Tavis Lachlan smiled.

"Oh, lass, I think I have in mind the very way to get him to listen. Use your feminine wiles."

4

"WILES?"

Joelle repeated the word, frowning. She wasn't exactly sure what these wiles were, but she didn't like the sound of it, or the cunning look that stole over her uncle's face.

"I'll do no such thing."

Tavis took her refusal lightly. "Now, Joey-lass, what better way for a woman to work her will upon a man?"

Her lips pursed into an uncertain moue. It was humbling for her to ask, "How do I know I even have these wiles?"

Tavis gave a great booming laugh. "Oh, girl, you've got 'em all right. Been using 'em since you been out of the cradle. Heaven help the men when you find out what to do with 'em."

Joelle scowled. She didn't like being laughed at for her naïveté. And she was beginning to suspect what wiles were all about. They had to do with female flirting. Now, there was a ridiculous notion. As if she could make an impression upon a man like Marshall Cameron with the fluttering of her eyelashes. Why, the man probably waded through pools of Eastern society belles on a daily basis. And her uncle thought he'd be charmed by the likes of her in her plaid mackinaw and cropped hair? Absurd. Anguish swelled within her when she thought of how different she must be from Marshall Cameron's ideal view of the female form. She tried to hide this unfamiliar hurt under a gruff facade.

"Really, Tavis. How could you suggest such a thing? I have no want to woo the man. I plan to go into business with him, not into bed."

Realizing what she'd said, she felt a hot flush spread across her cheeks because that *was* the direction her nightly musings about the new H&B agent had begun to take. She'd thought of little else since dropping him off a week ago. She'd lain awake experiencing the hard press of his body against hers in the privacy of her mind. The memory of being in the warm circle of his arms, smelling the leathery richness of his scent, and basking in the lambent glow of his dark eyes caused a desperate restlessness she could not explain. Was she attracted to Marshall Cameron simply because he was the only man she hadn't known like a brother all her life? The notion of Marshall Cameron in her arms and in her bed made nice fodder for dreams, but it also shamed and confused her so thoroughly that she was quick to put it from her mind.

"I want nothing of a personal nature to do with the man," she insisted a little too vigorously. "I need the security of the H and B behind my logging company. That's all."

"If you say so, lass."

Joelle gave him a sharp look. Why did he sound so disbelieving?

Because he didn't believe her. Tavis was not unfamiliar with a girl's blushes. They usually meant that just the opposite of what she was saying was true, and his niece was doing a keenly amount of protesting. So, the girl had taken a fancy to the dapper mine agent. For the moment, it was to his advantage to allow it. For the moment.

"Joey, I'm not asking you to seduce the man." If he hadn't been convinced before, her sudden gasp of mortification was all conclusive.

"Good, because . . . because I want to be taken seriously. I don't want him to get the idea that he's dealing with a weak, silly woman."

Tavis gaged the determined angle of her chin and the steely flash of her gaze. "No danger of that, lass."

Misinterpreting his claim, Joelle nodded curtly. She should have felt vindicated but instead felt deflated. No, Marshall Cameron didn't think he was dealing with a woman at all. He considered her a girl-child in lad's clothing, and she wasn't sure if it was her youth or the lack of femininity she objected to the most when viewed through those dark eyes.

Tavis took a moment to rethink his strategy. So the girl wouldn't play the seductress. He shouldn't have entertained the idea. His Joey had no idea a woman lurked inside her yet. If she was feeling urges of the female kind where Cameron was concerned, she likely wouldn't act on them if she knew how. Not that he'd want her all cozied up to any man, let alone this one. If passion wasn't the route, perhaps pride would serve him better. And the girl knew all about being prideful. He leaned back in his chair and smiled lazily.

"Lass, if you be wanting the man to take you serious, you best be showing him of what you're made. What better way than to take him to the cutting grounds to see your crews at work? To see you at work? Then he'll be knowing you're not all bluff and blow. You want to be keeping the Superior in the family, don't you?"

"You know I do," she claimed without hesitation.

"Go talk to the man. And if you doan feel right leading him on with your smiles, let him know there be a brain at work behind it."

So simple. Why hadn't she thought of it? Because she was too consumed with the memory of the man's dimples to be thinking direct thoughts. She chided herself for that silliness. What difference should it make that the man was appealing? She was interested in courting the H&B, not its agent.

Joelle slid from her chair and went to slip her arms about her uncle's thick neck. It was an impulsive hug, one expressing gratitude and affection. Tavis experienced only the slightest degree of guilt at manipulating it. After all, the girl would save her company, and he would save his place at the mine. What was so wrong in that? Marshall Cameron was the only one who stood to lose, and he felt no sorrow over it.

Tavis's smile lingered after the girl rushed out the door. Oh, aye, this would work well, it would. With the meddlesome Cameron gone, it would be business as usual until he had his response from Boston. He would send his own letter to the H&B Board via the daily winter run of the American Express Company. It would be in Green Bay in three days. He'd make sure Cameron's report and request were routed along the regular overland route by dog sled. They would reach the same destination 260 miles away in about eight days—if they got there at all. Items were known to get lost along that rugged trail, an annoyingly common occurrence.

If Colin Cameron's son had the poor judgment to be off frolicking in the woods while another plotted his downfall, he deserved what he got.

When Joelle knocked at Cameron's door, Spotted Fawn let her in. The Ojibway woman was the wife of one of the surface miners, and Cameron had apparently hired her on to do his housekeeping. Joelle found that amusing. How much tending could one man require? Or was he just used to having servants at his beck and call? Her own father had been a much better cook than she, and they had divided the domestic tasks equally between them in the woods and during the few months that they were under a roof. Theirs had been a true partnership, and she could not imagine humbling herself into a lesser role, not for any man. Especially one too lazy—or too helpless— to dish up his own beans.

Spotted Fawn ushered her into the small front room to wait. Was the delicate Easterner already abed? she wondered with some derision. Then she pictured Marshall Cameron's long form stretched out beneath clean sheets . . . Angrily she forced her thoughts from that enticing image and into a study of the room. He'd done something to it. She'd been in these agent's quarters with her father when he'd reluctantly come to hear Cameron's predecessor's offer. The room had been a dusty, spartan space, typical of the social indifference of the northwoods. The place was different now, not just swept clean of gritty hematite but actually inviting, the way she supposed a home would be. She noted the small details curiously, not having had a permanent home since her mother died.

A fire burned warmly in the grate. Several chairs were pulled up before it, inviting an intimate coze. Woven cushions softened the hard wood seats. A pipe with an intricately carved bowl perched on a humidor of the same design, had been left on a squat stool. Next to it was a stack of periodicals awaiting an evening read. She recognized recent copies of the *Portage*

Lake Mining Gazette among others. Imagine that. During the summer months, the northwoods' residents received papers and magazines on a regular basis; weeks, sometimes months out of date, but regularly. In the winter, the same dog-eared issue circulated from December to February. If she hadn't been so nervous about her meeting with Cameron, she would have gone through the magazines with interest. Instead she restlessly continued her inspection of the room.

Cameron had hung a painting above the stone fireplace and Joelle stepped closer to study it, a harbor scene looking down over steep-pitched roofs crowded close together near a bustling dockside. Was this Boston? How congested it appeared with nary a tree in sight. Was this where Marshall had grown up, then, amid the crammed quarters and cobbled streets? She marveled at the latter. Imagine a paved road. No wonder he'd expected a smoother ride. She smiled suddenly, remembering. Boston. So very far away and removed from her world, the place he'd return to after the spring thaws.

Sighing, she moved away from the painting and locked her eyes on a rare and wonderful sight. Books. Dozens of them. With excitement she knelt before the leather-bound stacks and ran a fingertip along the glittering gilt titles. She owned one hardbound book, her mother's family Bible. But here was a whole world of words: fiction, biographies, industry journals, plays, poems. With hands so eager they trembled, she lifted the top volume and reverently thumbed through the crisp pages. Sonnets. She was so engrossed in the flowing sentiments that she didn't realize she was no longer alone.

"You could borrow that if you like."

The smooth, masculine tone brought her about with a guilty gasp. The covers snapped shut between her palms. "I was just looking," she stammered as if expecting him to accuse her of stealing the words from the page.

"Be my guest. I must confess, I couldn't decide which of my books I wanted to reread for five months, so I brought all I could carry. A bit of an extravagance as far as freighting goes, but worth it. At least to me."

"Oh, yes." She sighed softly. The sound was like a caress.

For a long moment Marsh stood mesmerized by the silky passion in her voice, by the way the firelight detailed the

contour of one soft cheek. She'd taken off her ragged cap.
Though chopped to collar length, her glossy hair had a rich
blue-black sheen that invited a man's touch—the way her
unguarded gaze and gently parted lips invited a kiss. She'd
thrown off the heavy mackinaw coat, and while her wool shirt
was hardly form-fitted, her suspenders curved about the small
breasts beneath them.

His attraction to her was as unexpected as it was potent.
Heat seared through him like a long, delicious swallow of
brandy. But it settled and burned much lower than the region
of his belly. The way she was crouched before his fire, her
eyes uplifted to offer—hell, he must be crazy. He had a
fiancée in Boston and absolutely no business swelling up
like a pubescent boy obsessed with an unattainable fantasy.
And from what he knew of her, if Joelle Parry had any
idea of the direction of his thoughts, she'd most likely be
pitching that tome at his head instead of stirring his primitive
desires with her unintentionally sultry stare. He decided that
the invigorating northwoods air and his isolated state must
have made him so vulnerable to a pair of pouty wet lips
and revealing suspenders. But there was no need to react
to her like a bull moose in rut. To calm himself he drew a
deep breath, but it sounded suspiciously ragged.

"If you'd like to borrow that book, or any of the others,
please do," he restated gruffly.

Joelle set the treasured book aside. "I don't have time to
read." That came out with a hoarseness that matched his, and
she nervously cleared her throat. But the congestion wasn't
there. It was lower. Something was banging about her ribs
with frightening little lurches. The way he was looking at her,
all hot and smoky as if he were privy to what was hidden
under her bulky layers of wool, unnerved her. Defensively she
rose from her position at his feet to face him. Still he towered
over her, making her feel small and oddly powerless because
he was standing so close. They were toe to toe, with her nose
nearly pressed into the silky folds of his cravat. A cravat, she
thought in fluttery amusement. Who was he dressing for out
here in the wilderness? He looked inappropriately formal and
uncomfortable. She was tempted to reach up and loosen that
rigid knot . . .

What was she thinking?

She couldn't concentrate on business, not with him and his broad chest assaulting her senses. Retreat was impossible. She could feel the heat from the fire blistering against her backside, but the warmth emitting from Marshall Cameron was more dangerous. Since she couldn't go around him or step back, Joelle put her hands on his vested front and pushed. He took an awkward forced step, and she was able to slip by into the rescuing openness of the room. Her palms tingled. The satin fabric of his waistcoat seemed impressed upon her palms. She found herself rubbing them brusquely on her woolen trousers.

Marsh had seen the sudden flare of panic in her eyes, and yet he'd stood there barring her way like the rudest sort of dolt. What was wrong with him? He hadn't meant to come on aggressively or to intimidate her by his immobile stance. He simply hadn't been capable of movement until her shove woke him to his own behavior. He felt contrite, and she looked plainly furious.

"I hope I didn't keep you waiting long," he began lamely. "I was going over some tally sheets and I really wasn't expecting visitors."

Then why was he all gussied up? Surely a man wouldn't go through all the trouble to stay starched and stiff for his own company. She found her gaze assessing the fit of his coat, the way it molded to the broad expanse of shoulders and skimmed down his torso. There was no mistaking the lean fitness of his body, a form she remembered well for its unyielding contours. Good heavens, how her thoughts were digressing. What if he'd noticed the blatant way her eyes were caressing him? She'd heard Spotted Fawn leave—they were completely alone now. She swallowed hard.

"My uncle tells me you're ready to talk timber." Her words were an abrupt reflection of the angry turmoil inside her. Unconsciously she took a mannish stand, legs spraddled and arms akimbo, with her chin jutting at a stubborn angle.

The contrast to the kittenish figure curled on his hearth a moment ago made Marsh smile.

The dimples played along his cheeks, and Joelle struggled to deny the achy sensation forcing its way upward.

"And your uncle tells me you're the owner of Superior Lumbering. Why didn't you tell me yourself?"

"What, and cheat you out of the opportunity to bray like an arrogant . . . donkey?"

His grin grew rueful as he recalled his haughty confidence. He hadn't known he was speaking of *her* company when he vowed to take it over. He had the decency to look uncomfortable with the memory. "I thought you came to talk business, not to help me dine upon my own foolish foot."

With his embarrassment to bolster her, Joelle allowed a small smile. "Yes, business. What kind of deal are you willing to offer for Superior pine?"

"I wasn't planning to offer on the pine. I intended to buy out the whole company."

The smile stiffened on her lips. "I know that was what you intended, but it is quite impossible. The Superior is not for sale. Just the lumber."

"But I understood—"

He looked at her, and she could tell what he was seeing through his narrow Eastern eyes. A woman. A girl. In control of a logging outfit. Her temper simmered.

"You understood what, Mr. Cameron?"

He softened his tone to a kind timbre. "With your father gone, I naturally assumed—"

"You assumed wrong. I was more than a fixture in my father's home, as hard as you may find that to comprehend. I did his books, I drove his teams, I notched his logs. *Our* logs. I know as much if not more about timbering than any man in this region. And right now I need a contract, not your condescension."

Then he sapped the wind from her haughty sails. "I'm sorry, Miss Parry. *That* is quite impossible."

"What? W-why? You said you needed the lumber."

"I do, through a reputable company. Like the one owned by your father. Forgive me, but an operation of that size in the hands of a . . . a . . ."

"Female?" she supplied for him frostily.

"An inexperienced youth, regardless of gender, is too great a risk."

She stared at him, at his unsmiling face, and saw the

businessman in him. Inflexible. Inscrutable. Intolerable!

"Why you—"

"Please, Miss Parry," he interrupted, neatly severing a spew of the worst epithets she could bring to mind. "There is no need to vent your opinion, colorful though I am sure it is. I will buy you out, but I won't bid for your lumber."

She stood stunned by his flat decree. Then, to her horror, her eyes welled up with tears. He couldn't have missed the shimmering of quicksilver in that instant. His features didn't soften, and he didn't change his mind, but he did turn away so as not to embarrass her in her weakness.

Joelle groped behind her until her fingertips touched the arm of a chair. She collapsed onto its woven cushion, drained by the hopelessness of her position. *Papa, what am I going to do?* The H&B was her last chance. Without its business to sustain it, Superior would flounder and fold. Its jacks would drift to other camps for winter work. They wouldn't want to, but they had to look out for themselves, and she couldn't blame them. Without financial backing she couldn't keep her crews out; not without gear, not without food, not without the certainty of a payday in the spring. Where would she go? To the relatives in Detroit? No. She wouldn't be able to stand that. She'd feel caged after knowing the freedom of the northlands. Perhaps she could hire out to keep the books for some other company. Perhaps she could . . .

Who was she fooling? Joelle was at heart a realist. Without the H&B, she had no option but to close. And that would leave her adrift. She would not consider becoming a burden to her uncle, though she was sure he would take her in. What she wanted was to make her own way. What would Lyle Parry have had her do? Sell out to survive or hold to her pride and submit to ruin? She lost either way.

Marsh toed one of the logs back into the grate, sending up a shower of spark and ash. He'd done that to Joelle Parry, too. Rolled that vibrant flame of life over to deadened ash. Guilt twisted in his gut at the thought of her damp gaze. Well, what else could he do? It wasn't his money. Not yet. He had to act in the best interest of the mine. In the process he had broken the lively spirit of a woman he admired. God, he hated it.

"There are other mines that need good timber," he began quietly, offering that suggestion in a pallid attempt to ease his sense of obligation. She was silent. At least she wasn't weeping. He turned to find the forlorn evidence blinked away from her direct stare. She came up out of the chair with stiff dignity.

Never, ever, would she let him know the truth—that she had spent most of the week in search of adequate support through the neighboring mines. All the companies were of the same unyielding mind. A woman was useless at the helm of a business, and no one was willing to be shown otherwise. No one would give Lyle Parry's daughter the benefit of her years of experience in the forest. No one would allow her to prove her mettle in this, a man's world. She hated being snubbed, especially by this man. For some reason the insult felt worse coming from Marshall Cameron.

"I won't take up any more of your time," she said sharply.

She started for the door, only to have his hand close about her upper arm in a gentle, restraining cuff. His fingers curled just firmly enough to convince her he wouldn't be shaken off lightly. Her head came up, her eyes cutting toward him, glittering like freshly honed steel.

"You'll be all right, won't you?"

That touch of concern brought on a spasm of despairing fury. How dare he?

"I will be just fine, Mr. Cameron, no thanks to you. Now please let me go."

But he wouldn't. "Where? Where will you go?"

"I don't see that it's any of your— Haven't we been over this before?"

He made a rueful face, and his fingers loosened. "Yes, I suppose we have. Forgive me, Miss Parry."

With one last frigid look, she stormed to the entrance and wrenched open the door. The cold air struck her like a bracing slap. She gasped and almost reeled from the force. But the chill snapped something inside her, that thread of sullen pity that she chose to call pride.

What good was pride without the Superior?

Slowly she closed the door on that bitter wind and revolved back toward the silent figure watching her. She squared her shoulders and girded her will, needing every scrap of her courage and control to speak the words that could mean salvation.

"I will sell you the Superior."

Before he could respond in any manner, her chin angled up with determination.

"But there is a condition."

"And what might that be, Miss Parry?"

"I go with it."

5

"I BEG YOUR pardon." Surely he hadn't heard her right. The woman had a habit of saying the most outrageous things.

But she looked serious standing at the threshold of his home with her eyes cool as metal chips, with her posture framed up as if she were a prizefighter setting for a roundhouse punch, knowing it was coming yet daring it to do its worst. The woman had unshakable temerity.

"I'll let you buy the Superior, at a fair price, of course. But you will keep me on to manage it."

There, she'd said it. Joelle waited, not daring to take a breath watching Marshall Cameron's face for an answer. He had to say yes, she willed frantically. Everything she had rested upon this final sacrifice. Her heart was beating wildly behind the challenging calm of her facade.

He crossed the space between them, coming to stand over her. She held her ground, refusing to be intimidated by his size or his nearness, the latter being the most difficult. Marsh looked at her, long and with much bewilderment. Here was a young woman, a woman who could be a true beauty, seemingly content in her mannish clothes, in this isolated north. He couldn't figure it and spoke his confusion aloud. "Why, Miss Parry? With the money from the sale you could go just about anywhere, somewhere there's at least a trace of civilization and a chance of living comfortably."

She smiled then, showing a row of perfect white teeth. "And

do what?" she chided. "Find some nice man to take care of me?" His silence was answer enough. She sighed and shook her head. "I don't want to be taken care of, Mr. Cameron. I don't want to leave my home or the life my father made for me at the Superior. These woods are all I've ever known, and the Superior loggers are my family. I'm responsible for them and for keeping my father's hopes alive. I wouldn't be happy anywhere else, doing anything else. Lumbering is what I know."

He frowned, feeling so exasperated with her that it was an effort not to shake some sense into her stubborn little head. Or to turn her over his knee and swat the silly, impossible notion out of her thoughts. Or to jerk her up against him and kiss her pursed lips into recognizing the benefit of being cared for. Or simply to offer an embrace to salute her courage. He couldn't do any of those things. So he glowered down at her, angry at her plucky stand, frustrated at his desire to yield to it, and hating himself because he knew he couldn't.

"I was afraid you'd say something like that," he muttered. "And I'm afraid I'll have to say—"

Her fingers came up quickly to press over his mouth, halting that final word. She felt his breath suck in sharply beneath her touch, betraying his surprise, just as the sudden flare of intensity in his eyes spoke silently, explicitly, of other things born in that moment.

"No. Don't. Not yet," she urged breathlessly. How soft, how full his lips were, she realized in tangent wonder. Without consent, hers or his, her fingertips strayed slightly, testing those warm contours. "Don't say it until you hear me out."

Marsh wet his suddenly dry mouth, his tongue darting across the pads of her fingers in the process. She pulled her hand back, as alarmed as he had been by the contact. And she knew the moment saner thought returned to him. He blinked. He took a step back. But she knew she couldn't let him go. While she didn't understand completely, Joelle realized in that instant the power of feminine wiles. As long as she was close, as long as she was touching him, he couldn't think clearly. Somehow the effect she had on him detoured that rational process. She didn't want him thinking clearly, dispassionately, at this all-important impasse. She needed him off balance.

And so she took a matching step forward, reaching out to catch the front of his coat in an imploring gesture. Her gaze sought his and held it captive. She knew when his logic faltered. She could see it reflected back in the abrupt clouding of his wary gaze. But she wasn't as immune to it herself as she wished to be. There was something so compelling, so satisfying, about being engulfed by his dark eyes.

"Marshall, please," she entreated softly, her fingers gathering in the fine fabric, pulling him closer. "You owe me a chance to explain, don't you?"

No, he wanted to say. *No, I don't owe you anything.* But the words were jammed up in the tight swelling of his throat, along with his breath, along with his train of conscious thought. She had the most bewitching eyes, gray like the shadowed dawn, ringed with a sensual fringe of inky lashes. He wanted to help himself to their mysterious promise. What would desire look like, steeping in that smoky stare? The wondering held him hostage.

"You need me, Marshall," she told him with a husky certainty. The double-edged meaning made his breathing race and labor. "You don't know these woods. You don't know these men. I do. They're my woods, my people. Let me show you how to get the most from them."

"It's not my decision." His protest was vague, then completely useless. Her fingertips brushed over his lips again, scrambling coherent thoughts, inviting others of a more potent nature as they trailed lightly from his chin to the top of his very proper cravat.

"Yes, it is," she argued softly. "It is your decision. Give me the chance to prove myself to you. You won't regret it. Come with me. Join me and the Superior crew at the cutting grounds. Watch us work together. Give me one month. If you're not completely convinced about me by then, I'll let the Superior go. One month, Marshall. That's all I ask."

"You have no chance for another contract, do you?"

By telling the truth, she knew she might lose whatever bartering power she had, but Joelle couldn't bring a lie to her lips. She moistened them nervously before saying with quiet candor, "No. There's only you and the H and B. I need this chance. I need your help. You told me to ask, and I am. You've nothing to lose, and everything I have is in the balance." Looking up into his dark eyes, she couldn't believe he would use that helplessness against her.

"All right."

Incredibly he heard those raspy words come from his own mouth. He hadn't been aware of making any conscious decision.

"We can work out the details later," he went on in that same winded tone. "Have the papers drawn up with the figure you feel is fair. I'll submit the offer to the H and B."

"And if they won't accept it?" The edge of desperation returned to her voice. "We have to have a commitment now. If we wait, we won't be able to purchase supplies, and I won't be able to send out my crews again. I have to have a guarantee now that will give me a line of credit."

Silencing her mounting upset with the same means she'd chosen, Marsh placed his forefinger against the soft swell of her lips. "You have my guarantee. Is that enough? I'll front the money you need to get operations under way."

She turned her head slightly in order to speak, causing his finger to graze along the curve of her cheek. It was a smooth touch. There were no calluses on his hands. "But can you afford to take the risk? What if the H and B won't agree to buy?"

Her concern for him twisted the knot already lodged in his chest. Had she been merely greedy, she would have jumped without a thought to his situation. He liked her more for that hesitation.

"Then I guess I'll own myself a lumbering company."

Her sigh was like music. "Thank you, Marsh." Then her arms went quickly about him, hugging his shoulders tight to seal their arrangement. He let his face be coaxed into her short tousle of black hair as the feel of her against him proved the killing stroke to his control. He just had to have this provoking, impetuous creature. But even as his arms rose in hopes of claiming her, she stepped back from the grasp of temptation. He waited, uncertain whether to pursue what he daren't catch or to let her slip away.

Joelle smiled then, a soft, beguiling smile that wrought him up so tight inside he didn't have the presence of mind to stop her before she snatched up her coat and slipped out into the night.

The waft of cold air woke him from his sensual daze. He closed his mouth—he hadn't known his jaw had slackened—and gave his head a brisk shake. What had happened? He felt as though he were struggling against the stunning effects of an uppercut. His thoughts were buzzing. He was disoriented. Without so much as a kiss or an overt caress, the little witch had seduced him into compromising his judgment. And she had done it so neatly that he hadn't felt the effects until he'd given in to her will.

He should have been furious. He should have stormed after her to flatly refuse to honor the vow she'd extorted from him. As a man who prided himself on the divorce of wisdom from want, he should have been humiliated by the easy way she'd played upon his passions, making him a fool in the face of her feminine persuasions.

But Marshall Cameron was amused. And impossibly aroused. Both mentally and physically. The sly minx had circumvented his logic and his arguments with the oldest ploy known to womankind. He'd fallen captive to her big, beautiful eyes. If she was clever enough to make him do that unwittingly, just maybe she could manage a lumbering outfit.

Marsh went to pour himself a good stiff drink, hoping its balm would soothe the friction of his meeting with Joelle Parry. It helped. Some. He began to think seriously about the situation at hand and about the woman who had forced it. He'd been sent to Eagle River to tend the interests of the H&B. He owed them a thorough investigation before investing any of their funds. If he was buying the Superior, he needed to know all there was to know and didn't have the time for an impartial study.

He could now call himself a lumber baron. That was rich. He took another long sip. So much for his get-in-and-get-out plan. Why he'd court ties here in this wilderness, he didn't know. But then there was no use applying logic to Joelle Parry. He couldn't believe what he was entertaining at this late hour, in this desolate setting—keeping the Superior for his own investment and subcontracting the lumber to the H&B. Was this a sound move or simply the result of an irresistible interest in the company's female manager? But he hadn't promised to give her that title yet. He wasn't quite that far gone to her charms. The staid Bostonian in him rebelled against the thought of contributing to her folly. She should take his money and make a more comfortable life for herself. But that was her decision. He had no right to disqualify her from the job just because he didn't believe it suited a woman. But Joelle Parry wasn't like any of the women he knew. He couldn't imagine those parlor pretties surviving a day, let alone a lifetime, in this brutal clime. Not when there was a chance it would chafe their creamy skin or add one premature wrinkle to their pristine brows. They were delicate, pampered, in need of protection. But not this female. Not this little spitfire with her candid speech and stubborn stance.

A month in the woods, where it was probably blistering cold. What had he been thinking? He was unprepared for such a venture, but he would manage. If Joelle Parry could thrive in the harsh northlands, he surely wouldn't perish. But the thought of the primitive conditions even farther away from his few comforts here wasn't at all appealing, not as appealing as the surprisingly seductive Miss Parry.

In truth, he knew nothing about logging, and she'd been raised in the midst of it. In spite of his reluctance to place such responsibility on a woman, and such a young one at that, he was smart enough to know he could learn from her. It was to his advantage to have a working knowledge of any enterprise he meant to sink money into, whether the funds were his or the company's. Soon they would be one and the same. And as for being off in the northern wilderness with Joelle Parry for an entire month, perhaps there were a few things he could teach her as well, such as not to play games with a man's desires.

Joelle ran back to her uncle's company house. The hour was too late to begin the ride to the Superior offices so she would stay overnight at the H&B. She preferred to blame the sprint or the cold evening air for her breathlessness, but it was Marshall Cameron who had her gasping for control.

How could she have sidled up to him, touched him as she had, and led him to believe she had bartered her person for his promise? He'd agreed to the exchange. Now what would she do should he choose to act upon her invitation?

She'd thrown away pride and shame the moment she put her hand to his lips, an innocent gesture at first. Then she'd discovered how potent such a touch could be. She had had no idea he'd react the way he did, as if she'd struck him an unexpected blow. She had had no idea so simple a touch could bring such a fiery longing to burn in a man's eyes. She had no experience with a man's passion, only with playful taunting, friend to friend. This was very different.

She had enjoyed his closeness, his scent, the feel of him, in her first venture toward maturity of an intimate kind, and she found it exhilarating. She'd wanted to go beyond the exploration of fingertips, to taste the generous curve of his mouth with her own, another first. The last time someone had stolen a kiss, he and she had been little more than children, and she'd blackened his eye. She hadn't liked the kiss at all and remembered how repulsed she'd been by the boy's sloppy inexperience. Kissing would be pleasureable with Marshall Cameron. She just knew it. But kissing, her father had told her in no uncertain terms, led to other forms of male-female entanglements, and he'd always threatened to tan her hide if he caught her experimenting. That was when she was a girl— now her father was no longer here, and the feelings Marshall Cameron stirred inside her were by no means girlish. She was a woman, and he was no fumbling lad.

He was the mine agent for the H&B.

How could she have forgotten that? She'd played loose and fast with his sensibilities. By now he would have his faculties back. What if he was angry about the tricks she'd employed to gain his agreement? What if he was angry enough to change his mind about wanting the Superior at all? Panic hurried her steps and brought a mental scourging. She'd gone to him to impress him with a business arrangement and had secured him with an altogether different promise. How could she ever convince him of her capability after playing such a game?

Then a cool, saving logic intervened. Her pace slowed. Her breathing grew less frantic. What did she care what he thought of her, as long as the Superior was secured? So what if he considered her morals questionable. She had the backing she needed to get her crews into the woods. And once she had

Marshall Cameron there, he could see for himself what kind of manager she was. His opinion wasn't the important thing. Saving her father's company was.

So she continued to tell herself.

By the time she reached her uncle's door, she was once again feeling confident and in control. She'd done what she'd set out to do. Pride began to swell within her, crowding out her anxiety of moments ago. Tomorrow she would travel into Eagle River to order up, on the H&B's account, the supplies they needed before everything was picked over by the other lumbering firms heading for the trees. She would gather the foremen to explain the change in owners and assure them of her continued stability at their helm. The timber cruisers already had the best site selected. Advance crews had secured the area, putting up bunks and stables, cutting roads from the camp into the cutting grounds, and marking the trees they would take down. They'd done that much while waiting for Lyle Parry to return from Duluth. He'd let them down. She wouldn't.

Excitement sang inside her. By week's end, crews would be deep in the embrace of the woodlands where they would live and work for the next five months, surrounded by the sharp pitch scent of the pines and the crisp bite of winter.

Where she would prove herself to Marshall Cameron.

"How did it go, lass?"

Tavis was waiting for her by the radiating warmth of the stove. She felt heat fire her cheeks again and prayed their high color wouldn't betray her. But then, why was she worried over what he thought? Hadn't he been the one to suggest using wiles?

"I sold the Superior."

His expression didn't alter at that soft statement. There was, however, a certain tension in his tone. "Did you now?"

"It was the only way. The stubborn man flatly refused to contract with us." She plopped gracelessly into a chair, scowling. Then her features grew rueful. "I shouldn't blame him. None of the others would either, and they know me. They just wouldn't trust a woman in a man's job."

Tavis pursed his lips around the stem of his pipe. "It's a mighty big job for a wee girl."

"I could have done it. If I'd had the funds."

"I'm sure you could have, darlin'. You've that much of your father in you. So you sold the H and B." So much for his plans.

Joelle brightened, a smug suggestion of a smile playing about her lips. "But I'm to stay on as its manager."

"Cameron went along with that, did he?"

Her smile grew wry. "For the moment. I have to prove my worth to him in the woods. As if the likes of him would know how to judge me. Honestly, Tavis, I don't know how I'll survive tutoring such a greenhorn for the next month."

"He's going with you, then?"

"We leave at week's end."

"Good girl, lass. Good girl. You do your daddy proud."

Tavis sat back in his chair, puffing his pipe, mentally washing his hands of the problem of Marshall Cameron. *I got you now, Colin, me boy. It took a while, but I got you.*

A rough wagon came to collect Marsh that Sunday. Its driver was a growling soul who questioned every piece of banded luggage with a haughty lift of his brow. Where did the dapper fellow think he was bound? For a bloody picnic? To a right proper resort? He, like all the other shantymen, carried his earthly belongings in his turkey, and what he couldn't fit into that shapeless bag he bought on credit at the camp van. What was this blighter toting along? His feather bed?

His gaze summed up Marshall Cameron in a single sweep. Eastern. Educated. Useless. The man wouldn't last a day holding his own in the woods. An observer, Jo had told them. Did that mean the man meant to place his pampered arse on a stump and watch them sweat and toil for a living? Miss Jo had warned them to treat the man with respect. She should know better than to make such a demand. Respect wasn't something you gave, it was something that had to be earned. And this soft touch didn't look to be deserving of it. But for Lyle Parry's daughter he would make nice with the tenderfoot. Even if it stuck in his craw.

The wagon jerked forward, nearly spilling Marsh into the bed. He noted the driver's poorly veiled smile and decided then and there to voice no complaints. He was along for the ride, more a nuisance then a guest. It was best he remembered that, if he planned to survive among these gruff sorts for an entire month.

God help him.

Just as he made that vow, the wheels struck a bump a blind man would have seen.

"Sorry," the man at the reins drawled with as much sincerity as a February thaw. "Looks to be a rough ride."

Yes, Marsh was sure it would be. He forced a smile over teeth clenched to prevent the biting of his tongue. He'd already bitten off more than he could chew with this wilderness jaunt. No sense adding insult to injury.

The driver began a tuneless whistle and steered the team toward the second of an endless series of ruts.

Marsh gritted his teeth and hung on.

6

THIS WAS WHERE he was going to spend the next thirty days.

Marsh looked about the camp, at the buildings of board and tar paper that held no promise of warmth or comfort. Oh, no, he moaned to himself. Never again would he allow himself to be led astray by a pair of bewitching gray eyes. What madness had worked upon him to lure him from the now familiar ease of his mine office home to this copse of barbarity?

His gaze tracked Joelle as she mingled with the rough shantyboys—and from their rude living quarters, he could guess where lumberjacks had come by that name. Joelle stopped to speak with each man who arrived at the camp to work. She would squeeze his beefy arms with fondness and smile. When the mellow tones of her laughter reached him, Marshall experienced the queer tension in his middle all over again. While there was nothing wrong with appreciating a lovely woman, he wasn't happy about wanting this one quite so much.

When she saw him, her features stiffened, revealing displeasure rather than welcome. After the intensity of their last meeting, he'd prepared for flirtation or embarrassment but not that cut of cold winter that froze him clear across the camp.

Joelle couldn't miss seeing him. He stood out in his Eastern finery like a bird of paradise amid dull brown sparrows. Knowing she couldn't avoid him forever yet feeling ill-prepared for this first meeting, she stared at him across the clearing. To hide her anxiety, she encouraged a prick of anger. What could he expect, after all? Theirs was to be a business arrangement, and he should know that from the start. She needed to control her wayward emotions as well; otherwise, the next month would be sheer hell.

Realizing that some of the men had noticed their awkward stalemate, Joelle forced herself to cross the frozen ground. Anxiety starched her spine. By the time she reached Cameron her nerves were stretched as taut as a toggle chain.

"I see you survived the ride."

Marsh rubbed the small of his back tenderly. "I'll let you know when my spine quits clattering."

Damn, there were those dimples dancing mischievously along his cheeks. She had to look away. Her gaze shifted to the pile of bags the disgruntled driver had tossed to the snowy ground. "Are all those yours?"

Seeing her reprehensible frown, he rallied with a casual shrug. "Just the barest necessities I require to get by."

"You'll have to get by on a lot less unless you can convince half your bunkmates to forfeit their storage space. This is not exactly a hotel, Cameron."

"So I have noticed, Miss Parry."

Since she couldn't seem to shame him for his excess, Joelle gave up. "I suppose you can stick some of it in my quarters." As his brow rose askance, she quickly clarified that arrangement. "You, of course, will be bunking with the rest of the men."

He grinned at the discomfiture hidden beneath her bluster. "Of course."

"It's the best we can do. We're not set up for houseguests. If you find the situation totally unacceptable, I suppose we could erect some sort of temporary rooms for you."

Because her tone let him know that such an effort would be considered wasteful and inappropriate, he assured her, "I'll bunk with the crew. Don't go to any trouble. This isn't a hotel, as you said I don't require any special attention."

Joelle glanced at the mound of baggage and lifted a doubtful brow. That remained to be seen. "Why don't I show you where you'll be quartered, and then you can decide what you have to have with you. Be warned, it's rough."

Rough was an incredible understatement. Crowded, without an inch of privacy and totally lacking in personal space would have been a more accurate summation. As Marsh surveyed his new home, he tried not to reveal his dismay. For the next month he was going to be stacked in like cordwood among a hundred other men.

The bunkhouse was about seventy-five feet long, made of log and roofed with tar paper. It was windowless and gloomy. A huge iron stove squatted in the center of the room. The stovepipe went up then divided to run the length of the building in either direction, to a smokestack at each end. Rows of upper and lower bunks filled both sides of the long room, an idea borrowed from the Pullman car. In front of the lower bunks a deacon seat ran, where Marsh assumed the crew would gather beneath the string of kerosene lamps in the evening. He tested the mattress of the bed closet him and heard a suspicious crunching sound. Leaves? Branches? And from the looks of it a hay sack for a pillow and bedbugs for bunkmates. He made a grim face.

"Wishing for that hotel about now?" Joelle teased softly. How primitive things must look to him. She tried to view the room through his eyes and could understand his horror. Or at least she attempted to. For that he was grateful and because there was no malice in her tone, he responded with a wry smile.

"Or at least a feather bed."

"Sorry." She did sound sincere if not amused. "But I did warn you."

"So you did." He gave a determined sigh. "This will be fine. Which one is mine?"

Joelle cleared her throat uncomfortably. "Actually, you'll be sharing that one there with one of the others."

Marsh looked to the top bunk, which seemed too narrow for intimate lovers let alone two strangers of the same gender. He'd need heroic effort to retain his humor. "I suppose it's too much to hope that he won't snore."

Joelle's lips twitched. "That I couldn't tell you."

Marsh tossed his smallest travel case upon the rustling bunk. "I guess I'll just have to store the others. How about a tour of the rest of the camp? I'm sure I'll be quite familiar with this room by morning." And familiar with all its occupants the way they were smashed together like ticking in one gigantic bed.

The camp was full of activity now that work would begin early the next morn. The axmen were busy honing the tools of their trade, and several groups had banded together for an energetic game of cards. No one failed to notice the foreigner among them, walking at the side of their new boss lady. A new game of chance arose as the men began a betting pool—to see how long the Easterner would last.

Marsh found the camp to be compact and surprisingly self-sufficient. A large log barn without a floor housed the logging horses. These medium-sized animals were kept well shod, well fed, and well groomed. A corner of the barn made a makeshift blacksmith shop. It's smithy repaired logging chains, helped build bobsleds to carry the felled trees, and fastened on the large iron runners, as well as kept the horses sharply shod. Joelle lifted up one of the sturdy hoofs and showed Marsh the spiked shoes the animals needed to work the woods and iced roads. She displayed a natural ease around the teams, speaking to them, stroking their heavy coats of winter hair, and calling some by name.

After the stables they toured the cookshack and dining room. The "dingle," Joelle called it, was the domain of a surly, rotund tyrant by the name of Fergus. One of his bellowed blasphemies brought a trio of anxious cookees running to do his bidding. Several supply and storage sheds sat close to the kitchen, and next to them were the camp office and store, housed beneath one roof. This "van," Joelle explained, was where the men could buy needed socks, mittens, shirts, and tobacco against the pay they would draw in the spring. All was placed on an account. To pay them earlier would encourage reckless gambling and indulgent drinking.

Joelle had her quarters in the back of the store. Those she did not offer to show Marsh, which made him, of course, wonder about them all the more. Did she sleep on a bed of sticks? Was her room as austere as the bunkhouse, or did she hide some feminine touches there? Somehow, he doubted it. Were those doors off-limits to all, or just him?

That wondering grew acute when they were greeted by a loud cry.

"Eh! Jolie!"

Joelle turned, grinning, and was swept up into the embrace of a black-bearded man. She hugged the stocky fellow about the neck with unbridled joy, and Marsh experienced a sharp thrust of what could only be envy. How very pretty she looked all flushed and laughing with pleasure.

"Put me down, Guy!" she shouted gleefully. "Have you lost your wits?"

"That is what happens when I am with you, *cheri.*"

She laughed as if the words were meant to tease, but one look at the man's face told Marsh they were said with all sincerity. The black eyes of the French-Canadian were steeped with adoration. They darkened with something else altogether when they flashed to Marshall Cameron.

Restored to her feet, Joelle kept one arm about the waist of her friend. "Guy, this is Marshall Cameron. He's the new owner of the Superior. Marsh, this roguish fellow is Guy Sonnier. You won't find a better sawyer in all the northwoods. His brother, Chauncey, is one of our crew foremen."

The two men exchanged glances and stiff nods. Joelle frowned between them, wondering about the current of hostility she sensed. Guy was usually generous by nature. Chauncey was the one who could be counted upon to stir up an ugly mood.

Just then, the bell-like tones of the Gabriel horn sounded to call everyone to the evening meal. In a surprisingly short time, the camp was empty and the dining room full of hungry men. Marsh found himself wedged on a narrow plank between Joelle and a sullen Guy Sonnier. The hearty meal was served up from the kitchen and wordlessly devoured by the gathering at the long, high tables. Then just as quickly the room emptied out, and the cookees began to clear the spotless plates.

Finding himself abandoned as Joelle went to speak to Guy and a huge burly fellow whose resemblance to Guy unmistakably named him as Chauncey Sonnier, Marsh carried his tin of bitter coffee into the cold twilight air. Conversation flowed on all sides in a colorful patchwork of Finnish and French blended with a thick Cornish dialect. Darkness was quick to settle in the new December sky, edging the treetops with a fiery glow, then plunging all into gray silhouette. The temperature dipped accordingly, and in his thin wool suit of Eastern clothes, Marsh was soon shivering. Finally, with dread but resigned to give his new rough life a try, he walked to the bunkhouse to settle in for the night.

The deacon benches were crowded with men playing cards and swapping stories. Though nothing was said to him directly, Marsh felt the eddy of curiosity he stirred among them. Purposefully excluded from the camaraderie of the others, he shrugged out of his cutaway suit and folded it away with care before clamoring up into his bed. The mattress gave with a crunch and crackle as he shifted on the coarse covering. Finally he made a fairly comfortable hollow and closed his eyes. Sleep was instantly upon him, but his rest was short-lived.

He was abruptly bounced from his exhausted slumber as a mountainous form hit the mattress at his side. Marsh found himself looking into a pair of lively blue eyes framed by shaggy white-blond hair.

"Evening," boomed the big fellow in a heavily accented voice. "I be Olen Thurston. I buck on Chauncey's crew."

Marsh introduced himself and allowed his hand to be mangled in the other man's grasp. Olen grinned at him, noting the way Marsh tried to keep his distance as the mattress tilted toward the Olen's bulkier frame.

The lamps were put out, leaving a wafting pungency in the airless room. The darkness was complete, with only the grumbles and rustling of bedding to disturb it. Olen rolled suddenly. The wave of momentum rocked Marsh up against him, and he quickly scrambled to the edge of the bed frame. The Swedish giant chuckled.

"'Tis goot to share a bed with one who smells as goot as you," he noted good-naturedly. His broad palm slapped down on Marsh's chest, nearly driving the breath from him. "But not so goot as my woman back in Ontonagon, so you needn't be sleeping with one eye open." Chuckling to himself, Olen eased over on his opposite side, aware of the nervous Easterner staring at his back.

Then Thurston began to snore loudly and with great gusto.

* * *

Marsh had just closed his eyes, it seemed, when a blaring cry of "Roll out!" snapped them open again. It was still dark, but the warmth radiating from the stovepipes had eased to a seeping chill. He muttered a choice curse. It couldn't be more than four o'clock, yet the bunks were rapidly emptied by men bound for work in the woods. Well, he had no work to get to, and he'd be hanged if he was crawling out from under the negligible comfort of his covers. Olen was gone, freeing up an inviting space beside him. With a luxurious stretch, Marsh sprawled into it and let himself drift back to sleep. By the time he stirred again, the big room was filled with a pale light and silent as a church on a weekday. He was alone.

Muttering to himself, he yawned and lingered a few moments more. He reached for the watch he'd tucked under his mattress and squinted at the dial. Six. Still early by his standards, but he supposed he should make an effort to rouse himself and face the day—and Joelle Parry. He stretched out a languid hand for his shirt and found nothing. Not a shirt, not a vest, not a coat, not a pair of fine wool trousers.

That swiftly brought him out of bed. He swung down from the top bunk, thinking his belongings might have been knocked to the floor; but there was nothing on the two-inch rough-sawn pine boards.

Not even his shoes.

Joelle looked up from her ledger, then frankly stared at the sight of Marshall Cameron clad in well-fitting underclothes. He stood on the other side of her desk, huddled inside a rough blanket and the cotton-and-silk undershirt and drawers. His feet were bare and blue, with the toes curled under. His expression was thunderous.

"Good morning, Mr. Cameron," she remarked sweetly as if nothing were amiss. Even before he spoke in angry, roaring tones, she knew what he would say.

"Some no-good son of a bitch stole my clothes!"

"Well, now," she mused, leaning back in her chair to enjoy his fury. "The villain should be easy enough to find. All we have to do is look for a dapperly dressed gentleman who sticks out like a sore thumb."

Marsh huffed noisily for a moment then begrudgingly began to smile along with her. "If the ruffians took an exception to my mode of dress, they could have said so."

"I think they just did," was her smooth retort.

"Marsh's anger dissolved in an instant. "My feet are freezing. Have you got something in the store that won't offend my bunkmates' sensibilities?"

"I think I can fix you up."

Very aware that there would be nothing between her avid stare and Marshall Cameron's skin beyond a thin slip of revealing silk, Joelle was careful to keep her eyes averted from his. But that didn't stop her from continuing to look at his long, well-shaped legs, lean hips, and other intriguing contours. She fought to control her blushes as she assembled a stack of practical logging garb. Marsh looked with chagrin at the assortment. Not at all to his taste, he had to admit, but he had no choice. And better than being almost naked in front of Joelle Parry. He snatched up the clothes and was ready to head back out into the snow.

"Why don't you just change in my office," she suggested reasonably. "No sense in losing your toes to frostbite on your first day."

Grumbling, he complied and in moments was dressed to the envy of any shantyman. The coarse woolen underclothes chafed against his skin but promised uncompromising warmth. Over them he had pulled a pair of loose trousers, and he'd slipped the bright red braces up over the shoulders of his snug gray wool shirt. He eased his puckered toes into two pairs of thick socks, then crammed his feet into rubber-soled shoes with leather leggings that rose to his knees. All that he covered with a weighty blue-and-black-checked mackinaw. He stood for Joelle's approval in the storeroom and saw her nod.

"You'll do, Cameron. Here, take these." She passed him a knit cap with turned-up ear flaps and two pairs of mittens; one wool for next to the skin and one leather to waterproof the outside. He held them for a moment, again looking chagrined.

"Since I've lost my chance to make a favorable impression today, perhaps you'd show me around the cutting grounds. I don't mind a good joke, but I don't plan to be the butt of them for twenty-nine more days. The sooner I learn, the sooner I can

sleep nights without worrying about waking up in little more
than my birthday suit."

There was a lot of wisdom in what he said, and Joelle
wholly approved of his attitude. The men were testing him,
seeing if he could be pushed and goaded into some rash
or foolish action. If he kept his head and his temper and
his sense of humor, he could well be accepted among their
number. Looking at him now in his northern Michigan finery,
Joelle placed her money on him succeeding and surprising
everyone.

"Give me a minute to put my books away. Then I'll show
you what the Superior is all about."

Marsh quickly realized he couldn't have found a more
knowledgeable guide—or a prettier one—among the Superior
workers. From the cold plank of the wagon seat, Joelle took
him through each step of lumbering. The men worked in
gangs of nine under the direction of a foreman. The fellers
determined the direction in which a chosen tree would fall
and chopped a notch in that side with their ax. Then a pair
of sawyers manning a six-foot cross saw cut from the opposite
side until the mighty length of pine plummeted to the ground
with an earth-shaking bounce. At once the limbers set upon it
to strip it of its branches so the buckers could follow in sawing
the trunk or bole of the tree into sawlogs of twelve-, fourteen-,
sixteen-, eighteen- or twenty-foot lengths. Two men with the
skill of Olen Thurston could buck a hundred sawlogs a day in
what Joelle called fondly the "Canadian way." Her father had
brought his methods with him from the great Canadian forests.

Once the logs were divided up, swampers cut a path to
the fallen tree so a horse team could reach it, dragging the
skidding tongs. Marsh watched in fascination as the large
pincers with their fishhook barbs were fastened to the smaller
end of the log and then snaked from the woods to the cross
haul, where the logs would be loaded onto bobsleds. It was
continuous, brutal work for both man and beast, and as the day
progressed, mackinaws and woolen shirts littered the snowy
ground as the shantymen's exertion warmed them.

At noontime a cookee brought a hot lunch to the men on
the swing-dingle, a rude kitchen on runners. The jacks took

servings of meat, potatoes, beans, and bread, then seated themselves on the stumps left from the morning's work. Soon they went back into the trees to toil until the early winter dusk, when a blast on the cook's horn brought them back to the home camp for their evening meal. The menu was the same as the midday one, but it was warm and filling, and there were no complaints. There was also no dinner conversation, the same as the night before. Marsh did, however, garner his share of amused glances as he sat in his checked wool and suspenders. He paid them no mind, nor did he appear to hold a grudge toward those who had appropriated his expensive clothes. That earned him the men's reluctant respect, especially since Jo Parry chose to sit next to him for the second night in a row.

As Joelle had matured awkwardly into womanhood, she'd been careful never to play favorites among the crew. She divided her smiles and her time equally, as if the men were part of one large family in her care. Though some, Guy Sonnier foremost among them, sought to encourage a lingering attention, she brushed off their overtures with a gentle laugh that caused no hard feelings. But this one, this outsider, he was different. Guy in particular vowed to keep a watchful eye on him now that Lyle Parry wasn't on hand to see it done. Joelle was in a fragile state, and none of the gruff shantymen wanted to see her tender emotions bruised. If she treated them like brothers, they thought of her like a spirited daughter or younger sister—except Guy, who thought of her in more romantic terms.

What did Marsh think of them, Joelle wondered as she ate beside him in silence. They must look like barbarians to someone as cultivated as he, like beasts of burden to one softened by the ease of wealth. Yet there had been no contempt in his gaze as he watched the men labor in the woods. Indeed, she had thought she saw a burgeoning respect for what they did. The men viewed him as a curiosity. Their trick that morning had been played in harmless fun, but she knew sometimes such playfulness got out of hand when tempers shortened. Did Marshall Cameron have a temper beneath that polished surface, or had civilization bred such basic emotions out of him? Would being in the wilds stir them back to life? she wondered.

What was it like where he came from, in those cities that

held no charm for her? What did a man like Marsh do day to day to keep his body so lean and toned and yet leave his hands smooth to the touch? What were the women like who shared his past and would occupy his future? From the deferent way he treated her, she guessed they were weak, shallow creatures with little spirit and no opinions. Was that what he liked about them? Was there one particular woman for him already?

Did he have a wife? Even children?

Joelle frowned into her forkful of beans. She wondered if he were used to coming home at day's end to a cozy meal set with silver, to a woman in starched and dainty frills who would listen with a rapt smile as he spoke of his work, then fuss over him as he settled with his papers before the fireplace. What would it be like to retire at the end of the day with Marshall Cameron?

Her musings were interrupted as the men rose from the tables. She had hardly touched her own meal. She hurried to scoop up the mass of cold potatoes so the cookees could have her plate. Soon only she and Marsh remained in the big room; she with her tin of cold food and he with his cup of bitter coffee.

"Is there some taboo against table talk?" Marsh wanted to know.

"Silence speeds the meal along and prevents arguments," she explained with her mouth full. After swallowing, she elaborated. "The Cornish fight with the Irish. The Irish fight with the Finns. The Finns fight with the Canadians. Better they all stay quiet and keep their opinions to themselves."

He was leaning an elbow on the table, studying her profile. His intense gaze brought warm color to her face. She ate faster.

"And how do you fit in here? I see no other women."

"Not at the camp. Many of the men have families down by the mill site. Some travel back to visit them on Sundays when we're not too far into the woods and the weather is mild."

Thinking of how a pretty thing like Joelle Parry, who was all alone in the world, would begin to look to a bunch of woman-starved men after several months of isolation made him mutter, "Let's hope it stays mild."

She looked to him in surprise. "Oh, no, the more snow, the

better. It keeps the roads passable. Otherwise we'd lose costly man-hours shoveling it onto the roads so we could trail the logs down to the river. Better we stand in four-foot drifts than suffer a light winter."

Just then a rumbling and roar of voices could be heard from outside. Marsh started up, but Joelle placed a steady hand on his arm. "Just the men letting off a little vinegar. The Cornish fancy themselves as the world's best wrestlers, and the Canadians are always spoiling to prove them wrong. It's harmless."

Most of the time it was. But not this time.

Joelle looked up to see a grim-faced Guy with hat in hand. He looked repentant and angry.

"What happened, Guy?"

"Karl and Cecil got into a bit of a mixer."

"And?" Joelle prompted tersely.

"Karl broke his wrist."

Karl was Guy's partner on the cross saw, and now would be incapacitated for weeks, perhaps months. Joelle sighed heavily.

"I can work the saw alone," Guy offered staunchly.

"No," she began wearily. It was a bad omen for their luck to sour so early in the season. They were short of men as it was, and now one of her best sawyers was down. Illness and injury always took a toll, but she'd hoped to last at least a few months without feeling its bite.

"I can man the other end of the saw."

Guy and Joelle looked blankly at Marsh as if they'd heard him suddenly begin to speak in a foreign tongue. He scowled at their obvious disbelief.

"It's not as though I have anything better to do," he added crossly.

Joelle assessed him candidly for a long moment. Then she turned to the Frenchman. "Marsh will partner you. At least for tomorrow. Then we'll see."

Guy flushed an unbecoming shade of purple and angrily let loose a flurry of French that Marsh couldn't begin to follow. He understood the gist of it well enough, though. It was not a pairing the sawyer would take lightly. Or silently.

Finally Joelle had heard enough. She put up her hand and

spoke with authority. "Marsh will work with you until Karl is able or until we have another man free."

Guy sputtered like a hot wick in a pool of wax, but he knew there could be no further argument. It was then he saw the way Joelle Parry regarded the Easterner with a warm and glowing admiration. Outrage lodged bitterly in the Frenchman's throat.

So the greenhorn wanted to work. Well, Guy would make sure he got a day he'd not soon forget.

7

ONE THING ABOUT pines made an immediate impression upon Marsh. They were unyielding. As soon as he began working with Guy Sonnier, he was jerked forward into the rough bark with enough force to split the skin of his forehead. The blow dazed him, but he instantly had to haul back on his end of the saw for all he was worth. The jagged teeth sang through pitch and pulp, giving him scant time to recover his stance. His temper flared easily, however, and his fierce pride remained intact.

Guy Sonnier was not going to wear him down.

Sonnier obviously meant to give until Marsh couldn't take anymore. With his black eyes shooting enough sparks to set the forest ablaze, the compact Canadian made the teamwork into an angry challenge. There was no smooth push and pull of the big blade through the thick trunks. The handle was nearly yanked from Marsh's hands then immediately thrust back at him. By the time Marsh caught on to the rhythm, his ribs felt splintered from the sharp cracks of the handle, his nose and brow were bleeding from abrupt meetings with the tree trunks, and his shoulders felt as if they'd been wrested from their sockets. He forced himself not to reveal any outward show of relief at the sight of the awkward swing-dingle transporting lunch into the cutting grounds and a chance for him to recoup his flagging energy.

Without a word, Guy cleaned the blade of his saw and stalked off toward the meal wagon. A single word of praise or thanks would have gone far in that moment to douse the seething hostility warming in Marsh's belly.

"You're welcome, you son of a bitch," Marsh mumbled as he slowly rolled his aching shoulders. "Remind me not to do you any more favors."

But he hadn't made the offer just to help Guy Sonnier. He'd done it to impress a certain lady logging manager, and so he deserved every bit of the agony his pride had brought to bear. Grinning wryly at his own foolishness, he joined the others in line before the runnered buffet and carried his steaming plate to a freshly cut dining table. Balancing his meal on his knees, he wrestled off his gloves and almost winced at the red, pulpy state of his palms. There'd be hell to pay for his pride tomorrow when those blisters were full-blown. He let the gloves drop and applied himself eagerly to the hot meat and potatoes. The cold air and brutal exercise had built up his appetite, and the sight of Joelle Parry striding lithely through the company stirred another kind of hunger altogether—one that couldn't be satisfied easily or caused by the chilliness of the air.

He watched her move through the gathering of men while he continued to devour his meal. The dazzling smile she bestowed upon everyone she greeted was a balm for his bodily miseries. The quicksilver softening of her gaze when it brushed across him was a cure for his sore spirit. But before he could offer a smile in return, her attention was called elsewhere. He felt its loss with a curious degree of deflation as she went to discuss the morning's work with the crew foremen. He didn't realize at first that she spoke to none of the other workers. He only knew he would have liked some measure of notice to make up for the abuse at Guy Sonnier's hands. As much as he wanted to blend in with the gruff batch of loggers when it came to sweat and camaraderie, he sought to be different in Joelle's discerning eyes. Why? He wasn't sure. Maybe because he was so used to drawing a woman's interest, and when it was denied him, he chafed at its absence. He had no reason for desiring affection from Joelle Parry. No reason and no right. But for the first time in his regimented life, thought and feeling were a world apart, and that troubled him no little bit as he swallowed down the last of his meal.

Joelle was not unaware of Marshall Cameron's hot regard. The way his eyes followed her should have caused the frosty fortress around her heart to melt. Hang the man for being so obvious. The one thing she could scarce afford as the only woman in a camp full of red-blooded men was to show any kind of partiality or response. Marsh had come to her just the other morning seeking a way to be accepted among the shantymen. He claimed to be a smart man, yet he was displaying a singular lack of insight.

He should have looked slightly foolish, a Boston-bred aristocrat sitting on a tree stump, eating bland fare from a tin plate. He should have looked glaringly out of place among all the brawny loggers who'd discarded gloves and mackinaws to apply themselves with mannerless gusto to their meal. The sight of him sitting so comfortably in the grim surroundings acted oddly upon her sensibilities. A man like Marsh Cameron had no business looking so at home in a Northern Michigan lumber camp, so aggressively male in the way he devoured his meal with a single cheap utensil, or so rugged in the snug stretch of wool that banded his chest and shoulders. She had no business admiring him with such fascination. As she forced her gaze to skim over him, she noted the way his smile lifted and fell in confusion at her casual disregard. Better he suffer a moment's pique than the sullen envy of his fellow workers. Better he know from the outset that he was one of many, not one in a million, in the mind of Joelle Parry. Though he might well claim the latter status in her innocent heart, she stubbornly vowed never to let him know of it.

She was conscious of his dark, burning stare as she talked with Chauncey and the other foremen. Her pledge to ignore him was about as successful as a blanketing snow against the sear of summer sun. Her willpower dissolved. Angrily she concluded her meeting and turned to freeze Marshall Cameron with a single icy glare. His reaction wasn't what she'd hoped for. He didn't recoil from her censure but instead returned a slow smile that curved up his mouth with a sensuous bow of satisfaction, as if despite her annoyance she'd given him some great compliment. Never would she understand the strange workings of that man's mind! Nor would she try, she promised herself as she stormed out of the camp. Let him smirk and simmer.

Made content by her telling fury, Marsh tugged his gloves back on and went to dispose of his empty plate. Then he met Guy Sonnier's black stare and knew with cold certainty what the timberman held against him. The problem wasn't the differences in their education or social status, and not simply contempt toward an outsider. Competition for Joelle Parry's attention wedged bitterly between them. Marsh sighed to himself and went to join the other man at the saw, readying himself for the pummeling of the dark Canadian's jealousy.

By the time the evening table was cleared, Marsh knew he'd done a day's work. Every muscle in his body screamed with pain. He'd never considered himself soft and prided himself on a regiment of daily exercise to tone form and mind. None of those civilized pursuits had prepared him for the grueling strain of this primitive workout. The effort of lifting a fork to his mouth was almost more than he could sustain. He could hardly hold his eyelids open. He was sure even his bunkmate's rumbling snores couldn't penetrate this evening's complete exhaustion.

Olen's thunderous chuckle distracted Marsh from the painful toil of unbuttoning his shirt.

"You have the look of a man in misery, my friend," the big Scandinavian mused from where he reclined on the upper bunk.

"I'll not argue there," Marsh returned with a faint smile. Was it so obvious that his pride had driven him to the limit of endurance? If so, was he destined to ride out the ridicule of his cabinmates for another night? What deviltry would he discover upon waking to the new day? And could he in all fairness begrudge them their mirth? He must have been some sight; all stiff and sore and aching from the arrogance that made him compete where he was so lacking. He should have stuck to his Eastern finery. At least it fit him more honestly than these rough woolens made to be worn by better men.

Some of his chagrin must have shown in his glum features, for Olen immediately clucked in sympathy. "It is no shame to boast of honorably won blisters. You have done a man's work today and have won the respect of every man here."

Marsh was tempted to scoff, but something in the big Swede's manner held him. Admiration. That sentiment surprised him. It was one almost unknown to him. He'd been the envy of other men before. He'd felt their begrudging obedience and carefully veiled resentment. He knew they groveled because of his father and because of the position he was marrying into. But never on his own, through his own accomplishments, had he earned the esteem of his peers—and here in these rugged woods, crude timbermen were more than his equal. He had gained some measure of respect not by his wealth or privilege but through his own hard work. And it felt good, better than anything he'd ever achieved before. He swelled with pride and at the same time, humility.

"If anyone's earned respect this day, it's all of you from me," Marsh said with absolute candor. Unable to express himself any better, and to avoid embarrassing the husky Swede, he concluded simply, "I had no idea."

Olen nodded at the compliment, his pleasure betrayed by the squaring of his mammoth shoulders. "You will make a goot woodsman, I am thinking." He put down his huge hand, and Marsh gave his without hesitation. He nearly swooned at the crush of surrounding fingers on his tender palm. Olen saw his wince and turned the slender hand up. He pursed his lips knowingly. "You will be goot for nothing tomorrow unless you see to these hands tonight."

Marsh tried to flex his fingers by way of a denial and was instantly shocked into believing the other's words. His tendons had cramped, and his skin felt stretched. He'd be a fool to ignore such signs of abuse. By morning he'd be lucky if he could make a fist let alone wield a saw. He looked up at Olen for an answer and wasn't pleased with what he heard.

"You go see Miss Jo. She fix you up but goot." When Marsh began to frown, the blond giant gave him a push. "Go on with you. You think you be the first greenhorn to pop a blister? If you want to work tomorrow, you tend your ails tonight." With that final word he dropped back on the makeshift mattress and closed his eyes. His manner indicated that Marsh would be ten times the fool if such good advice were not heeded.

Marsh might have been prideful, but he was not stupid.

The walk across the quiet camp to the company van was a long one, especially since the last thing Marsh wanted to do was bring his complaints to Joelle Parry—particularly when she'd been so cool to him in the woods. Would she think he'd come crying to her just to gain her attention? Or would she laugh at him now that his boastful actions had taken their toll? He recalled his early boasts and knew she was going to love feeding his words back to him. He vowed to choke down each and every one of them without rebuttal. She'd been right. He was no lumberman. He knew ledger sheets and business deals and stock options. A world of blisters and overstressed muscles was completely foreign to him.

The van was dark, but the door had been left unlocked. He frowned. To his big-city thinking, an unlocked door was an invitation to mischief. He thought of the young woman inside, alone, in a camp full of men, and his frown deepened. Did she care so little about her own safety? Or was she so naive that she didn't understand the temptation she offered? His strides were long and angry as they carried him through the stacks of goods to the room at the rear. His brusque knock echoed. Without so much as an inquiry as to who stood on the other side, the door was pulled open. He heard no grate of a latch and could only assume that this door, the one leading to her private rooms, had also been unlocked.

"Haven't you got a lick of sense? Leaving all these doors open, you might as well post a sign: 'Come in and take what you want.' "

Eyes wide from the fierceness of his greeting, Joelle blinked and drawled softly, "That's why you're here?"

"No, of course not, but—"

"Good, because you would not look nearly as nice with another hole in your head." She lowered the pistol in her hand from its ready position and eased off the hammer. Her words were heavy with amusement. And irritation. "Or did you just stop by to give me a lecture on how to take care of myself? I thought we'd settled that."

Marsh drew a breath, prepared to launch into a stern reproof. He felt it strangle in his throat. Slowly his gaze took in the sight of her, braced defiantly in the door frame. Her slender form was clad in faded long johns over which a man's plaid shirt swam. It was ridiculous attire, but somehow on her it was as seductive as the thin scraps of lace and linen he'd been teased with on more provocatively feminine figures. The long underwear hugged to the clean line of her legs in a manner that tempted hands to follow each gentle curve. Without the bulky boy's cap, her dark hair grazed the crisp angle of her jaw, lending a piquant beauty to her features. She looked vulnerable standing there like that—if one discounted the potential danger of the pistol and her steely eyes.

"Well, Mr. Cameron? If not to chastise me for my inability to protect myself and mine, why are you here at this hour?" There was an edge to her tone, as if she had seen into the hot images in his mind and were suddenly wary.

Marsh was uncomfortable with the reminder. He almost left right then and there rather than admit to the truth. But that would have been more foolish than the thoughts he had entertained so briefly. His voice was a grumble of displeasure.

"Olen told me to see you about my hands."

She didn't need further explanation. She reached out and caught one of his hands between her own. He felt a shock of warmth as her fingers gently manipulated his palm. The pain was nothing compared to the sensation of her thumb riding the swells of broken skin. If she were aware of what she was doing to him, he couldn't tell, for her expression was all concentration and concern.

"I've just the thing. Come in."

He hesitated after she dropped his hand, then followed her retreating figure into her private quarters. Mellow firelight revealed all the bare necessities of the room: log-hewn furniture, a few hand-braided rugs on the planked floor, a single table with chair pulled back, atop which a ledger was opened as if she'd been making entries when he disturbed her. Nothing of a personal nature adorned the walls, no female clutter, just stark and efficient basics. He could feel the loneliness of the room and of the single soul held within its walls.

"Sit down." Without looking his way, she gestured toward a stocky chair angled by the fire and strode from the room.

By the time he'd settled in it, she was back, carrying a jar of ointment and a stack of clean cloths. She knelt between his straddled knees and positioned one of his hands, palm up, atop his thigh. "This will burn, but believe me, you'll be glad for it tomorrow."

Burn was too mild a word for the searing bite of pain penetrating his raw nerve endings. As if anticipating the jerk and quiver of his arm, Joelle gripped his wrist in a surprisingly strong grasp to hold his hand steady. Then, before he had the presence of mind to object, she caught his other hand and applied the same stinging cream to that tortured flesh. Quickly, while he was blinking the dampness from his eyes, she bound his hands with linen strips, her ease of movement telling him she'd performed this same service hundreds of times.

"Leave these wrappings on tomorrow and the day after if there is any soreness. The liniment will ease the tenderness and draw out any poisons."

"I'm not surprised," Marsh ground out between clenched teeth.

She smiled up at him with a warming sympathy. Then she frowned and touched the split of skin discoloring his brow. "What happened here?"

"An introduction to your Northern pines," he said wryly. He could have said more but didn't. He didn't have to.

Joelle's gray eyes grew stormy and confused. "It isn't like Guy to mistreat his partner on the cross saw. What on earth could have gotten into him?" She was musing aloud, not expecting an answer. It occurred to Marsh then that she didn't know. She wasn't aware that the Canadian was in love with her. He was amazed. How could she not see it? The man fairly smoldered when she was near. And she treated him with all the warmth due a brother. "I'll speak to him."

"No," Marsh said quickly. "I'm sure it was just one of those tests these fellows are so fond of. If you reprimand him, I'll be treated worse. I can handle myself, Miss Parry."

"I'll bet you can."

Their eyes met and held for a second; hers softened, and his simmered. Then, as if abruptly conscious of her intimate position within the vee of his thighs, Joelle clamored to her feet, blushing.

"If that's all, Mr. Cameron, I have some work to finish." Her tone held all the sting of the ointment in her hand.

"That's enough, Miss Parry." *For now,* his gaze warned. When he stood, she retreated a cautious step. "Good night, Jo."

"Marsh."

"I'll lock up on my way out."

A reluctant smile quirked her lips. "Do that."

After he'd gone, Joelle couldn't return her thoughts to her books.

Blast the man! What was it about him? She tended the bruised flesh of every newcomer in camp. The sight of puffy blisters and angry sores had never affected her the way the angry redness on his smooth palms had. His hands weren't meant to suffer the harshness of labor. He didn't need to prove anything to the men or to her. He didn't need to strive for their respect. A man like Marshall Cameron commanded it with his presence and his pride. He was a leader born and bred, yet he allowed himself to be humbled by the jests of crude lumbermen and the harassment of Guy Sonnier. What manner of man was he to lower himself so, and by doing so, raise himself in her eyes?

Unable to concentrate on her figures, Joelle closed the ledger and blew out the single lamp. She padded on silent bare feet into her bedroom. Huddled beneath a heavy quilt, she tried to close her eyes to summon sleep, but the image of Marsh Cameron wouldn't leave her. She tossed restlessly and beat down her pillow, frowning into the darkness. She remembered how he'd berated her for not locking her door. She could almost hear the staunch tones of her father, and tears pricked behind her eyes. She had no father, and she was not about to take on a pompous Easterner in his stead. She was perfectly capable of taking care of herself. She had nothing to fear from the men in these northwoods, but the Easterner quickened her worries.

She flung herself over on her belly and scowled with a fierce determination. One month. She had only to put up with him that long, then things would be back to normal.

Or wouldn't be.

Her life would never be normal again. Her father was dead, and her sparse rooms would echo with emptiness. When Marshall Cameron left as soon as Lake Superior thawed, that spark of life he'd brought would never warm her again.

8

"DAYLIGHT IN THE swamp!"

Marsh groaned and forced his eyes to open to darkness. He'd slept like the dead, the cry of the cookee the first sound to penetrate his consciousness since he dropped into his blankets. The wood fire in the bunkhouse had died down to a soft gray ash, leaving an unwelcomed wintery chill in the room. He pulled his blankets tighter about him but couldn't ignore the activity around him as the shantymen stirred for breakfast and work. Grumbles, jaw-popping yawns, and the sounds of serious scratching filled the dim quarters as a hundred pairs of legs clad in long red underwear swung down to the floor. Rough hands rubbed sleep from weary eyes and shoved through mussed hair. Socks were pulled off the wire overhead, all dry and stiff. And when Olen Thurston's bulk heaved up beside Marsh, the momentum was great enough to push him out of the blankets.

His eyes still glazed and his mind still clouded with sleep, Marsh tugged on his two pair's of socks, heavy woolen pants, and rubber-soled boots. He was buttoning his second heavy wool shirt across his longies when he realized he had movement in his hands. He took a moment to marvel at it, wiggling and flexing his fingers, then said a brief thanksgiving for Joelle Parry as he let his bright suspenders snap along his chest.

The room's single washbasin was set upon a bench at one end of the building. One by one those who wished to wash dipped the basin into the barrel of water, drawn only that morning through a hole cut in the ice. When they were finished, the contents were pitched out the door, where they froze into a steadily growing pile of ice that wouldn't melt until spring. By the time Marsh reached the tin dish, twelve men had used the company-provided towel before him. With the chill water dripping down his chin, he lifted the sodden bit of soiled cloth in obvious dismay. Suddenly someone snatched it from his hand.

"Afraid of a little honest man's grime, Mr. Fancy Down Easter?" Guy Sonnier sneered as he wiped his own heavily bearded face. He slapped the towel at a spindly choreboy. "Get him a fresh one, boy. We can't afford to offend this one's tender face."

Clamping down on his temper as best he could, Marsh dried his features with a swipe of his sleeve and pushed past the arrogant Canadian. He stomped with the others to the cookshack and was quick about silently devouring thick pancakes with a heavy coating of blackstrap molasses. If Joelle was among the group of hungry men, he purposefully didn't notice. He was still simmering as he joined in the march of log gangs as they picked up axes and swung saws over their shoulders to walk behind the bobsleds to the cutting grounds. Crisp air mingled with heated blood, chafing an aliveness inside Marsh that he'd never known before. Ribbons of fog threaded between the majestic pines on either side of the road and rose in a chill haze as the first weak shafts of sunlight cut through them. He couldn't remember ever seeing a dawn quite so beautiful as those gray and pink pastels lifting through the trees. God's country, his father called it. Yes, it was.

Guy was waiting impatiently beside a notched pine. When Marsh picked up the other end of the saw, he rubbed off the bark where they would cut with a slow lining draw of the blade, and the Canadian settled his feet to make the initial pull that would bite deep and sure into the resinous wood. Then Guy was abruptly jerked off his feet as Marsh applied his weight on the handle to bring it toward him with a rapid rasp. The look of surprise on the other man's face was worth the wrench of agony through Marsh's shoulders. Marsh gave a grim smile, one that would remain throughout the long, arduous day. His features set in a dark scowl, Guy wrestled the blade his way, and the two of them began an efficient rhythm.

Production was good all week. The weather remained cold and clear with several dustings of snow during the nighttime hours to keep the pull of logs from the woods smooth and continuous. By week's end, Joelle had every reason for celebration, but her spirits refused to lift. Her melancholy had two names—Lyle Parry and Marshall Cameron.

She listened to the reports of the gang chiefs every evening and dutifully listed figures in the company books. As she sat back with what should have been satisfaction, she realized there was no one there with whom to share each daily triumph. She and her father had been a team. Without him nothing seemed complete. Sitting alone in her rooms, she longed for the hours they'd sat before a warming fire, laughing, planning or just enjoying the lazy silence of a winter's night. He'd been her best friend, her confidant, her sounding board for dreams. Without him there was an empty echo.

With whom could she share those quiet times? With Guy? No. He was a friend. Inviting him away from the crew into the privacy of her life would alter the ease they had with each other. She knew he'd come to care for her in the way of a man seeking a wife, but she didn't feel the same way. She'd known him for too long. He was as familiar as the scent of tobacco from her father's pipe, as comfortable as the stocking cap she wore over her dark bobbed hair. He was just too much a part of everything she knew to become the person she sought.

In the stillness of her evening hours, Joelle wondered what it would be like if Marshall Cameron were beside her. How quickly those minutes would fly provoked by his sharp banter. He'd been places, seen things, experienced delights beyond the pines and cold, cruel lake. They could talk of things in books. She could listen to him speak of his home in Boston, and she could tell him her dreams, dreams that ached for the telling. And then there'd be the silences when gazes met and lips stilled from speech, eager to begin a more intimate conversation. What would she have to say to a man who had spoken the language of love with probably scores of educated ladies? What words of affection could move upon lips that had never tasted another's kiss?

Joelle sat in her shadowed rooms, brooding in the waning hours of Saturday afternoon. From outside she could hear the stirrings of merriment that would escalate throughout the night. As there was no work on Sunday and the roads were still good, many of the wives and sweethearts had come up to the camp for the evening. There would be much laughter, many languishing looks, music, dancing, and sips of forbidden drink. The gay mood was just the answer to her dire musings, yet she was reluctant to embrace it because Marsh would be there among them.

She'd scarcely seen him since he'd come for the ointment for his hands. She'd heard his praises from those who weren't usually free with compliments. In one week, he'd made a place for himself among the clannish loggers, carving it out with sheer determination and brute strength. Sparked by the hostility between them, his efforts on the cross saw he shared with Guy were the most productive of all the rival gangs. And with every grudging word of admiration, her own feelings for him grew. He was one of the men, not the owner of Superior Lumber, and as such she was restrained from showing him any extra attention. By her own strict rules, he could not know a moment of her private time, nor could she let her smile or eager gaze linger a second longer upon him than on others. Bound by her own convictions, she remained alone and miserable, imagining herself with Marsh.

A knock on her door startled her from her thoughts. Burly Chauncey Sonnier stood in the storehouse, hat in hand.

"Evening, Miss Jo. I have me a fellow here who is looking for work."

She looked beyond him to where a large figure lingered in the shadows of the store. She could see mammoth shoulders carrying a patched mackinaw and ham-sized hands holding the turkey with all the man's worldly goods stuffed inside. She could see an outline of shaggy hair and heavy beard, but none of his features were visible in the dim light.

"What can he do?"

"Says he be a sawyer."

Joelle peered curiously at the sketchy form. "And you say?"

"Could be he is. Has the hands for it. Could be he looks for a hot meal and a roof over his head at our expense."

Every lumber camp fell prey to "inspectors," the hobo lumberjacks who applied for work, ate their fill, slept in a good bed, and disappeared without ever toting a saw in payment. There was no sure way to tell if a man's intent was honest or if he would be gone to another camp the minute it came time to report to the cutting grounds. Joelle never begrudged a hungry man a meal, but she resented trickery of any sort.

"What name does he use?"

"Kenny Craig."

"Mr. Craig," she called out and waited for him to come forward into the brightness. He did so with reluctance, moving with surprising grace for a man so huge. When he came abreast of Chauncey, she was able to get a good look at him. Not much to see, she thought to herself. A stony face pocked by childhood disease, dark eyes hardened by the struggle to live day to day, and lips thinned into a surly line by a pride that would not be humbled to beg for work. He had a face like those of half the men she employed. But when his dark eyes bored into hers, she felt a shiver run clear through her. As he observed her, a spark kindled with lurid interest, gleaming, feral, and the woman in her cried out in alarm, warning her to step back to a safe distance. She suppressed that quiver of uneasiness by taking an offensive stance. Her slight shoulders squared, and her eyes narrowed as they swept over his hulking figure with critical thoroughness. Her manner was designed to throw a haughty male off balance, but this one seemed unperturbed. In fact, a small quirk of amusement touched his thin lips as if to say he was not intimidated by this one little female. Joelle knew right then that Kenny Craig spelled trouble.

But he was a sawyer.

"He can team with Guy. Give him a bunk and see that Fergus supplies him with a hearty meal. Welcome to the Superior, Mr. Craig."

He took the hand she offered in his roughened grasp, holding it just a second too long. The moment her features began to tighten, he released it and gave her a wide, broken grin. Several of his front teeth were missing, giving him the appearance of a swarthy jack-o'-lantern.

"Thanky, ma'am," he said in a husky whisper.

After he left with Chauncey, Joelle found herself wiping her palm upon her woolen trouser leg. She would have to watch that one. She usually didn't ignore her instincts, but in this case she overruled her sense of misgiving. The man was a sawyer—if he teamed with Guy, Marsh would no longer be working among the jacks. She could then invite him to share the companionship of her fire. For that she was willing to hire on a man who gave her flesh a nervous crawl. To slake her present loneliness, she felt as if she were willing to chance most anything.

As her mood was lifted by anticipation, she hurriedly dressed to join the others in the center of the camp, where they'd built a huge fire. High leaping flames bronzed the mirthful faces of those seated on log benches, creating a warmth of body and spirit within their circle. Many a couple were cozied up just beyond the reach of light. The murmurs from those dusky shadows acted strangely upon Joelle. Oh, to be one of those lucky souls, so absorbed in one man's gaze that the world around ceased to exist. She wondered what they said to each other to provoke those smoldering stares and breathy little chuckles. Her curiosity flared an odd excitement inside her as she scanned the perimeter of the clearing for one particular face.

"Jolie!"

Her smile was forced as she turned toward Guy, then became genuine as she beheld him. He was clad in his French-Canadian finery, a costume worn along the waterways for generations; yellow plaid mackinaw, woolen trousers tucked into knee-high heavy socks, and a sash of bright yarns wound about a sturdy waist, with mits tucked behind it. His head was bare, and the firelight shimmered with an almost bluish sheen on his black hair. His broad white grin was in sharp, appealing contrast to his heavy dark beard. His joy in seeing her was impossible to miss.

"Lookit you, missy," he cooed with an admiring sweep of his dark eyes. "Get ready to lift dem skirts for a do-si-do and *laissez les bons temps rouler.*"

She laughed as he spun her in a full circle. The hem of her wine-colored wool skirt flared wide, exposing heavy stockings and rubber-soled boots and layer upon layer of ruffles on her single, stiff petticoat. As she came to a stop within the loose curve of his arms, her gaze flashed to the other side of the fire and was held captive. Guy frowned his displeasure, knowing without seeing what had changed her eyes from glittering animation to smoky yearning. Or rather *who*. His embrace tightened, calling her back to him.

"Come, *ma cherie*. I play a song for you."

His eagerness pulled her away from the study of Marsh Cameron, but she couldn't erase the sight of him from her mind. The way he straddled one of the upended log butts, resting his forearms casually on his thighs. The way the flickering fire teased highlights of gold through his tawny hair and played with intense mystery in his dark stare, which fixed on her and never wavered. She felt it follow the path she took halfway around the fire, to where several musicians plucked energetically upon their fiddles and dulcimers and wheezed out wavery notes on the mouth organ. Guy enthroned her upon a place of honor, a low stump at his feet where he could command her presence if not her complete attention. He picked up his small French accordion and squeezed soft sighs of sound from it. Then he looked down at her expectantly.

"What can I play for you? Something for the heart or something for the feet?"

"The feet," she urged him with a smile.

"*Eh bien.*" Obligingly he forced a groaning note from the accordion's pleated bellows then pumped out a lively tune that had her toes twitching in time and couples swirling about the fire in a lively dance. He crooned out the words in French, his voice a sultry baritone pitched to make the mademoiselles swoon. But the one he wanted most to affect seemed immune to seductive serenade. Her toes were tapping, her lips were smiling, but her gaze was lost to him. If he couldn't win her heart through song, then perhaps he could do so within the possessive circle of his arms. Before he could seize an opportunity, one of his fellow sawyers stepped up to claim her hand. The grinning Canadian whirled her through the fancy combinations of turns and dips until she was flushed and laughing.

Marsh watched Joelle move lightly in the guiding arms of her partner. He'd seen various sides of her personality— the hard business owner, the shy seductress, the vulnerable child—but this new facet was equally intriguing, the free-spirited woman. He'd never seen her in a skirt before. He liked the way it belled out around her trim calves and showed off the slenderness of her waist. She wore a tempting wool top scooped wide at the neck so that it slid along her shoulders in a dance of its own, dropping away just far enough to display a tease of bosom. A pair of silver hoop earrings grazed along her graceful neck and played in the swing of her cropped hair. All these things were so natural, free of all contrivance. She wasn't flirting, she was enjoying, and that joy of life flowed from her. When Marsh thought of all the seasoned Boston coquettes he'd known, he had to smile. Joelle Parry could teach each and every one of them a thing or two about enticing a man.

"Guard the way your heart shines in your eyes, my friend, lest yon sawyer choose to carve it on the morrow."

Marsh glanced up at Olen and let his smile tip at a wry angle. "You're seeing things."

The big Swede gave a snort of disbelief. "'Tis you, I'm thinking, that sees things that cannot be."

Marsh's laugh was short and harsh. "You talk in foolish riddles tonight. There's nothing wrong with my eyesight."

"And an eyeful there is, too. Remember that you can do no more than look."

Marsh scowled at him and returned a more guarded gaze to the dancing pair. Was his reaction to her that obvious? His frown grew worried. He had no right to display what could never be more than a heart's wish. He respected Joelle too much ever to bring her any hurt. How easily he forgot that the aggressive ploys he used with parlor flirts would confuse an unschooled innocent. She would construe such overtures to be sincere, and then her pride and tender spirit would be crushed when she learned the truth. He would never risk that.

Nor did he care to have Guy Sonnier drag him through the narrow cut of wood behind his saw blade.

Perhaps he should go to the bunkhouse. There, he could enjoy a moment of peaceful reflection or a bit of long overdue reading while the bulk of the crew was caught up in merry-making. But a martyred solitude had much less appeal than seeing the flash of pleasure in Joelle Parry's eyes.

Noting the direction of Cameron's gaze, Guy glowered and seethed as his fingers flew over the last few keys. Then he called out the name of a tune to his accompanists and went to claim a dance for himself. Joelle slipped easily into his arms and smiled up at him with fond delight. Nothing more. She looked at him with happiness, not simmering desire. A dark anger quickened in his heart that could not be quieted by the boisterous steps of the dance or by Joelle's laughter.

They made an attractive pair, Marsh noted with some cha-grin as they threaded through the crowd of couples; they were both dark and filled with the passionate joie de vivre of the French. Guy Sonnier was the kind of man Joelle should belong to, one who shared her past and understood the needs of her future. But the sight of them together galled Marsh. It wasn't as though he had any plans to lay his own claim to the fiery Miss Parry. Still he ground his teeth in irritation.

When the tune ended, another started up with a peppery cadence and beckoning beat. Guy left Joelle to take up his accordion, and she immediately searched for a partner among those who had none. She sidled up to big blond Olen with a playful shake of her skirts and pouted when he grinned and shook his head. The slap of the Swede's palm between his shoulder blades knocked Marsh forward off his seat, and Joelle took advantage of his staggering attempt to catch himself by seizing both his forearms. Before he could protest that he hadn't the slightest idea of how to move through the romping turns of the lively reel, she was towing him into the crowd of dancers, laughing up at his stricken expression. After a few fumbling tries to pick up the tempo, he was laughing, too, at his own clumsiness, out of sheer enjoyment. Then it didn't matter so much if he turned right as she twirled left or that his arm smacked into her forehead as she spun around him. Or that he was standing on her feet more often than on his own. He was having fun, and the laughter was contagious. By the time the music softened into a booming waltz, he had no intention of surrendering the feel of her within his arms.

This tempo was easier to follow. Marsh had the chance to watch his partner more than where he was placing his awkward feet. And he liked what he saw. Unconsciously his hold on her clinched up until her hem was brushing over the toes of his boots. She didn't object, and his confidence soared. He was engulfed by the warmth of her smiling eyes, lost in those crystal-dawn depths until he couldn't see his way to tomorrow. There was only this moment, this woman, this hurried excitement in his blood. He pulled her closer still.

For Joelle, this closeness was remembered bliss. She leaned into him, yearning to feel the hard wall of his chest beneath her cheek the way she had on the snow-whipped boardwalk in Copper Harbor. Only this time there was no tearing grief to distract her from how wondrously Marshall Cameron was made. Broad of shoulder, firm of chest, lean of middle. His hands had been toughened by days of hard labor; his arms swelled with that newfound strength. He had been a strong man before, but now he had a power about him that made her weaken in response. Oh, to feel those bulging arms close about her in a raptured embrace. She shut her eyes and sighed with the compelling want of it. As her head nestled within the hollow of his shoulder, he complied without conscious thought. The fingers of one hand spread wide and sure along the curve of her lower back while his others twined with her own. Moving together, they forgot that other couples shared the same clear evening, that others knew the same restless beating of hearts, that the music feeding the pulse of their heated blood came from the man who would pry them apart. They weren't aware of the discordant sound heaving from the French accordion or when it stopped playing altogether, not until Guy Sonnier took hold of Marsh's shirt collar and jerked him back from Joelle's arms.

So angry he could only spit a fierce challenge in French, Guy squared off against the taller man and waited with clenched fists. Marsh may not have understood the words, but he took the man's meaning well enough and was more than ready to answer him right then and there. He assumed a wide, flat-footed stance, balling his own hands.

"Stop it!" Joelle planted a palm on each man's shoulder and shoved hard to disturb their warring pose. She was all too aware that the evening's entertainment had shifted from music and dance to the possibility of a brawl. She lowered her voice so that only the two men could hear her.

"Enough! What is wrong with the two of you that you must fight over a dance? I won't have it, do you hear? I won't be growled over like a morsel between two wolverines. And I won't choose either of you, so don't flatter yourselves to think I would cheerfully reward the winner of this ridiculous contest with my favors. Arrogant fools."

With that sharp condemnation, she marched away from the two stunned rivals and from the circle of hushed company. Chuckling to himself, Chauncey Sonnier motioned to the musicians to take up a lively song, and he went to shake the stiffness from his brother's pride. Guy was coaxed into playing another tune, but his seething stare never left the equally taut Easterner.

To her dismay, Joelle found her vision blurred by an annoying wash of tears. Most likely it was from the sudden slap of cold that had struck the moment she left the circle of friendship and fire. Brushing at the dampness with the back of her hand, she continued to stride furiously toward her office. How dare they make spectacles of themselves over her affection! As if she cared a hoot for either of the pompous, preening idiots! She would not admit it, even to herself, but she was angry she'd been wrested from the haven of Marshall Cameron's embrace. She'd waited forever to return to that comforting spot and then, had the pleasure torn from her over a pique of male pride. Fools! Did they think she'd been pleased by their show of puffed-up importance? Did they think she'd welcome their announcement to every jack in the camp that she was an object to be fought over and coveted? She worked so hard to be taken seriously, not for the dubious honor of being a prize in a squabble of dominance between two rutting bulls of the woods. She'd given neither of them the right to be so bold.

She was so angry that she paid no attention to her surroundings. Otherwise she would have noticed the dim light in the far corner of the camp store and would have seen something amiss when she almost stumbled over a large sack of collected goods lying in the middle of the van floor. But she was preoccupied, and only as she walked in did she recognize the shadowy figure of Kenny Craig as he was robbing the company store.

9

JOELLE FROZE. SHE tried not to tremble as she realized her danger. Standing very still, she quickly assessed her options as Kenny Craig advanced toward her in his long, gliding stride. She could bolt for her private rooms and grab her gun. She could run for the door and try to outdistance him and reach the others. Screaming would be a waste of precious air because no one would hear her over the merrymaking. Seconds ticked away as she stood still, indecisive and paralyzed by fright. Then he smiled that horrible gap-toothed smile.

"Well, now, this was unexpected," came his raspy whisper. "Things was just too good to be true with all of you enjoying yourself too much to care if I was to borrow a few things. What am I to do with you? Can't have you running off to warn them, can I?" The path of his eyes drew a cold chill along the rounded neck of her blouse. "Guess I could spare a few more minutes. Considering."

Then he reached for her.

He was fast. Joelle barely had time to dodge the thrust of his huge open hands. Because he was expecting her to head for the safety of the door, she darted to the side and raced around a stack of barrels in an effort to avoid him. She wished she had her gun. She could picture it so clearly, tucked beneath her pillows. If she could get to it—

Rough fingers clamped about her wrist. Desperately she flung her other hand out, seeking anything she could use as a weapon as he hauled her toward him. Her fingers closed around the smooth wood of the ax handle, and she swung it with all her might, hearing his satisfying grunt of surprise and pain as it struck his shoulder. His grip slackened only for an instant, but that was long enough. She twisted wildly and ran, her unsteady knees tangling in her petticoat, almost making her fall. Her heart was knocking with a forceful panic inside her chest, its loud beats filling her ears even as she heard Craig's rumbling curse and the scuffle of his pursuit. Her breath came in raw sobs as she flung open her door and whirled to throw her weight against it. But before she could get it closed, he struck the other side with the force of a runaway bobsled carrying a full load. The wood shuddered and gave way, caving inward, knocking her off her feet. My God, he was in her rooms!

She sprawled hard on the floor, banging her knees and scraping her palms, but she immediately scrambled in the hampering skirts to gain her feet. Her attacker caught her waistband, and she screamed once, loudly, in an involuntary rush of terror. Struggling, she lunged ahead, hearing stitches give, feeling fabric tear. Then she was loose and racing for her bedroom. She didn't pause to shut the door. It wouldn't keep him out. There was only one way to stop him from doing what he planned. Joelle dove for the bed, her hands spearing under the pillows, closing on the comfort of cold metal as she rolled and twisted to face Craig.

The pistol discharged with a thunderous boom and a blinding flash and fog of black powder. Through the bitter bite of tears, Joelle saw a spot of bright crimson blossom on the front of Kenny Craig's shirt. But to her horror the impact didn't slow his charge.

The pistol was wrenched from her with bone-snapping violence. Joelle's fear-dazed eyes registered the sight of his hand swinging in a downward arc. Pain shattered through the side of her face, exploding along her jaw, numbing it, silencing her cries. He fell atop her, his weight squeezing the breath from her as if her lungs were the compressed bellows of Guy's accordion. She fought with every part of her she could move. She slapped at him. Her nails tore his flesh. Her elbows flailed. She used her head to butt his leering face. But none of that was enough to stop him, just as the bullet hadn't stopped him.

She felt his hands in her skirt, shoving it up to her knees, up over her thighs. Understanding brought a wave of nausea and a helpless terror such as she had never known. She fought the fear with anger. No, she would not let this happen! Crazy things flashed through her mind; Marsh cautioning her to lock her doors, her own proud vow that she could take care of herself, the shiver of alarm she felt from Kenny Craig's dark stare. Why hadn't she listened to Marsh? Why hadn't she heeded her own instincts? She'd allowed this to happen as surely as if she'd opened the door to him herself.

Hot breath grazed her cheek. She jerked her head to the side, trying to avoid the swooping descent of his mouth, her hands pushing uselessly at his pinning bulk. He yanked her hair, twisting her face up. His kiss ground brutally. She could taste her own blood from the cut of her teeth as she refused to part her lips. *Her first kiss.* Her mind reacted to that with a wild hysteria. Body writhing, head thrashing, she tried to squirm free. Another sharp blow sent blackness spiraling upward. Fingers clawed at the edge of her bodice, curling, pulling, rending material. Joelle tried to scream, but horror swelled her throat shut. She squeezed her eyes tight against the sight of his dark, vicious features, the way her numbed thoughts tried to block out the reality of what was happening. *Let this be over soon,* she prayed frantically. *Don't let him kill me. Please God!*

Then, miraculously, the crushing pressure was gone, lifted from her with an abruptness that left her gasping desperately for air. She forced her eyes to open, stunned then overwhelmed by the vision of Marshall Cameron wrestling her assailant. A fierce, murderous fury contorted his features in a way she wouldn't have thought possible as he locked his forearm about Craig's thick neck. Marsh was no match for the brute strength of the other man, even wounded as he was. Leaner and lighter, Marsh was plucked from the broad back and sent spinning with one mighty blow. He stumbled and fell, landing spread-eagle across Joelle on the bed.

But Kenny Craig had had enough. Staggering, stumbling, he lurched out of Joelle's rooms. They could hear him crashing through the store. Then he was gone.

Marsh started up, intent upon following, but Joelle snagged his neck, holding him fast. For a moment he was torn between the desire to vent a black vengeance and the need to respond to the ragged sobs of the woman in his arms. A single moan from Joelle and the whisper of his name decided for him.

"It's all right, Jo. He's gone. You're safe now." He hoped she hadn't noticed how his voice faltered. He was panting, shaking, stunned and furious about what he'd seen. If he hadn't come to apologize . . . If he hadn't grown curious at the sight of the opened door and sounds of struggle . . . If his pride had held him just a minute longer . . . He shut his eyes tight and hugged her. He wouldn't think of what could have been.

She was making small snuffling sounds into his shirt collar. Her body shook, and her fingers bit deep into his flesh. He forced the anger to leave him. Her attacker wouldn't get far, not bleeding and afoot. Marsh suspected that nothing short of a block and tackle would pry Joelle from his chest anyway. She needed him here, and he would hold her for as long as it took for the fear to subside. Hers . . . and his.

She quieted gradually. The shaking eased to fitful tremors. She was silent save for an occasional sniff. But her grip on him didn't lessen. His rocking movement was instinctive, as was the gentle stroke of his hand upon her hair. She responded to those calming gestures, and little by little the tension in her rigid limbs relaxed.

"He was stealing from the store," she began in a hoarse whisper. "I surprised him when I came in. He was going . . . he was going to—"

"Shhh, it's all right, Jo. Don't."

"I tried to stop him. I shot him. I did everything I could, but he was so strong . . . Marsh . . ."

"Shhh, it's all right now."

"If you hadn't come—"

"I did. And you're safe. You're safe, Jo."

The breath sighed from her as she finally believed it was true. Only then did she allow him to ease her away to assess the damage for himself. His features tightened. Fury beat a hard pulse along his jaw when he saw the discolorations on her face and the swimming anguish in her eyes. With whisper-soft tenderness, his thumbs brushed the tracks of tears from her cheeks. His gaze dropped, taking in the rents in her skirt, the rip in her bodice. And the blood. He forced himself to say the words.

"Did he hurt you, Jo? Other than hit you, I mean."

Her head gave a jerky shake, and he felt an overwhelming relief. He could deal with her fright, with her bruises. Those he could handle with a level head because both would fade in time.

"Do you have any coffee? Any brandy?"

"In the cupboard by the window," she replied faintly. When he stood, she came up quickly on her knees, fingers clutching at his sleeve. "Marsh . . ."

He rubbed a hand over hers in a soothing motion. "I'm going to put on some water and make some coffee. And I'll lock up. I'll be right back. I will." Uncomfortably aware of the amount of fair skin showing through the tear in her blouse, he reached for the woolen shirt folded over the back of a nearby chair. "Here. Put this on while I'm gone and try to keep warm." She'd started to shake again, great telling spasms of shock and lingering fright.

"Marsh—"

"I'll just be in the other room. I won't leave you. All right?"

She managed a nod and released him. He smiled in appreciation of that courage and lightly touched his palm to her tearstained cheek. Both of her hands covered the back of his, delaying his leave-taking for just a moment longer. Then she sat back, hugging the plaid shirt to the front of her ruined blouse.

He found the coffee and the brandy, and once the water was heating, he went out into the storeroom. He straightened the strewn items that marked Joelle's frantic flight, steeling his emotions as he did, to hold his anger in check. God help the man if he ever caught up to him again. He couldn't think of a torture severe enough to serve as ample punishment for what he'd seen in Joelle's eyes. His mood darkened as he lifted the goods from the thief's sack. Clothing mostly, some gunpowder, lamp oil; survival basics. Things she probably would have given a man in need had he asked. But he hadn't.

He'd just taken them and probably would have taken more had Marsh not come in when he did.

Solemnly Marsh turned the latch on the outside door. In the morning he would insist she add a bolt. He would put it on himself if he had to. When he went to shut the door leading to her quarters, he noticed that it hung ajar, nearly ripped from its hinges. He would fix that too. But no locks, no doors, no amount of caution could keep a single female safe in a world that meant to do her harm. Maybe now Joelle would understand that. He wished the lesson hadn't been learned in quite so severe a manner.

With a cup of heavily laced coffee in hand, Marsh tapped lightly on the door to Joelle's bedroom and was bade by a soft voice to enter. She had put on the plaid shirt and was huddled under the covers. With her knees hugged to her chest and her features drawn, she looked like a child upon her parents' bed, waiting to be comforted. The tug at his heart was tremendous. He managed to smile.

"Here you go. This will steady your insides some."

"Thank you," she murmured in a hushed voice. She took the cup from him. Trembling hands betrayed her. When he looked about for a place to sit, she reached out and drew him down beside her. He perched there on the edge of her bed, feeling awkward, feeling incredibly protective yet unable to display it as Joelle sipped then finally drank all the contents of the cup. He took it from her and set it on the floor for lack of another place.

As her eyelids lowered heavily, Joelle asked, "How much of that was coffee and how much brandy?"

"About a ten-ninety mix," he confessed with a smile. "It should fell you like a good-sized tree."

She smiled, too, and snuggled down into her quilts, willing to surrender to her weariness as long as he was with her. She gave a small sigh and tried to close her eyes. The images lying there in wait for her brought them back open with a despairing snap. Her chest jerked with remembered terror. It was almost as if Kenny Craig hid in her unconscious, ready to spring again the moment she was unprepared. She couldn't face the feel of his hands, the sweat of her helplessness, the stale heat of his breath upon her face. Not alone.

Marsh had gotten up to turn down the light. He found her staring at him with an odd intensity.

"Don't go."

With the quiver of anxiety in her tone and the marks of violence upon her face, how could he walk away? He settled back on the edge of the mattress. "I'll sit with you until you're asleep."

The thought of waking in the darkness with no one to chase her dreams away urged her to plead, "Don't leave me, Marsh. Please."

So he would not mistake her again, she turned back the quilts to offer innocently the space next to her.

Without a word Marsh removed his shoes and eased, fully dressed, beneath her pristine covers. He extended his arm, and she was quick to roll up into the haven it represented, her head resting on his shoulder, her arm tightly banding his middle. Then she felt safe enough to shut her eyes, and no threat awaited in that encompassing darkness.

Marsh lay awake long after her breathing grew soft and regular. He tried to ignore the pleasurable feel of her pressed against him by concentrating on less appealing matters. Like what he was going to do about this attack. At the end of the month she was going to expect him to make a choice regarding her future—whether or not she would be kept on as manager of the Superior. How could he in good conscience say yes? She was a seventeen-year-old girl, alone in the world, trying to run a man's business that would place her in this same situation time and time again. Who would be around to protect her after he was gone? Who would she have to talk sense to her, to curb her impulsive stubbornness? Who would hold her when the memories of this night rose to haunt her? And they would. Who would take care of this beautiful, brave woman-child after Lake Superior thawed and he returned to his planned life?

He'd have to tell her no. She would just have to accept it as a fact of life she couldn't change. She was more than capable of doing the job; she was wonderful at it, as a matter of fact. She had a real genius for figures and the respect of her crews. She just couldn't alter the fact that she hadn't been born Lyle Parry's son.

Just then Joelle muttered restlessly in her sleep. The sudden jerk of her slender form told of her rude awakening. She gave a startled gasp at his closeness and began to scuttle back in fear. Carefully, so as not to increase her fright, he touched her hair and spoke in a low whisper.

"Jo, it's Marsh. It's all right. You asked me to stay. Remember?"

He heard her breathing pull and ebb in quick little pants, then slowly deepen. "Marsh?"

"Yes."

She sighed thankfully and let the chill of terror shiver through her in a final wave. She'd been dreaming—no, remembering—and it had seemed so real. Waking to feel his firm male form beside her had brought the panic home. But it was Marsh, just Marsh. Trembling, she rolled tightly against his ribs. Her face fit into the hollow of his throat, where she could breathe in the warm, clean scent of him. She could feel his smooth chin rubbing over the crown of her head, and that gesture brought contentment. This was how she'd wanted to learn of things between a man and a woman, unhurriedly, tenderly, not through an abrupt act of violence. Damn Kenny Craig for almost cheating her of her chance. She did feel cheated and angry and unaccountably dirtied by what he'd done, by what he'd tried to do. She needed something to wash away the stain of guilt and distaste, something to wash away the feel of Kenny Craig.

"Would you kiss me, Marsh?"

He was silent for a long moment, afraid he hadn't understood her. "What?"

She tipped back her head. Although she couldn't see his face in the dark, she could feel his hesitation in the way his breathing altered. Would he say no? Perhaps she should just forget the whole thing. Embarrassed, she had started to dip her reddening face back into the safety of his shoulder when his hand rose and skimmed lightly along her swollen jaw.

"What did you say?" he asked again, his words scarcely a whisper.

"Kiss me, Marsh. Please."

There was no passion, no coquetry in her small voice, but rather an urgent desperation. Again he was quiet, thinking about what she had said and why she had said it. It was because of the attack, he was sure, not because of him personally. So he very gently lifted her chin in the cup of his palm and leaned down to find her lips in the darkness. It was the tenderest of touches, a soft cushioning of his mouth upon hers. When she moaned from the sheer wonder of it, Marsh felt a desire surge inside that was so fierce, so hot, it scorched him to the soul. Deliberately he pulled back then. That wasn't what she needed from him now. She proved it by burrowing into the cove of his shoulder. Her quiet voice did to his heart what the press of her body did to his loins.

"I knew it would be like that," she murmured contentedly. "Thank you, Marsh." Then she fell asleep.

Marsh fought the desire to groan aloud. Lord, what had she done to him? He was twisting inside with a confusion of longing and lust. He wanted to roll atop her and show her with all the considerable passion he possessed what it was to know the loving of a man. He needed to hold her, to keep her safe, even from his own pounding urgency. His hand moved restlessly through her cropped hair, but what he wanted to do was let it glide down the length of her supple form, to where the oversized shirt ended. He wanted to slip beneath that covering of rough wool to the satin softness of her warm skin, to feel the sleek contour of her hip where it nudged innocently into his. He wanted to explore the rounded glory of breasts that tantalized through a rent of cloth and hear her moan of awe become a rumble of passion. But not tonight, his sensibilities warned.

Not ever, reason commanded.

"Ah, Jo," he whispered hoarsely into the night, "how am I going to survive until spring?"

There was a brightness in her room that quite confused her. Slitting her eyes, Joelle peered about and realized in some surprise that it was daylight. She couldn't remember a time when she'd slept past dawn, yet here it was closer to noon. What—

She moved, and the entire side of her face seemed to come alive with agony. Then she remembered. Feeling the swell of abuse on her jaw, the horror of last night came back to her— struggling with Kenny Craig, the acrid bite of gunpowder, the sour smell of his breath. As her heartbeat quickened at the memory, she gathered her covers close. She also recalled the rest of the incident.

"Marsh?"

He was gone. She lay back in the pillows unsure of whether to be relieved or remorseful. He'd stayed the night in her bed, just holding her. Thinking of his warm, unyielding presence stirred a sense of peace within her. But there was more—the kiss. Her tongue touched her lips as if she could taste his soft mouth upon hers even now. He'd kissed her, and the sensation had been wonderful beyond belief. She wouldn't fool herself into thinking he had intended to offer anything beyond comfort. But she couldn't keep herself from wondering what it would be like to experience passion from that firm, masterful mouth. She'd spent her first night in the arms of a man, and she could see one of the distinct pleasures marriage had to offer. If only he'd stayed so she could have looked upon his face in slumber. But no, better he was gone. What would she have said to him, to the man who had seen her tears, who had responded to her needy plea for a kiss? Then, realizing he must have looked upon her while she slept, a flush warmed her cheeks.

Her hand touched the neckline of her baggy shirt. Though it covered her completely, she was aware of her own nakedness beneath it. Had he known? If he had, would it have swayed him from his pose of gentleman protector? She thought of his newly roughened fingertips skimming along her jaw, and she knew she wanted more from Marshall Cameron than a comforting kiss. But wanting Marsh was not something that pleased her. Wanting meant dependence, and she'd have none of that, no matter how good it felt.

When she climbed out of bed, a host of new miseries came to her attention. Her knees burned from skidding on the floorboards. Her shoulders ached, and her neck felt wrenched. All along the length of her, sundry bruises appeared as badges earned in battle—a battle she'd lost, a surrender to disgrace that Marsh had saved her from. Angrily she washed herself, scrubbing her skin until it stung; then she finished dressing in her typical mannish garb. She didn't want to feel feminine today. The sight of her torn skirt and blouse was enough of a reminder of what it was like to be female. She wadded the clothing and flung it away. Later she would see it burned, as if the memory of Kenny Craig's hands upon the garments could be consumed as well. But she knew it couldn't and her fury intensified.

Now, Joelle heard the sound of pounding in the storehouse. After her initial alarm passed, she went curiously to see what was going on. She found one of her men installing a heavy bolt on the main door. He looked up when he saw her, his features registering his shock at her ragged appearance, then softening in sympathy.

"Morning, Miss Jo. Cameron told me to see this fit first thing. Hope my banging didn't wake you."

"Cameron?" she said, frowning.

"Said I was to rehang your door when you was up and about and put another one of these here bolts on the inside of it."

"Did he?" She took that news with an odd mix of indignation and gratitude. His concern touched her heart, but his boldness rubbed raw upon her temper. "And where is Mr. Cameron?"

"He and some of the others went out looking for that no-good what—well, you know." He looked down uncomfortably, and Joelle wondered in dismay exactly what Marsh had told him and the others.

She didn't have long to wait and wonder. Joelle ate quietly in her quarters, having asked one of the cookees to bring her lunch. He did so, wearing the same sympathetic expression as the fellow who had fixed her doors. Finally, exasperated by the men's skittishness, she went to appraise the damage for herself. She spent a good long minute staring, aghast, into the mirror. There was a purplish lump the size of a small potato on her jaw and an equally unsightly bruise high on her cheekbone. It gave her face a sorry, lopsided look that made one wince to see it. Dejectedly she packed a towel with ice and held it to the sore contusions, hoping to alleviate some of the swelling and the sympathy. She was sitting at the table holding the ice to her face when she heard Marsh speaking to another man in the storeroom. Before she could go out to confront him, he was there, tapping upon her door.

Joelle wasn't quite sure how to greet him—as rescuing hero or annoying meddler? She settled for brusqueness.

"Did you find him?"

Marsh nodded. She didn't know what to make of his chagrin.

"He made it about ten miles before he dropped on the trail from loss of blood. Froze to death." His hands clenched at his side until his knuckles popped, as if he were angry at being denied the chance to deal out that justice more personally. But that didn't matter to Joelle. Dead was dead. Now she wouldn't have to watch for Kenny Craig's shadow every time she came into the van after dark. Now he would only haunt her dreams.

To distract himself from his impotent rage, Marsh tested the new lock and nodded his satisfaction. "Good and strong. That ought to do it."

Joelle refrained from commenting on the benefit of locking the barn door once the horse was gone. Instead, she said in a neutral voice, "I suppose I should thank you."

"You want to thank me, you keep these latched."

"I suppose the time has come to endure your lecture." She did her best to adopt a lop-sided scowl. She shouldn't be complaining, but his manner ruffled her independent feathers.

He looked at her, taking in the bag of ice and the pinch of weariness around her eyes. "Would a lecture do any good?"

"No."

"Then I'll save my breath."

Joelle waited. He didn't sound angry or irritated, just resigned. Still, she proceeded with caution. "What did you tell everyone? About what happened, I mean." Had he painted her as the helpless victim and he the brave hero? Would he have been wrong if he had? She started to clench her teeth, but it hurt too much.

Marsh shrugged. "I told them you came in on the fellow while he was robbing you, that he slugged you, and you winged him to drive him off."

"That's it?" she asked faintly.

"I figured that was all anyone needed to know unless you wanted to elaborate."

"And what did you say about your part in all of it?"

"I told them I heard the shot and showed up in time to see Craig running off. And that after I helped you pick up the place, I bunked down in the store in case he came back. And that you wanted to make sure I got someone to put better locks on the door first thing this morning."

Gratitude brought tears to her eyes. His version of the truth went far to save her dignity. He'd made her sound capable of fending off any threat and keeping control of the Superior. Only the two of them knew different. For the first time she considered what this whole mess might mean to Marsh and her position.

"I was unprepared, careless," she began carefully. "It won't happen again."

"No," he agreed softly, "it won't."

A cold uneasiness seeped through her like a chill. She studied his expressionless eyes, the somber set of his mouth, a mouth that had kissed her so sweetly the night before. There was no gentleness in either now. She knew the direction of his thoughts, but she had to hear him speak it plain.

"Meaning what?"

"It means I can't recommend that you stay on as manager of the Superior."

10

JOELLE FELT A terrible sense of helplessness rise up inside of her all over again. And again she would not endure it without a fight.

"That's not fair," she spat out tersely.

"No, it isn't," he told her with flat candor. "None of it's been fair, not the fact that your father drowned, not the fact that there are men out there who don't give a damn about abusing women, not my decision that a seventeen-year-old girl can't run a lumbering company by herself. But being unfair doesn't change any of those things."

"I can run this company as well as any man!"

"But you aren't one."

She couldn't argue, but she wouldn't apologize either. "No, I'm not. Had I been a man, Kenny Craig would have probably killed me on the spot. But being a woman, there was a chance he'd leave me alive."

"At what cost?" He was almost shouting. Damn the woman, couldn't she understand he was doing this for her own good? Not to hurt her, not to humiliate her, but because he cared about her. Because he was tortured by chest-clutching visions of what he would have found if he'd arrived a minute later.

"My cost! Not the company's mine. And that's my decision, not one you or anyone else can make for me."

"And would you have been so eager to pay the cost last night if I hadn't come in when I did? I don't think so."

Her glare was venomous. And worse, it was filled with an anguish of truth. No. Nothing was worth enduring what Kenny Craig had put her through. She hated Marsh for knowing that and making her see it as well. She placed the towel with its cold melt of ice down on the tabletop and stared at him for a long, unwavering moment.

He could almost hear the frantic workings of her mind. Such a clever mind. Such an impossibly stubborn woman. How he admired and was infuriated by her.

"So, because I am a woman alone I'm to be cast from the only security and family I've ever known. That serves your version of fairness, does it?"

Marsh had no reply. No, of course it didn't. A paralyzing ache clenched like a fist around his throat. That was the last thing he wanted. If only there were some other way around it. If only she weren't so vulnerable, so young. So beautiful. If only she didn't make his pulse go crazy.

"You promised me a month, and I insist you honor that agreement."

"I will," he said softly.

"And I warn you, Marsh, I mean to do everything I can in the next three weeks to change your mind."

He dragged up a ghost of a smile. "I'm sure you will." He turned to go, stopping at the door when she called his name.

"I almost forgot," she said with a soul-wrenching humility. "Thank you, Marsh."

He saluted her with a crooked grin, and his heart ricocheted off his ribs. "My pleasure, Miss Parry."

Three weeks. Three weeks to prove herself in Marshall Cameron's jaded view. It wouldn't be easy. He'd seen her at her absolute worst. She'd sobbed on his shirtfront and clung to him for comfort. She'd behaved like the type of mewling female she professed to loathe. She depended on him for her livelihood and now had to put last night's episode into perspective, consider it a lapse of judgment and control that would never, ever happen again. Joelle couldn't let his faith be shaken by her weakness. She would show him.

In the following days there were no signs that the terror of that night left her chest so heavy at times she could barely

breathe or that night shadows stretched her nerves to the limit.
She did what she could. She kept her doors latched. She took
to wearing the heavy pistol slung about her slender hips like
one of the Western cowboys she'd read about. She felt foolish
at first, but there was no denying the confidence she gained
from that heavy weight of steel slapping against her thigh. She
vowed to be no one's victim and would not look like one.

The attitude of the Superior crew heartened her as well. The
men had always shown her respect, had always treated her like
a little sister or a daughter. But since the shooting of Kenny
Craig, they looked at her differently, with a deeper admiration.
"Ma'am" was often tacked on to the end of their sentences.
They were more apt to tip their caps when she passed by than
to toss her a ribald quip.

If Marsh noticed, he said nothing. He said nothing at all. He
worked the woods with Guy, and as long as Joelle remained at
a distance, they worked with a sullen sense of camaraderie. He
made no effort to resume their conversation about her leader-
ship ability, and he certainly didn't try to follow up on the kiss;
and because she thought of both almost constantly, Joelle was
as surly as a bear whenever Marsh's name was mentioned. The
knowledge that he was watching her goaded her into action.
She would force him into admitting her value to the company
if she had to run the whole place single-handedly. And that
was becoming a frightening possibility.

Illness and accidents had taken an early toll on the crew. A
sprained back, a twisted ankle, a rattly cough, and one, two,
three days, a week, were missed when not so much as an hour
of absence could be afforded. Joelle filled in wherever she was
needed. On several mornings she was up at four o'clock to
build fires in the cookshack and bunkhouse and to saw holes in
the ice to draw wash water for the men. She showed up on the
swing-dingle at lunchtime to serve up dried-apple-and-raisin
pie. What she did best was work the horses. She was out on
the roads at night, driving the team that sprinkled water along
the sled tracks to make a good hard surface by morning. It was
a common sight to see her guiding the pair, dragging skidding
tongs into the cutting grounds. There she would fasten the
fishhooklike barbs into the small end of a log and snake
it from the woods to the crosshaul spot, where it would

be loaded onto a bobsled. She even hefted an ax, working beside the limbers to strip branches from downed trees. The only thing she didn't tackle was the cross saw, and that was purely practical. She was too small to hold her own there.

Marsh might not have said anything, but he was always well aware what Joelle Parry was doing—and aware of how his pride in her determination swelled. She belonged in this place, in these wild, untamed woods. He couldn't picture her in any other setting, not with her cropped hair, long masculine stride, and that thumb-busting pistol she toted on her hip. Hers was the spirit of the northwoods, free and indomitable. Yet he was trying to challenge that spirit, restrain it, break it, and wondered if he had the right. The Superior belonged to her regardless of who owned the paper on it. The men knew it. They deferred to her on every decision and followed her without quarrel or question. Even the brusque Chauncey Sonnier yielded to her will. How could Marsh say she couldn't run the company? He couldn't imagine anyone being more competent or more motivated to see it succeed. The Superior was like her father's other child, and as long as she could be a part of keeping it alive, she probably felt she could keep his memory alive, too.

Marsh knew all these things, but all of them stacked together could not overrule the terror he'd felt in his heart when he'd burst into her bedroom to find Joelle beneath the brutal bulk of Kenny Craig. No matter what she might say, no matter what she might do to prove otherwise, he would not be convinced that she could do without a man's protection. A crazy part of him wanted to be that man; crazy because he would be leaving in the spring and he had an entirely different life—and a different woman—waiting for him in Boston. Knowing didn't ease the savage pang of wanting.

Knowing he couldn't have Joelle didn't ease the jealousy curling in his gut when he saw Guy Sonnier fall in step beside her as they began their evening march back into camp. For here was the answer, whether he like it or not. Guy Sonnier would provide what he wished he could.

Joelle was thinking much the same thing while the stocky Canadian strode silently beside her. Guy wasn't a stranger to her, and she loved him like a brother. But with the slightest encouragement from her, he would propose. He'd been hinting at it since her figure started to develop womanly curves. He was a good man, she knew. He would provide companionship, laughter, warmth, and a means to stay in the world she'd grown up in. She'd have everything but the kind of love she knew should exist between a man and a woman. Guy would be good to her and longed to be a man with her. She'd seen that hot gleam of desire in his dark eyes, but there was no answering spark within her. But his presence would keep the shadow of Kenny Craig at bay and the Superior in her hands. Wasn't that enough?

"You are quiet, Jolie. Something troubles you?"

She looked up into the handsome bearded face. Immediately the simmer started in his gaze. She tried to summon some responsive warmth, but she felt nothing. Her smile was strained.

"Too many things to mention, I'm afraid."

Seeing an opening, he was quick to take it. In a casual move, his arm draped along her shoulders, tugging her into the sheltering firmness of his side. "You should not have to face them all alone, *cherie*. Have I not made it plain that I would happily fill your father's spot within your heart?"

"I'm not looking for another father, Guy," she replied with wry humor. She knew the direction he was heading. Distress wadded in her throat. Logic told her to let him continue, but emotion bade her to stop him now before he endangered their friendship.

But Guy's voice deepened, becoming an intimate rumble, suggesting exactly what she feared. "And what is it you are looking for, *ma petite*? What would you have me be?" His blunt fingertips stroked along her jaw, and she was stricken by the memory of another man's touch.

"I'm not looking for anything," she replied curtly.

His arm jerked away, and his features darkened with uncomfortable understanding. "Not from me, perhaps, but you lie to yourself if you say you do not look elsewhere."

"Guy—"

He was already striding ahead with big, angry steps, unwilling to hear more. Regret clogged within her chest and brought a dampness to her lashes. What could she have told him? Not what he wanted to hear. When the moment came, she found she couldn't encourage him unfairly. He loved her, and she didn't love him. He was too good a friend to saddle with such a bad bargain. He deserved a woman who would do more than keep his house and warm his bed companionably. He deserved a reflection of the passion blazing in his eyes. And she couldn't give it.

He had said something else that created panic in her soul. There was no use lying to herself. She couldn't love Guy Sonnier because her affections were held by another.

By Marshal Cameron.

A rare and fiery fury built inside Guy Sonnier as he sat at the evening meal. Across from him sat the reason for his rage. For two weeks he had worked the saw with Marshall Cameron. He'd come to a grudging respect for the man's grit and depended upon the strength of his pull. They had forged a bond of odd and mostly silent friendship, and there was nothing he would not uncomplainingly share with the man—except the woman he held in his heart.

Guy had known he wanted Joelle Parry for his wife from the time she was a gangly twelve-year-old. It wasn't because women were scarce in the North. He was a handsome man. He'd had plenty of opportunities with women who were more willing. But he preferred to wait until Joelle was old enough to court. He'd had patience because he knew they were destined to marry. Even as a child there was a strength and a spirit to her that captivated him. And then there was the Superior. A man could do no better than to have such a wife and such a legacy. Since there were no others she favored above him, he'd been content to go slow. Now it seemed he'd waited too long. The fancy Easterner had slipped in and stolen her right out of his ready arms. Maybe he could have understood it better if it had been one of his own who had won her, but this man, this Easterner, what could he give her but sorrow?

He'd always admired Joelle for her sensibleness above all things, but in this case she lacked a grain of common sense. Couldn't she see there was no future with Cameron? He was not of the North, and she would not survive in his city. Logic told Guy that all he had to do was wait until Cameron left in the spring, but instinct cautioned that he didn't have that much time. There was an impatience in the way Joelle looked at Cameron. She would not long be content to keep her distance. That would force him to step in when prudence warned against it, to take on a man he had no real desire to harm.

Then he intercepted the look Joelle gave Marsh, a smoldering glance of promise Guy would have given his all to possess. But she would not give that to him as long as Marshall Cameron stood between them.

Guy wasn't the only one aware of Joelle's speaking stare. Purposefully Marsh kept his eyes fixed upon his plate. Damn, why hadn't he seen the danger earlier? Because he'd wanted to be blind to it? As if that were an excuse. It was the kiss, that damned chivalrous kiss, that should have meant nothing. Thinking of her sweet lips brought a pleasure so raw it wrung his soul. Remembering the fit of her slight figure against him made his breathing painful. He shouldn't have let it happen. He should have . . . what? Left her to fend off the terror of that night alone? No, of course not. But he should have applied some degree of distancing restraint. He shouldn't have let her get so close that he now wore the feel of her against his skin like a tight pair of long johns. He shouldn't have let her stir his emotions into such a frenzy that they jammed up thick around his heart. She was barely beyond the blush of childhood, and he . . . he knew better. He had no right to tempt her with confusing passions. But it had been so easy to immerse himself in this life, to become one of the Superior's crew, to be a man without a past who could court the fair Joelle Parry. He'd let himself forget he had to go back to Boston. He'd let himself forget his responsibilities, and that wasn't like him at all; he was a man to whom duty was everything.

Except now, it wasn't. Everything was the dewy glistening of dawn in Joelle Parry's eyes.

Marsh thrust back from the table and stalked from the cookshack. He was so absorbed in his self-castigation that he plowed straight into the solid barrier of Guy Sonnier— and he was just crazy enough from frustration to shove hard to clear the way.

Guy pushed back. The abrupt force of rough palms smacking into his chest drove the breath from him and knocked all trace of reason out of his head. He swung. The unexpected blow rocked the smaller Canadian back on his heels. His dark head shook off the dazing effects of the punch. Then Guy smiled. This was the confrontation he'd been waiting for.

Before the two men could assume aggressive stances, Chauncey Sonnier wedged himself between them, grabbing up a shirt collar in each of his massive fists.

"Eh, now, enough of this. There'll be no brawling in this camp." He looked at both men's hardened faces and saw the uselessness of his gruff warning. They were already braced and tensed for a fight. Whether here or later in the cutting grounds, the explosion would come. Better here, he decided in an instant. Better to get it done with. He shook them roughly to unbalance their threatening poses, then let them go.

"I say again, there'll be no brawling, but if it's a little bit of honest sparring you need to wear off the vinegar, that we can arrange."

Guy stood down, grinning fiercely. "*Eh, bien.* What say you, city boy? Care to face me for a few rounds of bare knuckling?"

Marsh flung off the last of his civility. He returned the dangerous smile. "Anytime you're ready."

Joelle was slow to leave the cookhouse. It seemed she was viewing everything through a film of exhaustion. For days, she'd driven herself beyond the edge of endurance, mercilessly draining her body of strength. Only when she was ready to drop could she sleep in the room where Kenny Craig had shaken the sense of safety from her life.

She was vaguely aware of the sound of excitement brewing in the camp. That taut ripple tugged at her weary consciousness. She knew the rumble of a fight when she heard one. It was nothing new, nothing she cared to see. Men with tempers stretched fine by the isolation of the woods were prone to aggressive fits of pride. It seemed they could find no solution to their stress other than beating it out with another willing party. Some primal male urge, she assumed without understanding, as if they didn't get enough exercise to work their energies off at the saw and ax. Her father had seen the bouts of fisticuffs as a means to burn the bitterness of a

disagreement. He said it was safer to have two men square
off with bare fists than with an ax. She saw the wisdom of that,
so she'd do nothing to interfere with this evening's barbarity
whether she approved or not. Let the two empty-headed brutes
pummel themselves to pulp. She needed some sleep or she'd
be ready to throw a few punches of her own.

As she crossed the open camp, she couldn't help taking a
curious glance at the combatants. Shock froze her in place.
There in the circle of shantymen, stripping off coats and
limbering lethal limbs, stood Guy and Marshall; and from
the glazed looks glinting in their eyes, they were set to do
each other some serious bodily harm.

Men parted as soon as they saw who pushed between them.
Joelle was in a rare fury, intent on reprimanding both fools
within an inch of their lives. She'd reached the edge of the
ring when a huge hand closed about her arm. She glared up
at Chauncey Sonnier as he shook his head.

"Ah, no, missy. Let them play, or they'll be good for
nothing in the morning."

Play? There was nothing playful in the looks of the two men
fired between each other. "If you don't stop them, they'll be
good for nothing for weeks."

He only smiled. "I'll not step in. They need to settle things
between them. Better broken bones than broken hearts."

Joelle frowned for a moment, then a wild, fluttery sensation quickened in her belly. This fight was her fault. Guy's
shattered expression flashed though her memory with torturing
clarity. But that didn't explain why Marsh would indulge him
in this brutal display of jealousy. Unless he felt the same way.
The unexpected insight staggered her sensibilities. Could it be
Marshal Cameron cared for her? Why else would he be willing
to take the punishment Guy was aching to deliver? Why else
would his features be dark and intense with the same kind of
crippling fury?

She was still standing there stunned when Guy flung the
first jaw-cracking punch. Marsh spun from the force of it
then came back with startling resilience. Guy's teeth clacked
together, and his eyes rounded with surprise. He was used to
dropping a man with a single blow, yet this . . . this Easterner
had lashed out at him without missing a beat. He rubbed his

jaw and reassessed his opponent. He'd been misled by the
fine clothes and polished manner. Beneath them Marshall
Cameron was tensile steel. Somewhere he had learned to take
and throw a punch. Shifting from confidence to caution, Guy
feinted right and drove hard with his left only to find his wrist
deflected. Another of Marsh's jarring rights rattled though his
head. With a roar he threw himself bodily at the other man,
taking him unaware. Both of them went down hard, rolling,
flailing, cursing until a proper distance allowed them to regain
their feet. By then, skin had been broken, and tempers were
raw. Scenting blood, the circle of cheering lumbermen closed
in about the combatants.

Marsh's breathing grew harsh and jagged. He could feel his
face swelling. Every pull of air tore agonizingly through his
chest. Damn, the man had a fist like granite. He'd boxed on
the university team for three years and was a cool, skillful
pugilist. But that rushing lust for violence had shaken him
from his practiced stance. He was flinging his arms like a
back-street bruiser and taking a savage delight in the pulpy
feel of knuckles meeting flesh. That same frenzied rage made
him incautious, and Guy's fists slipped in to hammer like ax
bits. Marsh felt his ribs give and groan, sapping his wind,
buckling his knees. He went down on hands and knees on the
frozen ground, only to scramble out of the path of the sharp
steel calks of the boot swinging toward his face. Weaving like
a drunk, he hauled himself up by bracing his hands on his
thighs, and waited for the next felling wallop. But it didn't
come. He blinked hard and peered up through puffy eyes to
see Guy Sonnier in not much better shape, tottering just out
of reach. With a bellow of primal anger, Marsh lunged into
him, crashing like a felled tree through weaker timber to send
them both skidding on the wet earth.

It was all Joelle could do to helplessly watch them maul
each other with their fists and fury. She winced with the
delivery of each telling blow and swallowed back her cries for
it to stop until she could no longer stand the pressure building
in her chest. The slugging had been bad enough, but now they
were battered and spent, clouting each other with ineffective
blows, gripping each other by their torn shirtfronts to keep on
their feet. A strength of muscle and will honed by toiling in the

woods didn't wear down easily. They had just about exhausted the last of it, but neither would admit being close to collapse. Guy managed a half-head butt, flattening Marsh's nose and showering them both with a spurt of bright red blood. Marsh grabbed either side of Guy's heavy black beard and yanked his head down to meet Marsh's rising knee. They staggered apart, too disoriented to find each other and exact more weak punches. Seeing them bent double, arms swinging slackly at their knees like broken pendulums, Joelle seized Chauncey's arm. When he glanced down at her, the painful cramp in her throat forbade speech. Instead she mouthed the word *Please!*

Chauncey strode forward, catching his brother under the arms just as his feet went out from under him. Chuckling, he started to drag Guy out of the circle, ignoring his feeble protests the way he would dismiss the struggles of a gnat. "Come on, you great fool. I think the two of you have had all the fun you can stand for one night."

Muttering, the crowd of men began to disperse. Olen came up to help, but Marsh waved him away. He hurt. His insides felt as mashed as breakfast grits. All he wanted was to crawl away somewhere and die of his own stupidity. But he wasn't allowed that final dignity.

"Can you walk?"

He felt a slender arm go about his splintered ribs, and he groaned loudly.

"Don't expect me to feel sorry for you," Joelle warned crisply as she propelled him forward in a stumbling shuffle. His legs had gone to jelly. He didn't pay much attention to direction until his feet scuffled on floorboards. Raising his head took a major effort, like lifting a boulder atop a straw.

"Where . . . ?" he mumbled in confusion. His jaw wouldn't work right, and now he was doubting his other senses. He had the impression of warm firelight, and then there was an endless fall into a chair.

"Sit still and let me clean you up a little. I should have let you stand out there until you froze to the spot."

He reached out an awkward hand and caught her wrist, compelling her attention. "Why . . . why didn't you?"

Joelle looked from the curve of his fingers to the mess Guy had made of his face. The clogging fullness returned to her throat. She forced a whispering voice to cut through it. "Because you needed help and you were there for me when I needed someone."

He had no answer for that. He shut his eyes against what he was afraid he would see in her expression. Or was it in fear of what would show in his? The physical pain he felt was nothing compared to the agony of spirit her soft words betrayed. He vowed to endure her tender ministrations without a sound; then he would get the hell away from her before he gave her any further reason for remorse.

She was gentle. The blot of a warm cloth eased away most of the clotting blood and cleaned the worst of the gashes. He felt himself adrift on a cloud of comfort and complete exhaustion. He was past caring what she did as long as he didn't have to move. The faint feathering pleasure of her touch skirted the edges of hurt, making the exquisite misery just bearable. Her fingertips slightly caressed the split at his temple and soothed his bruised cheek and jaw. He was lulled into a stupor of contentment until a breath of warmth brushed upon his now bare chest. He pried his eyes open, battling soreness and swelling to stare in alarm.

"Just checking your ribs," Joelle chided lightly, but there was a certain thickening to her voice that made him uneasy. As she pressed along the dark discolorations on his side, he flinched and abruptly shifted. Her hand came up to steady him, sliding unintentionally across his firm chest. The contact was galvanizing. They both went still, their breathing arrested, heartbeats tripling as Joelle looked up and their gazes met and mingled. Marsh had a sudden insight into what it must feel like to drown in the gray depths of Lake Superior. Except this was warm, so warm, this sudden flood of emotion that swirled about his senses, sucking away all traces of will. He knew what it was like to be completely engulfed. Floating. Lost. Frightened yet so very free.

Joelle pulled in a sudden, raspy breath and straightened. Her face was white with agitation. She broke from his gaze and blurted huskily, "A snug wrap ought to hold things in place. I've got some supplies in the store."

As she turned away, Marsh fought the urge to catch her. To do what? Pull her to him, savage her sweet mouth with kisses? Now, that would be the way to cap the insanity of the evening. God, what was wrong with him? Had he lost his mind totally in that battering of blows? Exhaling a ragged breath, he tried to flush the rampaging need from his system and failed miserably. He was so swamped with feeling for her that he couldn't get himself untangled from the threads of it snarling about his heart. Desperately he grasped for anything that would keep him from caving in altogether. She was so young, so inexperienced. Maybe she was just experimenting, just flirting with the idea of seduction. Maybe he wasn't giving her enough credit. She was a female, and all the females he knew were experts at molding a man's emotions; they seemed to have been born with that talent and used it right from the cradle. Perhaps this was some game she would tire of. He hoped so. He hoped he was wrong about what he'd seen when their eyes held so intently.

Don't let her be in love with me!

11

WITH HIS EYES squeezed shut, Marsh was concentrating so hard upon that fervent prayer that he didn't know Joelle had returned until she nudged between his spraddled thighs to kneel close. She mistook his jerk of awareness for one of pain. The two feelings were very similar, both capable of forcing a deep, tight-chested breath from him. Before he could open wary eyes, she positioned a bulky towel over his eyes and throbbing nose, instructing him curtly to hold it in place. It took a moment for the chill of the ice packed inside to penetrate; then she stayed his hand when he started to remove it.

"Leave it on if you want to see tomorrow," she snapped with gruff impatience. The light stroke of her fingers over the top of his created a pleasant confusion when compared to that tone. "The cold will keep the swelling down. From the look of you, you should stick your whole head in a bucket of ice water. You're a mess, Cameron."

Yes, he was—in ways she didn't even realize. He sat still, blinded by the frigid mask over his sore features, yet acutely aware of her in every strained sense. He could smell the strong soap she'd used to wash her hair. He could hear the draw of her breathing, the way it shivered slightly each time she inhaled. He could feel the warmth of her care in each efficient brush of her hands, which for all their practical purposes seemed to linger just a second beyond what was

purely medicinal, as if she were taking advantage of the
chance to touch him. He might have enjoyed it, too, if he
hadn't been so battered in body and soul.

"Lean forward a bit," she coaxed in a less authoritative
voice. When he did, moaning slightly from the effort, she
worked an elastic bandage around and around the abused
rack of his ribs. Each time the bandage passed behind his
back, she stretched forward, tormenting him with the innocent
press of her breasts against him. When she tugged and tied
it snugly beneath one arm, she was leaning across his lap,
the softness of her hair tickling under his chin. Before he
could stop himself, he dipped his head slightly so his lips
touched that silken cascade. He ached to pull her against
him until she could feel exactly what she'd done to him
with her teasing nearness. That ache had shifted down from
a heaviness in his chest to a straining fullness in his loins.
Dear God, didn't she have any idea? Of course she didn't,
he realized with punishing contrition. He was the only one
thinking such things. But then how could he explain away
the leisure of her touch, her reluctance to move away now
that the wrapping was complete? She stayed in the vee of his
thighs, tucked beneath his jaw, hands splayed wide along the
rapid jerk of his ribs.

"Does it hurt terribly?" she asked at last. The velvety catch
in her voice set off a frenzy of sensation inside him.

"Like hell," he admitted with gritty candor. Most of his pain
was of her making, because she wouldn't move away to give
him room to breathe in anything but her fragrance, to think
of anything but how soft she'd feel beneath him, to recover
himself from this crazy path his passion had led him along.
He had to break free.

With a heaving groan, he dropped against the back of the
chair, at the same time moving his knees to prod her from
between them. He eased the towel away from his blackening
eyes to see her rock back on her heels, her features a study
of concern.

"Marsh?" Her hand pressed to the skin just above the stark
white bandage, over the chugging effort his heart was forced
to make to feed his galloping pulse. She couldn't help but feel
it. Her frown increased. "Are you all right?"

"No," he growled in an irritable frustration of want. He tried to stand, needing badly to escape this room, this woman. His legs shook and refused to hold him. Joelle came forward at the same time, readying to catch him should his balance give way. Their eyes met again. Their awareness of each other took on an intensity just short of cataclysmic. And what gave was his resolve.

"Jo . . ." His hand came up, his scraped knuckles following along the line of her stubborn jaw, his fingertips tortured by the remembered feel of her soft cheek. He let his fingers stretch out to explore that tender curve, gliding down to the slender column of her throat, where he could see her pulse pounding in erratic anticipation, and around to the blunt crop of her hair, where they drove up and spread wide to mesh in that thick, dark glory. He wasn't aware of drawing her toward him. She came forward as if her need and his melded their thinking into one. Their lips touched for a tentative taste. Passions whet by that brief temptation, they came together again to fulfill a pressing hunger, one that flared hot and out of control the moment Joelle sighed and sagged against him.

His arms cinched tightly about her tiny waist, pulling her more deeply into his hold. She felt so small, so damned fragile in his crushing embrace, and yet he couldn't for the life of him release her. Not when her mouth parted sweetly to invite him in. Not when he explored that moist recess and felt her shyly, then with increasing boldness, do the same with him. Her tongue slid like wet silk across his lower lip. It was enough to drive all thoughts of restraint from his mind. He'd known from the first, when he'd seen her crouched at the fireplace, when she came so boldly to save her father's company, that the attraction then would come to this. From the moment she'd touched her fingers to his lips, he'd felt an exquisite shiver of inevitability. He'd tried his best to fight it, to ignore it, to hide from it, but she kept drawing him back, the way the innocent abandon of her kisses drew him closer and closer, until there was no turning back. For the first time in his carefully regulated life, he wanted to throw off all vestiges of control and responsibility to pursue what beat hard and heavy in his heart. Ironically her willingness to do the same brought him back from that final step.

Joelle's arms found their way around his middle, and she squeezed tight in unthinking rapture. A splintering pain shot through him, shocking him into the reality of what he was about to do, of what he wanted with all his heart and soul to do. And consequence twisted so savagely within his chest that the other hurt was a mild nuisance in comparison. In an agony of gentleness, he captured Joelle's face between his hands and forced a saving distance. But that was worse, because he could see the tenderness, the yearning, the soft sheen of love in her heavy-lidded gaze. His heart cleaved in two with one swift, unexpected stroke.

"Jo." His voice was raw, hurting. "We can't do this."

A smile that was sensuality itself curved her swollen lips. "I want to," she said in a husky voice, as if that were the answer to his distress. She touched his face, learning its angles with a caressing sweep, encompassing the lumps and bruises as if they didn't mar the perfection she saw there. He surrendered to the reverent study as if he'd spent his entire life just dying to experience its cherishing thoroughness. His eyes closed in an anguish of need, giving her the opportunity to seek his mouth once more. He yielded to the intensity of her kiss, letting her discover its delights, surprised to find she could teach him a thing or two about desire as her lips teased his. He said her name again, this time in a low, yearning whisper. She shuddered in response and molded more firmly into his passion-inflamed form. The pressure was intolerable. He had to give it ease. His hands caught at her trouser-clad hips, rubbing her against him in a way that both relieved and increased his torment. He felt her stiffen in surprise and then instinctively begin to move in a rocking motion that drove him insane with frustrated urgency.

Her mouth opened wide to his plunging kisses, taking him in with maddening promise. She arched and moaned as his hands shifted upward with a rough eagerness to curve around her contours. A delicious tremor raced through her as the brush of his thumbs excited a tightening expectation in the sensitive tips of her breasts.

He'd imagined—no, that wasn't quite true. Nothing had prepared him for how good she felt in his arms; how vibrant, how alive, how soft and exciting. His emotions were on fire.

There seemed no way to cool them or to bring him back to the realm of reason—until she whispered a breathless declaration against his lips.

"Oh, Marsh, I love you."

He went still immediately. Sensation shut down with a jerk, as if a cog were caught in the machinery of passion. Feeling him withdraw in a way that was so much more than physical, Joelle leaned back in alarm. Her confusion bright in her gaze, she searched his face for an answer.

"Marsh?"

There was something deliberate and distancing in his lack of response.

"What is it?" she asked as her panic mounted. She sought some sign to help her understand the bleakness scoring his features.

"Jo, I'm sorry," he said in a dull tone. None of the muscles in his face would work. He watched uncertainty climb into her eyes, clouding the desire that had given them such a smoky darkness. As much as he hated it, as much as he wished to stay silent, he knew the time for truth had long since passed. There was no escaping the fact that he was going to hurt her unforgivably.

"Did I do something wrong?" Her voice was tremulous. Unshed tears brightened her anxious gaze. All Marsh's detachment deserted him. He wished suddenly and fervently that he'd let Guy Sonnier kill him, because that was what he was going to do to her—kill her trust and her tender feelings. For that there was no excuse. Regret thickened as he forced the words.

"No, Joelle, I did." His awareness of her was razor-edged. Even knowing he had to break the connection cleanly, he couldn't resist the need to touch her, to experience the softness of her cheek made dewy by the first trace of tears. The realization that he would never again feel the smooth curve of her cheek or the taste of her eager passion lent a shakiness to his hand. God, he wanted her, needed her with an ache so deep it defied reason and right. As the tenderness inside him just kept swelling, so did the reluctance and remorse. He had to tell her even if it meant losing this precious moment.

"I did something wrong, Jo," he continued in a constricted tone. "I let things get way out of hand. I should have stopped. I never wanted you to get hurt. I should have told you before . . . before . . ."

"You're married." She could barely get that out.

"No." He saw relief begin to lighten the tension in her face, but he couldn't allow it. "Almost."

"Oh."

"I have a fiancée in Boston. We're to be married when I go back in the spring."

"I see." Understanding shot across her features like a raw, lacerating pain. Then she got a grip on her devastation, determined to get it under a weak control, harnessing it with the only emotion stronger than a shattered love—the fury of humiliation. "You let me make a fool out of myself."

Marsh opened his mouth, but there were no words to exonerate himself. Drowning in guilt, wallowing in regret, he was saved by her remarkable poise. He'd broken her heart, and she was behaving far better than he could manage. He marveled at her strength, knowing the agony that writhed behind it.

Joelle stood. All the softness in her face hardened into a mask of icy anger. Her voice was brittle. "I don't appreciate being toyed with, Mr. Cameron. That's not part of the job I stayed on to do. I think you'd better get the hell out of here."

"Jo, I wasn't—" He caught himself. He had no business trying to lessen his blame. What he had to do was get the hell out before the false front of her bravery gave way. He dragged himself up out of the chair, pausing a moment to suck in air. The pain slicing through his ribs was nothing compared to what squeezed about his heart. He straightened slowly, cautiously, then faced Joelle. The wad of emotion in his throat was suffocating him.

She glared at him, her eyes glinting dangerously. Pride held the fractured bits and pieces of her dignity together, but it could only keep the storm of anguish contained for so long. She stepped back purposefully, making room for him to pass. Her chin notched up a degree, and it was that resourceful gesture that broke him.

"Oh, Jo, I wish . . . Dammit!" He clamped down on that. The truth of what churned inside him was better left unsaid.

It would do no good to force them both through that emotional wringer. Better he just walk away now. Only he couldn't.

Marsh framed the rigid set of her features with the gentleness of his palms. He kissed her. She didn't object, nor did she yield. Her lips tasted of tears. Still he savored them the way a condemned man would linger over a last meal. It was the first time he'd ever sampled from the piquant fare of love, and its sweetness was intoxicating. It filled him with an unexpected satisfaction and left him yearning for more. What good would it do to tell her his plans in Boston were more merger than marriage or that his lifelong code of honor and discipline was hanging in threads? That walking away from her was going to be the hardest thing he'd ever done? The tiny wedge she'd made in his heart had split it wide open, and he couldn't control the fall. After years of being with the most sophisticated and desirable women in the civilized East, an unspoiled, unpolished girl from the northwoods had brought him crashing down with the indignity of felled timber. He couldn't get up gracefully to save his life. She'd had him limbed, bucked, and skidded almost from their first meeting. But that didn't change a damned thing.

Feeling her tremble, Marsh dragged his mouth away from hers and gathered Joelle close against him. He used his hand on the back of her neck to hold her head tight to his shoulder. She continued to shiver in his embrace for a timeless moment. Her hands moved over him restlessly, stroking up his arms, touching his bruised cheek, twining in his hair, then finally bracing against his chest to push him away valiantly as if it cost her every scrap of will to do so. He let his arms drop heavily and stepped back. She refused to look up at him, sparing him the sight of her misery which was plain in the taut line of her shoulders and in the ragged sound of her breathing.

"Please go." She sounded near tears.

Fighting down the wrenching need to throw everything away just to ease her pain, Marsh said simply, once again, "I'm sorry," and was gone.

Her composure couldn't withstand the soft sound of the door closing. As a sob gurgled in her throat, Joelle let the stiffness drop from her shoulders. Her head hung, bobbing slightly with the force of her silent weeping. She stood letting the tremors of shock buffet her until she was too weak and drained to feel anything. On legs that wobbled almost too much to support her, she made her way into her bedroom and crawled under her covers, not even bothering to remove her clothes. She cried herself into an empty achiness, and then slowly she was able to regain some control.

For one glorious moment she'd thought everything were possible. For the first time since Lake Superior had taken her father from her, she'd felt secure and loved. In Marsh's arms she'd found the haven of a lifetime. Beneath his kisses, the woman in her awoke without awkwardness or apology. His attention made her feel beautiful, even desirable. He'd been tender and passionate, and in her naïveté she'd assumed because he wanted to make love to her that he fully loved her. How wrong she'd been.

She'd always known he'd be going back to Boston. The knowledge that he was returning to the arms of the woman he would marry brought that home with a cruel certainty. Before she had secretly hoped he could be persuaded to stay, that he would make his home here, with her. She no longer had the luxury of that belief. A man like Marshall Cameron would not choose a life of hardship with a rough-edged backwoods orphan who preferred long johns rather than silk next to her skin, not when he had a soft, sophisticated beauty waiting in some posh drawing room. She forced herself not to think of the man who'd kissed her; the man who wore plaid wool and red suspenders and had calluses on his hands. That man wasn't Marshall Cameron, owner of Superior Lumbering. Marshall Cameron wore fine tailored suits and silk cravats. He ate off china and Chippendale, not tin and tree stumps. He cut figures at the bottom of ledger sheets, not pine trees in a Michigan forest. He sailed on pleasure yachts in warm salt waters, not lumber barges upon the merciless cold of Lake Superior. She and Marsh were worlds apart. He was here on the Keweenaw for five months, playing out a role, playing upon her heart. When the waters thawed, they would carry him away, and he would never look back. He had family in Boston, a home and a woman waiting. He had no place in his life for a needy woman alone in the northwoods. And that's what he'd meant when he said he was sorry.

What did that leave her besides a heart full of misery and a memory wrung with shame? It left her with the Superior. But for how long? Her eyes squeezed shut, staving off fresh, useless tears. She'd managed to do everything wrong. The harder she had tried to impress upon Marsh that she was as capable as any man, the more she had exposed her frailty as a woman. Her instincts had failed her with Kenny Craig. Her inexperience had misled her with Marsh. *I love you.* Of all things to say, she had to blurt that out. He would never take her seriously again. How it must have amused a man of his sophistication to think a simple woodcutter's daughter was awestruck over him. She balled up tight in an agony of disgrace and let the tears come.

I love you.

Amusement was not what Marsh was feeling. The words "I love you" had humbled him to the core. He'd never heard them spoken, not from a father who demanded perfection, from a mother who insisted on discreet gentility, nor from a fiancée who would gladly take his arm but shrank from his embrace. Never had three words struck such a chord of emptiness in his heart. As he made his way in slow, shuffling steps to the dark bunkhouse, he was tormented by an unwelcoming clarity of thought.

He didn't want to go home.

That was ridiculous, of course. Guy's punches must have addled him worse then he'd suspected. They must have fractured his skull and his logic along with it. The blow to his ribs must have punctured his heart, considering the way it floundered so painfully. Or maybe it had been snagged and torn on the sharp accusation in Joelle's eyes. He would have preferred having her come at him with her fists the way Guy had, or even with that pistol she'd grown so fond of toting. He couldn't point to any apparent wound and say, "Look what you did to me," and so she didn't believe he suffered any pain.

He hadn't meant to hurt her. He hadn't meant for either of them to twist in this particular misery of futile circumstance.

It had happened so fast that he hadn't had time to prepare, to protect himself from feelings that should never have matured. Joelle had him off balance from the very first. With other women he'd known what to expect. He'd known the consequence of each playfully bantered word, each insincere kiss. But here he'd been lost from the instant he'd stumbled over her. She'd touched some part of him that he'd never explored, and the discoveries had been as big a surprise to him as they'd been to her. How was he to know that a case of blisters and a brusque, opinionated brat of a girl in men's trousers would drive him to distraction? Who would have suspected that in leaving the familiar sanctity of Boston and crossing a bitter inland sea, he would find himself in a raw new world that so beguiled his senses he couldn't face being anywhere else? Had he lost his mind or simply found his soul?

Marsh dragged himself into the room filled with slumbering men. The air was thick and almost unbreathable from the fumes of the now extinguished kerosene lamps and the drying wool socks and mitts hung along the stovepipes. The smell didn't bother him as it once had, nor did the sound of lusty snores grate upon his nerves. Both seemed a part of the camaraderie he'd found in this crude forest dwelling. How odd it was to consider these burly and mostly illiterate men as his friends, stranger still when he looked back and could see no similar relationships in his past. He'd had no time for friends. He'd been too ambitious, too intense, to cultivate a sense of closeness, too cold and selfish to inspire intimacy. The people he knew either feared him for who he was or envied him for what he had. No one sought him out unless there was something to gain from an association with him. What a shock this place had been to his cynical, suspicious mind.

Here there was a candor nothing short of brutal. Men were honest in their likes and dislikes and sincere in their respect once it was earned. And damn if he didn't like them for their straightforward opinions and their stoic acceptance of a hard life. There were the Frenchmen who clung to their culture, zealously keeping their societies, their newspaper and Roman Catholic religion; the Cornish who were staunchly independent and devoutly Methodist, preferring the dark chill of the mines to the green airiness of the woods; and the Finns who held to strict discipline, temperance associations, and working men's unions. They were all so different, all meshing together in these distant wilds. He was as much a foreigner as any of them, so their acceptance meant more than any corporate promotion, any inherited seat on the Board.

He hobbled like an arthritic old man to the edge of his bunk then looked up in despair. He might as well have been looking at a climb to the moon. He tried to lift one foot then the other, and both times the pain in his side was intolerable. "Oh, hell," he muttered to himself as he snatched down one of the heavier blankets.

The deacon's bench was harder than it looked. With the blankets wrapped about him Indian fashion, Marsh slouched down on it, letting his unregistering stare fix on the glowing belly of the stove. What a mess. How had he been so seduced by the back-breaking routine of the Michigan woods? He might play at lumberjack, might find a wonderful, freeing relief in the physical requirements and a contentment in its rough camaraderie, but he was no sawyer. He couldn't hide in these snowy pines pretending he had no life to return to. Even if nothing beyond the demands of duty waited, it was a duty he couldn't ignore.

This wasn't his world. It was Joelle's and Guy's and Olen's and Tavis Lachlan's. There was no place for him or his made-to-order suits here. He wasn't the man Joelle needed to fill her days and warm her nights. He couldn't stay beyond the greening of spring to act as her protector or her lover. His groggy mind or his aching heart suddenly made him beset by the most insane idea. He could take Joelle with him. He had a salacious image of them rolling together in his big feather bed, of waking to find her beside him beneath his fat, fluffy quilts. Even as his emotions rallied behind that notion, another part of his mind formed an objection. He forced himself to consider what it would be like beyond the bedroom. He tried to picture Joelle at his mother's pristine table and the crowded little social affairs he'd be obligated to attend. How would she spend her time while he was at work? Would she tend the spindly little annuals planted in his mother's flower boxes when she was used to having a forest at her command? She'd hate it. She'd grow to hate him for transplanting her to a place where she couldn't flourish.

His face ached mercilessly. The dull throbbing pulsed all the way to his toes. God, he felt awful. Wretched. Worse. He tried to close his eyes, but the memory of Joelle's anguished stare was right there ready to torment him. What was he going to do? What could he do? He couldn't give her anything. He was leaving in April, May at the latest. Lake Superior was going to take someone dear from her again. He only had a short time left to be with her, but something about Joelle Parry stirred images of a lifetime together, and that he couldn't offer.

So how the hell was he going to keep his hands off and his heart unbroken?

12

THE CREW WOKE to a world that was intensely white. Winds whipped with blizzard force through the small camp, driving the snow in a fierce, stinging fury. A man couldn't see beyond the reach of his arm. Within a half hour the roads were completely blocked. Superior Lumbering was at a temporary standstill.

That suited Marsh just fine. Moving himself was hard enough. He couldn't imagine drawing a deep breath, let alone a six-foot saw. Overnight every muscle in his body seemed to have fused together in one great clogging ache. When Olen saw him, he gave a low whistle.

"My friend, I think you are what the French refer to when they speak of the walking dead."

Marsh managed a grimace. "Except I can't walk."

"Are we to carry you to breakfast then?" The man's good humor was almost unbearable.

"Can't eat." How could he when he felt as if his jaw were broken in at least a dozen places?

"Is there anything you can do?" Olen was grinning, not even trying to hide his unholy amusement.

"I think I could probably sleep for a week if I could find a way to get into bed."

Before Marsh could protest, Olen caught him by the collar and the seat of his trousers and slung him up into the top bunk as if he weighed nothing. After the initial shock to his abused body, a tremendous sigh of satisfaction rippled through him. He melted right into the covers.

Olen chuckled and pulled up the coarse blankets. "I'll wake you in a week."

Marsh gave a grunt of agreement and was fast asleep.

His hibernation didn't last quite that long, but it was nearly dark when his senses stirred. He could hear the rumbling conversations of men made restless by the weather. He tried to sink back into the blackness of oblivion, but the rumblings coming from his own belly prodded him out of the warm blankets. When he had literally crawled down from the bunk, Marsh was forced to endure the attentions of men eager to lessen their boredom. Their ribbing over the state of his face and the unsteadiness of his walk and the simple fact that he was alive after facing down Guy Sonnier followed like a ribald wake as he wobbled along the row of bunks and idle loggers. He tried to grin at their rough humor, and they took the pitiful grimace on his face as a sign of his good sportsmanship. Then he hesitated at the foot of Guy's bunk.

The Canadian was stretched out on his back in a painful pose similar to what Marsh's had been. Though his thick beard hid most of the damage, there was evidence of a massively swollen lip. The one eye he could open was black with hostility when it settled on the tottering Easterner. Marsh offered a nod, indicating a truce, but the other man turned from it with a jerky roll onto his side and a very satisfying groan.

Sighing as deeply as his taped ribs would allow, Marsh moved on. At the door he paused long enough to struggle into his mackinaw, but that heavy wool coat was no protection from the bluster of the early evening chill. It cut right through him the moment he stepped out of the bunkhouse, cold but bracing and just what he needed to strip the varnish of lethargy. Huddling down inside his coat, he waded across the yard to the cookhouse, where welcoming fires yet burned.

The big room was empty, row after row of high tables all scrubbed down. At the sound of his scuffling step, one of the spindly cookees peered out and nodded in recognition.

"Can I get something to eat?" Marsh managed to call out. Moving his jaw was like crunching on grated glass.

When the cookee relayed his request back to the kitchen, a big bellow shook the rafters in response. "What the hell do he think this is? A gawddamn fancy hotel diner? He eats when we all eats! Breakfast is at four-thirty. Tell him to make sure he ain't late in getting his lazy arse outta bed!"

It wasn't the most delicately put refusal he'd ever heard. Disheartened and starving, Marsh stood in the cavernous room trying to decide if it would be better to gnaw bark off the side of the nearest tree or have Olen toss him out of bed for the noisy snarling of his stomach. What he wouldn't give for a sympathetic maitre d' eager to be bribed into humble groveling by the power of a man's fatted purse. Marsh closed his sore eyes, envisioning starched table linen, the clatter of heavy silver, the tantalizing scent of a thick, oozing prime rib, and a bubbly glass of a stimulating red wine.

"You look like hell, boy."

He glanced up at the glowering cook, Fergus, not denying the obvious. "Feel worse."

"Charlie, what the hell's wrong with you?" the burly man hollered behind him, sending ashes showering down from the tip of his squat cigar. "Get this man some coffee!"

Dazed by the sudden offer of hospitality, Marsh just stood dumbly and stared until a bench was jerked out for him.

"Sit afore you fall," Fergus growled, and Marsh obeyed. Fergus laughed at his confusion and explained in his gruff, booming voice, "My kitchen ain't never closed to a man who has grit enough to toe-to-toe with a Sonnier. Had me a go-round with Chauncey once. Took exception to a piece of beef I served him. Damn if the son didn't have me sipping mine through a straw for the better part of three weeks. What can I make up for you?"

"Got a straw?"

Fergus's laugh echoed through Marsh's skull like cannon fire. "I'll fix you up a stew so tender the meat'll dissolve on the spoon. Yer gums won't have to do no work at all. Jus' sit tight, and I'll start it steaming."

Marsh smiled gratefully. The moment the husky cook disappeared into his lair, he let his head drop down on his forearm. If he didn't move or breathe too deeply, he could convince himself that he would survive. Not that he deserved to. Closing his eyes, he let his awareness drift.

Surprise stopped Joelle in the doorway, and distress held her there for a good minute as she tried to dredge up the strength to confront Marshall Cameron. Shame knotted in her throat, urging her to make a quick and cowardly retreat. Her knees trembled. Angrily she forced them to steady. She would not run from him. She would not hide as if she'd done something dishonorable. If there were any blame, it rested with him for not telling her the truth of his situation. Had she known he belonged to another, she wouldn't have made that humiliating declaration of love. She had no reason to cringe from this meeting, and she wouldn't.

In short, stiff strides, Joelle crossed the dining hall. She'd all but forgotten why she'd come to talk to Fergus. Her concentration was consumed by the man sprawled bonelessly upon the tabletop before her. As she looked down on him, the dispassionate edge of her anger dissolved. A gut-wrenching need rose in its place along with a terrible tenderness. He looked so helpless, so worn out. She longed to brush back his tawny hair and linger over the twenty-four-hour stubble on his chin and cheeks. She'd never seen him quite so unkempt, and the effect was searingly masculine. Remembrance returned, overwhelming her with sensations; the way his roughened hands created a delicious friction on her untried flesh, the wild taste of desire he shared as his tongue explored intimately inside her mouth, the fluttery yearning that stirred where her hips pressed into the hard ridge of his groin. *Damn you Marshall Cameron for making me want you still.*

The arrival of Charlie from the kitchen was a saving grace. Pride kept her from showing the face of her misery before any other. She felt an uncomfortable smile stiffen on her features as she nodded to him and reached out to take the cup of coffee he'd brought for Marsh. When he'd gone, she clamped down on her wayward thoughts. She'd not make a fool of herself twice. Marshall Cameron was not hers to fuss and fawn over. She had to start getting used to that idea, but acknowledging and accepting were two different things.

Joelle set the cup down before Marsh's distorted nose. It took only a second for his nostrils to flare and his chest to expand in appreciation of the rich, dark scent. His sighing moan sent a shiver of response through her.

"Don't suppose you'd have anything a hundred proof to sweeten this with, would you?"

"Sorry. Against the Superior's rules."

She watched the effect her presence had upon him. Without him opening his eyes, she could see awareness in the tensing of his body. Muscles bunched beneath his shirtsleeves and stiffened in his back. His expression hardened as slowly he struggled to look up at her through a puffy rainbow of swollen eyelids. Discomfort was evident in the way he eased himself off the tabletop.

"Evening, Jo," he uttered in a neutral tone, helping her firm her own resolve.

"Cameron. I hope you don't feel as bad as you look."

He gave a wheezy laugh. "Worse, I'm afraid. What are you doing out on a night like this?"

For a moment Joelle was struck dumb. She couldn't remember what had brought her to the cookhouse. Seeing him had skewed her purpose. Then she recalled the papers she held. "I came to discuss a supply order with Fergus."

"You never take time off, do you?"

She scrutinized him warily for a second, trying to weigh the implications of his words, then said simply, "I can't afford to."

Marsh broke eye contact then. His brow furrowed with a moody concentration as he stared into his steaming coffee cup. She didn't want to know what he was thinking. Frowning, she started to move around the table, heading toward the kitchen. The movement startled him from his musings, and he reached out, his hand grazing her hip unthinkingly.

"Jo . . ."

She froze at the contact. The pace of her heartbeat tripled.

At her reaction, Marsh dropped his hand. The amount of time it took him to do so showed an obvious reluctance. The detachment left his voice. It was now low and gruff with concern.

"Are you all right?"

She stared at him straight on. Emotion gathered in her gray eyes like a massing storm, an angry storm. Her smile was thin, almost painfully so. "Of course I am. I'm not the one who got himself beaten to a pulp for no apparent reason."

"I had one—a damned good one—at the time."

Her throat convulsed. *Don't do this, Marsh. I can't stand it.* His fingers brushed her empty hand. Hers twitched and carelessly threaded through them, clutching for dear life. Lord, he felt good; warm, strong, and solid. And he belonged to someone else, she reminded herself. She tried to free her hand, but this time he was the one to cling. Hard. Her pulse quickened with trepidation as their gazes met and held. His was dark, intense, searching. Asking for what? Forgiveness? Compliance? She jerked her hand away.

"Jo, I said I was sorry. I didn't plan to hurt you. I didn't plan to—"

"And that makes everything all right." Her sharp retort cut off his regretful words. She couldn't bear to hear them again. Disappointment damned in around her heart, plugging her chest as solidly as an ice block. Her response was frigid with it. "Save your apologies, Cameron. It's not your fault I acted so foolishly last night. I was actually naive enough to think a man like you . . . that I was good enough . . . ." She let that trail off in hot humiliation. The tears she'd sworn she wouldn't shed threatened to fall. She blinked them back, and a bitter parody of a smile curved her lips. "I'm the one who should apologize to you."

"Don't!" The force of his quiet anger startled her, as did the sudden crush of his fingers about her wrist. His hand was unsteady, as if fighting the need to shake her or pull her to him. "Don't ever belittle yourself like that. Not to me, not to anyone. You've got nothing to apologize for, do you hear?"

Stunned, she merely nodded.

He stood gingerly, still favoring his side. He hadn't released her. It wasn't really necessary. She couldn't have moved. His nearness had a gripping effect. She was lost in his dark, compelling stare.

"Jo, any man would be lucky to have you. You've no idea how honored I am that you'd care for me."

Honored. Her features clenched tight. A word that soothed her pride but did nothing to lessen her longing. She was brutally aware that that passive emotion was all he could admit to. It was insultingly weak after his body's passionate communication of the night before. That diluting sentiment was worse than the thought of his amusement at her expense. It smacked of pity, and that she couldn't tolerate.

"I don't need your charity, Cameron. Be assured I'll survive just fine without it."

A spasm of frustration jumped along his battered jaw. His fingers bit into her arm. "Dammit, Jo—"

"Here be your dinner, boy. Tender enough for an old man to gum without the benefit of his choppers."

At Fergus's bellow, Marsh was forced to cut his angry plea short. Joelle took advantage of the distraction to end the connection flaring between them. She stepped out of his grasp and turned all her attention to the burly, rather perplexed cook.

"Fergus, when you've finished coddling Cameron, we have some figures to go over."

The stocky tyrant actually flushed. "Yes, ma'am, Miss Jo. I be right with you. Tell that lazy good-for-nothing Charlie to put on some more coffee."

When Joelle stormed off into the kitchen, Fergus laid the plate down in front of a seething Marshall Cameron and shook his head. T'weren't none of his business. But damn, if this weren't spicy food for speculation.

Temperatures plunged overnight, ending the snow but not the cutting wind. It rattled through the walls of the bunkhouse, making the boards snap like rifle shots as the chill bent them. For once Marsh was glad for the closeness of quarters and Olen Thurston's bulky warmth beside him. Even the fully stoked stove couldn't keep up with a cold that seeped under covers and into bones until the men's teeth chattered. The most unwelcome sound in the whole world was the sudden loud cry of "Roll out!"

Grumbling, still aching more than he cared to admit, Marsh fell in with the others to wait his turn at the washbasin. He dipped a fresh pan for himself and scrubbed the sleep from his face. He longed to duck his head, for his scalp felt fairly crawling, but he was afraid his hair would freeze during the walk between the bunkhouse and the dining hall. He could stand the scratching better than pneumonia. He dried his face on the damp towel without a thought to its much-used mustiness and trudged the frigid few feet into the warmth of the cookhouse. Stoked by one of Fergus's massive meals and fortified with strong, bitter coffee, he braced himself against the elements with a grim determination as the men marched down the newly cleared road to the cutting grounds. He was warmed as well by the heat of Guy Sonnier's stare as it burned between his shoulder blades.

"You wear your rage like a bad-tempered boy, my brother."

Guy scowled at Chauncey but said nothing.

The big Canadian pursed his lips in amusement and marched silently beside his brother for several yards. Then Chauncey couldn't resist a little more needling. "He fought you fair and well. You should swallow your pride and shake his hand."

"Is that what you would do?" Guy snapped back.

"No. I would not have let him walk away from a fight with me."

That fed Guy's stormy mood. He tried to glare up at his brother's smirking features, but his swollen eye turned his expression into a grimace.

"You go about winning the woman all wrong."

"And you are so experienced when it comes to an *affaire de coeur*." His tone was searing, but Chauncey only chuckled.

"I know you will not gain her admiration by pounding on the man she fancies herself in love with."

Guy ground his jaw. His stare perforated Marshall Cameron's back the way he'd have liked to ventilate it with something much sharper. "She does *not* love him!"

Chauncey shrugged philosophically. "It does not matter as he will be gone from her sight in a week's time and from her life in three, four months. Unless she goes with him."

Guy jerked up. He'd never considered that. The thought of her gone forever was beyond imagining. "No. She would not."

"What has she here? A woman alone?"

"She has me!" Guy began walking again, his strides stiff with agitation. His brows made a black slash above his angry and unusually fearful eyes. "But it is not enough. I cannot offer what he does."

Chauncey snorted at that. He was a surly brute of a man. Most men shivered at the thought of his consistent mean-spiritedness. If there was one warm spot in his cold heart, it was for his baby brother. And the thought of any man boasting of being better than him was a slap at their entire family.

"Book learning and fancy clothes? Miss Jo will not be swayed by such things. Pah!"

But Guy's brooding didn't lessen. "He has more than that. He can give her security. The Superior is in trouble, and he saves it from ruin. I could not do that for her. I have nothing but what I am to give her. And I'm thinking it is not enough."

Chauncey, too, began to frown. "Then we must find a way to get what you need to support her."

Guy said nothing. He was looking thoughtfully toward a future in which he could provide generously for Joelle Parry.

The morning's work went better than Marsh had expected. Drawing the big saw back and forth felt as though the razor-sharp teeth were cutting along his rib cage, but he managed. The bigger surprise was the lack of antagonism from his partner. Guy Sonnier was silent and preoccupied all morning, doing little more than lining up the blade and going through the motions. He never even looked at Marsh to acknowledge what had passed between them, which was fine by him.

By noontime an icy sleet was falling steadily to compound the misery of the morning. A quick-forming, heavy glaze clung to everything it touched—men, tools, and trees. The swing-dingle was late arriving due to the treacherous conditions, and the men were eager to hunch protectively over their plates of hot food.

"Eh, Yank."

Marsh glanced up to give Olen a smile of greeting. The Swede skidded a few feet on the slick crust of snow and dropped gratefully down upon a newly shorn stump.

"Some kind of weather to welcome Father Christmas," the blond giant grumbled.

Marsh stared at him. Christmas? Already? Strange how he'd been unaware of time's passage, isolated as he was here in the trees. Christmas in Boston had always been such an elaborate event, beginning months in advance with a deluge of invitations and ending in a fever pitch of social visits. There would be a frantic search for just the right tree for the parlor and just the right goose for the table. The scent of balsam and pine he'd grown so used to in the last weeks wasn't associated now with anything but labor and the luxury of crisp air. Christmas at his home was heralded by an increasing tension in his parents, because his grandfather would arrive on Christmas Eve and stay through the New Year to drive everyone insane trying to please him. That made him think of his mother's gentle kiss on the cheek and his father's firm handshake and a dozen impersonal and expensive gifts that never came as surprises. Buttered rum, spiced grog, and hard cider encouraged the holiday spirit, but he'd also endure Grandfather Hewlett's querulous moods to receive a pompously presented stock portfolio. This was the first year he wouldn't be celebrating with family, and his lack of melancholy surprised him. He hadn't even written to send his best wishes. That brought a twinge of guilt. He'd do so as soon as they got back to camp, even though it would be closer to February by the time his greetings reached his home.

To take his mind off his odd turn of feelings, he asked, "What are your plans, Olen?"

The big Swede sighed. "I'd planned to go to Ontonagon to be with my Evie and the children."

"Children?"

Olen swelled up with pride. "Two sons. Fine, strapping boys. They be joining me in the woods in a matter of a few years. But for now I must be missing them and my fine wife. And if the weather does not get better, I will not be there to wish them happy Christmas."

The sadness in his tone touched a responsive chord in Marsh. That was what he should have been feeling when he thought of his family, but he didn't. Strange how he was no farther away here in the wilds of Michigan than he'd been in the snug harbor of their front room surrounded by all the trappings of the season.

He was chewing his ration of beef pensively when his attention was caught by the bobsled that came to pick up the morning's cuttings. The team of six nervous horses was controlled by Joelle Parry. He watched her work them in close to the boles of pine. The bobsled, even empty, was an awkward conveyance. Two pairs of large runners eight inches wide by eight feet long were fastened together by cross chains and a swiveling king bolt to the ten-foot-wide bunk above. Marsh didn't envy the top and bottom loaders who had the dangerous job of guiding the logs onto the sled by way of a team pulling a chain at right angles—especially today when the trunks were ice coated. A noticeable frown puckered his forehead when he saw Guy Sonnier approach the pretty teamster. Her smile to him was a rough cut across the heart. Marsh returned to his meal with a vengeance yet couldn't keep his stare from canting toward the darkly handsome couple.

"Jolie, you should not be out in this nastiness," Guy scolded as he reached up for her. She took his hands easily and allowed him to swing her down but not to hold her close as he intended. She moved to a comfortable distance before chiding him for his worry.

"Do you know anyone better at the reins on such a day?"

"Ah, no. I wish I could say I did, but you are the best, *ma cherie.*"

She sighed in aggravation. "You're beginning to sound just like—" She broke off but not before he glowered in irritation. To give him time to get himself under control, she called out to the road monkeys who'd traveled the icy trail with her. "I want some straw put down on those hills, or the sled will be running right up over the horses. I don't want them spooked. It'll be hard enough to keep them in hand on this ice." She looked back at Guy with an arched brow, challenging him to continue.

"Jolie, you make me crazy," he complained with an exasperated smile. "You need a dozen children underfoot to keep you busy. Then maybe you would leave men's work to the men."

"Guy Sonnier," she began with huffy indignation, planning to give him a good verbal lashing for voicing such an arrogant opinion. The rest was never spoken. Above them came an ominous rumble and a harsh curse. Her gaze flew upward to see the binding chain on the newly loaded logs swinging free and the top bole tottering. In that fraction of a second, the whole load shifted and rushed down on them.

13

NEVER HAD TWENTY yards stretched so into a lifetime.

Pure chance had Marsh's gaze shift from Joelle and Guy to the pile of logs towering above them. His restless stare touched briefly on the top loader, who struggled to secure the toggle chain about the slippery stack of pine boles. He saw the man's foot slide on the ice-glazed bark and started to his feet even as the binding chain came loose. The pile of logs quivered, and Marsh's insides were taken by the same harsh tremor.

"Oh, my God."

Olen glanced up in surprise to see the plate fall from Marsh's hands. He followed the other man's stricken stare, then needed no explanation.

It was an impossible distance, even if it hadn't been slick as glass underfoot. Marsh's steel-calked boots found little traction as he scrambled and skidded frantically in a race to reach the cross haul. Keeping his footing was a peripheral concern to him as he charged recklessly across the patch of frozen ground. All his energy was concentrated in one spot—on the couple who stood unaware of their danger. A cry of warning came from someone close by, probably Olen. Marsh couldn't force anything beyond a ragged breath through the tight constriction in his own throat. That suffocating clutch of terror banded his chest fiercely when he saw Joelle look up toward the tumble of logs, saw her beloved features go stark with fear. And he knew, horribly, in that second that he couldn't reach her in time.

It happened so fast. Joelle was out of reach but not Guy, who was closer. Even as he gripped Guy Sonnier by the back of his mackinaw, Marsh could hear the thunder of descending pine. He planted the sharp spikes in his boots and heaved with all his might, swinging the stocky Canadian around the way an athlete would throw a weighty hammer. He let go, watching Guy windmill backward, falling hard on his rump to skid a good ten feet, well clear of the avalance of logs. The momentum kept him turning, spinning out of control on the glossy surface of ice. Then Marsh saw the butt of an eighteen-foot pine bole as it hit the ground and bounced high, striking him in the face.

A sense of desperation woke Marsh. Jo. He drew in a deep, hoarse breath as memories flooded back. He could see her wide gray eyes lifting upward toward the deadly spill of logs. He could hear her cry echo, just a soft whisper of fright compared to the crashing reverberations inside his mind. His breath caught in a panic of despair and was expelled with a sobbing moan.

"No. Oh, God. Jo . . ."

Something soft brushed away the dampness on his face. For a moment, he let the gliding caress soothe the fever of his thoughts, lulling them back into the velvety blackness beyond the reach of hurt and memory. He didn't want to wake. He shifted restlessly, trying to remain in oblivion, but the world was intruding. He could feel warmth enveloping him, carrying him gently. He sensed murmurs of sound—voices, movement, life. Pain, terrible and ceaseless, hammered through his head.

"He's coming around. Go get the doctor."

Doctor. Where was he? He couldn't smell the forest or the cold. The bed he was in sank, deep and comfortable. Lemon oil and something tart and medicinal teased him. And there was that tender touch moving lightly upon the side of his face.

"It's all right. Lie still."

Jo.

But that couldn't be.

"Jo?" He whispered it, not quite believing.

"Stay still, Marsh. I'm right here."

He forced his eyes to open, blinded by a shock of light and hurt stabbing viciously with the movement. At first he couldn't focus. A hazy distortion allowed him to see a shape bending close but not its identity. His hand rose up, unsteady and undirected. Fingers laced through his, holding tight. He used that contact as a fulcrum for his concentration, blinking hard, fighting his way through the fuzziness of pain. And she was there, just as she had said, perched upon the edge of the bed. His relief was so intense it brought a burning blur back to his vision, but he fought that, too, just as he would anything that stole away a sight so precious. He reached again, and, as if understanding his need to assure himself that what he saw was real, Joelle lifted his palm to her cheek, where her skin was soft and warm. Alive.

"Jo. God, I thought . . ." A spasm rode up through his chest, lodging thickly in his throat to silence the rest of his words. To supply an ending, he slid his hand until his fingers meshed in her bobbed hair. Because he couldn't lift himself from the bank of pillows, he tugged her down to him, into a clumsy embrace, into a hasty kiss. A kiss that lingered sweetly to the extent of his strength. Then his hand loosened and thumped slackly upon the coverlet, and his eyes slid shut.

Joelle didn't straighten immediately. She needed reassurance, too. The sight of him sprawled in the snow, blood pooling from a tremendous gash in his forehead, had shaken her to the soul. She'd been sure he was dead. Even when she'd found a faint pulse, she was certain he would never survive the frantic trip from the cutting grounds. Yet he had. Miraculously, his eyes had opened. The doctor had promised that if he regained his senses, chances were good he'd pull through. She wasn't going to lose him, at least not to a tragic accident in the woods.

She couldn't resist the inviting part of his lips. She kissed them with delicate brevity, just long enough to delight in his weak response. Her fingertips stroked his temples and toyed with the tawny hair escaping the heavy bandage above his brows. Her emotions soared on an updraft of joy, peaking at the sight of his slight, lopsided smile.

"I'm glad you're alive, Cameron. So much nicer than thanking a corpse."

His rusty chuckle rattled up on a sigh of good humor. "I must admit I prefer a living hero to a dead martyr myself." When she kissed him again, he tried to prolong the luxurious taste of her mouth by opening his, but she too quickly sat back. Then he, too, heard the approach of others.

"Waking up, is he?" The unfamiliar voice was followed by the press of a large thumb on his eyelid. Marsh winced as a piercing light was applied to his naked eye. "Good. Normal contraction," the voice announced cheerfully and the owner of it began probing Marsh's lacerated scalp.

I'd like to put you in traction, you heavy-handed son of a bitch, Marsh groaned to himself, flinching from the none-too-gentle handling. He endured an endless battery of reflex testing only because Joelle held his hand, chafing it methodically between hers. What a marvelous friction she fired inside the ash-cold recesses of his heart. Let the miserable quack do his worst as long as she continued to buffer his irritation with her tender care.

"Good. Everything looks good." The doctor gloated as if he were responsible for some miracle of medicine. Actually, Joelle thought, he'd done little more than bind the gaping tear after stitching it together, that and rebreak Marsh's nose. He'd taken that liberty upon himself after observing the misalignment, sure his patient would be in too much pain to notice a little extra throbbing. He'd been just as sure that a man of Marshall Cameron's fine looks would thank him generously later. "Total bedrest for at least a couple of days, then whatever movement he feels up to. Take it slow. If there's any dizziness or problems with sight, I want to know about it."

Marsh heard Joelle agree and was half tempted to grumble about being ignored, except it felt good to have her answer for him. It implied a bond of responsibility, and there was no place he'd rather be at that moment than in Joelle Parry's hands. He tried not to smile too smugly in his contentment but continued to lie still, his eyes closed as he tried to gather strength.

"I'll leave you some powders to give him when the pain gets bad. Have him take one before bedtime. That's about all

I can do beyond letting nature take its course in healing."

"Thank you, Doctor." Joelle stood, and Marsh's eyes flew open as he readied a protest. Then he saw Guy Sonnier standing at Joelle's side. Guy, whose life he thought he'd saved at the sacrifice of Joelle's. Guy, who was still covered liberally with the blood that had leaked all over him as he'd cradled Marsh's torn head in his lap on the rough ride to get aid. Seeing awareness in Marsh's dark eyes, Guy nodded stiffly, still reluctant to voice his appreciation to the man Joelle had wept over so passionately, even if he owed the man his life.

There was a long lapse of silence while the doctor was shown to the door. Marsh used the time to hoard his resource's which wasn't easy considering how even the pulse of his blood had intensified to a roar inside his skull, and oddly in his face as well.

Without opening his eyes, he knew she'd returned. Her tread was light and graceful, and suddenly his pain wasn't so bothersome. He reached out with his senses to follow her movements around the strange room. He heard the rattle of brass rings as she drew the curtains, the scuff of her boots on the bare floorboards, her steps muffled as she stepped onto the runner at the side of the bed, the cool sound of water. He felt the slight give of the mattress beneath her settling weight, and the reviving compress of a wet cloth over . . . his nose?

"Are you awake?" The question was asked softly, in case he wasn't.

Marsh started to nod then was urged to be still by the stabbing complaint in his head. The damp cloth soothed his brow, then was stroked down either cheek to blot along his neck. Its chill warned of his body's fever, which increased when she moved the cloth down his chest, bared by the open buttons of his long johns.

"That was a very brave thing you did," Joelle continued in a soft tone. "You might have been killed yourself."

"Didn't have time to think that far ahead or I probably would have finished my beans," he mumbled, covering his modesty with a wry touch of humor. He couldn't stand the suspense any longer and parted his lids to look upon her concern-softened features. She was smiling, too, albeit faintly.

"You saved Guy's life."

He ignored that admiring claim and frowned. His fingers eased over the back of her hand, squeezing tight to convey his anguish. "I couldn't get to you, Jo. There just wasn't time. He was closer."

"I know." There was no trace of accusation in the gentle dusk-colored gaze.

"I don't understand," he muttered at last. "How did you . . . I thought you'd . . ." The words swelled in his throat. He couldn't speak of the vision torturing his unconscious mind, of Joelle crushed and broken beneath the tumble of logs because she'd been standing on the far side of Guy Sonnier and just out of reach.

"Olen," she explained in a word. "He hit me like a freight train. I was sure he'd mashed every one of my ribs to pieces when he knocked me clear."

"Did he?" His grip tightened.

"No. Just a few bruises in places I'll not show you." She blushed prettily, which provoked his smile as he imagined where the bruises might be. Then his gaze left hers with reluctance, to take in his surroundings. They were in a small, neat room papered with a faded pattern of flowers and stripes. He was lying in a big canopied bed, beneath a downy quilt.

"Where are we? I don't know this place."

"A settlement between the camp and Eagle River. I knew there was a doctor here. I didn't know how badly you were hurt." Her voice grew strained, and she swallowed hard. She made herself move on past that moment when she'd believed him dead. "Guy and I brought you and Olen here on the bob-sled." That was all she said of the terrifying ride through the trees, over trails so slick with ice she feared they'd all careen to their deaths before reaching aid. But they'd made it.

"Olen?"

"He was struck after pushing me clear. His leg was broken, quite badly I'm afraid. He's across the hall. We're in a boardinghouse. I took a couple of rooms so you both could get proper care."

Marsh started to push himself up on his elbows. "Can I—"

"Later," she crooned, putting cautioning hands upon either shoulder to ease him back to the mattress. "You can see him later."

Marsh couldn't struggle, nor did he argue. He just hurt too damn bad to do either. He rolled his head on the pillow in his restlessness. He tried to think of something besides his pain. "Olen has a family in Ontanogan. He was going to see them for the holidays."

"He can't be moved. I'll send someone for them."

That satisfied him. He let his eyes drift shut. The discomfort was overwhelming, fogging his senses, making it hard to breathe without moaning. He didn't want Joelle to see him in such miserable condition. "Why don't you go tell him? It'll make him feel better."

Hesitant to leave him, Joelle lingered, searching for an excuse to stay but finding none. Marsh was clearly exhausted and in no shape for conversation. He needed quiet and rest more than she needed to be near him to ease her fears.

"All right," she said finally. She couldn't resist caressing his stubbled cheek one more time. "While I'm gone, I want you to sleep. Promise?"

"Promise," he lied. He doubted sleep could best the insistent agony. But he was surprised when it seeped around him in a comforting embrace, holding him snugly even before Joelle reached the door.

The next three days left Joelle weary and worried. Olen was a grumpy patient. He had to be watched carefully to keep him abed even with heavy wrappings going all the way up his thigh. His leg ached, he would complain, and needed stretching. No admonishment could convince him that rest was in his best interest, but Joelle's authoritative presence kept him sullenly submissive. As only two rooms were available and Olen would chuck Guy out the window before obeying his commands, Joelle was forced to remain with him, spending restless nights on a sagging cot while fretting about the man across the hall.

Marsh's fever soared. There were times when he was lucid and would speak for short intervals before tiring. Then he had frightening lapses into hot delirium, when his frantic cries would wake the other boarders at all hours of the night. Guy sat with him, feeling obligated to care for him and also determined to keep Joelle safely across the hall. When he was burning, the stoic sawyer bathed him with cool water. When he was wracked by chills, he bound him in blankets. When rantings made him toss wildly, Guy secured him to the mattress to keep him from harming himself with the jerky thrashing. Guilt held the stocky Canadian at the injured man's side, guilt over being the cause of his pain, guilt over his fierce want to hold a pillow over Marsh's face to smother the life out of him when he called out Joelle's name in his frenzied ramblings. It was a relief to find him awake and aware on the morning of the fourth day, asking for breakfast, the morning of Christmas Eve.

Joelle was still dozing when she felt the cover she'd kicked off during the night drawn back up about her. She made a sighing sound of thanks and burrowed deeper into slumber. Thinking it was Guy or the kindly landlady come to check on Olen, she didn't bother to stir, lost to her first decent rest in days. Some time later she became aware of men's voices pitched low in conversation. Olen's and Marsh's.

Marsh looked awful, she observed through slitted eyelids. Untidy hair straggled over the bandage at his brow. His complexion was nearly as pale as that white wrap. In contrast, bruises ringed his eyes and banded the swollen bridge of his nose in a colorful array. But he was grinning at something Olen had said, and dimples puckered his cheeks, making him the most heart-wrenchingly handsome man she'd ever seen. That lazy smile stilled, turning into something softer, something sultry, when he saw her moving upon her narrow corner cot.

"Morning, Miss Parry. Didn't mean to wake you."

Wondering how awful she looked, she replied, "It's not as though I need sleep after days of taking care of you two great complaining oxen."

"I think we may have overstretched our welcome, Yank," Olen said with a chuckle.

Marsh merely smiled. He was captivated by the sight of a rumpled Joelle Parry. He'd watched her sleep before, awed by the sweet serenity her features claimed in soft repose. But this was different. Her voice was low and gritty with traces of fatigue. Heavy lids stayed at half-mast over her smoky eyes. With tousled hair and pouty lips, she looked like a kitten roused from a nap, an adorable kitten with needle-like claws and the temperament of a hungry bobcat. The thought of unruffling that prickly temper with a scattering of good morning kisses, beneath a shared quilt at the start of each new day, woke a dissimilar hunger inside him, one that growled with the desire to be satisfied.

Uncomfortable as the focus of Marsh's penetrating stare, Joelle held the blanket to her shoulders while reaching for her plaid shirt. She wiggled into it without dropping the shield from her flannel-clad form, then tugged on her mannish trousers as well. With suspenders dangling in coy loops about her hips, she was standing when they were all distracted by a loud clatter on the stairs. Made curious by the commotion, Joelle opened the door and stepped back from the charge of three exuberant Swedes all bent on hugging Olen at once. His Evie was a huge, buxom woman with a plain face and a wide, warming smile. His sons were sturdy as ship masts, promising all the height and breadth of their father. The group of them babbled noisily in their native tongue, quite overwhelming the two foreigners. Realizing they were intruding, Marsh and Joelle withdrew into the hall, both smiling at the pleasure the domestic scene evoked.

Joelle was suddenly and disturbingly aware of the man facing her. While he was abed and disoriented, she'd cared for him without a second thought. She hadn't tried to disguise the love in her tender touches or in the quiet murmurings she knew he didn't hear. She'd taken a bittersweet joy in those stolen moments when she didn't have to pretend or acknowledge he wasn't hers to fuss over. But that time was at an end, and she resented its passing almost as much as the reinstatement of her feigned indifference. It was a difficult wall to reconstruct, but she would manage.

"Cameron, you need a good bathing."

His mouth gave a mischievous quirk. "I hope you're volunteering because I've had all I can stand of your snarly friend's tender loving care. He about wore all the hide off me while I was at his mercy."

Joelle refused to blush even though an incredible warmth kindled within her. The thought of bathing Marshall Cameron incited provocative possibilities, until she remembered his fiancée. Her reply was less than charitable. "You look fit enough to do your own scrubbing. And while you're about it, you might consider having those clothes washed. A black bear would back down to you without a fight."

"Are you always this agreeable when you wake up in the morning?"

Her voice cracked like brittle ice. "You won't have the chance to discover that for yourself."

Marsh's features grew somber. His dark stare held the shadows of a man with sorrow in his soul. "No," he said softly, "I won't."

Silence stretched between them, broken when Guy approached with a look of sullen suspicion. Joelle greeted him with a tense smile. "Guy, Cameron needs a bath and a shave. Do you think you could handle a razor without cutting his throat?"

Black eyes gauged the open vee of Marsh's collar. "I could try." He scratched his own thick beard. "Shaving is not something I'm all too familiar with."

"I'll do it then," she grumbled, to Guy's everlasting regret. "Have some hot water brought up and see if Mrs. Brent is willing to do some laundering."

She was about to walk away when Guy caught her arm. "Jolie, I was thinking of returning to camp today. I would like to spend this sacred eve with my brother. We are all the family each other has."

Her look softened immediately, thinking of how much she wished she had family to go to. "Yes, of course, you go."

He began to scowl. "You'll not go with me?"

"I don't see how I can until I make arrangements for these men. Olen's family has just arrived, and I need to see to their comfort. You go. There are some things I'd like you to bring back for me."

Unhappy with the turn of events, Guy muttered, "Whatever you like, Jolie, you've but to name it." He glared at Marsh with a wariness that said plainly he would rather be leaving Joelle in the hands of starved wolves than with one battered Bostonian.

14

JOELLE PLIED THE razor strop, her face carefully stoic. For all her lack of expression, her insides were quavering wildly. She swallowed hard, angry at herself for being so emotional. This was just a shave, for God's sake. She could do this. She could. Her hand taking on the nervous attitude of her stomach, she approached the man in the chair.

Marsh turned toward her, and her heart collided with her ribs. She was sure he could hear the sound of it all the way across the room. She took a deep breath and poured every scrap of her will down into the arm and hand holding the razor, bidding it to still its trembling. A smile, unnatural and stiff, moved upon her lips. Marsh eyed her warily.

"Why do I feel you're about to say 'This is going to hurt you more than me'?"

She grimaced at his attempted humor. "Make jokes, Cameron. It's your face."

He saw her point and stopped laughing.

When had this sweet panic started wadding up in her throat? The moment she'd seen him come from the bath. The graying long johns lent to him by their landlady swam on his lean form, making him look smaller and younger than he was. With the hint of battle still discoloring his face and weariness tugging his shoulders into a vulnerable sag, all her maternal instincts had quickened in a poignant instant. But the sensation ignited with the connection of their eyes wasn't the least bit motherly. It was want, pure and powerful, the want of a woman for a man, so strong it crippled her resolve and left her trembling with needy desperation.

Now she was supposed to stand over him, touching him, breathing in the scent of his clean skin and damp hair while maintaining an impartial calm. Impossible. She should have let Guy do this, but he was gone and the razor wavered in her hand.

"Have you done this before?" Marsh asked with a transparent lack of confidence. He was watching the sharp blade jiggle in her grasp.

"Of course. Many times." Well, once or twice.

"Why am I not reassured?"

In spite of his wry words, Marsh laid his head against the back of the chair, baring the line of his throat with what he hoped wasn't misplaced trust. She struck a wide stance at the side of his chair and rested the blade against one rough cheek. Marsh's gaze rounded in dismay.

"Soap first!"

"Oh. Yes, of course." Her stammering didn't feed his plummeting faith. Joelle reached for the mug and stirred up a lather with the brush.

"Maybe I should be doing this for myself."

"Quit whining. You're weak as a cub. You'd have your face filleted out like a pan fish dinner."

He gave the quivering brush a jaundiced look. "Perhaps I'll grow a beard."

She slapped the soapy brush against his chin, just missing his mouth, and began to spread the lather along the intriguing angles of his jaw. "Do shut up if you value your tongue." She finished covering his whiskers with the softening soap and lifted the razor. His dark eyes followed the movement in some alarm. Then that intense stare fixed on her, and her scant control lessened. How was she supposed to concentrate on what she was doing?

"Close your eyes, please."

He blinked. "What?"

"If you want to keep your upper lip, close your eyes. You're making me nervous staring like that."

Reluctantly he did as he was told. That was better, she thought with a bracing sigh. There was a soft rasp as the blade scraped down one lean cheek, leaving a trail of weather-worn skin where the foam had been cleared away. She gave the razor a flick to clean it and began again with more confidence. After several draws and no bloodshed, she felt Marsh relax in her hands. And she grew as tense as an unsprung trap.

She moved his head from side to side without resistance from him. He might have been asleep except for the hurried pulse she felt when shaving along his neck. Every rapid beat bespoke his awareness of her. Was it worry or the same tightly wound tension twisting inside her? That betraying ache clenched her chest in a band that made breathing an agony.

Joelle knew the satisfaction a sculptor must feel as more of Marsh's chiseled features appeared with every stroke of her hand. Free from discovery, she let her fascination mold her expression. Even as misused as he was, Marsh Cameron was a work of art, shaped to strong perfection. His wet hair gleamed sleek and dark brushed back from a bared brow. He'd have a nasty scar when the gash healed just beneath his hairline. Fortunately it would be covered. He'd had to remove the wrapping to wash his hair. The stitches were holding nicely, minimizing the impact of the life-threatening wound that had caused her heart to falter. Once the bruising faded, there'd be little sign of what he'd suffered in the northwoods. Except . . . She paused, letting the razor rest beneath one ear while she studied the symmetry of his face more closely. Something was wrong. Oh no! It was his nose!

"Thinking about cutting my throat?"

Marsh's mild question nearly startled her into doing exactly that. He hadn't opened his eyes so he couldn't have seen the terrible guilt marking her features. She forced her hand to continue the last careful strokes along his jaw.

"There," she announced in an odd voice. She allowed her hand one last savoring feel of smoothed flesh. "All done."

Marsh tested the same taut lengths of jaw and cheek and nodded his satisfaction. "Not bad." He was smiling when his dark eyes lifted. "I was right to trust in your capability. You've made me into a believer."

Joelle's expression turned bland. She was angry that she needed a reminder of their relationship, that of employer and employee. But he'd said that soon would change, hadn't he? This was precious borrowed time, and she was spending it fawning over her nemesis instead of tending business as she should be. Was she condemned to be ever foolish around him? She slapped a clean towel across the bottom portion of his face, taking little delight in the startled dark eyes widening above it in confusion. Her tone was as sharp as the razor in her hand. "That was my intention, Cameron."

The damned company, Marsh thought with irrational pique. That was what she'd been thinking about when she offered her assistance. Neither care nor concern for him had motivated her. She was working on his trust along with his whiskers, and he didn't like the thought of being so neatly trimmed.

"I'll say this for you, Miss Parry," he drawled out in chill amusement. "You certainly know how to hone your point to a fine edge." He blotted his face with the ready towel then stood and tossed it into the vacated chair. "Thank you for the demonstration. And the reminder."

She was frowning as he stopped before the bureau mirror and stared for a long, perplexed moment. Slowly he turned his head from side to side as if puzzled by what he saw. Joelle drew an apprehensive breath and held it. Surely the difference wasn't that noticeable. There was no way she was going to volunteer the information that while he'd been unconscious, she'd agreed with the doctor's decision to do a little cosmetic repair. Nor could she convince herself that once the swelling left his nose, he wouldn't discover that although the doctor had cured the flattening, he had left that fine, noble appendage skewed to the right of center.

"Do you notice anything odd about my face?" he asked as he felt along the tender inflation at the bridge of his nose.

She swallowed hard and forced herself to use a bantering tone. "Other than the fact that it looks like you stuck it in a coffee grinder? Really, Cameron, you are so vain." Then she slipped quickly from the room.

The rest of the day was spent in a tense truce with the boisterous Thurstons as a buffer. To compensate their hostess for her kindness toward her husband, Evie Thurston insisted upon preparing a traditional feast for Christmas Eve. Wonderful aromas wafted up the steps to tantalize the boarders' appetites. With his family's help, Olen was able to join them at the big central table for dinner, but his condition forbade him from attending evening services at the small parish church. Instead they had an informal gathering of their own at his bedside. Marsh read verse in his low, pleasing baritone, then Olen echoed it in the language of his homeland. All present were suitably moved by the significance of the night, sharing a quiet company until it grew apparent that the Thurstons would appreciate their privacy. The two boys clomped downstairs to toss blankets in front of the parlor fire. Then, after she and Marsh closed the door to the hall, Joelle realized her uncomfortable position. She had no proper place to stay. There was no chance at this late hour to find a spare room within the tiny community.

"I could sure use some coffee," Marsh said suddenly.

Joelle murmured that she'd fix some, her mood quiet and distracted. Marsh touched her shoulder.

"Some of that special ninety-ten mix, I think." He smiled, coaxing one in return.

"All right. I'll be right back."

When she climbed the stairs with a mug in either hand, she found the door to his room open and Marsh partially reclined on the unmade bed. He was fully dressed. Still, the suggestion was impossibly tempting.

"Ummm. Smells good," he called. Joelle hesitated, but he made no move off the bed. At his patient, beckoning glance, she repressed an aggravated sigh and crossed to the bed. He reached out a hand but refused to bend, forcing her to climb up on the mattress to give him his cup. "Have a seat," he offered with seeming innocence.

Made cautious by his shift of mood from the afternoon chill to this simmering warmth, Joelle eased down beside him, leaning her back against the headboard. Marsh didn't look at her right away, giving his attention to the steaming cup. He took a sip, murmuring in appreciation. They sat side by side in silent contemplation, both pretending not to be so attuned to each other that awareness vibrated between them

like lightning-charged air. Faint strains of a Christmas carol
reached their ears.

Joelle was ill-prepared for the wrench of nostalgic longing the tune inspired. It brought memories of the last time
her family was all together; her parents, her aunt, and uncle
beneath one roof in cheery celebration. Her mother and aunt
had begun the lively carol, only to have the two men join in
with their booming off-key voices, lustily singing the wrong
verse. They'd all laughed so hard they hadn't been able to
finish. She remembered Lyle Parry's squeezing hug and the
tenderness of his kiss upon her forehead as he hurried her
off to bed. She would have gladly surrendered up every bit
of pine in the Peninsular forest just to have him tuck her in
once more.

She wasn't sure just when Marsh's arm became a bolster
about her shoulders. She only knew how grateful she was for
its strong circle.

"You must miss him terribly."

Words failed her, but her slight nod was answer enough.

"This is my first Christmas without family, too, so I think
I know a little of how you feel."

Joelle stared hard into her cup, willing the dampness in
her eyes to go away. At least he *had* family. And a fiancée.
Would he be spending this time with her if he were at home in
Boston, perhaps in a similarly intimate setting? The thickness
swelled in her chest until it felt plugged solid with misery.
Marshall would have many Christmases to spend with his
loved ones. With whom would she share hers?

Feeling her shoulders jerk with the struggle to suppress her
tears, Marsh was moved by an intense tenderness. He, too, was
thinking of her circumstance, and he was affected more strongly than he would have liked. He felt a responsibility to this
fragile-hearted roughneck and couldn't bear to see her proud
spirit humbled by loss. He touched the smooth curve of her
hair, rumpling it gently, enjoying the way it sighed through his
fingers like expensive silk, the same way his emotions sighed
through the last of his reservations. He found himself saying,
"Maybe we can help each other not to feel so all alone."

Carefully the circumference of his arm decreased until she
was drawn snugly into his side. The feeling of warmth radiating

from his body was like the warmth of brandy from within. Both lulled her into unwise contentment. She nestled her cheek against the hollow of his throat, and his chin came to rest atop her head. Theirs was a close, comfortable fit, one so familiar she never thought to object. It seemed so natural to turn into Marshall Cameron's embrace to subdue an anguished spirit. The door was opened to the hall, and the other boarders would be returning soon. Where was the harm? It felt so good to be surrounded by care, albeit temporarily. His heart beat strong beneath her palm, and his even breathing rocked away the misery steeped within her soul. It didn't matter what tomorrow would bring as long as she had this night when she needed him so badly.

"Happy Christmas, Jo." His wish brushed softly through her hair.

"And to you, Marsh."

She definitely felt a kiss stirring against her temple. Beguiled by that trace of tenderness and temptation, Joelle tipped her head back, her eyes closing, her lips parting in an offer she hoped no sane man could ignore, not even one tormented by his principles. She felt Marsh tense and feared that he would refuse her this small gift she desired above all others.

That tautness of his body and will didn't lessen even as he bent to accept the sweet promise of her kiss. His mouth molded briefly over hers, remaining still so as not to tantalize a flare of passion when he could scarce afford more than a suggestion of care. However brief, it was enough.

To Joelle the kiss was a taste of heaven, a teasing sample of potential paradise. When she would have had more of it, Marsh's hand cupped the back of her head, guiding it down to the safe cove of his shoulder. He held her there with a strength of purpose that would surely fail him if she were to seek his lips once more. She resisted. His grip tightened, anchoring her for her own good. The only thing that kept him from caving in completely to the desire they shared for each other was his need to protect her. He was playing with something powerful and explosive, and he knew it. Caution couldn't temper his longing to linger near the heart of danger. If holding and not having her was hell, feeling her slowly relax with a trusting sigh to nestle against him was bliss. By wary increments, he released the taut control cording his muscles and knotting his emotions. The forceful pounding of his pulse eased to a quiet rhythm. Then he was able to enjoy the feel of her in his arms.

After long, silent minutes had passed, Marsh could tell by the gradual softening of her position that Joelle was asleep. Though reluctant to leave her even for a second, he eased away from her to close the door and turn down the lights. Standing at the bedside, watching the way she burrowed into the pillows like a sleeping child, he felt rise within him once more the aching need to possess her. He should leave before things escalated. But then the sleeping beauty stirred. Her hand reached out, her palm running across the empty sheet where he had lain, as if in search of him. It was an incredibly intimate gesture, one that acted upon his senses like an encouraging caress. He stood transfixed, watching that questing hand.

"Marsh?"

Her voice was heavy, blurred by sleep and unintentionally seductive.

Muttering a strained curse, Marsh tugged off his bulky boots and slid into bed beside her. She turned instinctively toward the heat of his body, wiggling close until his every nerve was pulled to the limit of restraint. Finally she sighed and settled into the curve of his side, and he was able to expel a shaky breath. She fit full-length against him, a soft complement to the hardened line of his masculine form. It was all he could do not to touch her, not to seek out the exquisite contours he'd explored so briefly at a distant fireside in his Eagle River home. But that was before he had told her the truth. To take the same liberties would be more inexcusable now than it had been then. He had no right to act or even feel that way about a woman who was not his betrothed. And yet by telling her of his engagement, he'd discharged his responsibility. He'd made it clear that there was no future for them, that no physical or emotional ties could hold him in the northwoods. That left him free to take what she offered without a surfeit of guilt. It would be her choice, after all. If she wanted him under the conditions he'd named, he shouldn't feel obligated to his conscience.

But he did.

Because she loved him.

Dammit, because she loved him and he was terrified that he felt the same way.

The truth had all but destroyed her. She'd been furious and scornful. All the hate and indifference she tried to show him wasn't strong enough to hide the bruising of her childlike heart. She wasn't one given to fits of fanciful emotion. He figured that when she loved, she loved deeply, completely, and she wouldn't be easily shaken from it. Such a stubborn girl. He'd told her why he couldn't return her devotion. Though she might despise him for his poor keeping of them, he knew such vows would hold great meaning for her. She would hate him if he took unfair advantage, and he would hate himself. She would suffer more hurt experiencing his loving than he would suffer from never knowing it.

He'd made the right choice that morning. To stay any longer with the temptation of Joelle Parry ever at hand was to court disaster. Eventually he would weaken. He would cast honor aside to have the pleasures of the moment and in doing so would destroy them both.

Though weariness pulled at him, he fought it off. If this was to be the last time he held Joelle in his arms, he vowed to savor every second. He refused to miss one sleepy sigh of breath, one gentle murmur, one unintentional nudge of her hip against him. He had one whole night to fill himself with the feel of her beside him.

In the morning he would have to let her go.

"Leaving?"

The word hung between them, wavering like fragile sunlight on the frigid surface of the lake. She stared at Marshall Cameron over the remains of their morning meal and tried not to display what worked frantically through her mind. She was too aware of the others to let her feelings escape unchecked. She swallowed them back, choking on them, damning them for their bitterness. Damning him for choosing this time to tell her, when they were surrounded by the Thurstons.

"When?" was all she could manage. His answer nearly robbed her of all control.

"This afternoon, as soon as Guy gets back with my things."

"Guy?" She looked at him blankly. If he'd asked Guy to bring his things from the camp, he'd known he was leaving the day before when he held her in his arms and kissed her tenderly, letting her sleep in the charmed circle of his embrace. He'd left that shared bed before she awoke, saying nothing. He'd let their final moments alone together pass uneventfully while she slumbered!

He was going back to the H&B, and there was nothing she could do or say to stop him. He'd known she wouldn't make a scene in front of Olen and his family. It was better like this, more difficult but better. There would be no frantic pleas, no insincere promises, no desperate clutches, just a clean, detached good-bye. And, she thought with tears burning behind her glare, she would probably hate him forever for making that choice on his own. He'd placed himself safely out of reach. All she could do was bear up with dignity.

"I guess this is good-bye then." She heard herself mouthing the words almost pleasantly. A smile was frozen on the lips that he had shaped with passion. "Or will you still be on the Peninsula when we bring the logs down in the spring?"

"I don't know" was all he'd say. No promises. Nothing for her to cling to. "It depends on how things go with your uncle."

"Don't let him bully you." That was a ridiculous thing to say, she realized. Bully Marshall Cameron? As if anyone could. The man had a backbone as solid as the granite range of the Keweenaw.

"I think we understand each other fairly well," he told her with unfounded confidence. "I don't look for there to be any problems."

"Then I probably won't see you again."

He met her gaze with a concentrated effort, his dark stare complex, intense, and guarded. "No. Probably not."

"Then I can safely tell you you've been a royal pain in the backside ever since you bowled me over on the porch at McGinty's." Bowled her over? Oh, yes, he had. And she was still tumbling. But she wouldn't let him see anything beyond the mild amusement in her smile and the hard glacial surface of her eyes.

Olen gave a booming laugh, relieved by the prickly banter. He'd been afraid he'd seen tears in the plucky Joelle Parry's eyes when Marsh announced his plans. Perhaps he'd been wrong to suspect anything of a personal nature at play between these two. Then he looked more carefully and saw the tightness casting Marsh's jawline into sharp relief and the occasional tremor of Joelle's lower lip. Perhaps not. If not, this was going to be a long frigid winter for both of them. But he'd bet his last plug of tobacco that Marshall Cameron wouldn't sail on Lake Superior until the timber drive brought Joelle to Eagle River in the spring.

"Well, Yank, I for one will miss you. You've been a pleasure to sleep with. The little missus snores something awful, I'll have you know." He grunted as the brawny Evie Thurston smacked an elbow into his ribs with a splintering force.

Marsh grinned wide and clasped the Swede's huge hand. "Sorry I can't claim the same. I guess you have been a better bunkmate than the bedbugs. But I do feel better about leaving with the arrangements we've made."

"Arrangements?" Joelle's attention quickened. There was something the two of them had been careful not to mention since she'd awakened to find them in deep conversation the morning before. And now she had the uncomfortable impression that it had to do with her and the Superior.

Joelle looked at the big logger with a fearful astuteness. His broken leg would keep him from the cutting grounds for the rest of the season. For a man who had just lost the means of providing for his family, he didn't seem too distressed. In fact, he looked downright smug, like a man filled with good fortune, not despair. Like a man who'd just become the new manager of Superior Lumbering.

Her stare stabbed Marshall Cameron. Was this another little piece of information he was saving for the last minute? She would kill him! She would carve out his cowardly heart with Guy's six-foot saw—if the miserable skunk had a heart! She clung to that fury because it kept her panic at bay.

"What arrangements, Cameron?" she restated in a chill tone. He had the good grace to look uneasy before his natural arrogance reasserted itself.

"I've asked Olen to move over into the van. If that's all right with you."

All right? He was throwing her out of her lodgings and asked calmly if she minded. "It's your decision, isn't it?"

"I wouldn't want you to be uncomfortable with it."

"Uncomfortable?" Her voice cracked with an edge of near-hysteria. What gall the man had to ask such a thing.

"I know he does snore awfully loud—hell, he could wake the dead—but with him in the second room, I'd feel more . . ."

Joelle didn't dare snatch at the whisper of hope his words instilled. "Marsh, what are you talking about?" she demanded faintly.

"I've asked Olen if he could help you out for the rest of the season, you know, in the van, with the books, whatever. He's not bad company, if you can tolerate the snoring. He'd be close by if you were to . . . need anything." He didn't have to spell that out any clearer. She would have a big, intimidating man under her roof to discourage another attack like Kenny Craig's. He studied her stiff expression, trying to decide if she was in favor of the idea or not. He knew she hated to have decisions made for her, but, dammit, this was the only one he could live with. He continued in a taut tone. "Anyway, it would be just for this season. Later Olen will be itching to get back to the trees, and you . . . you can make other arrangements for yourself." He clamped his jaw down on that. He should have been pleased with his plan, but behind it was the bitter belief that by the next season she would be protected as the wife of Guy Sonnier.

Joelle was slow taking this information in. At last she said somewhat dazedly, "You're keeping me on as manager?"

Marsh allowed himself a smile. "I'd hire a man for the job if I could find one who'd do it half as well."

With a squeal of pure delight, she shot out of her chair and around the table. Her arms went about his neck with a strangling enthusiasm.

"Oh, Marsh, thank you! Thank you!"

Appearances were all but forgotten in that rush of excitement. She was exulted by the news and carried away by the encompassing feel and smell of him. She buried her face against his neck, breathing in the scent of soap and sensual

man. Before she could consider the consequences, her lips
were tasting the warm stretch of skin there and on his jaw,
angling purposefully for his mouth. Oh, how she wanted to
kiss him! But his hands settled upon her shoulders, and she
found herself pried away. He gave a ragged laugh, as if he
hadn't been pushed to the brink of surrendering all control.

"Don't thank me yet," he advised evenly. "You haven't
tried to sleep through his roof-rattling snores." With that rough
attempt at humor, he restored her senses, and she leaned
away, feeling awkward and chagrined by her display of honest
feeling.

The day sped by. Joelle preferred to spend it in her room
alone rather than endure the trial of making casual conversation with Marsh. She just couldn't maintain the pretense that
her heart wasn't breaking. She couldn't contain all the things
she wanted to say to him, and she knew he was too shrewd
to let her get him alone to speak them. They'd said everything
that needed saying. Why drag their goodbyes out indefinitely?
She was going to have to get used to him being gone.

It was hard to contain the tears when Guy returned, carrying
all Marsh's belongings. Now he'd go. She huddled in a small
ball of misery on the big bed and waited for him to ride out
of her life.

She responded to the tap on her door woodenly, thinking
her visitor must be Guy. She hoped he'd have the good sense
to be her friend rather than an ardent suitor. She couldn't deal
with his unrequited passions when her own were flickering to
a cold ash.

"You weren't going to say good-bye?"

Her head jerked up. She wasn't prepared for this. He was
standing in her doorway dressed in his Boston finery. Except
for the bruises marring his face and his swollen nose, he
looked much the same as he had stepping out of McGinty's
two months ago. It was as if he'd never been a sawyer clad in
rough wool and blisters. For an uneasy moment, Joelle feared
she would dissolve in tears, but she had a few remnants of
pride remaining, enough to see her through this last meeting.

"I thought we already did." She was proud of how firm her
voice sounded even with her heart beating frantically behind
it. She scooted off the bed. It was too personal a spot for

this final farewell. Instead she went to stand at a cautious distance, looking out the window. A sleigh was out front. His things were already strapped onto it. This was the end.

"Jo?"

She didn't want to turn around because she wasn't all that sure she could keep from throwing herself at him. He'd already made it clear that that wasn't what he wanted.

"I've something for you." He'd come to stand at her elbow. His nearness wrought an awareness in her so acute it was like torture to remain still and not cry out. When she didn't respond, he coaxed, "Here," and pushed something at her.

Through the veil of misery misting her vision, Joelle saw he held a book in his hands. She swallowed hard. Her hands were unsteady when she took it from him.

"Merry Christmas."

Blinking, nearly blinded, she peered down at it. Sonnets. Shakespeare. The book she'd coveted before his hearth long ago. And he'd remembered. She was going to start wailing at any moment, she knew it. Taking a stabilizing breath, she rasped, "It's too much." But even as she objected, her fingers were caressing the embossed leather with a possessive care.

"It's not nearly enough," he countered.

"I've nothing to give you," she mumbled, looking up just then to be struck by the intensity of his dark stare. She couldn't look away. Her eyes glittered with the threat of weeping.

"That's not true, Jo." His hand started to rise, his fingers stretching for her cheek.

"Everything's ready, Cameron," Guy announced brusquely from the hall. "Better get now if you're going to hold the light to the H and B."

Marsh cast a distracted glance his way. "Coming." He turned back to Joelle, but the moment was lost. She was already covering up her vulnerability with a steely gaze. "Good-bye, Jo."

She couldn't shove a reply through the thickness in her throat. Instead she put out her hand in an aggressive manner. Smiling, he took it in a firm clasp and held it long within the warm, callused hold of a man who worked the woods. Finally she whispered, "Take care, Cameron."

"I will."

Those damnable dimples creased his features; then he released her hand and strode to the door. She couldn't move and couldn't breathe as she heard his boots on the stairs. When at last she heard the door close upon all her dreams, she clutched his precious gift to her breast and said softly, "Good-bye, Marsh."

15

QUIET.

Marsh should have felt wonderful to be surrounded by it after a month when there'd been no such thing as even a private thought. He was so used to sharing everything from his towel to the direction he turned in his sleep that the solitary freedom of his first night back at the H&B should have been exquisite. So why was he pacing the floor?

On this late evening of Christmas Day, even the ground had been stilled from the usually tremors below. His head ached with enough volume to rival those reverberating blasts. His body was weak, yet his mind spun in circles, like a wheel on ice—all motion, no progress.

Damn, it was quiet!

Marsh prowled into his sitting room and spent several minutes prodding the fire. From those flames rose the image of Joelle Parry crouching on his hearth, her eyes impassioned by talk of the written word. Was she reading his sonnets even now? Or had she put them away, just as she would put the memory of him aside, as fanciful distractions?

Tension pulled through his shoulders and tightened like a painful band across his brow. He'd taken one of the doctor's powders but felt no soothing effect. Ignoring the common sense that told him to leave well enough alone, he reached for his bottle of fine liquor. Not even January and his supply was nearly gone. Might as well enjoy it while he could. He poured himself a liberal glass and settled into a fireside chair. He sat brooding for long, silent minutes until his dissatisfaction with his own company had him ready to chew glass in aggravation.

This was where he belonged, what he should be doing. He was an engineer, the agent for the H&B. He should be here upgrading production, not out in the woods cutting trees. This was his legacy as the Hewlett faction of Hewlett and Barnes, and one day he would preside over that long boardroom table as its chairman. Who in Boston would care if he could haul a cross saw or that he held the respect of a hundred illiterate shantymen? He'd been given an enviable education and guaranteed a solid future. All he had to do in return was carry out his responsibilities. No sacrifice, no great struggle, and absolutely no sense of anticipation.

Sighing, he set aside his empty glass. The hour was too late and he was too tired to be entertaining such thoughts. He'd feel better about his predicament in the morning when he got back into the business of mining. He hoped that in his absence he'd received the approval of the Board for all his improvements. There would be much to do. His hours would be too full for idle daydreams. The acrid bite of hematite would soon purge the fresh scent of the pines from his senses. And he'd forget the brief freedom he'd enjoyed while pretending to be someone he was not.

"Where's Lachlan?"

The roaring demand brought a startled response from the miners in the shaft house.

"He be already below," came one hesitant reply.

"Get him up to the surface and in front of me in one hour."

"Yessir, Mr. Cam—"

But Marsh had whirled away and was stomping furiously back out into the blustery dawn. For once he didn't notice the cold as it cut through his fine coat. He had his temper to heat him, and it flared to rival the best furnace. Whatever Lachlan was trying to get away with, it would stop now! All the plans he'd set in motion seemed to have stopped the moment he left the H&B, in direct disregard to his orders. It took no great thought to ferret out who was responsible, and he would have that man readied for judgment before the hour was out. The only thing that kept him from climbing down the ladder and personally doing the pulverizing was the fact that he needed Tavis Lachlan as an intermediary with the other miners. And, he was Joelle's uncle. Though he well deserved to be stripped of his arrogance, crushing a man's pride in public could easily make him a bitter enemy. Better it be done in private. Let Lachlan strut his power with his men, but when Marsh's interview with him was finished, there would be one boss in the H&B camp, and they would both know who it was.

Tavis Lachlan was more than ready to challenge Cameron's authority. His annoyance at being pulled from the mine was offset by his anticipation of the meeting to come. Without bothering to knock or shake the grime from his clothes, he strode into the mine agent's front room to announce himself with a searing drawl.

"So you're back." Cameron turned toward him from the fire, and Tavis's mouth twisted wryly. "I see the woods have treated you well." The man looked as if he'd been to Hell. Despite the dapper clothes, Marshall Cameron had a definite rough-edge appearance about him. Bruises mottled his clean-shaven cheeks and made smudged crescents beneath his eyes. His swollen nose told of a fierce battle. The savage split across his brow obviously caused him some discomfort, yet his dark eyes were unwavering in a stare as cold as the slice of his tone.

"Who the hell do you think you are?"

Tavis's smirk faltered.

Marsh took a bold, intimidating stride toward the bulkier man. "I gave very specific instructions before I left. As I assume you are not too stupid to have misunderstood, I have to believe you chose to disobey me. I want an accounting and I want it now."

"Do you?" Tavis's eyes narrowed. Something was different about the man. It was more than just the facial battering. It was a hardening of the spirit, a layer of toughness over his Eastern polish like calluses on smooth palms. It made for a more challenging foe but not an undefeatable one.

"Who gave the orders for production to resume on Six-teen?"

"I did," Tavis replied calmly.

"I told you to shut it down."

Tavis smiled thinly. He was enjoying this. Oh, he was enjoying this. Even secondhand, the victory was sweet. "So you did. I ordered it reopened."

"On whose authority?"

Tavis played out the moment to its fullest, savoring Cameron's outrage, relishing the knowledge and power that went with the paper he unfolded from his pocket. "The Board of Directors of the H and B."

Marsh's expression froze. He snatched the letter from Tavis's hand, and his fury increased by degrees as he scanned the contents. Tavis recognized the frustration and failure on the other man's grim face. He remembered its bite all too well. Finally frustration was gnawing on the backside of a Cameron after all the years of its festering into his hatred for Colin and his kin. *So how does it feel, spawn of my enemy, to know you've been tricked and bested by someone you thought you could trust?*

"As you can see," Tavis took delight in elaborating, "you can do whatever you like on the surface, but the underground is mine. There I'll tolerate none of your fancy book-bred interference. I answer to the Board alone."

Marsh reread the letter and saw everything Tavis said written in plain black and white. The Board had granted Tavis Lachlan independent authority over underground activities. This was unusual but not unheard of, if the company agent were deemed more of a businessman than a mining man. Marsh saw all his grand ideas ground beneath the crushing ignorance of Tavis Lachlan's ambition. The man had no conception of the harm he was doing. Without the needed improvements, the H&B would fold just like many of the mines before it. The treasured job the Cornish captain thought to protect with his treachery would be threatened as his niece's logging company would be. Marsh seethed when he thought of the consequences.

"Just how did you manage this bit of clever manipulation?" he asked through gritted teeth as he fought the urge to toss the offensive missive into the fire.

Tavis smiled. "Sent off a letter right after my pretty little Joey coaxed you into the woods. Should have been here minding business instead of seeking your pleasure."

Marsh went rigid. His heart rebelled against the insinuation his head could not ignore. Lachlan had a plan from the very first? Joelle had been the bait her uncle used to lure him to his own ruin? No, he didn't want to believe that. His lips thinned into a white line of pain. But the scheme made too much sense not to be believed. What he knew of women supported Lachlan's cruel claim. Joelle Parry was not the exception to that rule of womankind. He'd been wrong to think she was different.

Tavis was watching the taut jerks of emotion in the younger man's face. He recognized the agony he'd suffered at a similar age in a similar situation. Here was a man led by his infatuation, a man devastated by a woman's deceit. Oh, how well he remembered, and the anger flowed back through him, stoking his resentment, firing his need for retribution. How he wished it could have been the father and not the son writhing before him.

"I took the liberty of advising the Board that you were ill-equipped to direct the affairs of the mine," Tavis continued with a sneer. "Too easily distracted and inexperienced for such a big project, I think was how I phrased it. Let a slip of a girl lead you astray when you should have been taking a serious interest in your duty. A shame, too. Such a bright boy."

Marsh's teeth ground so hard he could feel the pressure tighten his scalp. Damn the man for his smugness and stupidity. And Joelle . . . He wouldn't think of her now. He'd let his interest in her draw him off once before but not now. He needed all his concentration in this tug of wills with her uncle. But even bringing her briefly to mind had him unbalanced. He couldn't free his thoughts from one anguished point. *How could she do that to him? How could she use and twist his heart to serve her uncle's purpose?*

"I'll apply to the Board to reverse its decision," he warned direly.

Tavis appeared unconcerned by the threat. "Oh, I would be disappointed if you didn't. But by the time you hear back from them, I'll have Sixteen producing so much copper, you'll look like a greenhorn fool for suggesting I didn't know my business."

"Is that what this is all about? Making me look the fool?"

"Oh, laddy, you've no idea." Tavis's eyes grew dark and his smile unpleasant. "Let's just say it's a debt long overdue I mean to collect from your old man."

"My father?" Now he was lost. "Do you know him?"

Marsh's genuine surprise cut worse than an intentional insult. "Yes, I knew him," Tavis growled. "I brought him here. You could say I made him everything he is today, and I mean to take the credit he never thought to give me. It might have cost me years of festering and my niece's reputation, but I finally have the satisfaction I deserve. Stay out of my way, Cameron, and maybe I'll be letting you keep a scrap of your respect."

He'd be lucky to retain even that, Marsh reflected bitterly. Tavis Lachlan was gone, leaving behind clods of rich earth and a wealth of ill feelings. Why hadn't he been more cautious where the man was concerned? Why hadn't he taken a little more time to woo the mine captain's good will before bluntly thrusting a whole world of change into his face? Or would that have made any difference? Tavis's grudge stemmed back a generation, and Marsh was only suffering its aftershocks. Had his father ever mentioned Tavis Lachlan? He couldn't recall. But then Colin Cameron's stories about the Keweenaw had bored the arrogant young Marsh near to death. He hadn't listened, and now it was too late to learn. All he could do was salvage what he could and accept the rest—the hell he would!

Putting pen to paper, Marsh struggled for just the right words to convey his competence not complaints, suggestions that were founded in truth not petulance. He didn't address his report to his father but to the Board. Lachlan had taken unfair advantage, but he wouldn't. Folding the paper, he gave vent to his frustrations. Tavis was right. The reply would come too late to save thousands in unnecessary expense. Shaft Sixteen was a dead end. He'd stake his education on it since his reputation had already been sullied. Thousands of man-hours would be lost pursuing Lachlan's folly, and Marsh was held helpless by a distant authority, betrayed by the poor judgment of his heart. He couldn't change that, but he could get on with what he could control. There wasn't much that could be done until navigational waters cleared in order to bring in new equipment, but when Lake Superior thawed and the locks opened to the industry below, he vowed to be ready to implement his plans—all of them, above and below ground.

With that decided, all that was left was the matter of Joelle Parry.

His agitation was too great to be contained within four walls. He pulled on his logging woolens and heavy boots with ease. The outside air was bracing, nearly frigid. He needed that cauterizing cold to stem the flood of his misery and to numb the raw edges of emotions torn beyond repair. So he began to walk, aimlessly at first, just to be moving, then with a direction in mind.

From the top of the bluff, Marsh had a perfect view of the lake. For as far as he could see, it was ice-covered and quiet, but he knew somewhere near the horizon its cold gray waters seethed. That fringe of ice held him captive on the bleak Michigan shore, kept him from returning home, kept civilization from reaching him here. Somewhere out there Lyle Parry lay in a watery grave.

Hunching his shoulders against a chill that was no match for the one encasing his heart, Marsh glared out over the frozen waters. Dammit, he'd cared for her! He'd gone so far as to think himself in love. How much of her feelings had been genuine and how much conceived between crafty uncle and desperate niece? She was the one who had challenged him to follow her into the trees. Was it to learn logging or to get him conveniently out of her uncle's way? He'd allowed a pair of bewitching gray eyes as unpredictable and dangerous as the far waters of Superior to lead him away from his responsibilities. That made him a fool. He'd wanted to believe what he saw in those turbulent depths. That made him twice damned for his naïveté. How he wished the channels would open on the big lake just long enough for him to go back to where he belonged, where he knew insincerity when he saw it, without risk to soul or heart.

The wind along the high crest pushed at his back, nudging him toward the rim of the rocky precipice. He held his ground when a more prudent man would have retreated to the safe shelter of the trees. He'd been buffeted about by this inhospitable and treacherous place long enough. No more. He was Marshall Cameron, son of Colin Cameron and Marion Hewlett, heir to his pride and her privilege. He would not forget that again, nor would he be swayed from the focus of his stay on the grim Peninsula. He was here to serve the interests of the H&B Board and his family, not to chase after fanciful illusions in the lush green woods or a pair of intriguing gray eyes.

He couldn't blame her for doing what she'd done. She'd seen an opportunity to make a place for herself and a future for her father's company. If there was fault to be found, it was his own. He should have kept things strictly business between them. He should have stuck with what he knew. He should have behaved like a man betrothed instead of one beguiled. Then only his pride would have ached at learning of her motive. Then he wouldn't have felt as though there were a hole in his chest big enough to drive a one-ton kibble through. He deserved every bit of humiliation Tavis Lachlan dealt him, because he couldn't have been tricked if he hadn't been so willing to betray those who'd placed their trust in him. He'd been willing to turn his back on his family and his fiancée for his own selfish pleasures, and now see where that had gotten him.

No more, he decided on that barren bluff. No more would he be ruled by frail emotion when reason would serve him better. His expression hardened, his features stiff with cold, his muscles taut with determination. He had a job to do here on this harsh ridge of rock, and when it was done, he would leave it behind without regrets.

Regrets were for fools.

The winter season was a profitable one for Superior Lumbering. The weather stayed cold, the ground frozen and snow-covered well into the end of March. Huge rollways of pine lay decked along the steep banks of the river waiting for the ice to crack. The forests had been cut back in a wide swatch all along that winding stream. Where the mighty pines once towered, tiny saplings stretched toward the weak spring sunshine, a sign of new life and continued prosperity on Superior land.

Lyle Parry had passed down to his daughter his reverence for the land. Never would the Superior be guilty of the "cut out and get out" attitude of some of the lumber kings. He had raised Joelle to care for the forests, not only for the work they provided but for the simple beauty of them. Extra care was taken to keep sparks away from drying branches and rotting bark and stumps. Nothing was worse than the scarred black ground left behind because of a second's carelessness. Once the mature trees had been cut from the land, ownership of the acres reverted to the state or was sold to immigrants eager to farm. So it was with pride not guilt that Joelle looked out over the cutting grounds, an area not denuded but seeded for the future. Where forests couldn't prosper, mankind would, so nothing went to waste in the Superior's wake.

The long months had created tedium and short tempers. Fights had become as commonplace as the Sunday boil-up to free dirt and kill lice in the laundry. There was little to break the sameness of the days and isolation of the nights. During the week, there was brutal work at the cutting ground. On Sunday the few men who could write took dictation so others could send letters to loved ones. When the weather was fair, itinerant sky pilots furnished religious services to all. The nuns were treated with respect and listened to with reverence, regardless of any man's individual beliefs. They ministered to men's soul's while the hand organs brought in on sleds lifted their spirits in song. The food supply was ample if not varied, and Fergus's gruff demeanor lessened the chances for discontent. But as the skies began to lighten and the daylight hours to lengthen, the men grew even more restless. Their days in the woods were almost at an end.

Joelle experienced that same disquiet. Though she filled her hours with all the labor she could handle, her nights seemed endless. She'd read and reread the book of sonnets she'd received for Christmas and spent long, dreamy hours reflecting upon its inscription: *Yours always, Marsh.*

Thank God for Olen. If not for his cheerful presence and rumbling snores, which the thickness of two closed doors could not restrain, she would have gone quite mad during those interminable nights. He made her laugh. He made her feel close to Marsh with his tales of the Easterner in the woods. Olen made her long for Marsh when he spoke with a low vibration of love about his family in Ontanogon. He kept her from feeling so desperately alone as the calendar days edged toward April. Would Marsh still be at the H&B when the thaws came? Olen's certainty stoked her own failing confidence.

In the evenings, when the book work was done and Olen had started his lusty snoring, Joelle's thoughts belonged to the sometime sawyer and owner of the Superior. Just as she had read and reread the book of sonnets, she replayed moments she and Marsh had spent together until they were ingrained like bold print upon her memory, recalling the inflections of his voice, the sureness of his step, the curving dimples that creased his lean cheeks. She lay awake wondering if thoughts of her passed through his mind on these deep, snowy eves. Did he wake up before dawn beset by a longing so intense it made the very marrow in his bones throb with wanting? He was a fever in her blood that rose every evening and burnt until daybreak. By the waning days of March, she was worn ragged for the want of him. Her nerves seemed frayed, and her heart filled near to bursting. Were he to have come to her on any of those desperate nights, she wouldn't have given a thought to the woman he had waiting in Boston. Perhaps it was a good thing that he hadn't been there, when conscience was no match for temptation.

She wanted to make love to Marshall Cameron more than she wanted to draw her next breath.

Both things were vital to her existence.

The ride to Eagle River in the company of the Sonniers was one long nightmare of nerves. She wasn't thinking about what needed to be done at the mill to ready it for the flow of logs to come. She wasn't concerned with the vast sums of money she'd carry back to camp to pay her steadfast workers. All her energies were directed toward one source, one hope: that the agent for the H&B would still be in residence. For three months, three barren months, she'd survived on memories. She wouldn't think of how she'd manage for a lifetime once he was gone. She only thought of the moment at hand.

But attending to business at the mill had to come first. With impatience she stopped in at the dwelling that served as her family's seasonal home and lingered only long enough to refresh her clothing and cool her excitement. She was stunned by the face she saw in the mirror as she combed out her blue-black hair. Her eyes were ablaze with expectation. High color flamed in her cheeks. Her hands shook with fretful tremors. She looked like a creature long starved and ravenous.

Steady, she cautioned. For three months her desire had simmered and steeped to an almost unbearable boil. What if the opposite were true of Marsh? What if in those ninety days of separation, his memories had faded instead of flared? What if his feelings for her had eased instead of intensified during that absence? She couldn't launch herself into his arms until she knew the state of his heart. *Yours always.* Was that still true? Nothing was certain until she saw him face-to-face.

Never had the miles between the Superior mill and the H&B mine seemed so vast. What if he'd already gone to Copper Harbor to book passage? The lanes would be open on the lakes within the next few weeks. What if he'd left the fate of the Superior and her heart in the hands of some indifferent bank in Eagle River? Oh, that was too cruel a thought to entertain. He had to be at the H&B. And he was.

Smoke rose from the chimney above the mine agent's modest house. She hesitated after tying up her horse-drawn sleigh. Maybe she should go see her uncle first. Maybe she could learn something from him without risking further wounding of her heart and soul. But she couldn't wait. Three months had been a hellish eternity. The need to become lost in Marsh's dark stare drew her to the door. Taking a deep breath to steady herself, she knocked.

There was a moment of respite. Spotted Fawn answered the door and took her inside. A terrible weakness seeped into Joelle's knees, making the steps toward the fire-basked parlor difficult. Her heart was knocking against her ribs with a bruising force. Then she saw him. He was seated before the hearth, reading. Firelight glazed his tawny hair with shafts of gold. For a moment she forgot to breathe, and when he turned, air gushed from her in a noisy rush. Oh, God, he looked—he looked wonderful, crooked nose and all.

"Hello, Marsh."

Was that her voice so soft and whispery?

Then she met his eyes, and confusion stilled the rapid flutter of her pulse. That intense, penetrating stare pierced right through her without a trace of gladness or welcome. His obvious cold dislike cut her to the core.

She tried to draw a breath, to somehow speak and defend against what she saw in that unswerving glare, but the shock was too great. His look was not without emotion. There was plenty of feeling there, too much to be contained by civility or even genial pretense. Passions sparked in that dark gaze and scorched her with their frigid fire.

What in God's good name had she done to make Marshall Cameron hate her?

16

STRICTLY BUSINESS.

Easier said than done, especially when the unexpected sight of her knocked the breath from him.

Staring at her from across the room, Marsh felt as if he'd taken the plunge over that high bluff where three months before he'd vowed to put her from his thoughts, to block her from his heart. He'd tried. But he was nowhere near succeeding. He knew that the minute he felt his sane and solid world drop away from him, leaving him to plummet into agony. His stomach shifted with a savage jerk until it seemed to have lodged in his throat. He wasn't going to make it. He couldn't catch himself. Inside every sense was scrambling in a frantic bid for survival. If only he'd had some warning!

But she was here, looking more beautiful then he'd remembered in those forbidden dreams. Her hair had grown out of its rough, boyish cut to softly brush her shoulders. The effect was staggeringly feminine. The scents of cold, clean air and fresh-cut pine that were a natural part of her struck him with an intoxicating force. She stood there gazing up at him through eyes as mysterious as morning mist rising off the lake, with an expression as heart-stirring as a new dawn. That look was a compelling mix of timid hope and sultry promise and hit him with the shattering strength of a ten-pound sledge.

Jo.

Marsh hauled in a stabilizing breath and exhaled a ragged hiss. The effort it took to control his erratic pulse was monumental, but he made it. He shut down the wild surge of his emotions, blanked it from his face, squeezed it out of his heart until his features were a hard mask betraying nothing. And then anger rose to fill that empty void, anger toward her for the way she bent his will with the whisper of his name, toward himself for wanting her so badly he had to lock his muscles tightly to fight off the need to pull her into his arms. But he wouldn't be her fool again.

Her reaction was subtle. He saw the flicker of surprise. Had she thought he'd welcome her warmly, after she'd helped sabotage him? Surprise was followed by confusion and finally a wariness. He wouldn't be misled by the shadow of hurt in her eyes. She wouldn't convince him with a dewy look and a wavery sigh that she was totally innocent of the reason for his wrath.

I love you, Marsh.

His jaw clenched. His eyes smoldered in a reflection of his soul. No, he wouldn't believe it. Better he cling to certainties.

"What can I do for you?" Even Marsh winced at the snap of his words. He couldn't help the way his voice cracked like brittle ice. His emotions and senses were strained to the breaking point. To his chagrin, she came about quickly to brace against his cool contempt. Her eyes slitted. Her jaw aligned in a confrontational square. All traces of vulnerability were tucked behind that staunchly presented shield of pride. If she held any regret for what she'd done, she hid it well. The knot of tension in Marsh's belly tightened more painfully. She didn't even pretend remorse. Nor would she show any fear of him. Damn plucky girl. Didn't she know he could yet destroy her?

"I've come for the payroll for the Superior. The work is done in the woods."

"You've come alone?"

A flicker sparked briefly in her gaze, like flint on steel. She answered as if annoyed that he would ask, "Guy and Chauncey are with me."

"Oh." The ache gripping inside him had nothing to do with business matters. Guy Sonnier. It hadn't taken her long. "If you'll put together some kind of accounting—"

"I have it all right here."

He took the list of names and wages, all neatly columned in her precise hand. He sucked in a shaky breath. "I'll draw up a draft and have it sent—"

"I'll wait. It's been a long winter, and the men are anxious to get home to their loved ones." Her tone had thickened slightly, but the firm angles of her face didn't falter.

"Wait if you like," he told her crisply as if it weren't the last thing in the world he wanted. How could he concentrate on a hundred facts and figures when only two played upon his soul. She was everything he desired and she'd betrayed him.

While he sat at the table checking over the men's names, a strange, bittersweet sorrow overcame him. The names were as familiar as family to him. For one brief month, he'd belonged with them, and now they were distant dollar amounts on paper. To be paid and dismissed from mind and memory. If he could. Then, on the last sheet, one entry struck right to the heart of him, notching it as with a feller's mark to direct the way he should fall.

Cameron, Marshall Sawyer $28

His wage for the most memorable month of his life. His first honestly earned pay. A wry thought twisted the melancholy in his soul. Perhaps he should have it framed and sent to his father as proof of his accomplishments here in the northwoods, or to his grandfather, who believed a Hewlett oughtn't toil in the common way. Perhaps this would amuse him. Perhaps not.

Marsh sat back in his chair and purposefully blinked the mist of nostalgia from his eyes. Then his gaze settled upon the slender figure bent like a graceful sapling to test the warmth of his fire. Joelle had taken off her bulky mackinaw. As she leaned toward the heat of the flames, her red suspenders pulled taut, making an enticing curve around the swell of each perfect breast—curves once sampled by his palms, which were suddenly damp and unsteady. He rubbed them together in a distracted anguish, and the sound caught her attention.

"Is everything all right?" she asked with an innocent lift of her brows. It took him an agonizing moment to realize she was speaking of the payroll accounting.

"Yes. Yes, it's fine. I'll write you up a draft on my account in Eagle River."

She gave him a narrow smile and nodded. Her stare lingered, searching his for just an instant as if desperate to find something there. Then with a jerk of her head, she fixed her attention on the blaze smoldering in his hearth.

Just as his attention smoldered. He should have written out the amount and sent her away without a word, but he couldn't let her go that easily. She'd been a preoccupation in his life for three desolate months, and he couldn't stand the thought of her walking out of it before he had the chance to savor again the sound of her voice and the pleasure of her company. Lord, they'd been lonely months.

"Now what?"

Joelle looked up, startled. Confusion melted the mask of her indifference into a wistful expression of hope. It took him unaware, sending a savage jolt of longing through his system. If only he could hold onto what he thought he saw in that fleeting moment. But then her look grew cautious, calling for him to explain.

"The Superior," he clarified as if that were all he was concerned with. "What will you do now that the cutting's done?"

She straightened until she stood as stiff and proud as one of her majestic pines. Her words were clipped and carefully impersonal. "The majority of the men will go home by way of the nearest tavern. Some will stay on to bring the logs to the mill. We'll start branding them when I return so we don't lose any to the other companies when they mingle in the rivers. We've always used the Superior S, but you can change that to H and B if you like."

"The S is fine," Marsh replied tersely. He didn't explain that he'd never transferred ownership of Superior Lumbering to the H&B holdings. He'd kept it in his name. He didn't explain because he wasn't sure he could.

Joelle nodded. There was a poignant haziness in her stare, as if she were unspeakably grateful for that small concession. Then she blinked it away. "We'll be breaking the rollways in a week or so, whenever the river is right. Then we'll bring the logs down to the mill for cutting, and you'll get your railroad ties and braces."

"It must be quite the adventure."

His softened tone prompted the offer of "You're welcome to see for yourself. As supervisor. I don't think we could afford you as an employee." She gave him a faint smile, and his heart flipped over neatly before he could stabilize it.

"I'm pretty busy here," he muttered, using gruffness to cover up the sudden expectancy lifting his spirits. How he'd like to be a part of it, to get his feet wet both figuratively and literally. But he knew the dangers—not to his body but to his heart and mind. Joelle would be there.

"Yes, of course," she murmured, lowering her gaze in dejection. "You'll be getting ready to leave."

Leave. The idea dammed up in his throat.

"Here." He extended the draft, and she came to take it from him. Their fingertips brushed. Sensation sizzled. They jerked back from the unintentional contact. Joelle snatched up her coat in agitation and shoved her arms inside. She wrapped the bulky front about her like a buffer between them.

"I'll be seeing you, Cameron." A ghost of a smile hovered about her lips. "I'll bring by your pay."

He responded with a mild grin of his own. "I'll try to survive until then."

The amusement left their entangled gaze, and the mood grew strained with emotional tension. Finally Joelle broke it with a quick, shallow breath and a hasty backward step. "I'd better go. Guy and Chauncey will be waiting, and I daren't leave them alone in a saloon for too long."

The chill returned to Marsh's eyes. Yes, Guy. How could he forget good old Guy Sonnier? The corner of his mouth gave a tic of irritation.

Joelle had started to turn but she looked back suddenly. "Oh, Olen said to tell the Yank hello for him. And you were right about the snoring. I'll have to re-chink all the logs from what he's rattled loose."

Marsh laughed, a natural sound gurgling up in a wellspring of relief. The warmth of sentiment caught him unprepared, and he relaxed completely. It felt good to let go of the tension. "Tell him I think of him fondly every time I wake from a good night's sleep." His expression sobered. "How's his leg?"

"Good. He walks with only a slight limp. He's anxious to be with his family, though he's promised to stay on until the logs are safely milled. He's been a great help to me, thanks to your suggestion." She looked uncomfortable with those words of praise and promptly hunched down inside her engulfing coat. "I won't keep you any longer. Good-bye, Cameron. I'll keep you informed of the count."

He didn't expel his breath until after she'd gone, and then it was with a gusty sigh. How could he pretend to dislike her? So she had tempted him into the trees to clear the way for her uncle's treachery. Who was he to her then? No one. A meddling Easterner looking to upset her already unsteady world. How could he blame her for siding with Tavis over a bothersome interloper? It would have been ironic justice to overthrow his authority in the mines after he'd dispatched hers in the forest. So why was he so angry? He didn't like the answer that came to him. It was easier to censure her than blame himself for his own infidelities. Anger put a distance between who he was and what he wanted to be to her. She had tried to deceive a stranger, and he'd attempted to cheat an absent lifelong friend. He couldn't lessen his own guilt because even now he would willingly tread upon vows made before man and sanctified by honor to consummate the overwhelming need he felt for Joelle Parry. Better he kept up the barriers. Better he kept out of arms reach for both their sakes.

She didn't understand. She didn't understand at all.

Joelle stomped across the still-frozen street. Her emotions were as brittle as the ice giving way beneath her feet with shattering crunches. What made Marshall Cameron's attitude run in a hot and cold confusion? She felt bad enough having had her expectations cruelly dashed, but she could find no reason for his abrupt change of heart. Upon their last parting, she would have sworn his yearning had matched her own. Now he shunned her with obvious distaste. Why? The question choked up inside her, creating a swelling ache. What had she done?

I love you, Marsh.

Joelle frowned. Had she ruined everything with her inexperienced passions? She'd backed him into an uneasy corner
with that carelessly blurted truth, and ever since then he'd
been trying to wiggle his way out. He'd tried to dissuade her
gently; she recalled how he'd evaded her demonstrations at the
boardinghouse. He'd told her he was involved with another,
yet his dark eyes still beckoned. He'd said he was marrying
another, yet he was drawn to her as she was to him. He would
resist her clumsy passions yet encourage her devotion with a
look, a touch, a tender act. She didn't understand him. And
now this harsh, inconsistent anger. Had his amusement at her
expense turned to annoyance? That notion hurt. She walked
faster, hugging her arms about her slender form. He was
going home. To *her*. Was he eager to put aside the past?
Was that why he was pushing her away with his moody
hostility? Was he afraid she was going to stage some grand
impassioned play to make their parting awkward? Well, she
would spare him that worry. She would not embarrass him
with her unworthy appeal for his attention. And she would
not embarrass herself. If he wanted to be rid of her, he didn't
have to spell it out any clearer. She wasn't dense. And she
wasn't about to drag her battered emotions around for the
entertainment of others.

That staunch vow of pride would not hold as she collapsed
upon the bench in her aunt's kitchen. She fought back tears.
Never had she brought her problems to her mother's sister.
The poor woman always seemed so overwhelmed by her
own problems. But Joelle had nowhere else to go, and she
desperately needed the advice of another woman.

When Sarah saw the girl's wet lashes, she was quick to
supply a comforting shoulder.

"Oh, Joelle dear, whatever's the matter?" She'd never seen
the girl cry before, not even as a babe. It stirred a wealth
of maternal feelings and a fierce protectiveness for her sister's child.

"I've been so stupid," Joelle wailed softly. She hid her face
in Sarah's bony embrace and struggled with her anguish as it
welled to overflowing.

"Surely not," the older woman soothed, as she stroked her
niece's glossy dark hair.

"I have. I've thrown myself at him, and now he hates me. What am I going to do? I love him, Aunt Sarah, and now he's going away and I'll never see him again!"

"Who, child?"

"Marshall C-Cameron."

Joelle felt the woman stiffen. "Oh."

"He has a fiancée in Boston. But he didn't tell me until after I'd already—"

"Joelle!" Her aunt held her away and stared in dismay. "Tell me you did not!"

Joelle sniffed. "Didn't what?"

Sarah flushed and looked uncomfortable, but she was compelled by her duty to her niece. She made her voice stern. "Did you let him bed you?"

"No."

There was enough dignity in that reply to convince Sarah it was true, but not enough to make her feel at ease. If the girl hadn't slept with him, it wasn't because she hadn't wanted to. Sarah struggled for wisdom. She had no experience in such things, and the girl's distress left her panicked in the face of her own inadequacy.

Joelle sat back and swiped at her dripping eyes. Her control was better now, but the grief continued to swell. So did her sense of helplessness. "I thought I could make him love me," she confessed miserably. "I even thought he might stay."

Sarah's thin features firmed with bitter knowledge. "No, my dear. In that you were wrong. A man like that wouldn't stay. He'd break your heart and take it with him if you allowed it. And you mustn't. It won't matter to him that he has destroyed your happiness. He won't look back. That's the way of them, those high and mighty Hewletts."

The latent fury in her pallid aunt's tone was as surprising as her revelation.

"Hewlett?" Joelle was confused. "But his name is Cameron."

"His father is a Cameron. His mother is a Hewlett."

To think she'd once worried that the purchase of the Superior would break him financially. And she had promised to bring him his month's meager pay of twenty-eight dollars, an amount he would probably squander on a decent bottle of wine. Her face flamed with horror. A Hewlett! She had

tried to entice him, had thought to charm him into remaining
in her arms. No wonder he was impatient with her attempts
at seduction. How he must have laughed at her ambitions. A
Hewlett and the lowly daughter of a Michigan logger—how
absurd! Her eyes and throat burned with that bitter truth.

"I have to go, Aunt Sarah," she announced brusquely as she
stood and brushed away the last of her foolish tears along with
the last of her foolish dreams.

Sarah Lachlan watched her go, watched her stumble beneath
the burden of her broken pride. Silently she damned them
both, mother and son, for having so little care for the tattered
and empty lives they left behind.

Joelle thrust herself, body and soul, into the arduous work
at hand. If she couldn't willfully force Marshall Cameron from
her thoughts, she would keep herself too busy to have time
for him. And there was plenty to do. The camp was quiet,
the winter's work in the woods done. Most of the men had
packed their belongings in their turkeys and headed for town
or home. Only a few remained to bring the logs downriver.
Among them were the Sonniers and Olen Thurston. One of
the ones who'd left, unfortunately, was their cook, Fergus, and
the men's tempers suffered for it. A contented stomach made
for a contented man, and there was a great deal of grumbling
over the bland beans and beef served up each day.

Joelle and Olen worked together, counting logs and seeing
them branded by the Superior axmen who notched a crude S
on them the same way a Westerner would brand his cattle to
separate theirs from the other companies using the same river
roadways. It was a good crop of timber. The numbers were
satisfying, and Lyle Parry would have been proud. Then the
thaw they'd been waiting for came. Ice broke in the streams,
cracking like pistol shots as great chunks of it popped up onto
the shores. All along Lake Superior turbulent waves worked
inland until the last of the freeze was swept away. Anxiously
Joelle and her men watched the river. Too little water meant
logs would grind on the bottom; too much flooding saw them
carried away and pushed into the swamps where retrieval took
time and money. When the time was right, Joelle gave the
order to begin breaking the rollways.

It was dangerous work with a dramatic result. The logs had been rolled by landing men into perfect stacks twenty to thirty feet high, where they sat, frozen pyramids along the banks, until spring. Some stacks melted into the water while some had to be pushed over the brink into it. The towering deck of logs went rumbling down the bank, splashing the frigid water high as the logs bobbed and churned. Logs piled farther back had to be dragged down to the edge with peaveys. Manipulating the massive lengths of pine with the steel-shod pikes was sweaty work. Once logs clogged the river, they were made up into rafts and the downstream journey to the sawmill began while the melt kept the water high and fast.

A path at the edge of the stream had been well worn by the river pigs who walked alongside the swell of logs, driving them with their peaveys. It was a dangerous job, requiring the drivers to walk out onto the rafts of pine to release jams, but paid well enough to compensate for the long sleepless nights in wet clothing. Since his leg was not yet strong enough for the hard labor and his size prevented too many complaints, Olen followed on the wanigan as cook. Joelle rode on the houseboat with the big Swede, watching over her timber like a proud mama, serving up food and sleeping in the cold, damp boat in restless stretches. She was always uneasy during the drives. It was the last leg of a long winter and one in which so many things could go wrong. If one log got hung up on a boulder, the others would pile into it, upending, grinding against one another until they were wedged so tight dynamite had to be used to break them apart. If their timing was just a little slow, the swollen torrent of water could reduce to a trickle in the span of a day, so narrow one could jump across it. Then they would have to construct a whole series of dams to carry the cut to the mill. More time lost. So she worried and watched, gleaning confidence from the drivers who skillfully moved about on the highway paved from bank to bank with Superior timber.

Joelle raised a hand to respond to Guy's cheery wave. She smiled as she followed his graceful movements across the flowing raft of logs, prodding the lagging lengths of pine with his peavey. She was glad he'd signed on to see the cut to the mill. He'd shrugged casually, saying he could use money, but she suspected he wanted a chance to spend some extra time with her. There was little time for wooing, however, as the logs rushed downriver. The only time she saw him was when he came to the wanigan, wet and shivering, for a change of clothing. Then he was quick with a smile but short on small talk. He seemed more preoccupied than usual. She could see him and his brother squatting beside their fire at twilight deep in conversation while brewing tea in a No.2 size tomato can wedged into the crotch of a stick. Nearly all the jacks carried that simplified teapot hooked to their rear suspender buttons and took every opportunity to pour something warm into their bellies.

At night the mood along the river grew more relaxed. Superstition held that jams never formed in the dark, so blankets were spread along the banks for a few brief hours of rest. Joelle didn't share that native belief, nor did she find any rest in a slumber haunted by the dark-eyed man she thrust from her thoughts during the day. She close to prowl the tiny deck of the wanigan, her senses alert to danger, her heart wary of the intrusion of wistful dreams. But still they came, tormenting her with the memory of Marshall Cameron's touch. Those nights seemed made for dreams, and like it or not, she found herself warmed by them as she huddled against the chill.

So she was understandably fighting exhaustion and a loaded-gun tenseness as their week-long journey culminated at the boom in the river mouth where their sawmill waited. She stood for long, tiring hours counting, sorting the brands to make sure the marks cut into them had been done by Superior's axmen. At first she thought her weariness had skewed the final count, so she did it a second time.

Furious she stalked into Marshall Cameron's office late that same evening. She had no patience with his look of heart-stopping surprise or with the smoldery fires that simmered be⟨…⟩ his gaze. There was only one thing on her mind.

⟨…⟩ short thirty thousand board feet of timber," she ⟨…⟩untly. "I've counted twice."

⟨…⟩hat happen?"

⟨…⟩ver pirates."

17

JOELLE PACED BEFORE the hearth, scarcely feeling the warmth from the cup clutched in her hand or from the gaze of the man seated off to one side.

"So how did they steal it?"

She responded to the question with a deepening frown. "There are several ways. The thieves alter the brands while the logs are still on the river to one that's registered in their name. Or they can misdirect logs into a pond, cut the ends off, and rebrand them. Usually it's difficult to pirate logs with so many rivermen on a drive, but we were working the stream alone with just a bare crew. Easy pickings for someone who knew what they were doing."

Marsh leaned back in his chair, watching her agitated strides. She was like something sleek and wild caged before his fire, a sight as dangerous as it was stimulating. He kept his tone neutral.

"What now? Write off the loss?"

Her eyes sparked like flint on steel as she turned to glare at him. "No. I want to know who did this. I have to know. We've got another drive coming down into the lake, and I can't afford to be picked clean of profits."

He noticed the possessive "I" she'd used when talking about his timber but made no comment. "What do you suggest, then? Is there a chance of catching these thieves?"

Joelle grimaced. "Not much. But if I can find out how they

did it, I might be able to figure out who."

"Just what do you mean by 'I'?"

She went on as if she hadn't heard his testy query. "By following along the stream, I might be able to come across some clue."

"There's that 'I' again. Would you care to explain exactly who you mean by that? Certainly you're not referring to yourself."

She glowered at him as if he were an imbecile. "Of course I mean me. Who else?"

"*Anyone* else. You're crazy if you think I'd allow you to crawl around in the bushes looking for log pirates."

"*Allow* me! Just who do you think you—" she began irritably then broke off to conclude, "It's my job."

"It's my timber," he countered quickly. To that she had no retort.

She stood with arms akimbo, tossing back the spill of inky black hair that curved about her jawline. She looked outraged. She looked gorgeous. "And just who do you plan to get to search out these thieves? A corner policeman? This is not Boston, Cameron. The nearest authority is the garrison of troops at Fort Wilkens, and I assure you they have better things to do than poke around in bushes."

"I'll take care of it."

"You?" Her bark of laughter was far from flattering. "You wouldn't be able to find your way to the river."

His eyes narrowed. Her opinion fueled him to act instantly on what had been just a passing thought. Yes, he would take care of it himself. "I can ask directions, Miss Parry," he drawled out in a less than civil tone. But she didn't heed the fact that his pride was pushing him beyond his capabilities. Instead she only goaded him further.

"And what will you look for? Have you the slightest idea? I suspect we'll be sending out a party of men to look for you soon after you leave the edge of camp."

"I can take care of myself."

Joelle couldn't supress her smile. She remembered speaking those same words a time or two, and he hadn't believed her when she said them. She gentled her voice so the criticism would be less cruel. "You're a greenhorn in the woods,

Cameron. You may be able to cut a tree, but that doesn't make you Paul Bunyan. I'm the only logical choice. I can't spare any men from the drive and I know the route blindfolded. I've walked it often enough over the years. I'll take my pistol along in case there's trouble, not that I think there'll be any. Surely you have to see the sense in it." She waited, searching the taut angles of his face. He looked angry. Then resigned. Her spirits soared.

"All right. All you say is true." He raised a hand to cut off her jubilant cry of thanks. "But there is one more thing I insist you take along for your own protection."

"Yes, anything. What is it?" She was anxious to be on her way before the tracks grew any colder and her ties to Marshall Cameron grew any warmer.

"Me."

"What?" She couldn't have heard right. Her heart beat wildly beneath her ribs.

He splayed his hands wide in a gesture of no quarter. "You can't go alone, and no one else can be spared. I'm the best you've got, Jo. Surely you have to see the sense in *that*."

She did. She also saw the impossibility. She and Marsh in the woods. Alone. No, her head protested. Oh, yes, her emotions countered.

"No arguments, Miss Parry?"

"I'm thinking," she snapped at his smug prod. But there was nothing to think about. It was his call. His company. Marshall Cameron could do whatever he liked. And since she knew he would be hopelessly lost at the first river fork, she had no option but to accept his vexing alliance.

Seeing his victory in the pouty fullness of her lips, Marsh restrained his urge to crow. "What time shall I be ready?" he asked in a well-modulated tone.

"Six."

"In the morning? But it's still dark—I'll be ready."

And he was, with a large pack strapped to his broad shoulders and an almost empty cup of coffee in his hand. He looked bright and eager, and Joelle, who hadn't slept at all, simmered with resentment. Wasn't he the least bit concerned about the two of them going off together? She glared at him, seeing the thirst for adventure in his dark eyes, not the suggestion of passions just dying to overwhelm them both. And that needled her temper sorely. Why, if Guy Sonnier were the man she was about to hike off into the woods with, he'd be bubbling at a low boil of anticipation. But not Marshall Cameron. He was looking forward to the chase, not to the starry nights ahead, as if she were just his guide and no more appealing than Fergus, the gruff cook. She cursed him roundly under her breath.

"Six o'clock and I'm ready," he told her with a grin.

"Good for you," she growled. His brows shot upward.

"Ah, I'd forgotten how surly you are in the morning. Well, Madam Grizzly Bear, let's drop the conversation and get going, shall we?"

"You're the boss."

With that, she started off at a brisk pace. Marsh smiled wryly and set his cup down. With a hitch of his pack to a more comfortable position, he strode after her, unwilling to lose her in the gathering shadows.

Joelle kept to her long strides. By the first pinks of dawn, they'd put the mining town far behind them. By mid-morning, they were winding along the river trail. She could hear Marsh's labored breathing behind her, but he neither slowed nor asked that they stop for a rest. She held to the fast pace because if he couldn't catch his breath, he couldn't talk; and if he couldn't talk, there was no chance that she'd want to believe what he had to say. She thought things would be easier if she stayed ahead, but even with him behind her she was acutely aware of him. That awareness played havoc with her heartbeat and her stamina.

"Are we running a race?" Marsh asked a bit breathlessly when they finally stopped at the edge of the water. Or was she just running from him? he wondered.

"I don't want to waste any time" was her terse reply as she bent down to cup some of the crystal cold water into her hands for a drink. Marsh followed suit, feeling as though his fingers had frozen when he dipped them into the stream. Never had he tasted anything quite so refreshing as that sip of north-country melt.

"Is there a chance that we'll catch the thieves in the act?" He was looking at her intently, gauging his ability to keep her safe should they stumble onto the logging pirates. He had no idea what sort of men they might be. An image of eye patches and a landlocked Jolly Roger seemed a little ridiculous. But the danger was real. He could tell by the grim way she gazed upstream.

"I doubt it. They've probably cut their logs and moved on to their next target. Most likely we'll get our chance to catch them on our second drive." Her features tensed, and she surged to her feet with impatience. "Come on. You should have your second wind by now."

"Don't feel you have to wait for me."

Joelle responded to his sarcasm with a piercing glance and a candid "I won't." Then she started upstream with that long, purposeful stride.

Sighing, Marsh repositioned his pack and went after her.

It was rough going afoot. The path was rocky and rutted, sometimes disappearing altogether where the waters swelled. But the scenery was beautiful. There was still plenty of snow piled between the trees. They waded hip-deep in it when the vanishing trail forced them to blaze their own way. During the morning, they had some sunshine, which gave almost no heat but created spindly shafts of brightness as it streamed through the high pine boughs. Those shifting fingers of light played through Joelle's hair, haloing it with a soft, beckoning aura. Marsh found himself mesmerized by that fanciful dance of brilliance surrounding her to the detriment of his footing. The toe of one boot snagged on an exposed root. Unbalanced as he was by the heavy pack, there was no way to catch himself. He went down hard, face-first into the frozen mud of the trail. A twinge of pain lanced through his ankle. The smack of unyielding earth skewed his senses. When they returned, he was aware of Joelle kneeling before him, her hands upon his shoulders.

"Marsh, are you all right?" Was that a quiver of concern in her voice?

"Fine," he lied through gritted teeth as he worked his foot free of the tangled root. He got his hands under him and lifted up, coming nose to nose with his companion. The pain in his ankle was forgotten. He noticed nothing beyond the cool gray of her gaze. "Just got distracted for a second," he managed to mutter through the constriction in his throat. She had the most lovely eyes, all fringed in feathery blackness, so cool and deep, like an inviting stream on a hot day. He felt his temperature rise in response. In that instant, all he wanted to do was kiss her and get the terrible agony of suspense over with. But her stare clouded as soon as his began to heat.

"Pay more attention to what you're doing," she growled as she pushed off his shoulders and rose to her feet in a picture of annoyance. "I don't have time to drag you back to the H and B if you break your leg. Try to remember that this is not a sightseeing trip."

"Yes, ma'am," he replied with syrupy insincerity. But she had already put her back to him and was stalking away, not even bothering to wait for him to gain his feet.

Cursing under his breath, Marsh hauled himself upright. Discomfort shot up his leg from the twist his ankle had taken, but he vowed to crawl before he voiced a complaint that would slow the tyrannical Miss Parry. He set his jaw and began hobbling as best he could.

The man had two left feet, Joelle told herself in a temper of irritation. He had no business being out here, fumbling about with all the grace of a newly foaled moose calf. It seemed she was forever picking up pieces of him. Why was he so stubbornly set upon doing things for which he had no skill? She heard his bitten-off oath and a rattle of stones but didn't look around. She said she wouldn't wait. He'd boasted that he could take care of himself, after all. And what was in that ridiculously bulky pack of his? Probably a half dozen books, a bottle of brandy, and a servant to pour for him. He should be sitting before a fire in some posh parlor with his feet up, not tramping about in the drifts, floundering after her. What was he trying to prove? He was leaving in a few short weeks anyway. Then who was going to fuss and fawn over her?

Joelle stumbled and angrily wiped her eyes. She needed to heed her own words. If she wasn't more mindful of what she was doing, someone would have to come and carry them both out on stretchers. Why had he looked at her that way, as if he'd wanted to grab her up in a rough embrace? He'd gone out of his way to put their personal business behind them. So why that desirous stare? It had rattled her more than she was willing to admit to herself, stirring up hopes best forgotten and needs best left unexplored. Her stomach in knots of agitation, she pushed onward, pretending not to hear his struggling pursuit.

When there was only an hour or so of daylight remaining, Joelle began to search for a campsite. A small cove provided shelter, dry ground, and fresh water. When she turned to Marsh to tell him of her decision to stop, she drew a short breath of dismay. He was limping so badly up the trail behind her she wondered if he had indeed broken something. His features were tight and flushed with pain. When he saw her staring at him in obvious distress, he forced a stalwart claim.

"You don't need to worry. I can keep up."

She made a sound of aggravation and came toward him. "You great fool. Why didn't you say something when we were close enough to turn back?"

"I didn't want to go back," he panted testily. He was reluctant to lean upon the shoulder she offered, but in the end he resigned himself to it. He knew he couldn't take another step on his own.

"So what am I supposed to do with you now that you're all crippled up?" Her words were harsh, but her assistance was born of compassion. She supported him almost totally until they came to a felled tree trunk. He couldn't help but groan when he was eased down on it.

"I guess you could always shoot me," he exclaimed with a grouchiness prompted by pain.

"Don't tempt me."

When she knelt before him and reached for his boot, Marsh was quick to say, "Leave it. I can hold out."

"But the daylight won't, so we might as well tend to it now. Is it broken?"

"I don't think so. Just hurts like the devil."

He gnashed his teeth together fiercely as she wrestled off his boot. The cold air shocked his fevered bare skin when she rolled down both pairs of thick wool socks. He might try to conceal his pain, but there was no disguising the puffy swell of his ankle. Without wasting words, Joelle pulled up one of the socks and began packing snow between it and the other pair. The relief was almost immediate.

"If we keep it chilled and you stay off it, you might be

able to walk on it tomorrow." Then, as if shocked by the fact that she was unconsciously massaging the firm calf of his leg, Joelle dropped his foot. Marsh howled as his heel hit the ground.

"Sorry," she told him brusquely and was quick to step away.

Her hands were shaking as she built up a warming fire. The man unsettled her, plain and simple. The feel of him, the scent of him, the sound of him and his near helplessness made it that much worse. Why was it so hard to remember she couldn't have him? Why was it so hard to view him as the unattainable heir to the Hewlett fortune rather than the brawling sawyer who'd come to her with a shattered nose and a devastating kiss? She knew he had a chosen bride awaiting him in Boston. So why did her bones go to liquid whenever he looked at her in that particular way? Why did her heart pound near to bursting with the desire to beat unfettered next to his?

Purposefully, she avoided glancing his way as she put the makings of a crude meal together over the fire; beans warmed in the can and tea brewed in the handy #2. It wasn't much, but why should she apologize? He was the one who had insisted on coming. He had no right to complain. And he didn't. He ate the unevenly cooked beans from a tin plate and washed them down with weak tea as if dining al fresco at a pricey restaurant on Nob Hill. She felt a curious turn of emotion as she watched him. As unprepared as he was for the roughness of the life she led, he seemed to relish it. When his plate was empty and his cup refilled, he leaned back against the log and sighed with an odd contentment. She couldn't understand him. He didn't complain. He didn't whine. He didn't pout about things he couldn't have his way. He made due. What kind of Boston blueblood was he? What kind of man who could buy and sell cities would take such satisfaction in a dish of plain beans and a backside chilled from the cold ground? And if he had a wife waiting, why did he keep watching her with such intensity?

"How's the foot?"

"What?" He blinked to end his study of her full lower lip. "Oh, it's fine. I'm sure I'll be able to walk come morning."

"I hope so, because you'll have no other choice."

He glanced around at the dark, inhospitable shadows and smiled ruefully. "Either keep up or get left behind, right?"

Her expression softened for a fleeting second. "I wouldn't leave you, Marsh." Then she looked away and busied herself with scraping the plates and scouring them clean in the snow. Her words had not been an expansive declaration, but they warmed him considerably—and he'd need warming, considering the way the temperature had begun to plunge as darkness settled. Even a built-up fire couldn't keep the chill at bay. Joelle was shivering in her heavy mackinaw. She finished untying the string of her pack so she could restore the plates and pull out her blankets. "We'd better get settled in. I want to get an early start. I hope you thought to bring blankets in that monstrosity you're carrying. Or do you have a whole feather bed with you?"

Marsh grinned at her tart humor. "Better."

What could be better on such a bitter night? She spread her own blankets next to the fire and watched covertly as he opened his bulging pack. Finally she gave up the pretense and stared openly as he drew out a series of poles and stakes and cord.

A tent.

In no time Marsh erected a snug little shelter with its flaps opening toward the fire. As he spread his bedroll upon its dry canvas floor, she had an unequalled view of his nicely formed trousered bottom. She was barely breathing by the time he backed out to give her a satisfied smile.

"Home sweet home."

"Leave it to a greenhorn to be afraid of a little fresh air," she grumbled with an envious look inside the airtight cave.

"There's room for two," he offered mildly.

Two? She sized up the opening with a jaundiced eye. Two malnourished children perhaps or two bird-thin old ladies, or two lovers who didn't mind the entwining closeness. Joelle swallowed hard. "No, thanks. I'm fine," she said rather hoarsely.

Marsh shrugged. "Okay. Good night then." With that he slid in on top of his bedroll and made a loud, disgustingly comfortable sound.

Joelle sat for a long minute staring at the soles of his boots and at the curve of his rump and shoulders beyond. The temptation was mighty. Was that exactly what he'd planned? With a mutter of irritation, she dropped down on her bottom blanket and pulled the other over her. Within a minute, the chill of the ground seeped right through her. It was hard and cold. No matter which way she wiggled, she found no yielding rest. Even with the covers clutched over her head, the night breeze was cutting, stealing her breath away. Another long, miserable night, she thought with a silent moan of discontent.

"Had enough fresh air for one evening?"

Joelle glared over to find the tent flaps lifted. The invitation was irresistible. Damning her pride, she snatched up her blankets and ducked into that dim interior filled with Marshall Cameron. She immediately heard the sound of his breathing and was assaulted by the clean scent of leather and the heat of his body. After securing the flap she paused uneasily until his amused chuckle goaded her into flinging out her blankets in the narrow space beside him. The steeply slanted sides of the tent forced her and Marsh together until they were pressed close shoulder to toe. There was no help for it. And it did feel good. So warm. So . . . familiar.

She struggled with her covers, and then he murmured, "Here, let me get that." He pulled them around her, anchoring them with the casual weight of his arm across her hip. A flare of heat pooled beneath that easy drape, intensifying because he seemed so unaware of it. Adding to her torment, he slipped his other arm under her head, crooking his elbow to hold her in the security of his embrace. There was no man-made haven like it. Quite naturally, she turned on her side so that her own arm banded his middle and her cheek found a resting place in the lee of his shoulder. The canopy of canvas kept out the wind. The warmth of the man beside her quelled the chill of the night. A feeling of comfort crept into her bones and relaxed muscles aching with weariness.

She should have dropped off to an immediate slumber, but Joelle had never felt so awake in her entire life. She was agonizingly aware of everything. Of the course nap of his wool shirt. Of the strong rhythm of his pulse beneath her palm. Of the heaviness of the air inside the tent as it filled with the moistness of their breathing. Of the way emotions churned within her breast. How on earth was she supposed to sleep confronted with such a sensory overload?

The edges around the tent flap had just enough of a gap between them to cast a bronze wedge of firelight across half of Marsh's face. From her vantage point, it was a perfect profile: high brow, fine nose, firm lips, strong jaw. More masculine with the burn of the wind and rugged texture of the cold to weather it. His eyes were open. He was staring with absolute concentration toward the center peak of the tent, but his altered breathing told her he was very much aware of her tucked in beside him. She wanted to touch his face, to feel the bold line of his chin rasp against her palm. She wanted to turn him toward her so she might see what he was thinking in the all-too-candid burn of his gaze. She wanted to feel his mouth move masterfully over hers just once more. Just one last time.

But what good would wanting do? Marsh Cameron wasn't hers to enjoy. Another woman would lie beside him each night, would feel his heat and share his kisses. Joelle was suddenly very angry with the knowledge that that woman would not be her. Could not be her. And she was angry that this fact should still hurt so much. She had to do something to distract herself from the urge to kiss or kill Marsh before the night was over.

"What's she like?" Her voice sounded unnaturally loud in the small space, startling him with its abruptness.

"What? Who?"

"Your fiancée," Joelle clarified with a touch of terseness.

"Lynette?" He paused as if uncertain of what to tell her. He decided upon the truth. "I've known her since we were children. I guess you might say she's the only real friend I ever had, the only one who liked me just for me and not for who I was or what I could give."

There was a warmth in his tone that disturbed her worse than the words. Proof that he cared for this faceless, formless woman who was her rival.

"We've always been close. I guess our parents always assumed we would marry." He'd begun to pull strands of her hair through his thumb and forefinger in an absent manner.

Just a slight tug, no pain except to the heart.

"Do you love her?"

"What?"

"This Lynette. Are you in love with her?"

Marsh was silent for a long moment. Joelle kept her head ducked down into the folds of his shirt, her eyes squeezed shut as she waited for his answer, for words he'd never spoken to her. But he didn't say them. Not quite.

"She's very dear to me. I would never do anything to hurt her."

Something in the soft, protective nuances of that claim set off a deep rage within her. "How very free you are with that sentiment. How easily you betrayed her." He tensed beside her, and she lashed out with her indignant fury. "I suppose you think she wouldn't be the least bit disturbed had she walked in to find us together the night you had that stupid fight with Guy. And that she'd have understood if she'd seen us sleeping in one another's arms on Christmas Eve. Or now. Would she, Marsh? Is she that trusting or that foolish? Would she believe you if you told her our kisses meant nothing to you? Doesn't she understand that you are one of the high and mighty Hewletts who think that having enough money means you can do what you damn well please with people and not care if you hurt them in the bargain? Well, she'd better learn and learn fast, or you're going to make her life hell."

Joelle shoved away from him and surged out of the tent, nearly bringing it down upon him in the process. She stormed across their small camp with no direction in mind. She just had to escape him and the incredible anguish he brought to bear upon her heart.

"Jo."

She struck at the hands that tried to catch her. Finally he forcefully backed her up against the rough trunk of a pine, his hands braced in tightly clenched fists on either side of her defiantly raised head. Firelight turned her damp glare to quicksilver.

"Meant nothing? Is that what you think?" he demanded harshly.

She refused to respond with anything but her stare, which cried for him to prove her wrong.

"Does this feel like nothing to you?"

His head bent and his mouth came crushing down on hers—grinding, searing, branding her with the heat of his desire. She made a small sound in her throat and then pushed at him. He didn't want to surrender the harsh pleasure the taste of her gave him. Not until he tasted the salt of her tears did he believe her protest. Then he eased back just far enough for them both to pant heavily for the return of breath and sanity.

"I'm sorry, Jo. I shouldn't have done that." He couldn't look up at her but stood with her slack body trapped between his forearms, with his forehead pressed against hers, with the rapid rasp of their breath mingling in vapor plumes. He wasn't prepared for how terribly vulnerable her voice sounded when she spoke at last.

"You have someone waiting in Boston to become your wife. Why are you doing this, Marsh? Can't you be satisfied with just one woman?"

He looked up then and saw that her eyes were tightly closed, tears gathering on the curve of her cheek.

He answered quietly, from the heart.

"I could be, Jo. If that woman was you."

18

JOELL'S EYES FLEW open. Shock and hope drove the breath from her. She wanted desperately to see the truth of what he was saying in his gaze, but his dark eyes were already closing. He angled his head, brushing her lips lightly with his own. When she gave a ragged little moan, he conquered her mouth sweetly, so sweetly. Everything inside Joelle melted and fused into a hard knot of longing as she opened herself to his kiss. She might pretend it wasn't so, but as he traced the bow of her upper lip with his tongue, no amount of denial, no word of protest could overcome the fact that she wanted this, wanted him, regardless of consequence. It no longer mattered that in a week or so he'd be gone from her life, that he was betrothed, that he would leave her without a backward glance because of who he was. What mattered was beneath those stirring, insatiable kisses, were feelings no other man had awakened, and which she feared no other could ever match. Marshall Cameron was her chance to experience all love had to offer.

Marsh leaned back, clearly fighting for control. He took a deep breath and said her name. His voice was rough with regret, and she knew she didn't want to hear the rest of what he might say, for fear it would stop the dizzying, passionate pull of drawing them together. She was fighting, too, fighting to know the conclusion of what he'd kindled deep inside her. And she had no intention of fighting fair.

"Oh, Marsh."

Her sigh was all liquid longing, searing his senses like molten steel. Her palms rode the taut planes of his face and settled in a locking vee beneath his jaw. The second she molded herself against him, Marsh knew it was too late for him. Much too late. A low, guttural sound was dragged up from his chest, speaking wordlessly of the raw emotions tearing at his heart. The brazen stroke of her tongue as it reached silkily between his lips knocked all reason and resistance from him. His hands moved over her, rough, restless, stroking and clutching at her hair, kneading the slope of her shoulders, lowering with hard little circles down the supple bend of her spine to grip her wool-clad buttocks. He hauled her up tightly against the ridge of his arousal, and when she shifted her hips to secure the fit, his every nerve caught fire.

"Oh, God, Jo," he gasped hoarsely into her greedy kisses. "I've wanted you, I've wanted this, for so long." Like the mounting of a sudden storm, emotions massed inside him, ripping him asunder with the violent rifts between conscience and need. He shook with indecision, wanting to do what was right for others, needing to do what was right for him. He pressed her face into his shoulder, securing her there while his thoughts chased one another wildly.

Joelle rode with the heaving plunge of his chest, hands enmeshed in his shirt collar, clinging for balance as the strength in her knees gave way. She could feel him battling against himself. To sway things in her favor, she whispered unevenly, "I want you, too." The last of his restraint caved in.

With a growl of desire rumbling in his throat, Marsh eased back her head. His mouth fell over hers with a bruising force, tongue thrust deep to demand a response, then moving more gently to savor it. She leaned into him, her breasts flattening with an enticing softness, her body moving with a promising sweetness. He never dreamed passion could flame to the edge of madness, but that's the way it was with Joelle Parry. He more than just wanted her. He craved her with the same vital desperation of life itself craving sun and rain.

"I love you, Jo," he whispered roughly and followed that claim with a self-deprecating sigh. "And I'm a selfish son of a bitch for telling you."

Joelle had gone very quiet in his arms. Her eyes opened slowly, glittering with a mercurial brilliance. She searched his expression, seeing more there, in the rigidly held lines than the simple truth of what he told her. Through the window of his dark eyes she saw a sorrow so deep it reached the soul.

"But you're still leaving, aren't you?"

She waited, holding her breath until he gave a jerky nod. Then she released a soft sob and blinked once, freeing the swelling dampness from her eyes. With infinite tenderness, his thumbs stroked the tears from her cheeks before they froze there, the way they once had on the boardwalk outside McGinty's saloon.

"I have to, Jo. I have no choice."

"There are always choices," she argued in a voice that was as weak and shaky as his resolve.

"Not for me."

As her eyes glistened with collecting tears and despair made her lips tremble, her words were firm, even bitter. "Because you're a Hewlett."

He expelled a ragged breath. "Partly. And partly because I've given my word to people I care about." He suppressed the need to confront her with his suspicious that she'd aided her uncle's scheme. There were too many complications to throw that in atop all else.

"And your word means more to you than I do?" Her accusation cut through him like a well-honed ax bit. The hands cradling her face tightened in a spasm of remorse.

"How can I make you understand? My word is everything I am. Once given, I can't break it. Even when I want to." His dark gaze probed hers, seeking some sign that she could comprehend just a piece of his dilemma. But all he saw there was misery, and it tore at his heart.

Joelle bit her lip, trying to summon enough bravery to get beyond this terrible moment of truth, a truth too cruel to bear. He loved her, but nothing had changed.

"So," she ventured gruffly, "where does that leave us, Marsh?"

He couldn't answer. No words could speak as well as the agony in his face.

She reached up for him, her fingertips grazing the slant of his jaw, twining in his tawny hair. Her words seemed to reach right inside to pluck the heart from him. "If you can't give me your word, if you can't give me your name, and you can't give me a part of your future, give me tonight. Love me tonight as if there were no tomorrow coming."

Marsh struggled for a proper breath and for the strength to say no. But honor and obligation were not what gave him pause. It was Joelle herself.

"Jo, it wouldn't be right. It would make things that much worse for you." Again he brushed away her tears, knowing he was responsible for her pain.

"Worse?" she cried out with a strangled little laugh. "What could be worse than letting you leave without ever knowing how it feels to be loved by you?" she shifted against him in a movement meant for seduction, but her voice was edged in an innocence that her gaze begged him to shed for her. "It would kill me, Marsh, that wondering and not knowing night after night. Can't you understand?"

Oh, yes. God, yes. For four long months his nights had held excruciating questions. What would it be like to hold her naked in his arms? Would her breasts yield a taste of heaven? How would it feel to sink his shaft deep within her and explore her wealth of untapped desires? He'd gone half mad trying to imagine the answers. How could he say no?

"And one night would be enough?" he asked in hushed concern. She looked so damned fragile with her big eyes shimmering up into his, pleading for him to impart a knowledge that couldn't help but forge them closer. Did she know once given, innocence could not be returned? He was ready to ask her when her fingertips stole across his lips to silence him.

"Yes," she told him with unwavering belief. "Tonight you love me and tomorrow I'll never ask for another thing. I'll let you leave without regrets. You see, Cameron, I'm used to making do. I'm used to taking what little I have and making the very most of it. I promise I won't complain or cling when the time comes for you to go. Just love me tonight. Please, Marsh."

It was that prideful declaration that finally broke him.

She was shaking. Her face was buried against his neck, and her breath darted quick and hot upon his bared skin. Her arms formed a tight band about his middle, clinging as if letting go might prove life-threatening. Tenderly he ran his fingers through her sleek black crop of hair and brushed across it with his lips. The fragrance of sharp soap and crisp air and tangy pines filled his mind to overflowing. He breathed it in deeply, as if he could pull her in with it, and held it in until his thoughts swam dizzily. He had to let it out eventually, just as he would have to let her go eventually. But not now. Not tonight.

"Jo, you're freezing. Go on back into the tent. I'll build up a fire that will last the night." He made his tone neutral. He was talking about adding wood. He was thinking about stoking passions. Damn, he had to let her go. But she was hanging on him like moss to a tree. "Jo, go on." He started to pry her arms loose, which was not an easy task.

"Marsh . . ."

"Go on," he scolded mildly. "Get warmed up. I'll be there in a minute." His hands ran down the sleeves of her mackinaw until their fingers met and meshed. His squeezed briefly; then he leaned forward to lightly kiss her brow.

Joelle hesitated. His carefully contained behavior confused her all the more. Was he saying no? Would they be wrapped in single blankets for the night or around each other? Uncertainty tore her confidence to shreds as she turned toward the tent after he released her hands. She wouldn't beg him to love her, but she feared from the way urgency throbbed through her that she would ask again. She wanted him so badly it frightened her, made her destroy her pride and name a bargain she wasn't sure she could keep. But she would worry about her dignity later. For now, she would wait for him to come to her for love or for simple comfort.

How long did it take a man to build a decent fire?

Joelle twisted restlessly on the blankets and fought the urge to peek out of the tent in search of him. He wasn't going anywhere. Not in the middle of the night. Not when he couldn't find his way around a tree trunk without getting lost. So why was he lingering out in the cold? Was he battling his conscience? Doubts assailed her. She was too much of a realist to believe she would pine away in celibacy for the rest of her days over Marshall Cameron. She would probably marry and probably bear children and be happy, just as he would. But she might never, ever, have another moment quite like this or a man like him, and she couldn't let the opportunity pass her by. She loved him with all her heart and soul, and he said he loved her, too. Didn't that count against the weight of guilt her upbringing told her to feel? She would feel guilty later if she must, for she could hear him approaching and she vowed not to spend this night untouched by the man she adored.

A snap of cold air followed as Marsh crawled inside the tent, then turned to keep the chill out by quickly tying up the flaps. The darkness became complete. Joelle lay still, listening to him move about, hearing the pull of his bootlaces and the harsh draw of his breath when he tugged the gear off his injured foot. The tent frame shivered as he struck it while tugging off his mackinaw. Then he settled down on his bedroll with an expansive sigh. Silence. Too much silence. Even their breathing was hushed.

After an almost unbearable pause, he reached for her, nearly poking her in the eye before finding the curve of her cheek. His touch was caressing, his words caring.

"Jo, are you sure?"

In answer, she caught his face between her hands and pulled him to her. Her fingers molded around his head, holding him in place for the reckless onslaught of her lips. She didn't just kiss him, she tried to devour him. She applied hungry, urgent pressure, deep, mind-drugging spears from her tongue, and hard then nibbly tugs to his bottom lip. It was all he could do to keep from slamming into her right then.

"Slow," he panted into her soul-snatching kiss. "Slow down, Jo. We've got all night."

All night. One night. She clung to his neck and tried not to sob out her distress. One night to stretch out into an eternity. She could no longer control her frantic anguish. It shook through her in violent tremors, choking up in her throat, stinging her eyes.

He held her. For a long time he just stroked her, soothing her with his calm. Finally, when she'd quieted, he laid her

back upon the blankets and came down to her with an ach-
ingly gentle kiss, so tender, yet it shook through the fibers
of her being like the fiercest storm. He kissed her mouth,
her cheeks, her temples, the tip of her nose, lavishing her
with those teasing whispers of passion, and she was wild
for more. Her breathing became uneven with excitement as
his fingers moved down the buttons to her shirt and then her
flannel underwear. He opened the bulky outer garments to
expose the brief linen chemise she wore to protect her soft
skin from harsh wool. His fingertips followed the unadorned
edges around the low scoop, then dipped beneath into the
warm, snug crevice between her breasts. Her heart fluttered
madly.

"Marsh . . ."

"Easy, Jo," he murmured softly as his lips skimmed along
the bodice edge. She felt close to swooning by the time he
lifted his head up. He gave her suspenders a sudden, playful
snap. "You're going to have to help me here. You're wrapped
up tighter than a package of smoked fish."

She thought she should protest the comparison, but his
fingers were running along beneath her bright red braces,
doing delicious things in passing. With unusual clumsiness,
she released the buttons securing them to her trousers then
sat up slightly so he could peel away her clothing until she
was bared to the middle.

Joelle hadn't thought about him undressing her. She felt
awkward and ashamed, even though she knew he couldn't see
her well. Heat rushed up her neck and face like flames over
dry tinder. As if he understood her embarrassment, he made
no immediate forays over that newly bared flesh. Instead he
kissed her some more, and some more, until she was gasping
and dazed. By then she didn't think to object when he lifted
up to give his hand access between their bodies. She arched
up eagerly, remembering now how it had felt when he touched
her through the layers of clothing, how she'd wished there
was nothing between her skin and his rough palm. Now there
wasn't, and the sensation was unbearably intense. By the time
he grazed her taut nipple, she was nearly mindless from it. Her
body jerked then shuddered as his mouth came down to lightly
feast upon the peak he'd aroused. She cried out his name, or

at least she thought she did, because he responded by saying hers. His voice was so low and harsh that it came out more a growl than a name. Now that he had suitably distracted her with the scrape of his teeth and tug of his lips, Marsh moved his hand lower, letting it rub over her restless thighs then up between them. When he applied pressure there, a jolt wracked her. When he moved the heel of his hand, she whimpered frantically. Hot spirals of longing shot up from her loins, shocking her, scaring her with their intensity.

"Marsh," she moaned uneasily as her hips twitched and trembled, "what are you doing?"

"Loving you," he mumbled into the soft swell of her breast. With one last devastating flicker of his tongue, he lifted up. "Let's get these off so I can do a better job of it." He was tugging at her trousers, so she arched her back, letting him work them off her hips and down the slender columns of her legs, followed quickly by the peel of flannel. Again he gave her time to adjust by returning to her lips. Slowly he eased her uncertainty with long, leisurely strokes of his hand. When he reached the juncture of her thighs to touch the heart of her passion, she was primed to move in time to the enticing rhythm he began. Her response had Marsh in an agony of arousal. Her impatient hands pulled at the rough wool of his shirt, but he stilled them, knowing that if he felt the hot silk of her skin against him, he couldn't trust himself to hold back. He could tell by her erratic breathing that she was on the edge of discovery. To gift her with that pleasure, he would rein in his own rampaging desires. But it sure as hell wasn't easy.

"Marsh . . . please," she gasped against the insistent pressure of his mouth. She wasn't sure what it was she needed, only that she needed and needed badly. There had to be some relief for the incredible tension screwing up tightly inside her.

Then his kiss deepened, and his tongue thrust hard and compellingly into her mouth. When he claimed her untried body with his touch in that same almost ruthless manner, her senses spun then wildly shattered. She cried out and clutched at him, waves of ecstasy shuddering through her before she went limp and trembling as he continued to caress her with his kiss. When he lifted up, Joelle sighed in exhaustion. Her candor, as always, surprised and delighted him.

"Is there much more to this loving? I don't know if I can hold up for it."

His chuckle rumbled in the darkness, and she could picture his grin and those delectable dimples. "Almost finished."

Joelle let herself float in a wonderful lethargy while he went through the frantic movements of disrobing beside her. All weariness fled the minute he came down over her in a gentle press of bared male flesh. He held himself above her on arms that shook with a rigid control that all but deserted him when she raised her hips to move with exultation against him. She made a small sound in her throat, one of anticipation, not anxiety, and snapped the restraining thread of his will. His last thought about gentleness escaped him when he felt the heat of her.

"Oh, God, Jo," he whispered gruffly. "Hang on."

He angled between her parted thighs and pushed, hard, until her untested flesh surrendered. Her slight gasp was swallowed up by his fierce, starved kisses. The stiffness of her shock abated the instant he moved inside her, stroking, stoking a passion untouched by anything she'd experienced so far. Her moan was muffled against his avid mouth. A desperate frenzy possessed her. Meeting the rough thrust of his hips seemed to ease it, so she moved with him, matching his urgent tempo, encouraging the sawing rasp of his breathing with her own uneven gasps. She choked out his name as the wild, now familiar pressure grew, building to an explosive conclusion that rocked the very foundations of her soul. She could feel him driving hard and determined through the spasming clutches of her body until a ragged groan was torn from him.

Then there was the marvelous quiet of a just passed storm. Marsh was kissing her, but Joelle was too dazed and drained to give back more than a weak response. He eased from her, drawing her close in a circle of care as her body trembled for long, intensely sensitive minutes. Then, with a soft murmur of contentment, she curled into him, whispering just before sleep overtook her, "I love you, Marshall."

19

COFFEE. STRONG. DARK. Close to scorching. The scent was a stark contrast to the crisp cold of morning, inviting but not tempting enough to lure Marsh out of the cozy cocoon of blankets. He pulled the covers up to warm his ears and listened for Olen's earthshaking snores. It must be close to dawn to be so frigid inside the bunkhouse, he thought, and the last thing he wanted was to crawl out of a toasty bed to let that chill air at his long johns.

Only he wasn't wearing long johns.

He wasn't wearing anything but his socks.

Shock did what coffee couldn't to snap the tightly wound spring blanking his mind. Awareness brought him upright, clutching the blanket around his naked shoulders. His head bashed into a low overhang, and his confusion was complete. A tent? What the—?

Jo.

With his memory came a flush of heat, warming him right down to those woolly socks. He lay back on the bedroll with a satisfied smile. Last night . . . last night had been incredible. Marsh closed his eyes, refusing to let conscience intrude as he savored every second in his memory. Nothing would ever sound so sweet as the echo of his name upon her lips, all faint and breathy in the throes of ecstasy, or be as satisfying as that first feel of her clasped tight and fiery around him. He hadn't meant to possess her quite so roughly, not her first time, but God . . . the exquisite madness of the moment had driven him beyond the brink of self-control. She was always doing that, knocking his sensibilities out from under him. He couldn't seem to catch his balance. But he was sure of one thing—she was made for him. And damn if she wasn't going to come back in to him, he was going out to get her!

One look at her stony features as she squatted before the fire made him quickly abandon that idea. Something was wrong. She stared at him through eyes as impenetrable as steel. Caution tempered his eagerness.

"Morning," he ventured as he climbed out of the tent, the blanket still around him.

Her reply was clipped and as cool as the dawn air. "Get dressed. We've got a lot of ground to cover." With that, she flung the contents of her cup into the fire. It sizzled hot and steamy, like the moment, as she rose up in a picture of impatience. "I want to be back on the trail in fifteen minutes."

His brows shot upward. "So much for a shave and a hot breakfast," he grumbled.

Her brows arched, too. "Let me remind you that you—"

"—were the one who insisted on coming. Right. I'll be ready in a minute." So much for a cozy toss in his bedroll. Her mood would have frozen a smelting furnace solid.

Marsh ducked back inside the tent. He yanked dry trousers from his pack and began to dress. He stuffed clothes still damp from the day before into a careless wad and snatched up the bedding. What the hell was the matter with her? He knew she was a bear when she first woke up, but he'd expected something a little warmer *this* morning. A whole hell of a lot warmer. Disappointment gave way to irritation. She was all business again, as if last night had never happened. He couldn't pretend that was true. His every nerve was taut and tingling with remembrance. He was so aware of her that his insides burned with longing. She might be in the mood for cool, distancing games, but he wasn't. Angrily he backed out of the tent and jerked up the stakes, collapsing the structure into a form as limp as his expectations. By the time he had it rolled and stowed, he still had five of his allotted minutes left. Time for coffee and an explanation.

She had the cup ready for him and extended it ginger-ly as if feeding raw meat to some dangerous creature that might devour her. In an attempt to bridge the frosty barrier she'd slammed between them, Marsh slid his palms over the backs of her hands. Her reaction was explosive. She jerked away, letting him fumble for the cup and curse as hot coffee sloshed out.

"How's your ankle?"

She jumped so quickly from one subject to another that his mind derailed. "What? My ankle?" He looked down somewhat blankly and gave it a testing twist. He felt a dull twinge, but it was holding up much better than his composure. "It's fine. Jo—"

"Then we'd better get going."

Joelle started to turn away, and Marsh's patience dissolved. She stood rigid when his hand closed about her wrist. Her eyes were wide and her expression somewhat frantic when she lifted her face to his intense gaze.

"Jo, talk to me."

A flare of panic brightened her stare then ebbed to a flinty opaque. "Everything's been said."

Her flat response ignited a flurry of confusion. He wanted to shake her, to hold her, but her stiff posturing forbid it. Instead he argued, "Nothing's been said. Jo, we made love last night. I want to know what you're feeling. It was your first time. Did I hurt you? Are you upset? Why the hell are you acting like we're strangers?"

"How should I act? What did you expect? We agreed on one night and no ties. I'll hold to that bargain. It's just . . . hard." She took a quick, ragged breath then continued evenly, as if she had rehearsed these words. "I promised I wouldn't cling and I won't. You have to let me cope the best way I can. Don't crowd me, Marsh. Please. Not now."

She turned away, tugging until he released her. He stood watching her shoulder her pack, seeing her arrange her fea-tures into grimly set lines. He couldn't let things alone. He had to know.

"Are you sorry?"

Joelle looked at him for a long, solemn moment. Her stare pierced through him.

"No," she told him frankly. "No, I'm not sorry."

Then she strode away, denying him the chance to reply or to see more of what worked behind her guarded eyes. He growled in frustration as he slipped on his heavy pack and followed her.

It was another long, arduous day of traipsing through drifts, investigating every slough, every tributary, walking over rough terrain and around emotions stretched tauter by the mile.

Though Joelle didn't look back, she did slow her pace to accommodate his bad ankle and her own discomfort. He'd loved her well and hard, but that slight, chafing pain wasn't what grieved her. It was the agony of easing out of his arms at dawn and the effort it took not to touch him as he lay sleeping. If she'd remained, she knew her will would have been worn down. She was hanging on by a figurative thread as it was. If the strain grew any greater on her heart, she feared she would fall into Marsh's arms and beg him shamelessly not to leave her. She couldn't endure that loss of pride or that lessening of his respect.

She would continue the sham of indifference and maintain her icy pose. But regrets? Lord, no. And deep within her, where tensions grew and yearning gnawed voraciously, she was confronted by the terrifying truth—once wasn't enough. As long as he was near, as long as he was within sight or earshot, and within the reach of her arms, she would want him. She would need incredible strength to resist him.

But she would. Because he was not the only one who valued his word once given.

They'd put almost another entire day behind them. They were cold, tired, and cross. The sky was as overcast as Joelle's glare, and a sleety rain spit down on them. It threatened to become as nasty as the storm of frustration tightening Marsh's gut. But Joelle plunged on upstream, afraid to stop, afraid of spending another night beneath that tented canvas with Marshall Cameron. For half the day she'd been blinking back the need to weep. The other half she'd spent swallowing down the desire to scream. Her emotions were on a razor-sharp edge when her foot slipped on a slick outcropping of rock. His hands were there to catch her around the waist, drawing her back into the steadying wall of his chest.

Long after the threat of danger passed, he kept her in that snug embrace, and she allowed herself the luxury of his care. With hours of tension behind them, it was a blissful relief to surrender, just for a moment. His cheek rubbed into her hair. His breath blew, warm and inviting, against the nearly frozen skin of her temple, rasping in a needy sigh.

"Jo . . ."

The low, seducing tone reached through her daze of compliance. Angrily Joelle jerked away from his devastating nearness. How could she have forgotten herself so easily with one touch? With one husky sigh? She started forward with a long, distancing stride . . . and disappeared.

"Jo?" Marsh stood, stunned into bewildered immobility. The ground had simply swallowed her up right before him. A sudden jolt of panic shattered his surprise. "Jo! Oh, God!"

Marsh fell to his knees on the slippery rocks. He reached into the tangle of brush and found not ground but frigid water, how deep he didn't know. Wild, terrifying images of her father being sucked beneath the fateful waves of Lake Superior sent cold tremors through his belly.

"No!" he cried hoarsely to fight off the vision, to deny the fates their chance to take Joelle from him. Furiously he rid himself of his pack, meaning to plunge into the icy unknown after her.

The shock of cold had struck the breath from Joelle. She wasn't sure at first what had hit her. Her shout of alarm had been instantly chocked off as liquid flooded her mouth and cut off the breath in her throat. Oh, God, she was under water, and she was going to drown. She struggled to overcome her terror, but her limbs were numb, and a gripping network of branches snagged her thrashing legs, beginning to drag her down. Something caught her pack, holding her fast like a sleek otter in a pelter's trap. She couldn't free herself. Her lungs burned. In desperation she wrestled out of the straps and gave her body a mighty twist. Her head and arms broke the surface. Before she could gasp for a gurgling breath of air, Marsh had her. He captured her flailing hands just as the cold waters surged in a deadly downward pull, and he heaved with all his strength.

Coughing and beset by great gulping sobs, Joelle was
hauled up into Marsh's frantic embrace. They clung together
for a timeless moment of thanksgiving, not minding the wet,
untouched by the cold.

"Jo, God, Jo, I thought I'd lost you." His fingers clenched in
the sodden strands of her hair. He was shaking almost as badly
as she was. His heart was beating so hard he feared it would
bruise her where she pressed against him. But he couldn't let
her go. He couldn't let her go. His eyes squeezed shut in an
agony of relief, and his arms tightened, trying to surround her
in safety, trying to engulf her with all the protective panic
thickening inside his chest.

For a while all Jo felt was the sweetness of fresh air and
the security of Marshall Cameron's embrace. She grabbed
greedily at both. Then, when his solid strength had convinced her that she was safe, her mind began to process
what had happened, first in jerky bits and pieces, then with
a cold logic.

"Water," she gasped against the warm flesh of Marsh's
neck. "It was water."

"Shh. It's all right."

"No. Marsh, you don't understand." It took some doing
to lever out of his fierce grip. She looked up at him in a
fever of clarity. The concern clouding his gaze told her he
was fearing for her sanity. He was quick to jerk one of the
blankets from his pack and begin to towel her hair before it
froze. She endured his care for a moment then pushed at him.
"No. I'm fine. Just think. Why would anyone go to the trouble
of making water look like solid ground?"

Comprehension dawned. "To try to hide something."

She struggled up, fighting against the drag of wet clothes
and the paralyzing chill quivering through her limbs. The
single blanket was scant insulation from the cold. Marsh rose
with her, his hands on her elbows, his support unwavering
but with objection tightening his face. She ignored him, just
as she ignored the gathering shock to her system as adrenaline
flowed.

"It's got to be here."

She pulled from him and abruptly started wading through
the snowy banks flanking the trail.

"Jo." She didn't respond. She just kept floundering onward. "Damn." Marsh lurched after her.

Soon it was apparent that she wasn't struck by madness. They came through an opening in the trees to a pond, a large natural cove that was crammed to overflowing with logs. Incensed by the sight, Joelle continued along the edge of the inlet until she found what she was looking for.

Marsh stared in puzzlement at the small portable sawmill erected in the woods and at the great pile of branded butt ends heaped nearby, all marked with the Superior S. Joelle lifted one of the thin discs of pine and studied it in a mounting rage.

"What is all this?" Marsh asked.

"Our den of thieves," she told him tersely. "They coax hundreds of logs into this pond then slice off the branded edges so they can cut another brand into the unmarked butts. Right under our noses. Clever. Very clever. And from the way they blocked the stream with brush, no one would ever guess there was an outlet here. All they had to do was wait for another drive to pass, then push these logs out into it. No one would have been the wiser."

"Now what?"

She looked out over the swell of logs and scowled dangerously. "We know how. Now we find out who."

Joelle snatched up an abandoned peavey in awkward, nearly frozen fingers and stalked to the edge of the water. She stretched out toward the nearest float of pine and nudged it until one of the freshly sawn ends turned toward them. She frowned.

"What?"

"See that mark?"

"A cross?"

"That's Tom Christiansen's brand. He cuts in the section upstream. He's been trying to buy out the Superior for years. Now he's found an easier way to make a profit off us. He probably planned to push these out when he brings his own downstream. Damn him. Well, he won't get away with it."

Marsh's thinking was a little less impassioned. "What are the chances that any of this will be left by the time the authorities get here?"

Joelle stabbed at the stolen log. "None."

"So how are we going to catch this pirate?"

She sighed harshly. A terrible quivering was beginning to seep along her bones. She fought it, hanging onto her fury to keep the tremors at bay at least a little longer. "By taking what evidence we can carry."

"Or," Marsh began thoughtfully, pulling the blanket tighter about her, "we can try to catch him red-handed." He smiled at her attentive look. She was starting to look very cold, and he wanted to get her away from here, back to where he could build a fire and strip the wet things off her. But she was so damned stubborn. The Superior came first. Urgency forced him to do some fast thinking. "What say we post some of the Superior's men and see who comes to get this equipment and move the logs?"

Joelle's initial enthusiasm dimmed to silence.

"What?" he asked when he saw her expression change.

"I'd rather not do that."

"Why?"

"Because I'm afraid some of the Superior's crew was involved in this. That's the only explanation. Who else would know exactly when we were moving our logs? Who else would blend in well enough to steal from us without arousing suspicion? That's a lot of timber. They must have been funneling it in night . . . and day."

Marsh was silent now. He was thinking of the men he knew, those who had befriended him, those he admired for their unflagging honesty. Who among them would do such a thing to him? To Lyle Parry's daughter?

It was the sight of Joelle's fitful trembling that finally jerked him from his glum considerations. "I'll pull some men from the H and B," he concluded. Then his mood grew stern. "We'd better get back and make camp before you freeze to death in those wet things."

Joelle simply stared at him as if she were readying to rebel against the suggestion. But when her teeth began to clatter, she knew the truth of what he was saying. She nodded and was about to leave the sight of someone's treachery when her eye caught something bright upon the ground. A tobacco pouch. Curious, she bent to pick it up then stiffened with recognition.

"Jo? What is that you have there?" When she didn't answer right away, he stepped closer and was alerted by her hard expression and by the sudden shadows that stole into her gaze. "Do you know whose that is?"

She clutched the bag tighter in her hands. Of course she did. It had been a gift from her. "It's Guy's."

The information hung tensely between them as they made their way back to where Marsh had shucked off his remaining supplies. Joelle's had been lost. He carried her most of the distance as her limbs gave in to the fearsome trembling. She huddled miserably, quaking with cold and delayed shock while he pitched the small tent. The damp clothes were beginning to freeze against her chilled flesh.

"Here." Marsh fished a pair of his dry long johns out of his pack and passed them to her. "Put these on while I get a fire going. Toss out the wet things so I can stake them up to dry."

Joelle eyed him in a moment of mulish caution, but he paid no heed as he hurried to gather up wood. She shook off her own foolishness, not about to die of exposure to salvage some nonexistent modesty. Crawling into the tent, she wiggled out of the cloying garments and flung them outside. Marsh's blanket chafed her numbed flesh as she rubbed it dry. The fit of his long underwear was far from perfect, but the feel of it was one of indescribable warmth. She was huddled down inside his bedroll, fighting down the wracking tremors, when Marsh slipped in.

"How are you doing?"

"F-f-fine."

He gave her a wry smile. "Sure." He adjusted the lacings on the flaps then eased down beside her. He was wearing dry wool flannels next to his skin, having hurried into them outside where he had more room to maneuver. The pitch of the tent wasn't high enough for him to sit naturally, so he lay back on his elbows. "Our things should be dry by morning providing the rain holds and nothing four-legged makes off with them."

"Now there's a c-comforting thought."

He grinned, his teeth flashing white in the dimness. He saw the way her hands shook as they clutched the edge of the bedroll to her throat, and his mood sobered. "'Fraid I don't have a handy number two to heat something up for you, even if we had something to heat up." He left the rest unsaid. All their foodstuffs had gone down with her pack. She shivered when she thought of it, but Marsh's cheeriness cut through her dark musings. "But . . . being ever prepared for emergencies, I did have the foresight to bring along something useful."

Joelle looked in amazement at the bottle of brandy he produced. Why should she be surprised, she thought with a rusty chuckle. "You'd be a real handy fellow to have around—if we were in a nice cozy parlor in the middle of B-Boston."

"Ah, now, don't be mean or you might find yourself sitting out by the fire with just your skin to keep you warm."

She scowled at his threat and muttered crossly, "I do apologize if I've insulted your ingenuity."

"That's better." He took a deep swallow from the bottle and made a warm, murmuring sound of appreciation. "Just the thing to cut the cold."

"And without food in our stomachs, we'll both be drunk as skunks." Even as she complained, she was reaching to take the bottle from him.

"I can think of worse things to be. We're warm, we're dry, we've got good liquor—what more do you want?"

Joelle didn't touch that one. As she tipped the bottle, she risked a glance at him. Stripped down to his longies, he was stretched out in a picture of lazy comfort. It was a very appealing picture. She took an unexpected breath and choked as the brandy burnt down the wrong way. Before he could question the cause of her distress, she returned the offering so he could indulge in another taste.

They shared their meager ration of comfort for a long, silent minute. As the contents in the bottle lowered, their awareness of each other heightened. The liquor created a fuzzy relaxation of their willpower, and Joelle began to wonder why she wasn't enjoying the companionable warmth of Marsh's arms. That digressing thought shocked her back to sobriety, and she staunchly refused the next pass of the bottle.

Marsh's mood had turned increasing dour as he contemplated what little brandy was left. While Joelle was preparing for an attack upon her resolve with some silkily seductive overture, he was considering something on an entirely different track that was far from flattering to the woman in her, but a relief to her flagging resistance.

"Jo, what are we going to do about what we found?"

His direct question brought an instant bridling of her defenses. "About what?" she replied testily.

"Guy's pouch."

"We don't know anything."

"Don't we?"

That challenge hung between them. Joelle squirmed uneasily, fighting the obvious truth with her inner faith. "I don't believe it, Marsh. I just don't. I can't imagine Guy doing such a thing."

Her stubbornness provoked Marsh's temper. He tried to rationalize in his foggy thinking that she was refusing to see reason—not because she was fiercely protecting his rival. "What do you need, Jo? His confession carved on the butt of one of the Superior's logs? Who had better opportunity? You said yourself that he doesn't usually work the downriver runs. Ask yourself why the sudden change. And who had better motive?"

"What motive?" she demanded, truly angry now because he was forcing her to consider things she didn't want to face, things that made too much sense to her mind and were unimaginable to her heart.

"To get back at me. My logs, my profit."

"That's crazy."

"Is it?"

She struggled for a way to support her instincts against circumstance. Guy? No. She knew he could never be guilty of such a thing. She just knew, even as the damning evidence overwhelmed her. Confusion shook the foundations of her faith, and her efforts to hold firm made her belligerent.

"Yes, it is. I've known Guy Sonnier all my life. He's a good, decent man." Marsh's doubting gaze prodded her into a harsh conclusion. "And I trust him more than I trust you."

Marsh didn't recoil visibly, but his eyes narrowed and the lines about his mouth tightened. "I'm sure he'll appreciate your loyalty when the troops come to arrest him."

Joelle's chest constricted with fear. If Guy were arrested, she would have no one when Marsh returned to Boston. There would be no one left on this harsh peninsula who cared for her. That unaccustomed fright manifested itself as anger, and she was quick to attack its source. "You're only after Guy because you know I'll be with him once you're gone."

That fact blew a hole in his confidence big enough to drive a six-horse team and bobsled through. He was instantly tormented by the image of Joelle and the dark Canadian entwined together in lustful pursuits. Everything inside him rebelled. Reason was overshadowed by consuming jealousy.

"Why should it matter to me who you bed down with after I leave?"

That was a cruel, inexcusable thing to say to her. He regretted speaking the words even before he heard her sharp intake of breath. He damned the spite in his heart that made him want to strike back at her for seeking happiness with another. But that didn't ease his misery.

"Jo—"

She made a low, anguished sound. It slashed his conscience with merciless intent. He reached for her, but she rolled away, curling protectively into the folds of his bedroll.

"Jo, I'm sorry. I'm sorry."

He touched her hair, and she shook her head, giving a harsh cry. Her body was wracked with fierce tremors of repressed weeping and lingering cold. Each jerking movement of her shoulders carved his blame more deeply. With an oath, he fit himself against her rigid back and wound his arms about her middle. She fought the closeness, but he overcame her struggles.

"Don't, Jo," he chastened softly. "You need the heat. You're still chilled to the bone."

Though she couldn't throw off his embrace, she rejected his comfort by lying still and stiff. Even as her heart pounded madly, she made her voice contrarily steady.

"I don't need you, Cameron."

He was silent for a long moment, his grip never easing. Then she felt his lips brush over the back of her head, just a slight stirring through her hair, and his words were a matching caress. "I know. You can take care of yourself."

She wished there had been insult rather than admiration in his tone. Then she could have kept her anger stoked high against the seditious warmth of his body curved behind her. But she was too weary and worn out to fight anymore. Her heavy sigh spoke of surrender but not defeat. Tucking her bare feet up to chafe a heating friction along his calves, she let her eyes close, shutting out her worries so her spirit could heal in slumber.

Marsh held her throughout the night. It was late before he was able to sleep. Even then his thoughts were troubled, making for a restless slumber. What if Guy Sonnier was their log pirate? How was Marsh going to pursue his punishment without damaging Joelle's heart? And if Guy were innocent, how was Marsh going to leave Michigan knowing Joelle would find comfort in the Canadian's arms? It was hard to know what to wish for.

20

JOELLE AND MARSH started off at daybreak like tense, wary strangers, leaving the stream to trek cross-country. By cutting across at an angle, they could meet up with the Superior crew as they brought the rest of the timber to the lake. The ground was higher now, so the snow was only knee-deep at its worst. As they didn't speak and there was no food to break for, they made good time. By late afternoon, they could hear the sound of rushing water. By dusk, they caught their first welcome sight of Superior logs crowding a swollen stream.

Guy was working the logs from the opposite bank and didn't see them. Marsh hid the churn of his misgivings as he watched Joelle's eyes darken in dismay. She was looking at a dear friend. She was wondering if he could have betrayed her for money. Marsh's grievances gave way to a gentler compassion. His arm became a bolster about her stiff shoulders. She started to pull away, but something in the set of his features stilled her.

"We don't know anything for sure, Jo," he said softly.

She searched his eyes with a needy urgency, then sighed. Her voice was flat, resigned. "Yes, we do. He came down to Eagle River with me when we came to pick up the pay. I saw him talking to Christiansen in town. No one else left camp, so he was the only one who could have arranged things. Dammit, Marsh, I've known him all my life!"

She didn't resist this time as he enfolded her close into the wool of his mackinaw. He held her tight as a hard spasm of remorse rocked through her. Then with a hearty sniff she pulled away, her expression set and determined.

"We won't let on we know anything. Let him believe he's safe. Then we can have some men follow him and others watch the pond. We'll let him convict himself."

Marsh said nothing. He could see how hard she was struggling, and his respect for her soared. He put a mittened palm to one cheek, and she rewarded him with a grim smile that said she was going to be fine. He wished he could believe that.

Olen spotted them from the deck of the wanigan.

"Ho, Yank!" he bellowed and gave his arms a windmilling wave. By the time they reached the river's edge, he'd maneuvered the barge ashore. He scooped Marsh up in a rib-crushing hug and held him with feet dangling helplessly until his former bunkmate groaned in wheezy protest. "Goot to see you, Cameron. I thoughts for sure you'd be bound for Boston by now, but it's glad I am you still be here." He set the smaller man down and let him catch his breath.

"I hope there's food aboard," Marsh said with a grin. "I'm hungry enough to eat boiled boot soles."

"I fix you up but goot. Come, you and Miss Jo, I make you big meal."

True to his word, Olen had them stuffed like holiday birds within the hour. Though he kept a happy booming chatter going, he was well aware that something was not right with his friend and his lady boss. They didn't offer an explanation, so he didn't ask. But he did wonder. Having spent so much of his married life away from his home, he knew the signs of lovesickness when he saw them.

"Jolie!"

The three of them looked up to see Guy Sonnier leap lightly from shore to deck. Four great strides brought him inside the cabin, where he swept Joelle up into a welcoming embrace. She clung to him, her emotions twisting desperately. Her eyes squeezed shut as she pressed her face to his bearded throat.

As pleased as he was by her greeting, Guy was less than excited to see the company she kept. His black eyes glinted as he nodded to Marsh. Then he said softly to the woman in his arms, "Jolie, I would speak to you. Come outside into the moonlight with me."

She stepped down, unwinding her arms from his broad shoulders. "All right." She saw Marsh tense and gave him a quick, staying glance before leaving the small cabin with her suitor.

"You love her?"

Marsh surprised the big Swede by saying without a pause, "I love her."

"So?"

"So?"

Olen frowned slightly, not understanding. "Why do you let him steal the moonlight with your woman?"

"She's not my woman, Olen. My woman is in Boston." There was finality in the way he said that as well as great sadness. Olen's big heart broke for his friend.

"But not a woman such as this, I wager."

"No, not such as this."

"So, you will do what?"

Marsh shoved out of his chair brusquely and moved toward one of the filmy windows. From it he could see the silhouette of Joelle and Guy standing close together at the edge of the deck. He tried to ignore the way his chest jerked. "I'll do the right thing."

"For whom?"

He said nothing then, but the big logger's words would haunt him throughout the night. And echo through many others.

"This is a surprise, Jolie. I did not expect to see you here. My eyes are always glad for the sight of you."

Joelle smiled at that crooning bit of flattery, and at the same time she fought to steel her heart and betray none of its anguish. She made herself stand unflinchingly as his hand brushed across the fan of her shoulders. *Oh, Guy, how could you do such a thing?*

"I have something to say to you, Jolie, and I would speak it now before my courage fails me."

Her head jerked up, and her eyes scanned his painfully familiar face. Was he going to confess? A burn of remorse quickened in her eyes, making his features waver. And she almost stopped him from saying more. But she waited and listened, pretending not to know the vileness he was about to admit.

"Joelle, I have made no secret of how I feel for you. I have gone about it in many wrong ways when I should have told you straight what is in my heart. I love you, Jolie."

She stared at him. This wasn't the confession she'd prepared for. She couldn't speak, and after a moment's silence Guy continued with mounting awkwardness.

"I know you have . . . feelings for the Yank, and I respect them. He is a good man, but he will be gone soon, and I would not see your heart broken. I do not mind that you cannot love me now, but I know it will come in time. We are of the same people, of the same spirit. And we are friends, no? I would care for you, Jo. I would give you my name along with my heart, and that he will not do. Marry me, Joelle."

She swallowed, and it was like trying to force a calked boot down her constricted throat.

His rough hand stroked along a very pale cheek, his fingertips gliding with sensitive care. "I see you were not ready to hear these words. Do not answer now. Think on what I ask. I will not always be the man you see now. I will be able to buy you nice things, a fine house if you will have patience and trust me."

Trust you? You would provide for me with money stolen from my father's woods? The anguish just kept building. *How could you, Guy? How could you think I would never find out the truth?*

Gently his hand curved about the back of her head, holding it tipped upward so he could bend his own to touch his lips to her brow, to her temple, to her cheek, and finally to her own chill lips. His beard was softly abrasive on her tender skin and his kiss, softer still. Her eyes remained closed when he leaned away, and when she heard his step and felt the boat sway with the shift of his weight as he jumped ashore, tears pooled along the sweep of her dark lashes.

Watching her proud shoulders quake, Marsh ground his teeth in helplessness. He had no right to offer comfort, and her firm stance implied she would not welcome it from him.

So he let her stand there, bracing the cold wind and the bitter truth alone long after darkness settled.

It took two days for the caravan of timber to reach Lake Superior. Marsh was awed, as always, by the vast stretch of clear water, now freed of its winter cover. The slightest breeze ruffled the calm surface, creating an agitation that sent the logs bobbing as they pushed out from the mouth of the stream. While a crew of sackers went back to ferret out the logs that had drifted and gotten hung up in swampy places, the rest of the jacks herded the rafts of pine toward the Superior mill.

It had been a tension-fraught two days for Marsh, being so close to Joelle as she worked on the wanigan with Olen, but unable to express any of the passion beating hard within him. His mood grew unbearably surly whenever the pretty manager spent time with Guy. Olen watched over Marsh, offering quiet companionship when Marsh was of a mild temper and standing clear when he grew explosive. Emotions massed and boiled until Marsh couldn't sit beside Jo at the table without longing to grab her up tight and never let go. Joelle was wise enough to stay out of sight and out of reach for most of the long hours, but when they came together for even the most innocent of reasons, the air thickened with a raw intensity, as charged as the gray clouds gathering over the lake. Their attraction grew by the minute, worsened by the hour, into a dangerous thunderhead just waiting to tear loose.

It couldn't continue, Marsh finally admitted. His concentration wavered, and his willpower was practically nonexistent. God, he wanted her. She was driving him mad. His brain grew feverish when she was near. His heart felt hollow when she was not. She said she would not succumb again to the passion they'd shared, and he had to respect that wish, even if it made him pace all night long like a caged and cornered animal.

The storm broke in full fury when the logs were within hours of the mill. The water rose from faint ripples into dangerous waves as they boiled toward shore. Driven on the cutting force of the gale, sheets of icy sleet slashed at those who tried to hold the rafts of pine together. If the chains snapped, the logs would spill hither and yon, riding the wild pull and ebb of the current until left to litter the shoreline for miles. Every inlet would be yellow with Superior pulp logs, and it would take weeks and the cost of hiring tugs to pick up the lost pine.

Standing on the bow of the wanigan, Joelle cast an anxious eye over the roiling float of timber. Her crew was out in the middle of it, locking in their stance with the calks on their boots, using their peaveys to minimize the damage and hold the mass together. Her cheeks were scorched by the punishing weather, and her drenched hair was plastered to her skull. Wind molded her woolen coat against her and threatened to tear her grip from the wooden rail.

"Come inside, Jo," Marsh shouted into the scream of the wind. "There's nothing you can do out there."

Joelle looked up at him through wide eyes. His rain-whipped hair clung in frozen strands along his creased brow. His words kindled a fierce objection inside her.

"Nothing I can do here," she yelled back, "but plenty I can help with out there."

Marsh followed her glance to the undulating roll of the logs and the men who fought not to fall between them. As he watched, he saw Chauncey Sonnier's footing slip on the wet bark. A quick stab of his peavey to anchor him was all that prevented the experienced logger from being mashed by the seething boles, that and the brute strength it took to hang on.

"The hell there is!"

By the time he looked back, she was reaching for one of the extra peaveys lashed to the rail. Believing that her slender bones would snap at a bump from one of those wave-tossed logs, Marsh grabbed her wrist. Her eyes flashed, alarmed then angry.

"Let go."

"Not until you give up this foolishness."

She didn't have time to argue and was annoyed by his interference. "I've been walking logs since I was ten and I've never fallen."

"It only takes once."

"Let go. I know what I'm doing."

"Stop trying to prove that you're a better man than anyone here and accept the fact that you're not one."

With a snarl of outrage, she shifted to one side to draw him off balance, then flailed hard with the free end of the peavey. It cracked against his ribs with enough force to slam him into the rail, but he didn't let go. Instead he lost what was left of his temper.

Cursing, he gave her captive wrist a merciless twist then wrenched the peavey from her. It clattered to the deck. She swung wildly at his head, but he dodged the blow.

"Jo, stop it! I don't want to hurt you, but I'm not going to let you get yourself killed."

A roar of rage burst from her, and a savage clench-fisted punch narrowly missed rebreaking his nose. Her fist caught him on the cheek with enough velocity to send him skidding backward. Their feet tangled on the wet deck, and they clung together to keep from going down.

As soon as his feet were under him, Marsh wrapped one arm about her, pinning her arms tightly to her side. He jerked her up and, with all the dignity he'd have shown a sack of grain carried her into the shelter of the cabin. Olen took one look at his friend's granite expression and the spitting wildcat he held under his arm and started searching for a means to abandon ship.

"Olen, get us to the mill," Marsh commanded.

"Don't you dare! Stay here. That's an order, Thurston!" Joelle ranted as she wiggled helplessly in the banding embrace.

"I give orders, and you take them, Jo," Marsh reminded her crisply. "Do it, Olen. I've got faith in our crew. They don't need us here in their way. And they don't need the help of a bullheaded girl determined to break her beautiful neck."

Olen looked nervously between them then nodded. "You be the boss, Cameron. I do like you say."

"The boss. The boss!" Joelle hissed venomously at her captor, still trying to land a kick to a vital body part. "You're a greenhorn. A meddlesome, hateful rich boy who's trying to prove he's a man. And I hate you. Do you hear me? I hate you!"

"I hear you, Jo," he said softly. He dragged his struggling burden over to a chair and sat down upon it. Joelle made a bolt for freedom but was quickly snagged about the waist and brought down with spine-cracking vehemence into his lap. He held her there, securing her arms with his and her kicks with the curl of his calves about her legs. She continued to writhe and spit and squirm, dealing out bruises and coloring the air with her descriptive curses. But he held her, keeping her safe until the wanigan left the churning lake and was pushed upstream to the mill.

"We be docked, Cameron," Olen called from the deck, forcing Marsh to face another problem, how to release an indignant Joelle Parry without suffering permanent damage in the process. He ended up carrying her, still pinned beneath his arm, out on deck. Then he realized his mistake. A dozen or so millworkers had gathered to greet the wanigan, and all were standing agog at the sight of him toting Joelle like a rebellious child.

"Put me down," she growled with a dangerous quiet, and cautiously Marsh complied. Her back was to him so he thought she meant to jump across to the dock. Instead, she whirled upon him, striking like a cyclone of pent-up rage. Her stunning slap was followed by a hard two-handed push that knocked him up against the rail and over. A tremendous splash heralded his descent into the icy stream.

The cold was paralyzing, but after the initial shock Marsh floundered to the surface, fighting the weight of his wet clothes and spitting out water. Above him he could see Joelle standing with hands on her hips arrogantly glaring down at him as he thrashed about.

"I am not some weak-willed girl to be bullied about by the likes of you, Marshall Cameron! You've no right to tell me what to do. Don't you ever get in my way again!"

With that she turned, sending the millworkers scattering as she stormed up the dock.

Olen was laughing as he put out his hand to haul Marsh from the water. "Be glad she's in love with you, Yank. Any man who made rough with her like that would have been slain and gutted on the spot."

"The ones she loves, she lets drown," he grumbled. When Olen's features grew grim, he considered what he'd said. Lyle Parry had been family to these men. "That was a thoughtless thing to say. I'm sorry."

The great blond head nodded as the giant hauled him, wet and dripping, from the stream. It took only a second for the air to start him shivering.

"Miss Jo may have the last laugh yet should you catch a chill and turn up your toes."

Marsh gave the Swede a wry smile. "I don't plan to oblige her."

"Then you must get dry and warm. I will send someone to the H and B to bring you clothes." He gave his friend a benign grin and looped an arm about his trembling shoulders. "Until then, I have just the place for you to cook out the chill."

Marsh breathed deep and felt the hot, humid air sear his nose and his lungs. He'd never experienced anything like it. A sauna, Olen had called it, built and enjoyed by his Norwegian coworkers just as they did in their homeland. A bathhouse filled with steaming air instead of hot water. He'd been dubious at first when Olen brought him, half-frozen and quaking, to the two-room log cabin erected near the mill. The first room, he explained, was for dressing and resting, and the second was the bath proper. It took some doing for Olen to convince him to strip off his wet things in exchange for a towel and to advance into the small second room, where benches lined the walls and the smell of pitch was almost overpowering. Olen goaded him inside and shut the door. Remembering what the Swede had told him, Marsh advanced upon the boiler roaring in one corner and ladled water onto red-hot boulders the size of cantaloupes. Steam billowed up to envelop him, and perspiration broke out where his skin had been puckered with cold. He felt like a lobster boiling contentedly in its shell. But he hoped the results would not be as disastrous for him as for his crustacean friend.

Gingerly he eased down on one of the benches, stretching out on his back to hear the dry wood sizzle where he settled. Olen had said his countrymen used the sauna for social gatherings. The miners had quickly adapted to it to get hematite from their pores and to cure hangovers. This ice-cold Yank inhaled deeply to restore the warmth of life to limbs numbed beyond feeling.

He must have grown drowsy, for the next thing he knew there was a sharp hiss as a thick cloud of vapor rose from freshly dampened rocks. A figure emerged from that heated mist—a figure with unmistakably trim legs ending at a thigh-length wrap of towel. Marsh sat up too quickly and was beset by a vague light-headedness. The movement wrung a startled gasp from the newcomer, and he found himself staring up into the bewildered eyes of Joelle Parry.

"What are you doing in here?" The tremor of her voice betrayed how her heart had taken to a wild flutter the moment her gaze touched on the long, bold length of him covered by the scant towel.

"Thawing out, thank you."

She hiked her towel higher, then realized how much more of her legs were exposed. Angrily she glowered at the last person she'd wanted to see. "How did you know about this place?" she demanded.

"Olen brought me."

"Olen?" Her voice was edged with tart suspicion. The big Swede, like all the mill and lumber men, knew she frequented the steamy bath to boil the bad temper from her system. And he'd brought Marsh. Hoping what? "I didn't see your clothes or I wouldn't have intruded."

Marsh was smiling now, letting his gaze appreciate the delicate turn of her calfs and elbows. "He must have taken them to get them dried."

"Or something convenient like that," she drawled sarcastically.

Marsh was just beginning to understand why his friend had been so insistent upon his taking this native cure. Indeed, there was little that ailed him that could not be healed by the contents of the little room.

"Well, I'd better go," Joelle began uneasily as her eyes detailed the firm bared line of lightly furred legs stretched out toward her. Her gaze traveled all the way up to where the towel swaddled his lean hips. If he'd thrown water on her at that moment, her flesh would have given off steam.

"No," he argued quickly. "You don't have to. I was just about done."

"But you have no clothes to put on," she pointed out.

"I guess I'll have to wait until they get here." He smiled with harmless welcome. "You don't have to go. I think we can behave ourselves for a few minutes, don't you?"

Still scowling, Joelle perched on an opposite bench then leaned back with her eyes closed. The tension cording her shapely limbs indicated that she was far from relaxed. Marsh let his eyelids sag to half-mast and continued to watch her, admiring the graceful curve of her throat and the seductive hollow of her collarbone. The towel was knotted above her left breast. One tug . . .

His sudden harsh breath made her eyes snap open. She regarded him warily then eased her guard down a second time. Marsh was feeling giddy by then. He was running with sweat, yet he felt baked and hot. His eyes and mouth were dry. His nose burned. But that was the effect of the sauna. The effect of Joelle Parry was much more devastating. The heat she stirred inside him was parboiling his internal organs. His heart was laboring like the corner oven, and the emotions steaming from it sizzled in intensity. He stared for a long, fascinated minute at a single bead of moisture, following its progress as it sped down the arc of her neck then slowed to a seductive trickle before sliding into the shadowed crevice between her breasts. He closed his eyes tight and struggled to contain pressures seething for release. There had to be some way to control them, some way to vent the passions before they blew. His mind groped for an answer.

Jo.

He couldn't do this to her. One night. They'd both agreed. But how was he supposed to have known that sampling would create a desperate hunger for more? He ached to slake that raging appetite and at the same time knew he couldn't. Knew he shouldn't. Because he was leaving. If it were up to him, he'd spend every minute between this one and that sating his need for her. Then maybe if he stored up enough loving, like a wilderness beast about to hibernate, he could survive the long, cold winter of emotions to come. But she'd said no. She'd begged him with her cool attitude and stiff manner not to push her—her control was just as frayed as his own. And if he couldn't honor vows made in Boston, he had to respect her plea that she be left some dignity. Even if it killed him!

He looked across the mist-filled room and was tortured anew by her image. God, she was beautiful, so unaware of her allure, so natural in her sexuality it made the primitive man in him growl to life. Bound in that brief twist of towel, she was like a precious gift just begging to be unwrapped and cherished. Desire coursed through him in a searing wave of fire, flaming wildly as it sought to devour the boundaries of his restraint. There had to be some way to beat it back, to squelch its heat without quenching its needs. He had to bring the chill back into the sultry woman simmering opposite, a chill founded in cold truth.

"Jo, I'm heading to Copper Harbor in the morning to book passage home."

She uttered no immediate response other than to draw a low hissing breath. Finally her eyes opened. They seemed to shimmer, or was that a trick of the heat? "Will you be back?" she asked.

"Just for my things. I've got some arrangements to make. I've wired the H and B to send a new agent, and I should have a reply waiting now that the lanes are open on the lake. I've got some reports to finish up and . . ."

It was just a small choking sound at first. Then the knot holding together Joelle's towel began to pitch as wildly as the logs out on the lake. The words burst out, unplanned and thick with despair, try as she would to hold them in.

"Oh, God, Marsh. Please. Please don't leave me. Don't go. Please don't go."

21

MARSH KNEW THAT the last thing he should do was go
to her. But there was no way he could not respond to the
incredible anguish in her tone. He crossed the room and sat
down on the bench beside her, hugging her close, feeling
heartbroken as her tears mingled with the sheen of dampness
on his neck. But even as she clutched him frantically, even
as awful sobs convulsed her, she was struggling to haul her
emotions under control.

"I'm sorry, Marsh," she wept miserably. "I know I promised
I wouldn't do this."

He squeezed his eyes shut and let his fingers clench in her
hair. "Shh, Jo. It's all right."

"No, it's not," she moaned softly. "I wish it could be."

"Jo—"

Fearing that her outburst had made him uncomfortable
enough to withdraw, Joelle tried to speak in an even tone.
Her voice was wavery but reasonably firm. "It's not your
fault, Marsh. I thought I could handle this better. And I will.
I promise. But don't leave tomorrow. Not tomorrow. It's too
soon. Can't you stay just a little longer?"

"Oh, God." He sighed, distraught. "I can't put it off anymore, Jo. It's just going to get harder. Don't you see? I have
to go. Tomorrow, a week from now, a month, it won't make
any difference."

Her slender form quaked as it pressed tighter to his, objection in every soft, molding contour. "But, Marsh, we've had no time since . . ." She left that unfinished. She didn't need to explain. Once wasn't enough. There was so much of what they felt for each other left unexplored and beckoning. She couldn't let him go until she'd charted more of that exciting territory, until she knew more of the combustible bliss she'd discovered with him. Her hand stroked restlessly along the sweat-slicked swell of his shoulder, down across the hard plane of his chest muscles, over which taut flesh stretched like hot, damp silk. She felt his breathing alter drastically as her fingertips reached the light furring on his firm abdomen. She let her hand come to rest there.

Joelle raised her head to look at him, feeling herself pierced by the intensity in his eyes. She wet her lips and spoke with a low, tugging urgency. "I love you, Marsh, and I want to love you." She touched his face, smoothing the dappling of moisture from the enticing angle of his cheek. "There are a lot of hours left before morning. Spend them with me."

His throat gave a jerky movement as he swallowed. His voice was hoarse. "Jo, I—"

"Marshall, don't say no."

Dimples danced beneath the spread of her fingers, and his dark gaze turned smoldering. "I wasn't going to."

The husky promise in those words ignited all the frantic feelings she'd held at bay since the night they'd made love out in the woods. Her lips parted, receiving the hard downward plunge of his mouth with a rapturous little moaning cry. There was no sense of time or place as his mouth worked her into a frenzy of need. There was nothing to hold onto except his broad, sweaty shoulders, no reality other than the hungry kisses that grew more mindlessly demanding with every forceful beat of their hearts. The hot, humid air made breathing difficult, and soon they were gasping for breath. But still he didn't stop the kisses, deep, thrusting, tongue-tangling kisses, until they were both light-headed. They slid with a liquid lethargy to the floor.

Suddenly there was a loud, rattling knock on the door, and an unfamiliar voice growled, "Here be your clothes, Mr. Cameron."

Marsh broke from the wet paradise of Joelle's mouth. His cheek slid damply against hers, and for a minute they both panted harshly. They were dripping with perspiration, their sensitive tissues steaming in the thick air.

"Jo, I can't breathe in here."

Her chuckle rasped against his ear. "I don't think this was designed for such . . . activity."

He returned her soft laugh and sagged upon her. There seemed to be so little strength left in his bones. "I feel like a chicken carcass left to boil in the soup. Everything's gone to mush."

Her hands lazily roamed the sleek breadth of his back. Her hips pushed lightly into the cove of his. "I don't know. You still feel pretty fleshed out to me."

"I won't be if we stay in here much longer."

Joelle pushed away. "Get dressed, Cameron."

He hesitated, his dark gaze searching her expression. The sly suggestion of a smile upon her lips sent ripples of relief trembling through him and made an expectation tighten in his groin when she added, "Then I can take my time undressing you someplace less public."

He nearly dragged her into the other room.

There the damp chill puckered their skin. Marsh reached for the tempting knot holding her towel together and gave it a determined yank. It fell open like the outer petals of a rose, revealing her soft and dewy body. It was all he could do to keep from dropping her down right there on the floor. Only the threat of company held his rampant desire in check. Still, he couldn't resist lowering his face to the pearlescent swell of her bosom. His tongue rasped across the tightened buds, licking up the taste of salt until she caught at his head with shaking hands.

"I think I could get dressed faster if you stopped doing that."

He straightened, meeting her stare. "Do you want me to stop?"

She forced herself to mouth the word *no*.

"Come on, then. Let's get the hell out of here and to someplace where we can do something about it."

She needed no further encouragement.

The cold air was more than bracing. It cut through them, heightening every sense to an unbearable degree. With nerves stretched to the limit of patience and pulses throbbing, they began at a walk and were nearly running by the time Joelle led him to her door. Their coats were discarded the second they crossed the entryway. They left their boots at the bottom of the stairs. Gloves, shirts, suspenders, trousers all fell at various intervals on the way up. Marsh removed his long johns outside the door to her room and he skinned hers down even as he backed her toward the bed. She stumbled over the tangle of flannel, and he fell with her. Before they'd finished the first bounce on the mattress, his hands were at her hips, jerking them up to meet the piercing thrust of his. He drove inside her so deeply she was screaming into the hot cavern of his mouth. It took less than two minutes to stoke the long-simmering fires to a blazing consummation. Then as they lay spent and gasping, both were surprised to find they were not exactly in Joelle's bed but rather draped at an awkward angle across the foot of it, more on the floor than atop the once neatly folded quilt. This struck Joelle as wildly funny as she ran distracted fingers through Marsh's damp hair.

"Do you always make love with your socks on, Cameron?"

His contented chuckle blew deliciously warm against her neck. "I might ask the same about your manner of wearing long johns." He bent one knee, raising her leg where it rested over the top of his. Her red flannels were hanging from her ankles, dangling like limp elastic on the prongs of a slingshot. She forgot all about them as he began nibbling along her throat. "Oh, God, Jo, you make me feel so good." He shifted over her, creating a slick, sensuous movement where they were yet joined together. "I could stay lost in you forever."

Joelle shut her eyes, squeezing back tears as she clasped his head to her breast. Forever was a luxury they didn't have. No, she wouldn't cry. She wouldn't reflect on the impossibility of his husky words, or on anything beyond this time they shared. She'd have plenty of time for weeping—later—when he was gone.

She felt him tense slightly, and then came his confused question. "What day is this?"

"What? F-Friday. Why?"

He groaned mightily and beat his forehead against her counterpane. "Oh, damn, damn."

"What, Marsh?"

"I've got to go." Even as he clamored up on his hands and knees, she was clinging to him, hanging about his neck in an attempt to bring him back to her. "Jo, I'm sorry. I forgot all about it. I'm supposed to meet with your uncle to go over some H and B business. He'll know I'm back by now, and we can't have him looking for me, can we?"

Her arms fell slack upon the rumpled bedcovers. Her voice was toneless. "No, of course we can't."

His regret was so strong it was almost physical. He bent to kiss her, but she turned her head aside. He turned her face toward him with the gentle brush of his fingers. "Jo, it won't take long," he promised. "Wait here for me and—"

"No."

He couldn't respond; he was totally speechless with disappointment. Then Joelle pushed him aside, reaching down to tug her long underwear up.

"I'm going with you."

Marsh sputtered. "But, Jo—"

"Oh, for heaven's sake, Cameron, you can be so thick sometimes," she snapped at him crossly as she buttoned the front placket together. "It's not as if I plan to greet him sprawled out naked on your hearth. I'll wait out of sight . . . in your bedroom."

He sucked a quick, raw breath. The innocent lift of her gaze completely undid him. "All right," he heard himself agreeing in hoarse syllables.

Silently they gathered up their scattered clothing and, bundled up once more, walked the mile between the mill and the H&B in the chill grays of twilight. He held her mittened hand tucked tightly in his until they reached the edge of the sleepy mining town. Then he dropped her hand. Joelle said nothing, but that automatic gesture fractured the fragile hold she had on her emotions. She was very quiet as he steered her inside his cabin, after first casting a cautious glance up and down the street. She went straight to the parlor fire without pausing to take off her coat. Huddled there, trying to absorb some of its warmth, she flinched when his hands settled with an intimate weight upon her shoulders.

"Jo?"

"I guess it shouldn't matter," she murmured to the flames.

"What?" He was easing the mackinaw from her, tossing it over a nearby chair. He put his hands on her upper arms and found her muscles taut and resistant.

"That you're ashamed to touch me in public."

"Ashamed?" He sounded geninely surprised. "Jo, I'm not ashamed of you. It's you I was thinking of. I was just trying to protect you from—"

"Talk?" She turned to face him. Her features were sharp with distress. "Do you think I care what anyone says?"

His knuckles grazed her cheek. "I care," he said with infinite tenderness. "If it makes you feel better, I'll step outside and shout up and down the street that I love you."

"That's not what I want," she muttered testily.

"What do you want, Jo? Anything I have is yours. Name it."

"I want you, Marsh."

She said that without hesitation, and he didn't know how to reply. She was looking up at him through great, glorious eyes, waiting for him to say something.

"You'll have my heart until the day I die, and you'll never have to share it with anyone." As he bent to kiss her, he whispered softly, "I wish it could be more."

As she gave herself over to his sweet, stirring kiss, she moaned inwardly, clear to her soul, *So do I, Marshall Cameron. So do I.*

He drew her slowly, steadily, from the room and down a short passageway to a small and intimate chamber. Rough furnishings were crammed into it. Shirtsleeves dangled from the drawers of his clothespress. Books overflowed from the night table. Papers lay scattered across the colorful blanket on his unmade bed. A soft smile touched her lips. *Why, Marshall,* she thought in tender surprise, *you're a slob.*

"It's obvious Spotted Fawn isn't allowed to tidy up in here," she teased softly.

"I like to relax in private." How defensive his muted reply sounded, edged as it was with a tinge of discomfort. Immediately he began to gather up the papers, the books, the clothes, stuffing them out of sight as if ashamed of their presence. Her heart was wrung with pity. Hadn't Marshall Cameron ever before been allowed the simple luxury of making a mess? Or was that considered beneath a Hewlett heir? Joelle touched his arm, halting his anxious, almost angry, movements.

"It's all right. I don't mind. When I first met you, I remember wondering if you knew how to relax. I'm glad to see you do."

He stood at a loss, a pair of suspenders in one hand, a mining periodical in the other. He let them drop and filled his hands with her instead.

"I love you, Jo."

Then with agonizing care he undressed her. When she reached for his shirt buttons, he caught her hands.

"No. I'm expecting company, but I'd be a bad host if I didn't make you comfortable first."

Comfortable didn't describe it.

Once she was naked, he tucked her under his covers and lay down atop them fully dressed. He moved over her, shifting, sliding in a way that had them both wild with desire within minutes. It was a frustration of delight—the friction of the linen against her nudity, the weight of him above her, the thickness of him prodding through the layers of blankets with a potent promise. Then came a loud, impatient pounding on the front door, and with a brief, apologetic kiss he was gone.

Joelle sighed restlessly and tried to force the expectant tension from her body. Was this what it would be like to be Marshall Cameron's wife? Left in an unfulfilled fever while he went to tend his business? What she wouldn't have given to discover that for herself. She rolled over and spent a minute enjoying the feel of the expensive linen. His sheets. He must have brought them with him from Boston because no mercantile in town sold such exquisite bedclothes. Not for the inhabitants of the Keweenaw. Who among the rough immigrants would appreciate such things? Fine, smooth, of the best quality. Not like the coarse stuff she slept between. It would be coarse linen for her and the finest weave for Marshall and his wife.

Joelle clutched at the big feathered pillow and repeated her vow that she would not think beyond this night. Tonight he was hers, and she wouldn't ruin a second of that time with melancholy thoughts, not when she was still wonderfully languorous from his earlier loving. Oh, how that man could excite her, until every inch of her tingled gloriously. Lucky the woman who would have him night after night. *You'll have my heart,* he said. Not much of consolation when she lay alone thinking of him in the arms of another.

But it was all she would ever have of him.

With a soft, bitter cry, she buried her face in his luxurious linen and sobbed.

Marsh paused long enough in the front hall to run a hand through his hair, then opened the door to Tavis Lachlan. The mine captain scowled and pushed his way inside without waiting for an offer.

"Been gone a while, Cameron. Something I should know about?"

Marsh gritted his teeth. "No."

"Close 'ome the door, boy, 'fore the chill gets in." Tavis ambled into the parlor and straight to the brandy. He poured himself a hefty drink, emptying the last of Marsh's supply into his glass.

Marsh let the door slam and stalked in to where his guest stood savoring his liquor. "Did you bring the reports?"

"Got 'em right here." He ignored Marsh's outstretched hand and let them drop next to the empty decanter.

"How's the production on Sixteen?"

Tavis let him pick up the grimy ledger and thumb through the first few pages before answering with a cocky confidence. "Nothing yet, but I know we be close to mineral."

"Yes, I know, your nose advised you of it," Marsh drawled in mild contempt. He studied the figures scrawled on the yellowing paper. Not bad. Actually quite impressive. But he didn't want to think about waste rock and purity percentages. His thoughts ran in another direction.

Tavis cleared his throat and began stiffly, as if it caused him considerable pain to do so. "The man-engine you had installed to carry the lads down into the tunnels, it . . . well, it seems to be a good investment."

Marsh stared at him.

"The men be less weary and work harder. That's all I gots to say."

That was more than enough for Tavis Lachlan.

Then the Cornishman caught sight of a wad of red-and-black plaid on a fireside chair. His brow lowered like a front of threatening clouds scudding across the lake. "That has the look of my Joey's mackinaw."

Marsh glanced at it and claimed easily, "It's mine."

"I ain't no fool, Cameron. What's my girl doing here with you at this time o' night and all alone?" Massive fists began flexing along the bulk of his thighs.

"I told you, the coat is mine. If you think your niece is tucked into my bed, by all means, satisfy yourself with a look." He managed to look just bored enough, just annoyed enough, for Tavis to have doubts. He studied the coat and the man, then held his tongue. His Joey had better sense.

"If that be all, I'll be going," he growled sullenly.

"I don't have anything else. Oh, you might be interested to know that the H and B will be getting a new agent. Someone I trust will not be as easily gulled as you found me to be."

"I won't be missing you, Cameron."

"I'll give my father your best."

Florid color flooded the miner's face. He looked as though he were considering taking a hammer to his rival's son just to see how nicely he'd split down the middle. Finally he smiled, a terrible, teeth-baring smile. "Do that."

After he'd gone, Marsh stood before the fire waiting for the tension to ease from him. He didn't need Tavis Lachlan to tell him how miserably he'd failed in his control of the H&B. The Board had never even seen fit to answer his request that they reassess their decision. That was how little confidence they had in his ability, how little respect they had for him when he wasn't standing in his father's encompassing shadow. Soon he'd be back in it, restrained by its boundaries, his actions dictated by the older man. He'd lost his chance to excel on his own, and now he would take his place as a puppet in the Hewlett organization. How much challenge was there in watching money making more money?

Moody with dissatisfaction, he wandered back into the bedroom and paused at the door. Joelle was curled beneath his covers, sleeping soundly. A wrenching tenderness twisted his middle into knots. He stood for a long while just watching her, thinking of how simple yet complex she was here amid his private clutter. An ache in his throat started swelling until he couldn't breathe properly. Then he crossed over and sat carefully on the edge of the bed. She stirred with a soft murmur, and he saw the dry traces of tears on her cheek. He brushed the back of his hand along that soft curve, erasing the sign of her misery but not its cause. The ache inside him shifted lower, settling, plugging his chest as solidly as ice plugged the Superior's water barrel when it was left out overnight. She and this place were the only good things he'd ever known in his life, the only claim he'd ever made outside that Hewlett shadow. He'd been so proud to make his mark, upon the Superior pines and upon Joelle Parry's heart. For a while everything had seemed so perfect.

Sick with anguish, he rose and returned to the front room. Bracing his palms against the mantlepiece, he stared into the darting flames and tried to convince himself that he was doing the right thing.

Joelle had awakened at the touch of his hand. She'd been groggy and disoriented at first, and by the time she realized where she was and who she was with, he'd risen and left the room. But not before she'd seen the terrible imprint of sorrow on his face. That had shaken her. She'd known, of course, that he was not unaffected by their impending separation. But she'd been so consumed by her own unhappiness that she'd never thought much about how he felt. The brief snatches she'd learned about his home life had left a cold, lonely impression upon her soul. How sad that he would let honor compel him where his heart had no desire to go. Except that he had a woman waiting for him, the woman he would wed and love and who would give him children. He cared for her and she for him. Perhaps she would give him the things lacking in his life.

Joelle hoped so.

Quietly she rose and slipped on her shirt. The floor was cold beneath her bare feet, encouraging her to move lightly, rapidly, into the heated parlor. Marsh stood with his back to her, too engrossed in his thoughts to hear her approach. His shoulders were a broad beam of tension. His neck was corded with it, his breathing shallow from it. She drew near and put a hand on his arm.

"Marsh?"

His head turned toward her slowly, as if it had attained some tremendous weight and were difficult to move. He stared for a silent moment through eyes black and glazed with desolation. Stripped to the soul by it, Joelle surrounded him with her arms, with her love, and held tight. She prayed it would be enough. It was all he would allow her to give him. He shifted, his body angling slightly so he could hug her against him. He let her bend his head down into the curve between his neck and shoulder, inhaling deeply of sleep-tousled warmth, the scent of fresh linens, the hint of acrid steam and salt. She stroked his hair, threaded her fingers through it, and finally brushed it with her lips before whispering, "Come to bed."

"In a minute." He straightened, taking control of their embrace, his hold on her fiercely enveloping. His cheek was pressed hard into her hair, and she could feel his ragged swallowing. It was too soon, too soon to be lost to this emptying despair. There would be time for that when they had to say good-bye. Joelle pulled away and tugged at his slack hands determinedly.

"Come on. Come on," she coaxed softly. She walked backward, clutching his hands, urging him to follow as if her quiet words were all that compelled him to take step after step. By the time they reached the bedroom, his expression had shut down completely. She could feel him drawing back internally, guarding himself against the agony already dulling his dark gaze. She wished she knew what worked within that keen mind of his, the demons dimming the life behind his eyes. Part of him would always be a mystery to her, an intriguing, terrifying mystery, and it was that part of him that would take him away from her.

Unsure if she had the power to reach him, let alone heal him, Joelle relied solely on instinct for the next few moments. He was a stranger now, and she was treading on very foreign, very fragile, ground. But she didn't waver. She moved forward with a bravery born of love. Slowly she undid each of his shirt buttons and eased the coarse wool from his shoulders, tugging the cuffs over his motionless hands. Then she peeled down his trousers, and all the while her gaze remained riveted to his. He sat when she gave a slight push and obediently lifted one foot then the other so she could remove his heavy boots. She left his socks on. With hands not quite so steady, she started down the fastenings of his long underwear, exposing bit by tantalizing bit his broad chest and bare middle. As she leaned forward to slide the faded flannel down his arms, Joelle let her lips hover close to his, brushing them with the light caress of her breathing and finally with a moist, inviting pressure. Before more could develop from it, Marsh turned his head aside.

"What is it? Can you tell me?"

He sucked in a noisy breath and for a moment was so still she was sure he wouldn't answer. Then he spoke in a low, raw voice.

"I don't want to go back. I don't know what to do, Jo."

They were the words she'd longed to hear, yet she couldn't celebrate them because of the lacerating pain she sensed in him.

"Everyone has choices, Marshall. Even you."

He flopped back onto the bed, his flannel-clad legs still dangling over its edge. His forearm covered the torment in his eyes. "I've done everything wrong. I was so damn sure of myself, so arrogant. I made the worst enemy I could have out of your uncle. I let him make a fool of me, let him strip me of my chance to prove myself when I fell head over feet into your arms, just the way the two of you planned it." He didn't see her sudden frown.

What was he talking about? What plan? And what was he mourning so intensely? Giving her up or losing prestige in his father's company? Joelle had an uncomfortable insight that swallowed up his other cryptic reference. It was the H&B. To become the man his father was, the man his grandfather had been, he would surrender everything that was uniquely and dearly him. And she couldn't stop him. Her voice was tight with disquieting pain.

"I'm sorry if loving me made you lose face with those who matter to you."

He looked up at her, and his eyes were alarmingly candid. "I lost more than that. I lost my soul to you, Jo, and I don't know how I'm going to go on without it."

He sounded accusatory, as if she'd purposefully set out to take his jaded soul from him like some tempting devil. Tears threatened but she fought to make her words strong and angry.

"Take it back. I don't want anything from you that isn't freely given. But you don't know how to give, do you? You just buy and sell. I don't know what you're worried about, Cameron. You're just like them, and they'll be very proud."

She never saw him actually move, but suddenly Joelle was flat on her back, and he was above her, pressing her deeply into the mattress with the weight of his torso. His face was mostly obscured by shadow, but what she could see was harshly drawn.

"No. I'm not like them. I'm nothing like them. Don't say that I am. Don't reduce me to someone who can't see beyond figures on a page. Don't force me to fit into a world where everything has to be in its place and perfect, where sentiment is a sign of the weak-minded, where manners are more important than motives. I'm not like that. I can't be like them."

His vehemence scared her. The spasms working the muscles of his face terrified her. The way he shoved her shoulders into the bedding with hard, hurtful fingers made her want to twist away. But beyond his anger and his dark, dangerous intensity, she saw a desperate need to be answered. She did so with one caring touch.

Her palm fit against his rigid cheek. "You're not. Or else I couldn't love you."

So simple. So direct. Marsh felt his heart cartwheel and collapse. With it went all his pent-up rage. All his impotent frustration faded. There was just Jo with her tender gaze and her loving touch. He came apart, his emotions shattering, and yet he felt so wonderfully whole in spirit.

"What am I going to do without you?"

With that soft whisper, everything about him was gentled; his features, his grip, his eyes, his mood. When he lowered himself to take her lips with his, their kiss was gentle, too. He spent the next hour unselfishly giving, giving of soul, of heart, of body. Joelle, having received sensation upon sizzling sensation beneath the attention of his skillful hands and devastating mouth, finally cried out his name in surrender, begging him to come to her and end the exquisite torment straining her every overstimulated nerve to the limit of pleasure.

When he did, he wasn't gentle about it. What they found in that violent burst of shared release destroyed the power of the past and future to interfere with this sweet, sweet time together.

It was daylight when Joelle finally stirred. She was still in Marsh's arms, curled into his side, her cheek pillowed on the swell of his shoulder, their legs entwined. Without lifting up, she couldn't tell if he was awake or asleep so she stayed where she was, absorbing the pleasure of being surrounded by him, by his belongings, by his world.

After a time, when just lying with him wasn't enough to feed the hunger gnawing through her, Joelle moved her hand, letting her fingertips follow the curve of his throat and test the harsh stubble on his chin. His mouth was slack and supple beneath that exploring touch, but when her fingers strayed to his unshaven cheek, they snagged on the deep crease of his smile. Her head rode with the magnitude of his contented sigh, but he didn't move a muscle. If he was determined to be lazy, she would take advantage of it.

During the course of the evening, he had learned her secrets but had shared few of his own. Curiosity emboldened her touch as it left his face and stroked along the hard surface of his chest. By the time she crossed the flat plane of his belly, the pose of lethargy had disappeared. His muscles tensed. His flesh grew taut. And when she put her hand over him, his chest jerked wildly beneath the weight of her head.

Hers was a light, cursory study, the feathery strokes and brief forays teasing him into an agony of expectation. She loved the feel of him, the exciting contrasts, like hot velvet and hard steel. She reveled in the power of her touch, the way it altered the pattern of his breathing from an indolent rhythm into quick, labored irregularity. His hand rose to the back of her head, fingers clenching, kneading, in agitated spasms.

Wanting to provoke him to the same keen edge of incoherent need he'd made her blanace upon for an excruciating eternity the night before, Joelle slowly licked his flat male nipple.

He went crazy.

With a ragged groan, Marsh snatched her hand away from him and dragged her up to press the hard slant of his mouth across hers. His body heaved, toppling her, rolling her beneath him with one conquering move. Her breasts flattened under the force of his chest. Her hips shifted restlessly as his ground over them, letting her feel the hard ridge of desire she'd tormented with her tempting caresses.

"Oh, Marsh," she moaned into his wet, uncontrolled kisses, and the sound seemed to echo back from a distant source.

"Marshall."

He went suddenly still, his head lifting, passion emptying from his expression. "What—?"

"Shh!"

"Marshall?"

The last came from outside the room, from outside the life he'd made for himself in this place, in this woman's arms. The intruding shock staggered him. His breath spilled out in a jagged shiver.

"Marsh, who—?"

"It's my father."

22

"HERE?" JOELLE GASPED as Marsh vaulted off her and began grabbing up his clothes. "What's he doing here?"

"Hell if I know," he replied tersely, stuffing his feet into his long underwear. His eyes were on the bedroom door as if he feared any minute it would burst inward. Joelle followed his gaze and abruptly pulled the covers up to her chin.

"Marsh? What are we going to do?"

He paused in his hurried buttoning to look at her, this woman who was not his Boston fiancée, huddled naked under his blankets. His first impulse was to pull them over her head and bid her to be silent. Then his panic quieted. No. He couldn't do that to her. He couldn't cheapen what they'd shared. He reached down and tossed her the faded flannels.

"Get dressed. I'll introduce you to Colin Cameron."

There was no time for careful grooming. Joelle raked trembling fingers through her rumpled hair, trying her best to slow the hammering of her heart. Marsh's father! What would he think as the two of them sauntered out of the bedroom still flushed from the heat of passion. There was only one thing he could think. Wishing she could just crawl under the bed and hide until he was gone, she finished shoving her shirttail into her trousers and risked a look up at Marsh.

The sudden tenderness of his gaze surprised her, and so did his soft, leisurely kiss. She hung onto him frantically, feeling that she'd rather face a whole team of river pirates than one Boston aristocrat. Marsh stepped back, severing their comfortable embrace. As his hand stroked her pale cheek, he advised, "Try not to look so scared." When she swallowed jerkily, he pinched her chin. "And don't look guilty."

That braced her. She wouldn't approach the Mighty Cameron Senior with her tail tucked between her legs and whimpering. Her posture straightened, and her jaw assumed its belligerent line. Seeing her square her shoulders with courage, Marsh felt a jolt of love shake through him with a cauterizing strength. He was ready to take on anything with this woman beside him. Even his father.

Colin was waiting in the parlor, studying the chunks of crude copper ore Marsh had displayed on the mantel. When he turned at the sound of their approach, the initial welcome warming his eyes chilled quickly. His mouth tightened in disapproval as he looked between his son and the lovely woman with him. Instead of a greeting, he supplied a cool apology.

"I wouldn't have made myself at home had I known you were entertaining. I wasn't expecting to find you with company at this time of the morning."

Marsh tensed at the smooth censure, but there was no hesitation in the way his hand rose to the middle of Joelle's back in unquestionable support. "Father, this is Joelle Parry. Her father owned Superior Lumbering, and now she's my manager there."

Shrewd blue eyes assessed her from head to toe, taking in every untidy strand of hair, every suspicious wrinkle in her unlikely garb. She felt heat climb into her face as she withstood his rude study. "Now I can understand your sudden passion for logging. Good morning, Miss Parry."

Joelle extended her hand with an aggression that set the older man back. Smiling slightly, he took her hand in a firm grip. She could see where Marsh got the rough edges to his handsome looks. Colin Cameron was a compelling man with the same intense gaze and charming dimples. He was dressed much as his son had been when he first arrived on the Peninsula, in expensive city finery, and toting a suave manner to complement it. But there was the same strength in him that she'd felt in Marsh—hard, uncompromising, and just this side of ruthless. She imagined he'd give off as much warmth as a cold slab of granite.

"I can understand much about the son from meeting the father," she replied with an equally chill civility. "It is a pleasure, sir, but you must excuse me. Cameron was about to issue me a draft for my crew's pay. I have a load of timber coming in today and would like to thank my men for a job well done. The days start early up here."

Colin scrutinized the impertinent girl then drawled easily, "So I remember." He glanced at his son, who had gone completely wooden as his young woman spun her lie, but his jaw was set in an intractable fashion just daring his father to challenge her words. Colin Cameron was no fool, either, and he knew good and well what he'd interrupted. Still, he had to admire the lass's quick mind and his son's temerity. "Then by all means don't let me get in the way of your business. But if you don't mind, I would like to bring in the rest of your company before they freeze solid."

Marsh frowned slightly at that cryptic statement. As his gaze followed his father to the door, his hand slipped down to give Joelle's a brief, hard press, as if he feared he wouldn't have another chance.

"Marshall!"

A stiff rustle of taffeta and a cloud of jasmine scent announced the advance of a striking older woman. She marched across the room with a posture a general would envy, to clasp her son by the shoulders and hold him, not to her bosom but at arm's length.

"Look at you! You look as though you haven't seen soap for days. Even here I would expect you to have a care for such things as proper grooming. And what you're wearing! Didn't you bring enough clothing with you? If you'd written, we could have sent some decent clothes. No need to adapt the ways of barbarians to live among them."

Marsh had gone increasingly stiff with each softly issued criticism. There was no surprise or hurt in his expression, so Joelle deduced that this behavior was typical for mother and son. And she was appalled. To greet a child with condemnation instead of affection was unnatural to her thinking.

Her hands had begun to ball into fists of fury when the elder woman stopped chastising Marsh to peer more closely into his face. Her eyes rounded with dismay.

"Oh, my poor darling! Your nose!"

Gloved hands fluttered up to that crooked appendage, and all traces of correct and proper behavior deserted Marion Cameron.

"It's fine, Mother. It got broken in a . . . an accident."

Her dark eyes going dewy with concern, she continued to fuss. "I'm sure it can be fixed. Don't you think so, Colin? We'll have it taken care of as soon as we get you home."

Marsh caught her hands and gently, firmly, lowered them. "It's fine, Mother."

A whisper of movement caught his gaze at the same time it did Joelle's. For the first time, both realized another woman was in the room. A simple oversight, seeing as how the young woman blended so timidly into the furnishings. She was so very pale. Yet when she saw Marsh, an appealing pink of animation touched her cheeks.

Shock jolted through Joelle. This couldn't be—

"Lynette."

The sound of genuine pleasure in his voice, the way he went to embrace her with obvious affection, shattered Joelle, giving her incredible pain. Lynette Barnes. His fiancée. She stood rooted to the spot, watching Marsh hold Lynette close, seeing him touch her cheek with a warm kiss. As Jo watched them, Colin Cameron watched her.

With his arm about the pallid woman, Marsh turned back. Only then did the smile leave his face and a tautness take its place. "Lynette Barnes, Mother, I'd like you to meet Joelle Parry. Jo manages my lumbering company."

Marion Cameron was quick to come to the same conclusion as her husband. She froze with a very proper dread at being confronted with her son's paramour. But Lynette was oblivious to the tension. She gave an astonished little "Ooh" and extended her hand.

"A female manager? Why, how very interesting," she gushed with painful innocence. Her hand was soft and flaccid in Joelle's sturdy grip. "I so hope you will have the time to show us what it is you do for Marshall."

Marion choked and pretended to cough daintily behind gloved fingers.

Joelle forced a smile and said, "It would be my pleasure, Miss Barnes." All the while, her mind was spinning wildly.

Lynette Barnes. Joelle had pictured her jealously a thousand times during her lonely nights. This was not what she had expected. No cool Boston beauty. No icy poise and perfection personified. Those qualities might have helped her understand Marsh's adamance about returning to her. But looking at this woman, she was confused. Lynette Barnes was quite plain and plump. There was nothing in her outward appearance that would drag a man halfway across a continent to be in her arms. Jo was too shaken to hold onto her composure. She had to escape Marsh's family with her dignity intact.

"I really must go."

She started for the door, trying not to run, not caring if she appeared rude, not thinking about the coat she left slung over one of Marsh's chairs. Marsh snatched it up and followed, draping it about her rigid shoulders as she reached the threshold. She couldn't look at him, not after she'd seen the fondness in his eyes when he looked at his betrothed.

"I'll send Olen over for the draft. I don't want to take up any more of your time."

"Jo—" he began softly and intently, but she silenced him with a cautioning look.

"Good-bye, Cameron."

She was out the door, running hell-bent down the muddy street. His emotions churned, spurring him to go after her, but the knowledge that his family waited held him. The time had come to let her go.

He turned back to find them all staring at him. An uncomfortable silence stretched thin. They were looking at him as though he were a stranger—an unkempt stranger, with an unshaven chin and a week of wear washed only briefly by his dunk in the river, sporting laborer's clothes and a broken nose and harboring a woman in his rooms. They must have thought he'd gone crazy from isolation, so far removed from their civilized world. And he didn't blame them.

"So, why are you here? I was just getting ready to book passage home."

"It was your father's idea," Marion began in a huff.

Colin ignored her. He was studying his son, noting the surety of his splayed stance, the way he held his hands half-curled as if to coddle blisters. Aggressive, wary, physical, more suited to rough plaids than smooth serge. His son.

"The Board got two letters, both from knowledgeable men, both with radically different views. For the good of the company and because of my personal involvement with both parties, I offered to settle the matter myself."

"So they did get my report."

"Oh, yes. And I might add they were all impressed, even your grandfather. But a few cautious voices sited Lachlan's experience." He gave a harsh snort. "They don't know him like I do."

"But, Colin," his wife protested, "I fail to see why it matters since Marshall will be leaving with us. It seems a great waste of time, just as this whole business forcing our son to stay up here has been a waste of time. He should have been at home, preparing himself to assume his seat on the Board. I fail to see the value in getting one's hands dirty."

"You always did, my dear," her husband replied, not unkindly. He sounded weary of this familiar argument, and for once Marsh actually listened beyond what they were saying. Colin was looking at him with a probing directness. "Well, my boy, you tell me. Was it a waste of your time?"

"No." That answer came without hesitation. There was no way to describe the value of all he'd learned during these five months in the north.

Colin put out his hand, and thinking his father wanted to shake his, Marsh reached out his own. Instead he found his wrist taken and his palm twisted up. A knowing thumb skirted the hard ridge of his calluses. Then Colin Cameron nodded and smiled in tight approval. Marsh stared at him, totally astounded. After all his hard work, after all his years slaving at school, after everything he'd sacrificed on his way to the top, a handful of old blisters had won him that nod he'd coveted all his life. He watched, still dazed, as his father walked back to the fire to heft one of the heavy rocks. There was a wistfulness to his expression that Marsh had never understood until now. It was the love of his memories, the same bittersweet memories Marsh had made for himself during the past winter.

"I came up from this, you know," Colin began quietly.

Marion looked between father and son and put her arm about Lynette's stout shoulders. "Yes, dear, we have all heard you tell of it before," she said impatiently, then quickly changed the subject. "Marshall, Lynette insisted upon coming with us. She has been quite worried. Colin, let's give the two of them a moment alone."

Lynette's eyes rolled toward her in panic, but the older woman smiled firmly and patted her shoulders. "I'm sure you have much to say to one another." Marion made that into a silk-clad order then towed her husband toward the door. When they were alone, Marsh looked at the blushing miss with a wry smile.

"So, you came all this way because you were worried about me."

Her blushes deepened. "Oh, Marshall, don't be ridiculous. I would never worry about you. You have always been so very capable." From beneath the downward sweep of her lashes, she studied him. Oh, yes, he did indeed look capable with those rugged clothes and that bristled chin. Rugged and intimidating. But still Marshall.

"Then why did you come? An eagerness to resume our courtship?"

His light teasing had the opposite effect. Lynette paled considerably. Her voice was hushed. "It was expected of me. And you know how hard it is to argue against what's expected of us."

His smile gave a grim twist. "Oh, yes." He remembered well their growing-up years, how they'd bemoaned the strict regulations that went hand-in-glove with being a Hewlett and a Barnes, the pressure, both external and internal, to be exactly what their families wanted. "Does that mean you're not glad to see me?"

Her eyes lifted then, warmed with feeling. "Marshall, you know I'm always glad to see you."

He came to embrace her then with the easy familiarity of their shared past, hugging tightly the one source of unfailing acceptance and affection he'd known. Lynette had listened with a quiet understanding to his frustrations, to his resentments, to his dreams, never judging, never crushing those softly spoken hopes with the truth that they could never materialize because of who he was. She in turn had trusted him enough to blossom from the timid bud of insecurity that plagued her in the company of others. He would never, ever, break that trust, not ever.

He stepped back and smiled down at her, seeing not a plain face but the beloved features of his friend. "So what do you think of this north country?"

She gave an expressive shiver. "It's not Boston."

Remembering his own first impressions, he laughed. "No. But you needn't fret. I won't let any fierce beasts or crazed woodsmen carry you off."

She gave him a slightly naughty glance. "I don't know. I might enjoy that latter part."

Marsh grinned. "For shame. And you a nearly married woman."

Those words brought an uncomfortable tension between them. It had been an almost silent agreement, ever since the matter had been decided by their parents, that they didn't speak of their upcoming nuptials. But they should, Marsh realized then. They needed to. This woman was going to be his wife, and that entailed much more than being an understanding confidante. It implied an intimacy they'd never explored. Purposefully he shoved the image of Joelle on his tangled sheets out of his traitorous mind. He'd never had any difficulty exploring with her.

With grim determination, he touched gentle fingertips to Lynette's chin, tipping her head up. She regarded him with a startled, almost fearful, look as he bent down to her. He heard her soft gasp as his lips brushed the curve of her cheek. She was as rigid as a stump in the curl of his arm and couldn't meet his gaze when he released her. Had she felt his reluctance? Had she somehow guessed about him and Jo? Dammit, why couldn't he bring himself to kiss her on the mouth?

Thankfully her upset was of short duration. Lynette stepped back, putting a distance between them, then was able to smile. "So, what does one do up here in this wilderness?"

"Cut logs, dig ore. Do you find yourself anxious to try one of those things?" Tension eased from him as their natural banter returned.

"I don't think so. I don't have the wardrobe for it. But there is one thing I would like."

"What's that?"

"I'd like to get to know your Miss Parry."

His stomach lurched. He felt the muscles of his face stiffen around his smile. "Jo? Why?"

"Because she's different. Because she's interesting. Do all the women up here wear trousers?"

He shook his head, trying not to meet her eyes.

"I think we could be friends, Miss Parry and I. After all, you like her."

"All right, Lynette," he mumbled with all the enthusiasm of a doomed man. "I'll see what I can do." He said a silent prayer that Joelle wouldn't rip the placid Miss Barnes to shreds.

"You want me to what?"

Joelle looked from Marsh's impassive features to the interior of the mill, where his father and fiancée were looking about with interest.

"I promised I would ask and I have," he told her tightly. "I know it's damned awkward."

"Awkward?" Her eyes flashed up at him. It was a nightmare! How could he casually ask her to entertain his betrothed? Hadn't he the slightest idea how horrible it felt just to acknowledge the woman's existence? Couldn't he guess at the long, miserable hours she'd spent alone in her bed the night before, remembering, oh, God, remembering how it had felt to be driven wild with passion on those very sheets? It had been enough to know he was leaving to begin a life with another, but to have that fact brought brutally before her while the heat of his hands yet warmed her body . . .

"You're asking too much, Cameron."

He heard the whisper of shaky control in that low reply. It took a moment for him to fight down the swell of emotion threatening to break loose inside him. It was all he could do to stand beside her and pretend he wasn't half-mad with the urge to touch her, just as she was struggling to pretend tears weren't hovering beneath the tempered steel of her manner.

"I know I am, Jo," came his equally hushed response. "I didn't expect this. I wasn't expecting them. What do you want me to do?"

She sighed. "Nothing. You belong to them, after all. Don't worry, I won't embarrass you."

"Jo—"

But she was already striding away toward the couple looking out of place in their Boston finery, dappled by bright yellow sawdust.

"Quite an efficient operation you have here, young lady."

Joelle smiled tightly at Colin Cameron. "We'll be on ten-to-twelve-hour days, six days a week, to keep up with the H and B's needs alone once the crew gets through spending their winter wages in town and comes back to work." She put her hand on one of the massive boles, rubbing the rough bark proudly. "Most of these are five-board trees. They'll make the cleanest knotless lumber in the world."

"Oh, what a heavenly smell," Lynette exclaimed, inhaling the fresh, sweet tang of pine.

Joelle found herself smiling at the other woman before she could stop herself. Then her expression stiffened, and she said, "A sailboat captain can tell a lumber port at night by the wind carrying the scent out over the water."

"So," the elder Cameron said to the younger, "you plan to be a lumber baron. Know much about logs?"

"I've been learning from the best."

Joelle ignored the complement, as Colin's words caught her attention. She stared at Marsh, trying to keep all emotion from her face. "You didn't buy the Superior for the H and B?"

Marsh returned her accusatory glare and said calmly, "I decided to retain ownership myself. What's the matter, Miss Parry? You don't like the idea of answering to me as your boss?"

"I don't like the idea of you not being up front with me about it." She drew a harsh breath. "But I guess it doesn't really matter. It would be owned by a Cameron either way."

Colin listened to her volley of tense words, then remarked, "A good investment, Marshall. Perhaps Miss Parry wouldn't mind giving us a short tour."

Joelle and Marsh backed down from their challenging stances, both afraid of giving away too much in even the most innocent exchange. Passions that ran so hard and fast weren't easy to control once they'd known unfettered freedom.

Her voice clipped and businesslike, Joelle escorted the trio through the mill, highlighting each phase of operation with obvious pride. She took them from the boom that lifted Superior timber from the river, through the series of saws that turned a log into a slab of usable wood. Each log had two edges removed to make it the same width for its entire length. After the slabs fell away from the band and circular saws, they were taken to smaller edgers set to cut boards to the desired width. The scrap material went through slash saws that cut it into lath or pickets, leaving only the large piles of yellow shavings that were later dumped into the lake. Miles of belts and an intricate arrangement of pulleys gave the machines the necessary power and speed, nursed by the belt lacers, who kept the mechanism in the best running order with the same meticulous care with which the filers tended the saws, to keep them sharp and true. The place was loud, the air filled with vibration and the fragrant bite of pine.

"We cut in the winter and mill in the summer," Joelle told them as they exited the noisy building and shook the yellow dust from their feet and clothing. "It keeps the crews employed year round and the profit in our hands. With our new alliance with the H and B, we'll be laying track to carry ties to the mine. The rest of the lumber will be sent down the lakes. The only thing that would substantially cut costs further would be owning our own lake barge. My father was in the process of purchasing one for the Superior when he . . . died." Even now, six months later, that fact was hard to say out loud. She swallowed down the fresh pain of losing him and looked toward the mouth of the river, to where the water rolled, cold and indifferent.

Unable to ease her loss, Marsh sought to give her the privacy to mourn it. "Father, we should be getting to the mine if you want to see it in full swing. Lynette, I can have someone drive you back into town."

"Oh, no," she said quickly. "I think I'll wait here for you. That is, if Miss Parry wouldn't mind the company. I promise I won't get in your way."

Even as the woman smiled hopefully at her, Joelle could feel her stomach clench and her throat constrict.

"I'm sure Jo's too busy," Marsh began.

"No." The sound of her voice surprised even her. Joelle forced a rigid smile. "It's all right. Miss Barnes can stay with me until you're finished at the H and B. I'm sure we can find something in common to discuss."

Her steely gaze cut over to Marsh as Lynette happily took up her arm in blissful ignorance. "Oh, I'm sure we'll have great fun. Do go along, Marshall. I'll be fine in Miss Parry's care."

Marsh grimaced, wondering.

Tavis Lachlan drank down the last gulp of forty-rod and shakily poured another. It was as if the Devil himself had suddenly come up through the rocks in the belly of the mine.

Colin.

He swallowed another hefty drink. It burned, but not nearly as hot as his temper.

Colin. With his fancy suit of clothes and his smooth palms and his smoother smile. *Damn him!*

He got up to begin pacing wobbly. Just out of sight, his wife snuck around like a mouse between the walls. He cursed her under his breath for not bringing him any of the things Colin Cameron flashed before him. Clothes. Wealth. A strapping boy. Success. Love. Colin had returned just to push his face into it. When his son hadn't been able to do the job, he'd come himself to ruin his old friend.

They'd poked around down there in the mine, him and his haughty boy. They'd talked big, fancy words between them, ignoring him as if he hadn't been there. They'd made light of his progress, sneering down on his know-how from the lofty realm of book learning. Useless stuff, that. How could a book clue a man to a fine keenly load of ore? His instincts had been born in the blood, bred in the bones. But Colin had forgotten that. He'd been away too long. All the hematite had been scrubbed from his pores, all the intuition from his soul. Now he had no more of the gift than his overweaned lad.

They were going to shut down Sixteen.

He knew it. The younger Cameron would see to it now that he had his father's ear. Tavis had hoped he could stall them long enough for the copper to come in. They were close. So close his nose was twitching! A few more days, a week at most. That was all he needed. If he could just keep the Camerons out of his business until then. If he could just have the time to expose that vein he knew was waiting. Then he would show them. Then they all would know who was valuable to the H&B. It wasn't the treacherous one who made good for himself by stepping on his friend's heart. It wasn't the college boy who knew graphs and numbers but not a damn thing about rock. He was the one who would save the H&B from an uncertain future. He, Tavis Lachlan, with his nose for ore and his hard-earned experience. He would show them all. He would double the shifts on Sixteen. He would make it pay if he had to crawl down there himself and dig with his bare hands!

Tavis emptied his glass and reached for the bottle. Empty. "Woman, bring me another bottle!"

There was a faint scurrying. His features twisted with loathing. Like a spiritless little mouse, she was. Then he thought of Colin and Marion Hewlett, and his look grew ugly.

23

JOELLE WAS DETERMINED to hate Lynette Barnes. All morning in the woman's company, she tried to hang onto the reasons. But one by one, they faded, down to the last and most devastating one; this was the woman who was taking Marsh from her. That should have been enough to kindle a raging fury of dislike. But somehow, it wasn't. Because Lynette Barnes was . . . nice.

Had Lynette been anything like her hated imaginings, Joelle could have despised her with a clear conscience—had she been so beautiful that Marsh was driven by lust alone to have her; had she been the picture of graceful poise, a man would be proud to show on his arm in the city's glittery social circles; had he been driven to the alliance by the lure of her money and her family connections. Any of those things she could have chafed against with an understanding. But none of them were true. The only truth was one she could not fight against, crippling her heart with despair. Marsh and Lynette were genuinely fond of each other. They showed a mutual respect for each other, a caring that went beyond anything physical or forced. Theirs was a bond Joelle could not break. Outward beauty hadn't drawn Marsh to his intended, her warmth had. How could Joelle hate the woman for that?

Lynette had a self-effacing manner that defied dislike. She took honest interest in Joelle and was oblivious to the threat the other woman might impose. Joelle tried to think of her as too stupid to know her betrothed was being unfaithful, but that cruel conclusion wouldn't hold. Lynette was simply too good to believe something so bad of someone she cared about. That made Joelle feel even more guilt. There was no way she could belittle the woman enough to make herself feel better about betraying the bond Lynette had with Marsh.

After just a few hours, Lynette had completely charmed her. She was warm and friendly and openly taken with a woman who was her complete opposite. Never having had a female friend, Joelle was too curious to remain cold for long. They might not have had anything but their love of Marsh in common, but that didn't stem the flow of conversation. Lynette wanted to know everything about her. She seemed fascinated by her independent lifestyle. Her questions appeared to be prompted by genuine interest, and her sympathy for Joelle's loss of her father seemed sincere. Her eyes even glimmered with tears when she listened to Jo speak of him. How could Joelle hate her? Worse was the way Lynette expressed her admiration. Jo was surprised to find that this woman who had everything envied her. Lynette unashamedly longed for even a particle of Joelle's lively spirit and openly praised her beauty. By the time Marsh and his father came to claim Lynette, Joelle was wallowing in remorse. She couldn't make herself look at Marsh and was unable to smile at Lynette without feeling as though her face would crack with the effort.

"You must come dine with us in town tonight," Lynette exclaimed excitedly. "There's so much we didn't have time to talk about."

Joelle went rigid. She had no choice but to cast a nervous glance at Marsh. His features were set as if carved in granite. No help at all. She tried to grasp for a reason to decline, but her mind had been slowed by shock. Imagine a dinner with Marsh and his family, seated beside his future bride. The idea was hysterically funny in a sad fashion.

"Don't say no, Joelle." Lynette took one of Jo's rough hands and petitioned with a squeeze. "There are so few people I genuinely enjoy. It's my only chance to keep Marshall and his father from talking business all night."

"All right."

Joelle was stunned by her own agreement. The reasons were such an unnatural combination—her longing to spend more time with Marsh, her curiosity about his parents, her growing fondness for Lynette. How could those things transcend the awkwardness of the situation?

But amazingly they did.

The meal was like a fantasy. The dining room of the hotel was dripping with elegance, from starched linen tables to lights bedazzling with crystal. The food was unlike any Joelle had ever tasted, rich with heavy sauces, complemented by wines so dry they parched her tongue. And the people . . . She had worn one of her few skirts and a crisp white bodice and had felt herself quite well dressed until she stepped into the hotel lobby. It was filled with the wealthy, who'd come to check up on their northern properties. The men wore stark black and white; the women were dressed in a rainbow of silks and satins. The looks Joelle drew as she clomped into the dining room wearing her heavy boots made her feel as though she should be waiting on the tables instead of sitting at one.

But the Camerons and especially Lynette chased away her discomfort. She hadn't expected to find a friend in Mrs. Cameron, but the woman seemed to go out of her way to make the awkward logger's daughter feel at ease. Maybe that was for Marsh's benefit or because Lynette had begged her to be kind, but whatever the reason, Joelle was grateful. And the dinner went exceptionally well.

Business was an unavoidable topic. There wasn't a facet they didn't discuss in lively discourse. Marsh and his father agreed and disagreed in crisp, intelligent sparring, and Joelle felt honored to have her opinion given merit by two such dynamic men. Lynette asked several questions, but for the most part was silent and attentive. Marion Cameron was politely bored. It was an enlightening evening.

Joelle was intrigued by Colin Cameron. For all his city polish and educated views, there were times when he talked sentimentally of the mines just as her uncle did. She was surprised to learn of his immigrant background and to discover that he and Tavis had once worked the Peninsula together.

How far the man had risen since those early days. No wonder Marsh was so driven to succeed, with such a powerful model to follow. There was a genuine respect between the two men and a tension she wasn't able to identify. Their relationship was guarded, filled with wariness and bitter references to things she didn't understand.

Marsh's mother was even more confusing in her signals. She went out of her way to be cordial to Joelle even though she must have considered her the lowest form of female. She fussed over superficial details yet had nothing to say about things that were truly important. Was this the kind of woman the cities bred—mannerly but emotionless? What must it have been like for Marsh to grow up amid such inconsistent affection? No wonder he turned so readily to Lynette's compassion. How could Marsh not care for a woman who supplied him with some of what he'd lacked in his own upbringing? How could Joelle resent the woman who'd given the man she loved the selfless attention he'd craved in his younger years? She couldn't. If the dinner accomplished anything, it made Joelle see with miserable clarity how good Lynette Barnes had been to Marsh and why he must love her. Perhaps Marion Cameron had been so obliging in order to show her son's lover why she had no chance of luring him away. The lesson was engraved on Joelle's heart by the time the meal was over.

"I must be going," she muttered with uncommon meekness. "It will be dark soon. I thank you all for the invitation."

"I'll see you back to the Superior, Jo."

It was hard to keep the apprehension and yearning from her gaze as it shot to Marsh in obvious dismay. "No. You don't have to do that."

"I'm heading that way, and besides, there's something I want to show you first." He spoke brusquely, in that authoritative manner that always made her feel rebellious. But this time she was too agitated to argue. It was a strain to act like a manager instead of a lover in view of the Camerons and the unsuspecting Lynette.

"All right," she growled at last. "You probably just want me to keep you from getting lost."

Marsh grinned wryly. He reached for her elbow unthinkingly as he bade his parents and his fiancée a good evening.

Joelle jerked at the unexpected contact and tried not to tremble. *Act as though this meant nothing,* she told herself sternly.

Bundled up against the chill of dusk, Marsh led her not to where she'd left her wagon but down toward the docks. He didn't speak, and she was too distracted to think of anything clever to say. Her mind was spinning with the image of him bending to kiss Lynette's pale cheek.

"There. What do you think of her?"

Joelle looked up at him in confusion. Her, who? Then she followed his gaze to the end of the dock where a sturdy barge was tied up. Her brow furrowed.

"It's yours, Jo," Marsh told her softly, "for the Superior." He watched her face closely, expectantly.

Joelle swallowed hard and managed to mumble, "She'll do, Cameron. Should make you a tidy profit." Then she turned and started hurriedly up toward the main street. Marsh hesitated then rushed to fall in step beside her. His tone was terse and anxious.

"If it won't suit, tell me. I can arrange for something else. Olen said it was the same kind of vessel your father meant to purchase." He paused, waiting for a comment but getting a stony silence. Her stride lengthened. "I thought you'd be pleased, but obviously I was wrong." He sounded peeved, confused. Hurt.

"It's fine, Marsh. It's just what the Superior needed to carry cargo across the lakes. It was a good investment for the company."

"I made the investment for you. It's registered in your name, yours and the Superior's. That way you'll never have to worry about how to take care of yourself."

"Why?" She drew up so abruptly that he skidded in the frozen mud and had to turn about. It wasn't dark enough to conceal the terrible turmoil in her expression. Or the anger.

"Why?"

"Why are you doing this? Because you feel obligated? Is this some kind of bribe to ease your conscience? I don't want anything from you, Marsh. How dare you think so! Or is it just a business arrangement, nothing personal at all?"

He studied her, wondering which answer would incur the least wrath. It was like standing before a double-barreled shotgun. A blast from either barrel would tear him apart. Diplomatically he said, "A little of both, I guess."

Fuming, Joelle resumed her rapid walk. The nerve of him, the sneaky cur. Going behind her back to make just the perfect gesture. She was of a mind to deny him the satisfaction. But cold logic argued that she couldn't afford the luxury. He was right. The barge would guarantee her a livelihood, the means to be independent. Damn his thoughtfulness. He was full of surprises today. First, the discovery that he'd retained ownership of the Superior. Again, a business decision or one of a more personal nature? Would he tell her if she asked or again say with annoying neutrality, "A little of both." And now the gift of the barge to both free her and tie her more closely to him. She was infuriated now, but the thought of his concern warmed her heart. How was she supposed to react?

"Thank you," she muttered at last.

"You're welcome," he drawled with equal enthusiasm.

They reached the wagon, and to Jo's surprise Marsh took up the reins. "Give me something safe to do with my hands," he grumbled in response to her pointed look. Joelle flushed and could think of no fitting retort. Instead she sat on the seat in silence, not daring to let her attention turn his way. He was fairly capable with the leads, so she couldn't complain. But she couldn't relax.

By the time he reined in the team before her lodgings in the Superior office, they were both on edge. They sat for a long, tense moment; then Marsh asked almost harshly, "Do you want me to come in?"

"No . . . yes. No."

"Better I don't."

"Yes," she agreed faintly.

With a kind of desperation, his fingers slid over the back of hers and laced tight. Holding to him, feeling those hard-won calluses, Joelle could almost pretend he wasn't sitting beside her in his fine suit. She could almost pretend he was the arrogant sawyer she'd fallen in love with. Almost.

"I like her, Marsh."

His grip tightened painfully.

"It's late," she observed, blinking her eyes to clear them. "I can take you over to the H and B."

"No," he said gruffly. "The walk will do me good."

They sat for a moment longer, hands and hearts entwined. "I'd better go," he said.

Joelle's fingers clutched then relaxed forcibly. "Yes." She turned and jumped down from her side of the wagon. She tried to gain control of her breathing before going around to where he stood. *Don't grab at him. Don't do it.* She shoved her hands deeply into the pockets of her mackinaw and smiled up at him rather grimly. "It was nice of your folks to ask me to dinner."

"I think they were curious about you."

"Curious or suspicious?"

Marsh looked uncomfortable and said nothing.

"Well . . . goodnight, then."

One week. Should he tell her? Marsh studied the way moonlight seemed to pool in her uplifted eyes. In one week's time, he would have everything in order; a new agent for the mine, his ideas implemented for the betterment of the H&B, Tavis Lachlan hopefully brought to heel. Then he would leave with his parents and his fiancée. It was all arranged. They'd come down to saying good-bye so many times, it seemed. It got worse every time. How in God's name was he going to walk away, on this night or the next six?

Joelle stiffened at the feel of his fingertips on her cheek. She didn't know if she should jerk away or lean into his touch. Her will was terribly close to collapse, having never been that strong to begin with where he was concerned. But in this case, it had to be. Firmly she caught his wrist and pulled his hand away.

"Goodnight, Marsh."

He gave a slight nod and turned from her, beginning his walk toward the H&B. He seemed to drag himself aimlessly along, as if he carried the heavy traces of some mighty load. He didn't look back to see her watching with her heart in her eyes, watching until his image disappeared in a haze of tears, and then into the distant darkness.

"Oh, please, Joelle. It will be fun," Lynette said with a forced intensity, as though she dreaded the thought every bit as much as the logger's daughter.

"For you, maybe. You're used to such things. I wouldn't fit in."

Lynette studied her hands and murmured, "I've never gotten used to such things. I just thought that perhaps if you went with me, I would somehow be braver. You are so courageous." She lifted her huge, pale eyes with unabashed admiration. "Nothing scares you."

Seeing you and Marsh together in your social element scares me, Jo thought. Then she would have to admit to herself just how impossible her dreams were. Perhaps, then, she should go. "What time?"

Lynette hugged her. It was a great, cushiony embrace, overflowing with natural good will. Joelle squeezed her eyes shut and endured it, then made herself smile. *Brave? I'm not so brave. If I were brave, I would tell you that your fiancé loves me. I would fight for him with every breath in my body. But like a coward, I will hold my tongue and bury my heart, and you will take him away with you forever. But I will have this night to shine for him—like a lady.*

"I'll have Marshall pick you up."

"No!" She swallowed hard and managed a rather coherent explanation. "I'll drive myself. That way if I decide to leave early, I won't be taking Marsh from you." *Even though it's what I wish for with every beat of my heart.*

"Seven o'clock, then. Bring your things and you can change in my room at the hotel. Then we can make a grand entrance together. It will be fun. I know it."

Joelle smiled thinly, plainly not at all sure she was right.

The box hadn't been disturbed in years. She still remembered so clearly laying her mother's belongings inside as if she were folding away her memories to keep them safe. The smell of camphor rose strongly from the brittle wrapping paper. But there it was, just as she recalled, her mother's favorite gown. She'd had it made for a trip to Copper Harbor. How excited she'd been. Her husband had just signed the lease for the lands he would cut, and he insisted that they celebrate. It was his way of saying their journey down the lakes would be delayed, at least for a while. Knowing it would probably be delayed forever, she had taken the opportunity to make the most of this one special night. How lovely she'd been when she tried it on. Joelle remembered standing with her Aunt Sarah, who was staying overnight, watching her father hand her mother up into their plain wagon with that beautiful gown held to her breast like a dear child. There were so few happy memories after that, which was why this one was so vivid.

Joelle took out the silver-plated brushes, the bits of lace, a fan, gloves, the scrap of fancy work her mother had stitched until her health grew too frail to continue. And then the dress, yards and yards of it. This one night would be her special night, too, for she would at least look as though she belonged on the arm of Marshall Cameron.

"Oh! How beautiful you are! Look for yourself."

Doubting Lynette's gushing claim, Joelle revolved slowly in the unwieldy swarm of petticoats. She stared at the figure in the glass, scarcely recognizing the woman reflected back.

It was the dress, of course. It created the illusion of a lovely lady within. Magenta satin hugged the trim line of her torso, belling out into a full skirt overlaid in tiers of frothy pink lace. Layers of that same gossamer stuff fell from the neckline, where it skimmed the outside edge of her shoulders and came to a low vee over her bosom. The dress seemed to show a scandalous amount of skin, but the effect was feminine to the extreme. Next to her mother's fairness, the dress had been a dainty confection; but Jo's dark coloring brought the satin alive with a rich vitality. Her hair had resisted all Lynette's efforts to give it a curl, so she'd simply swept it back in a sleek wave and secured it behind each ear with a borrowed comb. Without the benefit of wool socks and long johns, her legs felt uncommonly bare in the sheer silk stockings Lynette had loaned her, and her feet were swimming in the satin slippers she wore, even though the toes were packed with wadding to keep them from flopping. She felt sensations as foreign to her as the appearance of the woman in the mirror. But for one night, this was the illusion she wanted.

The glaze in Marsh's eyes told her it was the right one.

He was waiting for them at the foot of the stairs, arrestingly handsome in his dark evening clothes. For what seemed an eternity but was actually a few seconds, he stared at Joelle, emotion smoldering in his gaze, bringing an answering heat flooding through her unsteady limbs. She stopped trembling. That one blazing look told her she had no reason to fear she could not hold her own among his society peers.

Afraid that if he didn't pull his stare from her, he would be quite lost to the spell of Joelle's beauty, Marsh turned his attention to Lynette. Beside the devastating vision the other woman presented, the pale Lynette was unflatteringly garbed in blue-green taffeta, styled with flounces and frills and poofs and petal-and-bow trim that added more bulk to her already full figure. Sausage curls wadded beside her round cheeks, making her face seem puffy, but Marsh didn't notice. He saw only her inner glow, and that made her pretty in his eyes.

"If you ladies would do me the honor of allowing me to escort you, I will be the most envied man alive."

Lynette giggled and took his arm with a shy familiarity. Joelle hesitated. Marsh looked to her questioningly, and his melting stare freed her of her temporary paralysis. She slid her fingers over the swell of his forearm, trying not to clutch, trying not to betray how good it was to feel his strength beneath her hand. As he walked them toward the huge, open parlors that had been cleared for the evening's dance, she could pretend, just for a moment, that they were alone, that he didn't have his fiancée gracing his other sleeve.

The gathering was everything she had expected. The atmosphere fairly oozed wealth and elegance. Liveried servants carried tiny slivers of food upon heavy silver trays to bejeweled and bedazzling couples. Songs that sounded as though they belonged in a music box were played while people danced in the same stiffly correct style. She had her first taste of champagne and decided she preferred the bite of her uncle's whiskey to the bubbly nonsense, just as she preferred frank talk about timber and trade to the fluffy gossip bandied about her. She was approached by countless young men who tried to guess her lineage and thought they remembered seeing her at someone's seaside resort or debut ball. She smiled and allowed them their illusions, growing more and more restless with their prattle and more and more agitated by the sight of Marsh moving Lynette about the crowded floor to the strains of some pompous tune. So this was society, she thought, and was thoroughly unimpressed. No one seemed to be having much fun. There were no grins; no one laughed. Everything was as formal as the steel cage supporting her skirt. If not for the tortuous enjoyment of watching Marsh, she would have slipped out the nearest exit.

"You look as though you're having a marvelous time."

She gave Marsh a smile as wry as his observation. "Is anyone having a good time? This all seems such an incredible waste of effort for so many to be so properly bored."

Marsh chuckled. The sound rippled over her senses like a restoring spring thaw. "In proper circles, it is considered bad manners to have too much fun. Bad for the blood, you know."

"A bit of something to get their blood moving would do the lot of them some good." She looked about the glamorous setting and saw Lynette taking lemonade with Marion Cameron. The elder woman frowned slightly when she saw Jo with her son. "Do you really enjoy these affairs, Cameron?"

"I have been taught to endure them." He studied her features, suddenly struck by a longing to see them fired with animation. "Dance with me."

She eyed the sedately twirling couples with disfavor. "I don't know this dance."

"I'll teach you. Come. I've stomped on your toes. Don't be afraid to step on mine."

He took her arm and led her out onto a floor polished to a mirrorlike shine. Assuming the correct stance, he began to guide her awkwardly through the regimented turns. She was stiff, and he was too aware of her. After a turn about the floor, Joelle stepped out of his arms.

"Thank you, Cameron, but I've had enough of what you call dancing. It has all the charm of learning to cipher."

He smiled, retaining her elbow. "I guess it does at that." He glanced toward the musicians and had a wicked thought. "Wait here for me a minute."

She watched, bemused, while he crossed to the performers' platform and spoke to one of the men playing violin. She caught the discreet way money changed hands. Marsh turned back to her with a self-satisfied grin, and she understood the instant the music began. This was *music,* the kind that was made for dancing, with strings sawing out a peppery tune as native as the pines. Marsh crossed to her, bowed low, and then held her tiny waist as he whisked her out onto the dance floor.

People stared—startled, aghast, and scandalized—but Marsh and Jo didn't care. He moved his lively partner through the series of breathless circles, just as she'd moved him before a roaring fire and cheering group of timbermen. The steps were high and quick, and Joelle was forced to yank up the dragging hem of her dress to keep up, displaying an immodest amount of her trim, gartered calf, which made the matrons gasp in shock.

With her son galloping about the empty dance floor with that vivacious female in his arms, Marion Cameron paled and looked about at the censorious faces of her peers. In a hoarse voice, she demanded, "Colin, do something."

"Yes, my dear, I believe I will."

She gave a cry of surprise as his big hands clasped her waist, turning her out from the edge of the murmuring crowd and into the center of attention. He grinned at her dismay and challenged her with a lift of his brows.

"Come on, Mary. Surely you haven't forgotten how to let your hair down."

Defiantly she reached down for the edge of her skirt and hiked it knee-high while her other gloved hand sought his broad shoulder. "No, I haven't."

The dance might not have been in the height of good taste, but if it was good enough for Colin and Marion Cameron, who could object? One by one couples edged out onto the floor to attempt a conservative version of the unbridled dance. With flushed faces and pounding pulses, some of them even had fun.

When the music finally ended, Marsh was forced to release the woman in his arms. For a moment he could almost believe they were back in the woods, stepping to Guy Sonnier's accordion. He remembered with bittersweet clarity what had come after—their first kiss of passion. Would that they were back there now. Then he recalled the hurt he had brought her that night with the truth about Lynette. He continued to hurt her, every time he took her in his arms—because he always had to let her go again.

The pleasure of the moment gone for him, Marsh bowed to a bewildered Joelle and made his way back to his fiancée. He led her out in the staid pattern of a waltz and tried to cool the frantic pace of his heart.

24

FROM THE DARKENED terrace, Joelle could make out the ridge of the mountains and smell the restless lake. Familiar things, comforting things. She was so grateful to close the mood of stilted formality behind the double doors that she didn't even notice the cold. It felt good, bringing the tingle of life back to her. From where she leaned on the brick retaining wall, she could see down into the busy port. Masts stood out against the charcoal sky like mighty pines denuded of their greenery, like an unnatural forest planted by the wealthy as they came through the locks and across the yet-angry waters of Lake Superior, to see how their wilderness baronies had fared over the winter months. Down there was the timber barge Marsh had bought her, providing for her as her father had failed to.

The port was fairly quiet now, but in the morning hours it would ring with activity. White-winged schooners and heavy barges would crowd for the chance to dock and unload. Cargo the citizens of the Peninsula had starved for over the last few months would be handed down onto the decks, and mineral from the H&B would be loaded in its place. And soon Joelle would have to teach her crew the ways of the stevedores—for when they piled the first load of light, clean, sweet-smelling pine into the hold of her ship. If she closed her eyes, she could imagine it: freshly cut lumber stacked along the harbor, drying in the summer sun, the soft warm wind from the forest carrying the scent of newly sawn boards out over the blue waters of Lake Superior. Maybe she would follow that wealth of lumber up and around and down the series of lakes. Following . . .

Her eyes opened with a snap. No. She couldn't go chasing after Marshall Cameron. He was going back to a world like the one inside, one that excluded her with its rigid standards and the rites of the unimportantly proper. He was going there with Lynette, her friend. She would have to let him go, to be where he belonged, to love the woman he had chosen. It wasn't fair, but it was a fact she had to accept sooner or later. She might pretend for one night that she belonged inside with the others, but the charade wouldn't last for long. Here was where she belonged, admiring the majestic bristle of pine rising on the cliffs above, scenting the crisp waves of Lake Superior.

The sound of the doors opening distracted her from her glum thoughts. From where she stood in the shadows, Joelle had an unrestricted view of the figure crossing the stones, probably needing fresh air as much as she had. She stilled the fluttery excitement knocking about her ribs and watched, unobserved, as he leaned against the low wall to look down on the lake. She saw his shoulders rise and fall heavily within the superb cut of his coat. He looked so alone, so dejected, that she overcame her original plan to stay silent.

"The view is better from over here."

Marsh jerked upright and spun toward her. It took a moment for his eyes to adjust to the shadows, then he gave Joelle a wry smile. "Definitely better, but keeping a safe distance is much less dangerous."

He took a minute to appreciate the sights—the pearlescent curve of her shoulders, the shimmering mystery of her gaze, the way her stockinged feet stood on top of her satin slippers rather than within them. She made a thoroughly enticing, provokingly waifish figure, one he couldn't resist studying from a closer perspective.

Joelle felt her chest tighten as he came across the terrace toward her. This wasn't wise, not with moonlight creating golden highlights in his hair, not with the seducing bend his smile had taken. Still, she stood her ground and waited for him to come to her, watched him slip between the shadows like something sleek, compelling, and potentially lethal. He came to stand beside her, as close as he could get without actually touching her. Then he turned to admire the beauty of the lake.

"Deceiving, isn't it?" he murmured softly. "With all those ships down there, one would think we had it conquered, yet we are the ones at its mercy. We can make bigger, faster, stronger ships, we can grasp for better technology to guide us, we can grow careless in our arrogant confidence, yet the tides that moved along these shores centuries ago still control us. One could almost believe in the spirits the Indians claim prowl across its surface."

Joelle shivered then tried to make light of his mood. "Why, Marshall Cameron, what a romantic you are."

"That's my Longfellow showing." He grinned at her, daring her to interpret that any way she liked. "You know, *The Wreck of the Hesperus, The Song of Hiawatha.*" She shook her head, unfamiliar with the reference. "I'll lend them to you. I think you'd like Longfellow. Anyway, when I should have been tending to more practical stuff, I was sneaking Longfellow and Cooper's *Leatherstocking Tales.* Lynette gave them to me as gifts. She thought I was getting too unbearably haughty in my literary taste. Lyn and I used to—" The sudden spasm of her features made him stop and check the look of fond remembrance softening his expression. "I'll lend them to you."

"No, thanks. I won't have much time to read," she told him gruffly, then looked back over the lake to conceal the similar glimmer of her eyes.

"But you really would enjoy them, Jo."

"There are a lot of things I enjoy but have to get used to doing without."

He touched her arm and felt the quiver of gooseflesh move over it. "Here. You're cold."

"I'm fine," she began to protest, but Marsh had already taken off his coat and slipped it about her shoulders. There was no way she could object to being enveloped by the heat of him that lingered in its smooth lining, or the scent of him teasing her memories. Warm leather. That and fresh pine would always trigger all the tender emotions her heart could hold.

Marsh looked at her, the way she was bundled defensively inside his coat, at the way her stubborn chin squared in defiance of her dampening eyes. God, she made him crazy. Even with his family and his peers inside, just on the other side of double glass doors, all he could think of was holding her, loving her, showering her with all that beat so frantically inside him. They weren't the ones who demanded his restraint. She was the one. Her pride, her vulnerability—the pair of attributes twined into an intriguing whole that incited a fever of longing where none should exist. It became suddenly imperative for her to understand him.

"Jo, about Lynette . . ."

"You don't have to explain anything to me, Marsh."

"Yes, I do. I owe her the only happiness I knew as a boy. She was my best friend, Jo. God didn't give her a beautiful face or a shapely figure, but he gave her the biggest, most generous heart I've ever known. But the damn fools in Boston can't see that. Oh, some have courted her for her fortune, but she's not stupid enough to miss their motives. At least she never has to doubt that my feelings are genuine. I'll take good care of her and I can make sure she's happy. She deserves that, Jo, more than anyone I know. She's not independent like you are. She can't make her own way. She hasn't the looks to catch and hold any man she wants. She deserves someone who'll love her for herself."

"And that's you, Marsh?"

"Yes," he said somberly.

"And do you love her?"

"What?"

"I asked you that before, and you didn't answer. Do you love Lynette the way you love me?" She searched his face, seeing his hesitation, seeing his confusion, his caution. No. He didn't.

"Don't you think she deserves that from the man she marries?"

His features had hardened into that cool reserve that reminded her so much of Colin Cameron. "She deserves a man who won't hurt her."

"You don't think it's going to hurt her when she wakes up every morning for the rest of her life with a man she knows doesn't love her? With a man who married her out of pity?"

"That's not true, Jo!" He was getting angry, but he was also thinking, and it was worth the risk of one to have the other. His dark eyes narrowed dangerously. "What do you know about it?"

Suddenly, everything was very clear. She knew. It was she and Guy all over again. She had to make him see, to understand before it was too late. "Marshall, a woman doesn't want a man who'll protect her like a brother. She needs more. She needs this."

She caught his rigid face between her hands and pulled him to her. *I need this,* she thought wildly, desperately, as she kissed him. His smooth cool cheeks warmed quickly between the press of her palms, just as his mouth warmed to the urgent slant of hers. When she broke away, they were both breathing heavily from the abrupt influx of passion. Marsh's hands rose to cap her shoulders, kneading them through the weight of his coat. His forehead touched hers.

"Jo—"

"Do you kiss her like that, Marsh? Because if you don't, if you can't, you're not doing her any favor by taking her as your wife. You know the difference, and someday she will, too. And she'll resent you for preventing her from finding happiness. She'll feel guilty for keeping you from your own. Lynette is not stupid. She cares for you and she will understand the truth. Don't let your sense of honor get in the way of what's right."

"Damn you, Jo," he moaned. "Can't you leave things alone? You've done nothing but tear my life apart."

She swallowed hard, suffering his anguish with him but loving him too much to back down now. She tipped his head back, forcing him to look at her, to listen. "Was it a life worth living? Can you tell me honestly that you were happier with what you had and what you'll go back to than you were with what you've known these last few months? Can you make yourself believe that?"

He drew a deep, uneven breath. Recollection hit him hard and unfairly right in the solar plexus. He remembered the freeing scent of the pines and the painfully cold air filling his lungs, the rough camaraderie of the jacks as they teased him about his bruises and shattered nose. That damned broken nose that he wouldn't let the best surgeon in Boston try to straighten. He could feel his fury and frustration with Tavis Lachlan, the rivalry with Guy Sonnier, the deep satisfying friendship with Olen Thurston. No, nothing in his past or probable future could touch those crisp, candid emotions.

Then there was Joelle and her maddening stubbornness, her provoking impertinence, her unfailing frankness. The way she challenged him, the way she surrendered to him, the way she equaled him. Laughing with her, yelling at her . . . loving her. No, he would never know those heavenly delights and sweet aggravations in Boston.

He bent slowly, angling to fit his mouth to hers. He kissed her deeply, desperately, with all the agonized yearning in his soul. When her tender lips parted, welcoming him to savor more, to stay longer, to stake his claim where she'd allowed no others, he felt the weight of responsibility crumble from his shoulders. His arms banded her tightly, crushing her up to his chest, and she met his rough embrace with an eagerness of fearsome intensity. When he was finally forced to pull away, gasping for air and restraint, she hung as if dazed in his arms. Her eyes were closed, her thick lashes fluttering delicately. His palm slid along her jaw, his fingers reaching to pull the soft curve of her hair away from her neck, holding it back so his lips could rub over that taut, slender column. The sound of her breathy moan sent a flood of desire to swamp his senses.

Then suddenly she went stiff in his arms. Her murmurs of compliance became gasps of objection. Confused, he didn't release her when she began to push. It wasn't until he saw the incredible anguish in her eyes as she stared past him that reason returned. He let her go, turning as he did to face whatever made her features blanch to such an alarming degree. Then his own face drained of color.

At the open door to the hotel's crowded parlor rooms a startled Lynette Barnes stood with her hands clasped to her mouth. In a flash of blue-green taffeta, she was gone and with her went the magic of this unplanned rendezvous.

Feeling miserable, Joelle looked up at Marsh. She gave a small choking cry and ran after her new friend, throwing off Marsh's coat in her anguish. He stood for a long moment after she'd disappeared inside, then went to collect his discarded jacket. There was no trace of her warmth left inside it, just as there was no heat lingering from their brief embrace. Only the slated clouds over the sinister Superior could change as fast and furiously as the past few seconds. All he could do was weather the aftermath as best he could. Joelle had gone after Lynette. He couldn't interfere there. What could he say to Lynette? What excuses could he offer? His heart was in a terrible confusion. How could he convince her of something doubted now? She would see right through him. Hadn't she suffered enough hurt for one evening?

Marsh couldn't return to the gathering inside. Joelle was right about it. It was deadly dull. How had he ever partaken in the shallow conversations, the insincere flattery of society's upper crust? God, they were a boring bunch. He wanted to be surrounded by honest talk and earthy emotions, in a place where he could indulge in his moodiness without offending anyone. Lord, he was tired of pretending that nothing of value went on behind his fixed smile. Besides, his mother would be waiting to pounce upon him with questions about Lynette and Joelle. How could he answer her when he'd found no suitable reply to his own troubled thoughts? He didn't need a crowd of bothersome acquaintances. He wanted to get lost among caring strangers. And he knew just where to look.

Even at this late hour the muddy streets of Eagle River were thronged with gambling men and fancy women in their colorful silks and satins. Jacks with money burning holes in their pockets swaggered in and out of saloons, their steel-calked boots punching holes in the boardwalks. They were eager to get their fill of the liquor denied them in the lumber camps, of the rich food brought in on the sleek sailing ships, of the women looking to pick their pockets clean. But mostly they were anxious to meet the slightest insult with ready fists, to vent their spleenful of aggression upon any hapless miner who might cross their path before they had to report for work in the mills, when their money was gone.

It was hard for Marsh to blend in at the bar of the first saloon he came to. He was in full evening dress amid a sea of plaid mackinaws, flannel shirts, woolen trousers, and heavy boots. The talk growling around him in all manner of accents and rough speech was of mining and timber. He listened over his first mug of forty-rod—called that, he learned from the smug bartender, because its aroma would kill a greenhorn at forty rods. Marsh grinned into his glass. The liquor would have felled him six months ago, but now the alcohol just burned heartily all the way to his gullet. He was concentrating on his second swallow when he took a hard elbow to the ribs.

"Quite the fancy coat there, fella. Sure you ain't in the wrong place?"

That won the bearded Cornishman a ripple of gruff laughter from cronies close enough to overhear.

"You like it? It's yours. I'll trade it for the one you're wearing."

The miner raised a doubting brow, eyeing the fine serge and comparing it to his own worn wool. A coat like that would cost him a year's wage. But wouldn't his Sal go crazy for it. "Yer on, Yank. Crazy ye be, though. Don't come a-looking for me when ye've sobered up."

Marsh smiled and shrugged out of his jacket. "Doesn't fit very well anymore. Wear it with my blessing."

The miner stroked the smooth black fabric and made a great show of stuffing his bulky shirtsleeves inside it. Laughter rumbled from all sides at the spectacle he made, but the Cornishman was pleased with his trade. He brushed a bit of imaginary lint off his cuff and crowed, "Think I'll be off and about some fine courting."

Marsh slung the smelly mackinaw around his shoulders, drained his mug, and called for another. Those standing at his elbows relaxed, regarding him as eccentric but harmless. A few even muttered that damned if he didn't look like the H&B agent. He'd worked the woods with the man over the winter months, and danged if he couldn't draw a mean saw. Even toed the line with the younger Sonnier in a fair fight. No, scoffed another. Marsh let the talk ebb and flow. All he wanted was to get so drunk he couldn't think or feel or remember the pain in Lynette's eyes or the truth of Joelle's words.

"On Sam Hill's road, it was, halfway between Portage Lake and here," the man on his right was saying energetically to his companions. "Ol' Ed Hulbert, you know Ed, he done found it in a pit in the woods. Copper boulders different from any he'd ever seen."

Marsh slid a look at the chunk of stone the man smacked down on the bar. He blinked and looked closer.

"Heard tell some of the pigs strayed from Billy Royal's Wayside Saloon, and he was helping 'em search. It was them pigs what found the mineral, rooting like they was in the pit," another chuckled to make light of the discovery.

"Pudding stone," sneered another. "Me Cousin Jack captain said there ain't enough of it in the world to buy a shift boss a decent drink."

"May I see that?"

The miner glanced at Marsh and shrugged, pushing the stone his way. He picked it up curiously. It was copper, but like none he'd ever seen either. Pebbles of it were cemented in red sandstone. His first thought was that it was worthless, just as the miner had said. How could such a conglomerate be profitably mined? But he continued to weigh the hunk of rock.

"Buy an old man a drink?"

Marsh registered none of the shock catapulting through him. Calmly he raised his forefinger to motion the bartender, then added another to indicate two. "What brings you to such a place?"

"Some cheerful miner very much in his cups and wearing my son's coat. Thought I'd better see that you weren't facedown in some alley. Might ask you the same thing. This more to your taste in company?"

Marsh shrugged and reached for his third mug of the mind-numbing brew. His father frowned down at him slightly and took up his own drink. After a deep swallow, he released an expansive sigh.

"Now there's something that hasn't changed. Thank God. Could still strip the paint off wood." He turned so his elbows rested on the bar and he could observe the rowdy gathering. "No, hasn't changed at all. Spent many a night in spots just like this one."

"With Tavis Lachlan?"

Colin hesitated, then said, "Yes."

Marsh suddenly straightened, his gaze less than friendly. "What are you doing here, Father? Come to drag me back with you?"

"Thought I might enjoy a hearty glass and a few memories, if that's all right with you. I'll let your mama do the bird-dogging. You're a grown man, to my thinking, and can pretty much do as you please."

Odd words coming from Colin Cameron, who had also insisted his son fit the mold just right. Independent choice was not encouraged in the Cameron home. As the Hewlett heir, his choices had been made for him in the cradle: good education, good manners, a seat on the H&B Board, a wife who would give him a controlling share of stocks. Fairly cut and dried.

"I'm giving you back full authority over the H and B, above and below ground."

That clipped through Marsh's sullenness. "What?"

"Your ideas are sound and fresh. I see no reason to hamstring them because Lachlan has a twenty year score to settle with me. Your mother insisted I take a room for you at the hotel. Feared you'd get yourself lost in the dark, I suppose, what with no regular streetlights. I'll come by in the morning, not too early from the looks of you, and we'll make us a good list of the equipment we'll need."

Elation and pulse-pounding excitement shot up to Marsh's head, spinning his senses like a good quart of forty-rod. Full authority. To explore his ideas. To prove himself to the Board, to his father. God, a dream come true . . . almost. As quickly as his mood soared, it sank again.

"But we're leaving at the end of the week." He said that dully. He could put things in motion, but he wouldn't be there to see them take shape and prosper.

Colin gulped the rest of his drink with a practiced ease then set his glass on the scarred bar. "Aye, the boat sails, Marshall. That be a fact." The forty-rod had revived the thick brogue of his youth. "Now, I must be off afore your mama sends the troops out after me. Good night to you, me boy. And, Marshall . . . you've done me proud."

A great lump of emotion rose up in Marsh's throat at the same time he was trying to swallow a swig of brew. He nearly strangled before he could force one past the other. By then his father was gone. Marsh turned back to his drink and his original plan with grim determination. Colin Cameron had given him no gift. He'd given him another agonizing problem to solve in a brain too sodden to comprehend anything beyond the weight of misery in his heart. He closed his eyes, willing himself to become lost in the gut-wrenching liquor, in the coarse folds of a miner's mackinaw.

"Drinks," came a bellow from beside him. "Drinks for the house and for as far as my gold will stretch."

A handful of coins spun and clattered upon the bar. Marsh found himself watching with a hazy fascination. That voice . . . so familiar. He tried to drag himself up from his stupor to peer up at the generous gentleman at his elbow. Chauncey Sonnier? He couldn't turn his head that far without inviting a flood of dizziness. So he watched the spin of coins. Gold coins. A lot of gold coins. Something snapped inside his foggy brain.

As Chauncey reached for his first glass, a firm hand closed about his wrist.

"Where did you get this gold?"

Chauncey looked in some surprise at a drunken Marshall Cameron and grinned. "Wages for hard labor, Cameron. The timber be in and drying, and I be ready for some reward."

"Wages from whom?"

The hard edge of the man's voice deflated much of Chauncey's good cheer. His eyes narrowed cautiously. "You ought to know. 'Twas your draft that saw us paid."

"Not in gold."

The words sank deep and with dire warning. Marsh straightened, understanding pushing the effects of the liquor aside. Chauncey Sonnier had a good fifty pounds of muscle over him, but Marsh was past caring. He saw a stack of log butts branded with the Superior S. He saw Joelle disappearing before his eyes into what might have been the same cold grave that took her father. He saw red.

"You son of a bitch," he growled low in his throat. "I bet if I ask around I'll find that Christiansen pays in gold."

Chauncey's features grew hard as bedrock. "You won't be asking nobody nothing."

Sturdy fingers meshed in the front of Marsh's dress shirt, closing like a vise and twisting until Marsh's feet cleared the ground. Then glass was exploding all around him as Chauncey Sonnier heaved him bodily through the front window of the saloon.

Brawling was an acceptable outlet for men with too much hell-raising stored up over the winter months to be content with simple drinking. Cornish and Irish might work together during the day, but at night they fought like natural forest rivals. No one paid much mind to a little toe-to-toe slugging, and no one in his right mind would interfere with a Sonnier with blood-lust in his eyes. Though many would sympathize with the luckless fool Chauncey was about to pulverize, no one would make a move to aid him.

Marsh lay flat on his back in a glittering sea of broken glass, the wind knocked out of him. He could hear Chauncey's boots crunching on the scattered shards, but he couldn't make a move to defend himself.

"Why did you have to stick your nose in it, Cameron?" came a low, dangerous rumble. Chauncey reached down to sink his fingers into Marsh's hair, using that grip to haul him up to his feet. "I liked you. Why couldn't you have left it alone?"

Marsh had met Guy as a formidable foe, but against Chauncey he was about as effective as a raft of straw on the surface of Lake Superior. The man had fists like the smashing heads of a stamping mill. The first blow shredded the inside of his cheek against his teeth, filling his mouth with blood and his head with the image of Fergus the cook eating through a straw. The second sent his eyeballs rolling back into blackness. Chauncey flung him aside, and he staggered on weak legs to collapse finally in the cold mud. He'd managed to get his knees under him when a kick to the ribs shattered his insides, driving up a gutful of suffocating bile. He went over like a tipped stump, hugging his knees to his middle.

"Sorry, Cameron."

Marsh forced his eyes to open, then squeezed them shut against the sight of Chauncey Sonnier's steel-calked boot descending toward his face with enough power to crush his skull.

25

"No!"

The sudden cry was followed by a hurtling body, crashing into Chauncey with enough momentum to knock him off balance. The two brothers went down hard onto the street, Chauncey spitting mad and Guy wildly furious.

"What the hell are you trying to do? Kill him?"

"Mind your business, Guy," Chauncey snarled, tossing his brother aside like a gnat so he could scramble to his feet. "It was done for you, after all."

Marsh had managed to get his hands and knees under him and was crawling slowly, almost blindly, toward the lights of the saloon. He uttered a hoarse cry of protest when he felt a huge hand clap down on the back of his head, thrusting his face into the wet street that offered only cold darkness and no air.

With his features set in ruthless lines, Chauncey ignored the flailing arms, the scrabbling feet, the frantic gurgles of sound. What he couldn't ignore were his brother's twin fists laced together to form a felling club against the side of his head.

Marsh finally lifted himself up out of the filthy water, gasping and choking. Galvanized by a self-preserving panic, he half dragged himself on shaky limbs to the edge of the walk. Lacking the strength to pull himself to his feet, he flopped over to brace his back against the boards and readied for the continued punishing attack he couldn't fend off. Through the muddy water blurring his vision, he saw a figure approach and crouch low. Groaning with an angry helplessness, he tucked his knees up tight to protect his belly and crossed his forearms over his head.

"Easy, *mon ami*. I am not the sort to harm a man who's already beaten. I just want to see that Chauncey hasn't broken anything that can't be repaired."

Marsh relaxed the shield of his arms and let them fall limply to his heaving sides. He allowed Guy to fit his palm under his chin, manipulating his jaw back and forth, provoking a muttered oath. Satisfied that Marsh's jaw hadn't been shattered like the saloon window by his brother's grinding punch, the Canadian pressed against his rib cage until Marsh sucked a harsh breath and shoved him back.

"Dammit, I'm fine."

Guy snorted at that and rocked back on his heels. "So, Cameron, why was my brother trying to shorten your years?"

"As if you didn't know," Marsh growled, nursing the torn skin on the inside of his mouth with his tongue. "I found out what you bastards were up to."

Guy's black eyes blazed at that. "Riddles. Answer straight, or I'll wake him and let him finish you."

Marsh cast a wary glance at the figure sprawled in the street. He'd come too uncomfortably close to dying to face the man again. "Jo and I found the logs. You weren't as clever as you thought, especially letting him pay for drinks with your blood money."

Guy's hand balled up the front of Marsh's torn shirt. "I said answer."

"We know you and your brother pirated Superior logs for Christiansen." He spat out a mouthful of blood and a gutful of contempt.

"Ah, no. You are wrong! Why would you think such a thing?" He opened his fist, and Marsh slumped back against the porch.

"Your brother tossed around Christiansen gold and your tobacco pouch at the scene of the crime. Jo recognized it."

"But I lent it to—" He broke off and looked toward his fallen brother. "*Non. Mon Dieu.* He would not be so stupid.

He could not think—" But of course he would. Chauncey had looked out for him all his life, had supplied for him as best he could. Guy had bemoaned his lack of circumstance, had taken on the river drive to earn extra money. And Chauncey, the great fool, had taken it upon himself to secure his future for him regardless of the means. Guy looked back at Marsh, his expression grim. "I had no knowledge of it. I could never steal from Jo. From anyone! You thought so?"

"Yes."

"And Joelle? She thought me guilty, too?"

There was so much pain in the dark eyes and so much anguish in his question.

"No. No, she never believed it," Marsh lied softly.

"So, Cameron, what happens now?"

Marsh hurt all over. He just wanted things wrapped up neat and final. "I don't want to see your brother rot in jail. If he'll implicate Christiansen, I'll see he's not punished. As far as his job with the Superior goes, that's up to Jo. She's the boss now."

Guy nodded soberly. "I'll take him to Fort Wilkins and see he comes clean with all he knows." He ground his teeth. "I am in your debt once more."

"You can settle it by lifting me out of this mud and dragging me over to the hotel."

The thick black beard twitched slightly. "Fair enough, Cameron." He put out his hand to help.

"Lynette? It's Joelle. May I come in?"

There was a muffled reply behind the door that Jo took to mean yes. Drawing a deep breath, she entered the room, not sure what she'd find, but willing to accept the consequences. Her guilty conscience flared when the woman who'd befriended her looked up from where she sat in a pool of crumpled blue-green taffeta on the counterpane, eyes swimming in distress. Without a thought of her own pride, Joelle rushed to dropped down at her feet in a gesture of supplication.

"Oh, Lynette, I am so sorry," she began in a teary voice. "Please forgive me. Don't think badly of Marsh. He never meant to hurt you. It was my fault. Please let me explain what you saw."

"What I saw was fairly self-explanatory. Stop your weeping, my friend. I'm not angry with you and Marshall. I feel so foolish for having reacted so poorly. Get up. Please. Let me pour you some tea. We'll talk."

Wiping her eyes and sniffing miserably, Joelle climbed up out of the collapsed cage of hoops to sit docilely on the edge of the bed. Why was Lynette being so generous with her understanding? Jo wondered wretchedly. If Marsh had been her intended and she'd caught him in a similar position, she wouldn't have been. She would have slain them both on the spot! So why was Lynette being so nice, extending her hankie, bringing her tea? Joelle took both gratefully, using one and sipping the other while Lynette sat beside her.

"Please, Jo, don't distress yourself. I am not a total imbecile. You are a very, very beautiful woman, full of life I am sadly lacking. Of course Marshall would be drawn to you. What man wouldn't be? I don't need you to suffer an explanation of how such things happen. After all, I am not the sort of woman that men are dying to possess."

"Oh, don't say such a thing," Jo cried out in protest. She took up the other woman's hands and pressed them fiercely. "You are a warm, giving person. Any man would be lucky to have you care for him."

Lynette smiled doubtfully but didn't argue. "Drink your tea before it grows cold."

With shaking hands, Joelle did as she was told. What else could she say to this woman? That she and Marsh were in love with each other? That kissing in the darkness was the least of their crimes against her? Guilt roiled within her. She almost choked on her tea. What right had she to destroy Lynette Barnes's happiness and secure future? None of this was Lynette's fault. She wasn't to blame for their weakness, yet she would be the one to suffer for it. Joelle thought of the bold words she had preached to Marsh. Would Lynette be better off with or without him? Would it matter to her that he didn't harbor any grand passion inside their marriage? Maybe not. Maybe she would willingly settle for the warm camaraderie they already shared. But if Joelle spoke of the things ladening her heart, Lynette would be forced to act upon them. Maybe she would be forced out of pride to withdraw from a relationship she desired with all her heart. She had the prior claim. Joelle had ignored it willfully, and she was the one who should suffer the consequence, not Lynette.

And after all, Marsh had never told Joelle he would stay and marry her if he didn't wed Lynette.

Better she say nothing.

Lynette studied the downcast features of her vivacious friend. No, she wasn't angry with the two of them. If anything, she was grateful, grateful that this lovely woman of the woods had become a buffer between her and Marshall. She could see that Joelle was confused by her complacence. How to explain? She would have to start with how their families had manipulated them in order to control stock. A marriage merger, her father had called it. Though she was comfortable with Marshall as her friend, she found him intimidating as a man. He was so intense, so demanding of a response from her, so evidently virile. It was hardly his fault that she couldn't view him through a lover's eyes. He was like her brother! When he'd made no objections to their marriage, however, she was soon goaded into agreeing. But deep in her heart, she dreaded being Mrs. Marshall Cameron. It would mean night after night of occasions like the one she'd suffered tonight. All the people crowded together, expecting her to say something clever, to be entertaining, to be beautiful. She could do none of those things. Being Mrs. Cameron would thrust her into the focus of society's attention, and the thought of it was enough to send her fleeing for a box of her favorite bonbons.

But she wouldn't disappoint Marshall and she couldn't let her family down. She'd always felt like such a failure to them—plain, plump, ordinary. She would do this one thing to please them. She only wished she had an ounce of Joelle Parry's courage, just a pinch of her loveliness. Then maybe she could attract a man who would care for her and she wouldn't need to pretend. At least she had the comfort of knowing Marshall would understand. Once they were married, he wouldn't hate her for her weakness. So how could she object to his finding passion where he might, with a woman like Joelle?

"More tea?"

Joelle shook her head. She was stunned by Lynette's absolution. She wasn't deserving of it. Perhaps she needed Lynette to rant and rail at her to ease her guilt. But this kind sympathy and acceptance made her sink lower into despair. How could she and Marsh have betrayed such a woman? How had they let their desires carry them away?

"I have to go, Lynette. It's very late."

"Oh, dear, we wouldn't dream of allowing you to make a trip back to the mill at this time of night." When Joelle began to protest, Lynette squeezed her hands. "The room next to mine has been reserved in your name for the night. Please stay. We can breakfast together before you go. After all, we'll be leaving in just a few days and we won't have much time to spend together."

Joelle smiled wanly. Leaving. Lynette and Marsh, together. Proudly she lifted her head and vowed to behave graciously if it killed her. And it just might. But not until after they'd gone.

"You are too good to me, Lynette. I don't deserve it."

"Nonsense. I have so enjoyed our conversations. Sleep well, won't you?"

"I will," she lied.

When her mother's frothy gown was neatly folded aside and she was swaddled in familiar flannel, sleep was the farthest thing from Joelle's mind. She sat up against a bank of pillows, leaning on tented knees, half listening to the unfamiliar sounds of civilization. The noisy silence of the north country was much more to her liking, where she could hear the howl of the wolf, the bobcats that screamed out like children in pain, the wind in the pine boughs. Here it was tinny saloon music and drunken revelry punctuated by the occasional gunshot. It took a moment for the sounds in the hall to separate themselves from those disturbing rumbles of the night, for them to become the sounds of familiar voices—Guy's and Marsh's.

Joelle opened her door a cautious crack to look at them. Guy

was hauling Marsh down the hallway by a loose arm draped
across his shoulders and a grip on the band of his trousers.
The wobbly Easterner wasn't doing much to help. He toed the
expensive carpet in an irregular pattern and seemed to think
one place was as good a spot as any other to stop for the
night. His fine coat was gone, replaced by a dirty mackinaw.
He was covered in grime and blood and reeked of whiskey.
Joelle didn't know if she should be appalled or amused.

"Guy," she hissed, "how did he get into such sorry shape?"

The Canadian hoisted his dragging burden upright, relieved
to find his obligation nearly ended. The man was as heavy as a
length of five-board pine. "It is a long tale, Jolie. Where does
he belong?"

Joelle looked up and down the row of doors. She had no
idea which was his, if he even had a room. She drew a
resigned breath. "Bring him in here for now." She stepped
back and held her door wide. Guy took in the sight of her
in her clinging long johns and loose plaid shirt. Her room.
His gut clenched, but he lugged Cameron inside and let him
drop on the counterpane. Joelle quickly crouched beside the
senseless man she loved. Her eyes lifted after taking in the
sight of one bruised cheek.

"Have the two of you been fighting?"

Guy's gaze narrowed. He was watching her face carefully. "Ah, no. He and my brother had a disagreement. About
logs."

Understanding flickered on her face. Suspicion, too. Guy
knew now that Marsh had lied to him. Joelle had believed
the worst about him.

In a gruff voice, he told her, "When he wakes, tell him I
went to see our bargain met. Good night, Joelle."

Troubled by the distress in his black eyes, Joelle was about
to call to him when Marsh chose that moment to groan mightily. By the time she looked back up, Guy was gone. She sighed
and turned back to the problem at hand.

"Oh, Cameron, what a mess you are. What possessed you
to go up against a man like Chauncey Sonnier? I've buried
enough pieces of my heart this last year without mourning
you, too."

He gave a grumbling moan and flopped onto his back. His eyes opened, all blurry and unfocused. "Jo?"

"Who else would take you in smelling like you do? You have the scent of my father after a wedding or a wake. And where did you get that coat? It looks to be crawling with things I'd rather not think of."

"A gift from a friend," he said with a slur, then immediately began to drift again.

"Where is your room? You can't stay here." Her tone was unusually clipped. Oh, no, he couldn't stay in here with her, with Lynette next door.

"Doan know. This is fine. Soft." He rolled over and burrowed into the covers.

"Marshall! Oh, no, you don't." But he sighed in contentment, and she was lost. "All right, but you're not going to foul my bedding with whatever you've been crawling in. Let's get you cleaned up some."

He growled and muttered as she wrestled the coat off him. Holding it at arm's length, she carried it to the window and dropped it out. With it went a good deal of the objectionable odor. She poked and prodded him until he obliged her by turning onto his back. While he dozed, she gently sponged the muck from his face and neck, grimacing at the damage dealt by Chauncey Sonnier's fists. Traitorous fingertips lingered along the line of his jaw, then, realizing what she was doing, Joelle jerked them away.

What was she thinking? What was she doing? Marshall Cameron was sprawled out on her bed. She had to get him up and out. For both their sakes. Gripping one slack hand, she gave a Herculean tug. "Come on, Cameron. Up you go."

"Vile woman, leave me alone."

"Vile, am I? Get up off that bed, Marshall Cameron. Go lay out in the hall for all I care."

He finally sat up, but she had no time to express her relief, for his arm wrapped around her waist, pulling her to him so his head could rest on her midriff. "Love you, Jo," he mumbled with devastating candor.

She couldn't succumb to the frenzy of delight his words stirred within her. "You're drunk," she accused testily.

"As a skunk," he admitted.

Her irritation melted. With fingers combing through the tangle of his hair, she murmured, "What am I going to do with you, Marsh?"

He leaned back, looking up at her through great dark pools of longing. "Love me."

She sighed as she touched his discolored cheek. "I have no choice there."

He pressed into her palm for a long moment, his eyes closed, lying so still she began to wonder if he'd fallen asleep. When at last he spoke, his words sounded starkly sober.

"Jo, it was Chauncey who helped Christiansen pirate the logs. Guy had nothing to do with it. Now there's no reason . . . things can't work out for you."

"Things?" Joelle frowned down at him, not wanting to follow his direction. His glance shifted away uncomfortably. "Oh, you mean now I can marry Guy, and you can leave with a clear conscience."

"He loves you, Jo. He'd make you a good husband." How quietly that was said. He wouldn't look at her.

"That would take care of everything, wouldn't it? Is that what you want, Marsh, to go back to Boston and leave me to marry Guy?"

His eyes flashed up then, blazing with fierce intensity, darkened with an unspeakable anguish. "No. No, it's not." With hands clasping her face between them, he yanked her down between his thighs and kissed her full and hard until her brief flare of rebellion stilled. He felt her fingertips flutter against his throat, against his jaw, across his cheeks, finally gliding to mesh with his hair. When she touched her tongue to his lips, he drew back with an objecting twist of his head.

"I must taste awful," he mumbled, aware of the sour taste of drink inside his mouth. He reached to her night table for a small bottle of scent. After inhaling a fortifying breath, he took a deep swig of it, swished, gargled, winced as it burned the lacerations in his cheek and then spit it into the rust-colored wash water. He made a face. "Better, I guess."

Joelle leaned forward to sample his mouth and made an affirmative noise. Her arms went about his shoulders, her weight settling against his chest. He went down on his back, carrying her with him, then beneath him in an effortless move.

He deepened their kiss, making it piercingly intimate, exquis- itely thorough, until she pushed lightly at his chest.

"Marsh, don't. You're hurt."

"Can't feel a thing," he murmured. Then she felt his grin against her lips. "Nothing but the important things, that is. Probably *will* hurt like the devil tomorrow, so I'd best enjoy myself now."

"Marsh, we shouldn't."

"You don't want to?"

"We can't."

"I want you."

"No! You have to go. Now!"

She started to squirm out from under him, but he pinned her between his elbows. "Jo . . ."

"No!"

"Don't make me go. I'll behave. I just want to be with you tonight. I just want to hold you. We don't have to make love if you don't want to. I don't care."

But he was kissing her again, moving his hips above hers provocatively, the best intentions of his heart betrayed by his body. She couldn't pretend not to be tormented by a similar desire. The feel of him woke a frenzy of sensation crying to be satisfied. Vows and obligations were easily forgotten when pitted against such powerful passion.

"I want to," she told him in hushed earnest. "I love you."

His fingers hurried down the buttons keeping him from experiencing the satin sleekness of her skin. He sighed as his palms rode that smooth warmth right up to its hard, yearning peaks. He caressed her with his touch, with his gaze, with his mouth, then reluctantly moved aside so she could shed the bothersome flannel completely. She undid his buttons, peeling back the fine linen from his deliciously firm musculature. She adored him with her touch, her gaze, her lips.

"I love you, Jo. God, how I love you," he whispered rough- ly, filling her heart with those words and her anxious form with his magnificence. He moved within her with a teasing rhythm, coaxing forth her passions, bringing soft cries that were bold then beseeching as her pleasure approached its pin- nacle. Her fingers bit into the hard contour of his shoulders, her hips rising, arcing, wanting more, demanding more, needing more so badly she cried out at the moment of her release into his engulfing kisses. She felt him follow with a blind urgency into that same explosive paradise, and then, only then, was it enough.

He moaned his satisfaction, nuzzling into her neck, squeezing her tight. "The luckiest moment of my life was when your uncle sent you into the woods to seduce me," he murmured happily.

"What?" Surely she hadn't heard him right.

"I'm not angry about it anymore, though at the time I dearly wanted to beat you."

"Marsh, what are you talking about?"

"Your uncle. He's really a son of a bitch, you know. His own niece. Someone ought to shoot the man."

Joelle's insides froze. "Who told you I was plotting to seduce you, Marshall?"

He muttered thickly, sleepily, but the answer was all too clear. "Your uncle."

A long while after he'd fallen into a deep sleep, she held him at her breast, her thoughts jumping between the woman in the next room and the uncle she had trusted.

26

"JOELLE?"

Lynette tapped lightly on the door then pushed it open. The room was dark, the draperies drawn against the advent of daylight. There was a mutter of sound from the corner bed followed by the groan of the mattress. Smiling with exasperation, Lynette crossed to the window and jerked the curtains wide. Sunlight blasted through the windowpanes, throwing its strong glare over the figure huddled beneath the covers.

"Gracious," Lynette exclaimed. "It's almost ten o'clock. If you don't stir soon, we'll be sharing lunch instead of breakfast. I wouldn't have pegged you for a slugabed, my friend. Come on, rise and shine." She reached for the edge of the counterpane and gave it a tug. It was held determinedly in place, and an oath growled out from beneath it. Lynette blushed. She didn't think ladies knew such language. Becoming rather stubborn herself, she gave the quilt a hard wrench just as a very clear, very familiar voice sounded.

"Have mercy, Jo. My head is fairly splitting."

"Oh!" she said in a squeak, a sound so unlike anything he could imagine Joelle ever uttering, that it brought Marsh's eyes open to brave the brilliance of the day. He squinted. He stared. There stood Lynette, her mouth hanging open, the sheets she'd stripped off him dangling from her hand. If a single look could stop time, this was it. They stared at each other, too shocked for thoughts to register until Marsh became slowly aware of how cool the day was against his extremely bare flesh. He grabbed the covers and bundled them up to his chin as if his act of tardy modesty could erase what Lynette had already gotten a stunned eyeful of.

"L-Lynette," was all he could manage in a ridiculously redundant stammer.

Her mouth opened and closed once, twice, then she spoke with a reedy firmness. "Marshall, you and I have got to talk. I will be down in the breakfast room. I'll expect you in fifteen minutes. I'll have coffee poured." She left him staring after her.

Facing Chauncey Sonnier held more appeal than journeying down into that breakfast room to meet with Lynette Barnes. Marsh crawled out of bed, finding first his knees, then his feet. His head hammered from the pounding it had taken. The mugs of forty-rod had turned into a forty-gun salute fired every time he tried to move his head on his stiff, complaining neck. Last night the liquor had dulled his misery enough to allow that splendid moment with Jo, but now there was no buffer—only harsh daylight and harsher truth. His fiancée had found him in another woman's bed.

But where was that other woman?

"Jo?" Her name echoed. He might well have hollered it down the mine shaft for the way it came back at him in waves. Her evening gown was gone and, so was the bottle of cologne he'd drunk from last night. Why hadn't she awakened him? But then how much worse would this moment have been if Joelle had been tucked beside him when Lynette came peeping in? His mind was too dull for such complexity of thought. Better he just stick to the one important issue.

What the hell was he going to say to Lynette?

She was sitting primly in the hotel's breakfast parlor. Marsh hesitated before approaching her. She didn't look upset, no more than she had after her initial surprise had faded upstairs. There was an aura of simmering anger about her that had him quite bemused. He'd never known Lynette to have a temper. But then she'd never been confronted with a soon-to-be husband's infidelity.

"Lyn?"

She looked up at him, taking in his careless appearance. His face was unshaven and bruised like a roughly handled piece of ripe fruit. He'd had to put on his shirt and trousers from the night before. He had no idea what had happened to his coat. He looked ragged and repentant, but Lynette showed him no glimmer of sympathy.

"Sit down, Marshall. You look terrible."

He eased down into a chair, trying not to move his head, for fear it would explode. How could anyone feel so horrible and still be alive? His hands moved toward a cup of coffee and cradled the hot china gratefully. Lynette said nothing for a time, letting him take cautious sips and gather his scattered wits about him. He was hunched over that nearly emptied cup when a starched and proper server hovered over him, scowling his haughty disapproval.

"Will the gentleman be having creamed eggs, also?"

Lynette watched Marsh's face grow an alarming shade of green before she remarked calmly, "No. I believe the gentleman will be dining on humble pie."

The waiter gave her an equally disdainful glance and marched away.

Marsh cringed inwardly. He wished he could sink under the table, which was better dressed than he was. He wished he didn't have to live beyond the next seconds or look up into Lynette's eyes. Couldn't the ground just open and swallow him whole? He'd go peacefully, without the slightest fuss. But the Fates weren't so obliging.

"Well, Marshall?"

He elevated his dull gaze from the pudgy hands clasped patiently on the tabletop, the hands wearing his big engagement ring. Finally he looked at her. Her features would have done a gambler proud, so stoically were they arranged. If only she'd betray what she was feeling—as he'd betrayed her. Contrition welled helplessly in his eyes.

"Lyn, I never meant to hurt you," he began in a hoarse plea. How lame that sounded after what he'd done.

Her eyes narrowed ever so slightly. Her voice cut like a band saw. "Well, you have, Marshall. You have hurt me, and I don't know if I shall ever find it in my heart to forgive you. If not lovers, I thought at least we were friends."

"Oh, God, Lyn, we are. Please let me ex—"

"Explain? Oh, there's no need. I have just one question. A simple one."

Marsh braced himself for it. Guilt lanced his heart, and oddly he felt somewhat relieved. He'd hated hiding his feelings for Jo from Lynette. Now everything was painfully out in the open. All that was left was her response to what she'd learned.

Lynette came up out of her seat and walked around to the side of Marsh's chair. He looked up warily, flinching slightly when her palm fit beneath his chin. Then she bent and kissed him, full on his lips, a long, seeking kiss that searched right to his very soul . . . and came up empty. She straightened, her features puckered, her fingertips gentle beneath his jaw.

"Oh, Marshall, how could we have been so foolish? There's nothing there. There never would be, try as we would to make it so." She knelt down so that their eyes were even. Hers were steeped in understanding, his with confused anguish. "Why didn't you tell me? Why didn't you come to me with the truth—that you're in love with Joelle? We're friends, Marshall. We have been for a long, long time. Did you think I would hold my pride above your happiness? How could you? What have I done to make you think I would be so unfeeling, so selfish?"

He tried to speak, but the words, the emotions, jammed up in his throat as tightly as Superior logs. That dam just kept building as Lynette drew off his ring and pressed it into his hand.

"Give this to her with the proper feelings behind it."

He stared at the glittery piece of cold stone. Jo would never wear such a thing. Or maybe she would. His fingers closed about it tightly. An equally crushing fist constricted about his heart. "Lyn, what about your family?"

She touched his hair, raking a strand back along his temple. "I don't know about you, but I've grown weary of being a financial asset to them. I think I will take an extended seaside holiday. I seem to remember a certain quiet gentleman who worked behind the registry counter there. Not the type a woman of my social standing should have noticed, but he did have the most bewitching smile."

"Oh, Lyn." How had he forgotten how dear she was to him? The pressure of looming intimacy had scared it out of their relationship. They'd been stiff as strangers almost since the moment their betrothal was announced. Why hadn't he trusted the friendship that had spanned years? He hadn't betrayed her with Joelle as much as he'd betrayed her with his lack of faith. He'd been looking at her as an obstacle to his happiness instead of someone who would go to any length to see that he achieved it. Hadn't she always been the one he could count on, the one he knew would continue to love him no matter what? Yes. And she was telling him she still was. A sudden smile broke through the wad of misery, freeing him inside. His eyes shimmering with respect, with love, Marsh hugged her to him. "You're one hell of a woman. I don't know what I'd do without you, and I'm damned glad I don't have to find out."

They clung to each other for a long, satisfying while, then Lynette pushed away. "What will you do, Marshall? What will you tell your father? Will you still be coming back with us?"

He rolled the ring around and around in his callused palm. "My father can wait."

It was hard to see the road through the persistent burn of tears. Joelle found herself relying on her team's surefootedness more than once as she wiped her eyes and swallowed down her unhappiness. In leaving Marsh, she had left behind a piece of her heart. It would never be whole again. Cowardice hadn't forced her to sneak from the hotel before facing Marsh or his fiancée. It was the fear that she could no longer pretend to have a strength she didn't feel. If she'd allowed Marsh to wake while she was with him, she would have clung to him with needy pleas. She'd vowed not to do that. If she'd met Lynette Barnes for breakfast, she would have betrayed the truth with one glance. She couldn't do that, either. The time had come to sever herself from the happiness she'd known over the winter months. Marshall Cameron may have loved her with all his heart, but he would never claim her with the honor of his name. So what was the point in remaining?

She couldn't go right to the mill. What if he came looking for her there? What could she say to him? "Thank you for last night, but I can't bear the pain of seeing you again?" She knew Marsh. He wouldn't back away gracefully. He'd run her emotions to ground. And she just couldn't endure the pleasure and the parting another time.

She couldn't go to the mill, so she would go where he'd be least likely to search. Wiping her eyes, Joelle pulled the team up in front of her uncle's little house. She had a thing or two to discuss with him this morning. She needed to know the truth about his motives for chasing her off to the woods with the H&B's new agent. Her heart was already battered—why not let him break it too?

The delicious smell of fresh-baked pastries was a given in the Lachlans' home each morning. Sarah rose early to prepare the beef-and-potato pie her husband would put in his shirt still hot from the oven. There it would be kept at body temperature until lunchtime, when he would warm it on a shovel above a small fire. This morning there was no wafting odor of welcome. The interior of the house was strangely cold and silent.

"Aunt Sarah?"

"Is that you, Joelle?" came a fragile query from the rear bedroom.

"Has Tavis left for the mine already?" She moved closer to the hall. Something wasn't right.

"He didn't come home last night. He stayed down in Sixteen. He's determined to tap a vein of ore or die trying."

"Aunt Sarah, are you all right? You don't sound yourself." Joelle turned into the small bedroom to find her aunt huddled in the big bed, her pallid face turned toward the pillows. Even as the woman uttered a cry of protest, Joelle crossed to her and knelt down, frowning as Sarah Lachlan brought both hands up to the side of her face. "What is it, Aunt?"

Cold with suspicion, Joelle pulled her arms down. A vicious telltale bruise marred one pale cheek and swelled her eye half-closed.

"My God, Aunt Sarah, what happened?"

"I-I fell in the kitchen and—"

"He did this, didn't he? Tavis struck you!"

Sarah was immediately animated with excuses. "Oh, Joelle, dear, he didn't mean it. It's my fault. Sometimes I provoke him so. I'm slow and not very pleasing. He just lost his patience with me, is all. I deserved it. Next time I won't anger him."

"So you let him hit you?" Sarah shrank beneath the force of Joelle's fury. "This isn't the first time, is it?"

"Joelle, he's a good man. He really is. He's a good provider for me. He doesn't mean to let his temper get the best of him. Usually I just let him yell until his fury works itself out. This is the first time he's ever put a hand to me. It's never happened before. It's the Camerons, you see. They upset him so."

"That's his excuse for beating you? How dare he?" She surged to her feet, angrier than she could remember ever being. The feeling brought back the memory of Kenny Craig's abuse. No woman should suffer such brutality. Not for any reason! She made her voice gentle, though inside she shook with rage. "You just lay quiet, Aunt Sarah. Don't worry about anything. I'll make a nice lunch for us both when I get back."

"Joelle?" Sarah cried worriedly after the retreating figure of her niece. "Where are you going?"

"To Sixteen. To have a talk with my uncle.

Joelle disliked the mine. She would never say so, but she couldn't breathe easily at all once those tons of rock hung over her head. The hematite penetrated the air, falling like sediment to the bottom of her lungs. It was cold down there, a different kind of cold from above, a cold that chilled the very marrow in her bones. As she went down farther into the belly of the H&B, she was suddenly, irrationally, glad her father was somewhere out in Lake Superior's embrace rather than deep underground.

Her uncle was in one of the farthest-reaching shafts of the honeycomb. She could see his broad figure in the wavering candlelight. She had to pause for a moment to settle her emotions. She was angry and hurt, yet this was the man who had taken her up on his lap as a child. Bitter conflict roiled within her. Before she could reach some resolution, Tavis Lachlan turned, wiping a grimy hand across his eyes, and saw her.

"Joey! This is a surprise. What be you doing down here?" Then his features tightened, and he came to her in long, rapid strides. "Is everything all right up top? Is it your aunt?" His frantic mind flew back to Sarah as he had left her, packing her bruised cheek with ice, blinking back her tears of distress. He'd been too steeped in his own ire to pay much mind to her silent weeping. Dear God, if that one thoughtless blow of impotent fury had done her any harm . . .

Joelle's glare was severing. "I'm surprised she is the first one you would mention. It would seem she is the last one you consider."

Tavis drew up. He cast a quick glance back at the others, but they were occupied with their work. When he looked again at his niece, his face was chiseled in stern lines. "What are you talking about, girl? What has Sarah been saying?"

"Oh, she wouldn't say anything except what a good man you are." Her voice was thick with sarcasm. "Such a good man who beats his wife and betrays his niece."

His ruddy features paled. A terrible guilt assailed him, and being a prideful man, he fought it down with anger. "What's between me and Sarah's none of your business, lass. But what's this about betraying you? When have I done such a thing to you?"

"You used me to bait Cameron away from the H and B so you could undermine his authority."

His jaw tensed. "And what if I did? I was only thinking of your aunt and—"

"No! You were thinking of yourself and your pride. It has something—I don't know what—to do with the Camerons."

"No, lass, you don't know. You don't know that if it wasn't for the treachery of Colin Cameron, I would be where he is instead of down here sniffing out ore. I would be wearing them fancy clothes and bragging on my handsome laddy-boy."

"Tavis!"

The call came from the miners at the end of Sixteen. Tavis swallowed down his fiery emotions with several deep gulps of mineral-laced air and stalked back to see what had them so excited. Joelle followed determinedly. More was beneath this simple twist of rivalry between old friends. She would find out what it was, because Marsh was somehow involved.

Tavis Lachlan stared at the vein exposed in the wall of
Sixteen. So this was what his nose had scented out. Pudding
stone. Worthless pudding stone. His chest filled up with frustration. The men were looking at him, waiting, hopeful as he
weighed the conglomerate in his hand. He had driven them
and himself hard for endless days in search of this folly. He'd
been so sure, so ready to stake all in his effort to unseat the
arrogant son of Colin Cameron. And he'd been wrong. *Wrong!*
At that moment he wanted to bash his head against this wall
of fool's ore, as he'd bashed his head against the barrier of
unfairness erected by a traitorous friend. But one act would
have been as futile as the other. What good would the venting
of raw fury do? His dignity was all the Camerons had left
him, and he wouldn't lose it in front of his men. Wordlessly
he turned and began to walk away from them. He showed
the stone to Joelle, saying heavily, "There be my life, Joey.
Bits and pieces all jumbled together into something worthless.
Close 'er down, lads," he yelled behind him. "Let's get the
hell out of this hole."

He might have fooled the others, but Joelle knew him too
well. Never had she seen her uncle look so defeated. Before
he'd always bellowed in the face of obstacles. Now he was
walking away with his shoulders rounded dejectedly and his
head hanging low. Despite her anger, despite her own hurt,
she couldn't endure the emptiness of his surrender. Quickly
she caught up to him and looped her arm through his. His
glance flickered to her in some surprise. She returned the look
with a confident smile.

"There'll be other veins, Tavis. No one has a nose for them
like you do."

Tavis sighed, hugging her arm against his side. "Aye, that
may be, Joey, but a nose for ore can't compete with brains
on paper." His jaw squared in a sign of prideful rebellion
that no defeat could dull. The truth came hard and was taut
with resentment. "I should have listened to the lad. Too much
Lachlan stubbornness."

She leaned her head against his brawny shoulder and was
about to give more words of encouragement. But the words
were never spoken, for just then an incredible explosion tore
through the rocks, bringing the world down around them.

*   *   *

Where the hell was she?

Marsh drove back to the H&B in a surly temper. The thunder continued to roll through his head in loud, insistent waves. His whole body ached, and his pulse was still out of control. Was he going to have to track the woman all over the Peninsula just to propose?

All the way from Eagle River he'd practiced what he would say, but nothing seemed quite right. None of the words expressed his joyfulness, the urgency he felt when he thought of a lifetime spent with Joelle Parry. He wanted the words to be just right. They'd been swelling up around his heart for months, aching to be spoken. *I love you. I want you. I need you. I'm crazy for you. I can't imagine a day without you in it. I want to be linked to you in name the way we already are in heart. I want to spend the rest of my days arguing with you, loving you, caring for you.* They could work the particulars out later. For now, he needed to hear her say yes. That's all. Yes.

So where the hell was she, so he could ask the question?

Something was going on at the shaft house. Miners were running madly in and out without direction. Their voices were high and edged with unmistakable panic. For an instant Marsh forgot Joelle as he hurried the team toward the hub of confusion. Then he saw Sarah Lachlan. Her expression was stark and stricken. Glazed eyes rose up from her pale, pale face, a face sporting a bruise as nasty as the one on his own cheek, and for a second she just stared at him without recognition. He leapt down from the wagon and closed on her in an anxiety of unknowns.

"What is it? What's happened?"

Her narrow chest jerked soundlessly. Marsh's clutched tight. His hands curled about her upper arms, shaking her to free the awful truth she wasn't telling. Her head bobbed on the thin column of her neck.

"My God, tell me what happened!"

"My husband . . . my niece . . . down there." Her huge eyes rolled toward the shaft house in an agonized explanation. Underground.

Joelle.

Marsh fought the incredible terror running through his system. He had to know. God, he had to know.

"Alive?"

She stared at him as if she didn't understand, and he shook her hard in his impatience, nearly snapping her neck.

"Are they alive?" he shouted into her blank face.

"I don't know," she whispered.

Marsh's hands dropped. In fear he ran inside the shaft house, into the center of the turmoil. He asked man after man, trying to get a straight, coherent answer, trying to find out what had happened. But all he learned from one after another was that Tavis Lachlan, his crew, and his niece were below, trapped by an explosion in Sixteen.

Finally Marsh had to go down himself to see how bad it was. And it was bad. What he did for the next several hours remained a blur in his memory, a great void that actually kept him from going completely mad with panic and despair. Darkness had fallen by the time he surfaced topside. He collapsed on one of the shaft-house benches, filthy with ground-in hematite, shaking loosely with fatigue and delayed shock. His hands throbbed dully. Hour after hour he had chipped away at the mountain of unyielding rock with a pick and a shovel, and something had snapped in him. He'd begun clawing at the barrier with bare hands. The men had to restrain him, sending him up out of Sixteen for his own safety and theirs. He needed fresh air and a fresh perspective.

Joelle was dying down there, if she weren't already dead. And there wasn't a damned thing he could do to help her.

A sleeper, one of the men told him, an unexploded packing of black powder. The charge ignited when broken rock was carelessly shoveled into one of the cars in Sixteen. The uncontained force of it had shattered timbers and brought a ton of rock down to form a wall of unknown depth. Smoke and fumes were thick, unbreathable. Pumps had been crushed, and a cold seepage of water was soon standing in puddles. Survivors, if there were any, were on the other side of the cave-in, rapidly running out of air and out of time. So many unknowns—the shape of the supporting braces, the depth of the tunnel on the other side—all adding or subtracting from the seconds left to those trapped beyond the barricade of rock.

He had to think. He had to come up with some way to get to her—them. But rifts of grief and fear kept paralyzing his mind. Tormenting pictures of Jo plagued him—pictures of her crushed beneath the fall of stone, of her lying hurt in there, cold and frightened in the frigid darkness, not knowing he was trying to reach her. God, she had to be all right. She had to be! He could almost see her in that wet grave, choking on the foul air, listening to the trickle of loose rock overhead. *Marsh, where are you? Why haven't you come to get me?* Imagining her terror crippled him. His shaking grew more severe until his jaw ached with the effort to keep his teeth from chattering. He couldn't just sit here and let her suffocate! His fists balled helplessly at his sides.

"Marshall?"

The familiar voice cut through the haze of his misery. He raised his head and looked up through eyes that were gritty, forcing a swallow that tore all the way down.

"I just heard, son. What can I do?"

In answer, Marsh leaned into the crisp fabric of his father's coat and wept as if his soul had been ripped wide open.

"Set another charge? But that will bring the whole place down."

Marsh looked up from his hastily drawn sketch, his eyes moving from man to grim-faced man gathered around him. "Not if it's set properly. Not if the blast is directed."

The miners grumbled among themselves for a minute, then one spoke up for all. "What if you're wrong?"

"If I'm wrong, they're dead. If we do nothing, they're dead." Those were the harsh facts, and he had to make them see. "At least this way there's a chance."

"Might be we're snuffing out the only chance they have." The others muttered in uncertain agreement.

"Dammit, I'm an engineer. I know what I'm doing. There isn't any time to waste."

Colin put a hand on his son's shoulder, calming the flare of his temper. His own voice was low-pitched, confident, and thick with the accent of his youth. "Lads, he's right. Mad water's seeping in. We've no way of knowing how much good air they've left them. We cannot wait. We dare not use up more of their precious time in disagreement. All I know is if I was on the other side of that rock, I'd want to know this man was leading my rescue. I would trust him with my life. And I think you should listen."

Colin Cameron looked from face to face, pausing at each one until the man nodded. "Marshall? What do we do first?"

Marsh gave his father a tight, grateful smile then stabbed a dirty forefinger down on his drawing. "I want sturdy timbers braced and reinforced here and here. Who's our best blasting man?"

"That be Murphy."

"Murphy, you set your charge here. With the tunnel shored, the percussion should burrow right through that standing rock and hopefully clear the way to the other side."

"How are we going to let them know we're coming so they can stand clear?"

Marsh's features hardened. "We can't. We just have to believe they'll know we are."

The men studied the schematic, their doubts gradually lifting as their confidence in Colin Cameron's son grew.

"Let's get to it," Marsh said at last, and they all reached for their helmets.

"Marshall?"

He looked around to see Lynette flying toward him in a flutter of pink silk. He opened his arms just in time to receive her heedless rush, and she clung to him, not caring if the soil on his clothes ruined hers. She hugged him hard, her words firm and final.

"You'll bring her up, Marshall. I know it."

His arms tightened in a brief, spasm of thanks. "Yes, I will." Then he stepped back, lit the candle on the bill of his hat and, followed the others down into the mine.

27

WAS THIS DEATH?

Dark. So very dark. And cold. Then Joelle heard the rasping sound of her own breathing and felt a welcomed spear of pain through her shoulder. She was alive. Alive. But where? She remembered the reverberation of the explosion shattering through the rock. Then had come the terrible sound of the earth ripping open all around them. She'd been flung to the floor of the mine, by an explosion or by her uncle, she wasn't sure. Then she hadn't been sure of anything for long, dreadful minutes. Now at least she knew she'd survived. But was she alone?

"Tavis?"

Her voice wavered like a shadow through the blackness. No answer. Then she felt a pinning weight across her legs. Her hands crept downward, touching wool, flesh, hair, something warm and wet. Blood. Panic jerked up into her throat, and she swallowed her scream.

Moving very slowly because she wasn't sure of their position, Joelle sat up. She groped in the darkness for the unmoving shape of Tavis Lachlan, feeling for and finding his neck, feeling for and finding the strong pulse beating within it.

"Oh, thank God."

Were the other men still alive? She wasn't sure if the rock had come down in front or behind them. There was no light, so it must have been blocking their path to the surface. It was then that the full brunt of the accident hit home. They were trapped down in the cold belly of Sixteen. Joelle drew a few ragged gasps then forced herself to calm. No. Mustn't panic. Every breath of air would be· valuable. It would have to last until help came. Until Marsh came for her.

She had no doubt that he would.

But would he be in time?

There was water oozing underneath her. Joelle realized in some dismay that she'd been lulled close to unconsciousness by the rapidly thinning air. The floor of the mine was flooding. She almost laughed at that. Drowning was the least of her concerns. She took a judicious pull of breath. It barely fueled her greedy lungs. *Oh, Marsh, hurry!*

A low groan distracted her from her rising panic. She was quick to reach for her uncle, quieting him with her touch. "Don't move. I don't know how badly you're hurt."

"What . . . ?"

"There was an explosion, remember? But don't worry. Marsh will be here soon to get us out." She hugged her uncle's shoulders and prayed hard that she was right.

"Move. Got to move back."

"What?"

"Now. Back as far as we can go."

"I don't understand." Had he been hit on the head that badly? He was making no sense at all. Why should they move back farther into the mine when rescue was somewhere close up ahead?

"Smart lad, Cameron," Tavis rasped out weakly. "He'll come through with powder, if it can be done. Got to move away, back where it's safer."

A shower of small stones came down from above. Joelle put one arm over her head and the other over Tavis's for scant protection. They were just little pebbles. What would fall if Marsh was planting explosives on the other side?

"He can't! The whole mine will cave in on top of us." For the first time, Joelle was truly terrified. In his eagerness to reach them, Marsh was going to bring the entire roof of rock down to crush them.

*   *   *

"All set."

Marsh took a deep, stabilizing breath and called, "Light it."

There was a hiss from the fuse as they scrambled back into one of the cross-cutting tunnels. They sank down, ducking their heads between their raised knees, bracing their arms over the backs of their necks, holding their breath. Marsh squeezed his eyes shut, trying to block out all thoughts but one—the image of Joelle's beaming face when he asked her to be his wife. *God, give me that chance. Give me that chance!* He could hear his heartbeats echo as loudly as the hammers that had prepared the way for the blasting powder. He was doing the right thing. He knew it in his mind, but his soul was wracked with fear.

Then the very air vibrated with the tremendous force of the explosion. Even before the dust settled, he was up, racing for the hole blown through the wall of rubble.

"Get me a shovel and start bracing. Now! Shore up that loose rock. Hurry. I don't know how much time we'll have before it all comes down. Move!"

He started digging frantically through the dirt and stones. Shovelful after shoveful flew behind him. He was vaguely aware of the men working beside him. Then he hit something. He didn't need to uncover more to know what it was. It was a human body. He fell to his hands and knees, scooping away the soil, wheezing with effort and fear. A hand. A man's hand. Dizziness almost overcame him. For a minute everything went black and cold, and then he felt the firm grip of his father's hands on his shoulders.

"You can't help him, Marshall. There are others waiting inside who need you now. Come on, lad."

"What if I've killed them all?" He looked up in a daze of dread. "Did I do the right thing?" Then he answered himself with fierce certainty. "I did. I did the right thing. If they're alive, we'll get them out."

"Yes, we will, son. We will."

Marsh got up and began to shovel determinedly.

They came to two more bodies, both crushed, both miners. Colin was certain they'd been victims of the initial blast. They

kept digging and bracing, brutally aware of what each second
was costing those trapped on the other side. Suddenly the soil
and rock got looser, and one of the shovels broke through.
There was no cheering, not even any smiles. Were they in
time? Somber-faced, they continued to dig, opening up a hole
big enough for a man to wiggle through. One of the miners
grabbed a lantern and dropped down on his belly to snake
through the small crack. The rest of them waited, scarcely
breathing, some audibly praying. Then the news came back
to them.

"I've got seven men in here. All alive."

Marsh's knees gave. Jo . . . Colin gripped his elbows, holding
him up as he uttered a soft, moaning sob. Somewhere, under all
that rock, in a grave as anonymous as her father's . . .

"Make that six men and a woman."

Uttering an oath of thanksgiving, Marsh tore from his
father's grasp and knelt in front of the hole. "Well, don't
hold a reunion in there. Send them through!" He backed up
as the head of the first man popped out. He was gasping for air
like a newborn babe. Marsh grabbed his forearms and helped
him out, passing the wobbly miner back to the others waiting
with warm blankets and encouraging hugs. Two more grimy
men crawled through, and Marsh impatiently urged them to
move out of the way. Then he saw the top of her dark head.
Her glossy hair was filthy with dust and grainy pebbles. As
soon as he had enough of her to catch onto, Marsh dragged
her free of the hole and up against his chest, hugging her, just
holding her. When it became apparent that he wasn't about to
move, his father gripped him by the back of his trouser band
and hauled the two of them out of the way so the other three
men could be rescued.

At first even the dim candlelight hurt Joelle's eyes, so she
kept her face pressed into Marsh's shoulder. Soon, the desire
to see his face, to see for herself that he was really holding
her, overcame that small discomfort. Squinting, she pulled
back. It was like prying up a lid that was nailed down, so
tightly was he holding her. He looked so tired. His dark eyes
were rimmed with fatigue and strain. His face was caked with
grime and suspiciously streaked with what might have been

tears. But his smile was a bright white slash in the middle of all that dirt.

She touched his features, letting her fingers relearn each contour as if she'd been blind and had been granted the return of her eyesight. She drew a shaky breath and said, "You're a mess, Cameron."

His chest jerked. It might not have been the best time or the right time, but he blurted out the only thing that mattered within the pulse-pounding realm of that precious moment.

"Marry me, Jo."

Her fingers stilled on his cheeks. Her expression froze. For a long, agonizing minute, she said nothing. Then her hands stroked back into the unkempt mat of his hair. "I guess I'll have to," she told him softly. "Someone has to take care of you." She drew him forward to meet her lips in a fervid kiss.

They came up out of the mine to be engulfed by a confusion of condolences and happy tears. Superficial wounds were bound. The heartsick wails from the families of the three who'd died were overwhelmed by the noisy welcome for those who'd survived. More blankets were made available, and hot coffee was served, liberally laced with fortifying liquor. When Marsh and Joelle emerged from the dank shaft, they found Olen and Guy waiting, along with several dozen men from the Superior. But it was Lynette Barnes who pulled Joelle away from all of them, into her sheltering embrace and away from Marsh's side, where she yearned to linger. Joelle resisted, wanting to stay with him, needing the security of him beside her to make the words he'd spoken down in Sixteen real in this world of the living. But he was swarmed by grateful families, caught up in their babble of thanks, accepted into the close brotherhood of people who worked below ground, as he should have been. Joelle knew she should not take that moment from him. She was exhausted and filthy, and her knees wouldn't stop quivering. That wasn't how she wanted Marsh to see her.

Mindful of the way her friend was looking back at the grimy mine agent, Lynette smiled to herself. Aloud she said, "He was half crazy thinking of you trapped below. We both were. I'm so glad you're all right, especially now that Marshall's come to his senses."

"What?" Joelle glanced at her then paled. Whatever was Lynette talking about? Marsh had just asked her to marry him, and she'd agreed. Where did that leave Joelle's only woman friend? Lynette was relieved that her rival had survived. Joelle bit her lip, her happiness taking a bitter tumble. She'd wanted to hear those words from Marsh for so very, very long. Now it seemed so unfair to have them tarnished by the pain of another. The knowledge that her future would be built on the abandonment of this tenderhearted woman brought Joelle close to tears. Seeing the glimmer in those cloudy gray eyes, Lynette hugged her friend.

"I take it Marshall hasn't had the chance to tell you about our meeting this morning?" Joelle shook her head numbly. "Or about what we discussed at breakfast?" Again she shook her head. "No, of course he hasn't. Perhaps it isn't my place— but then, we're all friends, aren't we? There shouldn't be any secrets between us. We've got much to talk about." When Jo hesitated, looking back toward Marsh, Lynette gave her a good-natured tug. "Come on. You've got the rest of your life to fuss over him. Let his friends do it now. We need to talk. And you, if you don't mind me saying so, look dead on your feet. Some tea or maybe something a tad stronger will be just the thing. Besides, you don't want him to see you looking as if you've just been dug up from under some stump, do you? Of course not."

Joelle allowed herself to be pulled away from the noisy gathering in the shaft house, half dreading, half anticipating whatever it was Lynette Barnes had to say. She couldn't be with Marsh again until she worked everything out between them. She owed that much to the woman whose betrothed she'd unwittingly stolen.

"Marshall!"

Marsh was pulled from his visual search for Joelle by his mother's strangling embrace. For once she had no comment on the state of his appearance. She just squeezed the breath from him.

Behind Marion Cameron, Sarah Lachlan stood, plain and gaunt. But Tavis Lachlan didn't notice how poorly his wife fared next to his long-ago love. For once he didn't have a thought for the other woman. Marion Hewlett hadn't lived with him, slept beside him, cared and cooked for him all these many years without a complaint or a demand. Marion Hewlett didn't bear the shameful mark of his temper upon her undeserving cheek. All he remembered was how empty his world had seemed when Joelle had come down to him in the mine and he feared she was bringing some grim news about his Sarah. All he knew was there was no one he would rather have had waiting to welcome him back from the edge of death. Her appearance there, after what he'd done, humbled him to his core. Sarah still stood, her eyes shimmering with concern. She hung back out of habit, but when her burly husband opened his arms, she didn't hesitate to fill them.

"Oh, Tavis, I feared I had lost you." Tentative fingers brushed the fresh bandage on his brow.

"Sarah," he chided with a low rumble, "how could you think I'd not come back to you?"

Relieved and bewildered by the change she sensed in him, she just hugged him, happily, hopefully. Then, seeing how Tavis and Colin exchanged tense looks, she pulled away from his broad chest to offer meekly, "Mrs. Cameron, would you care for some tea while they finish up here? You must be half-frozen."

Marion stepped away from her son and regarded the mousy woman curiously. Then she, too, caught the undercurrent in the room, that ripple of unfinished business that had lingered over the years. "Yes, I think I might like that. But only if you call me Marion—Mary." She gave Marsh's sagging jaw a loving pat and went off with the wife of her husband's arch rival and oldest friend. Then it was just the three of them remaining.

"I've got a cask of the most god-awful whiskey you'd ever think to swallow at my office," Marsh suggested, and that sounded good to the other two. Wordlessly they left the shaft house and their hematite-encrusted work clothes to walk across the mining town to the comfort of Marsh's parlor. They were sampling the truly terrible liquor when Tavis drew out the sample he'd taken from Sixteen.

"You were right, Cameron. Sixteen was a waste of time and effort. Nothing down there but pudding stone. And the death of three fine lads."

Marsh took the rock, as intrigued by it as he'd been by the one he'd seen in the saloon. "Father, what do you make of this?" He passed it over. "It's copper. Good quality."

Colin turned the chunk in his hand. "It would be expensive to mine a conglomerate like this one. You'd have to extract the mineral from the waste."

"But it could be done," Marsh urged, suddenly excited.

"I suppose." He tossed the rock back to his son. "Why don't you try to find a way?"

Marsh caught the stone out of instinct and held it forgotten in his hand. He was staring at his father. "I thought you wanted me in Boston. I thought you wanted me to take over Grandfather's place on the Board of the H and B."

"Is that what you want, Marshall?"

"You never asked before."

Colin Cameron sighed. He'd been waiting a long, long time to have this conversation with his son. Now he saw someone man enough to hold up his end of it. "You were too busy trying to be what you thought I wanted, what your grandfather wanted, to have any ambitions of your own. I was waiting for you to stand up for yourself, to tell us to go to hell. But you didn't."

Marsh stared at him, at the father he thought he'd known so well and now didn't recognize at all.

"That's why I sent you here. Or at least one of the reasons. I wanted you to think, Marshall. I wanted you to know what you wanted to do with your life without anyone to influence you. I wanted you to know me better by seeing what I was before I got civilized by my own greed. It's my fault, I suppose, for wanting so much for you, for letting your mother spoil you so. She never wanted you to struggle, she never wanted you to touch the baser facts of life I sprang from. I should have put a stop to that long ago."

Marsh was totally confused by what he was hearing. "I don't understand."

"No? Pour me another, and I'll tell you a story about two friends from Cornwall who came to better themselves in the New Country." He saw Tavis stiffen, but the other man made no move to stop him from continuing the tale. Colin studied his glass, letting his voice thicken into its almost forgotten brogue. "They was hard times, right, Tavis? All of us hungered for something better, for something to wash the hematite from our pores. But I was hungrier than most. I wanted to escape the mines any way I could. When I saw your mother, I knew I'd found a way." He had to take a long, searing drink before he could go on. "I knew she and Tavis had an interest in one another, but I didn't care. All I could see was my ambition. I seduced Marion Hewlett and got her with child so I could get away from the harshness of this life. I turned my back on my friend, on everything I was, and it wasn't until much later that I learned what I'd thrown away. Oh, Marion's father insisted that we marry, but he made me vow I would never give them reason for shame. I worked harder than I had ever labored below ground to become a gentleman worthy of the name and got in return a troubled marriage and a life sentence of success. How I envied Tavis the simple purity of his existence. How I wished I could come back, but it was too late for me. Instead I sent you, Marshall. I sent you to make amends for the treacherous way I treated my best friend."

Tavis's lips curled harshly. "You sent him here to taunt me with all that you've achieved and you thought that would make amends?"

"No. I sent my son because he is smart and a brave keenly lad. I knew if anyone could make the H and B pay, he could. I sent my son to help you, Tavis. It was your stubbornness that made you refuse what he had to offer. It took a cave-in for you to admit he knows the mines as well as you, or could with your help."

Tavis shot a glowering glance at Marsh then grumbled, "Aye, he knows his way around a piece of paper, but he needs more dirt under his nails to make a miner out of him."

"You'll teach him?"

"If he'll stop growling like an arrogant young pup. Then maybe this old dog can learn something new as well."

Colin sobered, confronting his old friend with the shame he'd carried for too many long years. "I wronged you, Tavis. I would repay you now by giving my son to your niece. He can give her the things a daughter of yours might have had if you'd wed Marion instead of having me steal her from you. I can't change what I did to you, but I ask that you forgive me for the foolishness of youth."

Tavis scowled then put out his hand. "Aye, my Joey will take the lad. She could do better, of course, but you be owing me and all, we'll settle on him."

"Now, wait a minute," Marsh stuck in irately. "Don't Jo and I have anything to say about this?"

The two men looked at him in bemusement, as if they couldn't believe he'd have reason to object to their interference in his life. He threw up his hands, dismissing them with a shake of his head.

"To hell with the both of you. You just sit back and enjoy my liquor and your little schemes, but you'll have to excuse me. I have things to do."

As he stormed out, Tavis chuckled. "Reminds me of you, Colin, me boy."

"Aye. He'll more than do."

They hoisted their glasses and drank in agreement.

Lynette was being helped from a wagon by a solicitous Guy Sonnier when Marsh stomped across the street.

"Where's Jo?" he growled in annoyance. He'd wasted enough of this day without her in his arms, and he meant to remedy that loss immediately.

Lynette gave Guy a shy smile then looked distractedly at her former betrothed. "Oh, I believe she said something about a steam bath, whatever that means. Marshall, I— Marshall?"

But he was already vaulting up into the wagon. "My mother is at the Lachlans'," he shouted as he wrestled the team about.

"I'd be honored to show the lady the direction," Guy offered. His gallantry brought a host of delighted blushes from the lady in question.

"Be my guest," Marsh hollered as he slapped the reins down.

"Do forgive Marshall," Lynette was saying. "He's not normally so rude."

Guy tucked her hand into the bend of his elbow. "On the contrary, I've never known him to be anything else."

Hot, humid air billowed out the minute he opened the door. It enveloped him like a sultry embrace as Marsh stepped inside the sauna and closed the door behind him. He ladled a dippper of water onto the glowing rocks and was rewarded with a smoldery hiss. And a luxurious sigh.

"I didn't think things could get any steamier," Joelle murmured huskily. "Have you come to prove me wrong?"

"Do I need to?"

She smiled through the mists and held out her hands. "I'd like you to."

He came to her, resting his knees on either side of her on the bench and tipping up her face between his palms. His kiss was scorchingly intense, and it warmed her right to her toes.

"We'll stay here at the H and B this summer," he began between hungry kisses. "I want to keep an eye on your uncle." Joelle frowned at that but didn't argue. She was too intrigued by the feel of his bared back beneath her palms and the swaddling towel bound about his hips. And by what the towel covered. "Then we'll winter in the woods with your crew. Only I don't plan to bunk with Olen Thurston. I want to keep you warm at night. Besides, you don't snore."

"It sounds as if you have everything well in hand," she purred happily, for his hands were occupied with the knot of her towel.

"Almost." He gave a final tug then filled his palms with her eager breasts. After a moment of leisurely kneading, he murmured, "We need someone to marry us." He lowered to taste the taut, budded tips and growled huskily, "Soon."

She arched her back, trying not to lose herself to the sensations he was building inside her so insistently. At least, not yet. "There's a priest in Copper Harbor. I think he'd be more than happy to perform the ceremony. Tomorrow? Oh, Marsh . . ." For a moment she was unable to speak as her fingers tightened in his thatch of tawny hair. Then her words were as happily strained as the tension building between them. "Lynette wants to stand up with me. She said the two of you had decided that being friends was enough for both of you."

"Did she? Good. That just leaves tonight." He lifted himself to nuzzle her neck where it was good and slippery with beads of moisture. "I seem to be out a place to stay. My house is filled with Cornishmen determined to make up for twenty-odd years by toasting each other with gut-tearing drink."

"I suppose you could come home with me. If you'll behave."

He responded to her teasing smile with answering dimples. "Oh, Jo, I guarantee you my behavior will be exemplary."

"Well, then, what are we waiting for, Cameron? I suppose you need me to show the way. I wouldn't want you getting lost."

"No need, Jo. I know exactly where I'm going." His grin became a curve of smug promise and deeper confidence.

"Show me," she challenged softly.

Everything he showed her on that night and the others that followed was very much to her liking.

434